CRACK ONE OPEN AND GET STARTED . . .

"Two zombies are eating a clown. One turns to the other and asks, 'Does this brain taste funny to you?'"

"Braiiiins," Renee laughed, regarding her friends from the romance book club. "I want more heroes with braiiiiins."

"You and me both, sister," replied Alissa.

"Well, I don't care if the hero's got brains," Erin piped up, "as long as the heroine has enough for both of them. Bring on the bad boy. He's a little bit dark . . . but has a softer side." She winked.

Cindy wrinkled her nose. "Ew! Like, the decomposing bits? Zombies and romance don't mix!"

"Why the heck not?" Erin asked. "Love makes us all a little mindless."

"Well," Alissa said, glancing down at *My Zombie Valentine*, "if love makes you want to take a bite out of someone, have I got the book for you. . . ."

Katie MacAlister
Angie Fox

My Zombie Valentine

Marianne Mancusi
Lisa Cach

LEISURE BOOKS NEW YORK CITY

A LEISURE BOOK®

January 2010

Published by

Dorchester Publishing Co., Inc.
200 Madison Avenue
New York, NY 10016

ISBN 10: 0-8439-6360-3
ISBN 13: 978-0-8439-6360-1
E-ISBN: 978-1-4285-0793-7

The name "Leisure Books" and the stylized "L" with design are trademarks of Dorchester Publishing Co., Inc.

Printed in the United States of America.

10 9 8 7 6 5 4 3 2 1

Visit us online at www.dorchesterpub.com.

My Zombie Valentine

CONTENTS

Bring Out Your Dead

Katie MacAlister

Chapter One

"Braiiinssss."

"Yes, I know."

"Braaaaaainnnsss!"

"Ysabelle?" The front door thumped shut with an audible grunt from Noelle, one of my two flatmates. "One of these days we're going to get Mr. Sinclair to fix that door . . . Ysabelle?"

"*Elle est* right here *avec le* sitting *chambre du femmes*," Sally, my other flatmate, called out as she drifted through the room. Sally had issues.

"Braaaains!"

"*Vous parlez* a mouthful." Sally beamed at my client as she wafted past him, through the wall, and into the room beyond.

"Oh." The door to the sitting room opened and Noelle stuck her head in, a worried frown puckering her brow. "Did you know there's a small herd of zombies in the hall?"

I sighed, giving my client what I hoped was a reassuringly cheerful smile. "Yes, I know, and please, Noelle—zombie is so politically incorrect. The preferred term is revenant, or functionally deceased."

"Well, there's a group of *fuctionally deceased* in the hall playing strip poker, and if Mr. Sinclair sees them, he's going to have a fit. You know how he is about using the flat for business."

"Ahem! Brains!" Tim, a new revenant in need of counseling, glared at me.

"I apologize for the interruption," I said in a calm, reassuring voice as I waved Noelle away. She rolled her eyes and closed the door, leaving me with my client. "You were telling me about the taunting you experienced recently?"

"Yes, brains. Or rather, *braiiiiiiins*. Spoken in a slurred, repugnant voice that was accompanied by a fine spray of spittle. That's all they said, over and over again, as if I were supposed to stagger toward them with a fork and knife, and start hacking away at their heads. I am more than a little offended by the stereotype portrayed in modern films, and which people such as those at the bus stop wholeheartedly embrace. Isn't there something we can do about it? Must we endure such things without speaking up? Is there no way to educate the public about the true nature of revenants?"

"We're working very hard to do that, but as you know, public acceptance is a hard-fought battle, and frankly, I don't see an end in sight any time in the near future."

"*Qu'est que le* hell?" Sally, who had drifted back into the room on Noelle's heels, paused to look out the window.

"Sally, language, please!"

"*Pardonnez.* But holy *merde! Voici est* a whole boatload *du* zombies *en l'rue. J'allez* to get *le* cricket bat in case *ils* try breaking *dans le* flat."

"There, you see?" Tim pointed at Sally. She gave us a cheerful smile and flitted past to the next room. "Your . . . whatever she is. That's just the sort of negative stereotypical reaction I object to!"

"Sally is my spirit guide," I answered. "I apologize for her, as well. Some time ago she decided she wanted to be French, so she changed her name to Fleur and began speaking in that atrocious Franglais. We're hoping it's a phase that will pass. *Soon.*"

Tim's eyes, which reminded me of a particularly obnoxious form of boiled sweet, bugged out at me in the manner of an elderly pug. "Spirit guide? *You* have a spirit guide? I thought you worked for the Society for the Protection of Revenants."

"I do, but counseling is only a part-time position," I explained. "I also occasionally tutor English and history, and sometimes I act as a medium for persons wishing to contact the deceased. I'd probably have more of the latter work if I had a spirit guide who wasn't quite so . . . well, you saw Sally. But my personal problems are neither here nor there. We were discussing your successful reentry into a meaningful and productive life filled with satisfaction."

"It's neither successful, productive, nor meaningful thus far," he said in a rather petulant tone. "Surely there must be something we can do about the prejudice I've been forced to face?"

I gave a helpless shrug. "What would you suggest?"

"Well . . . I'm a pacifist, so I won't go the route of violence, despite what the public seems to believe of us. Perhaps a picket, or a boycott of nonrevenant companies, or oh! I know! An Internet letter–writing campaign! That worked wonders with the Save the Hedgehog folk! You should suggest that to the Society."

I opened my mouth to explain that the SPR had spent decades working to educate the public as to the true nature of their members with little success to date, but I bit back the inevitable lecture. It would do no good. Tim was newly reborn, as were many in this time of upheaval. He'd learn with time how to hide his present state. My job was not to teach him to pass as mortal—it was to get him past the first hurdles of rebirth. "I'll be sure to pass along your suggestions, but you know, something like that really needs someone with excellent organizational skills to head it up. Perhaps you'd like to start a grassroots campaign yourself? Your resume says you were very active with a human rights organization."

"Hmmm. That's an idea," Tim said with a thoughtful pause. "I suppose I could do something along those lines. Perhaps if we started small, say, a sit-in consisting of new revenants like myself to show the public that we aren't the mindless, brain-eating zombies popular movies paint us as."

"Excellent idea," I said, relieved that he was channeling his energies into something worthwhile. Most new revenants spent several months at a loss as to how to restart their lives.

"Somewhere popular, obviously. Leicester Square?"

I frowned. "There are a great many restaurants there . . ."

"Is that bad?" He looked puzzled for a moment, then nodded. "Ah, I see what you mean. You believe the proximity of fast food and other restaurants will be a temptation for us to leave the vegetarian lifestyle behind."

"It's been shown that revenants function much better in society if they severely limit their intake of animal flesh," I said gently. "It seems those who turn feral tend to indulge in feeding orgies at local fast-food restaurants. That's why the Society insists all members adhere to a strictly vegetarian diet. Most members have no problem, but for new people, it can be difficult to avoid the lure of a quarter-pounder with cheese. We recommend you avoid temptation for the first two months."

"Surely a hamburger now and again couldn't hurt?"

"You wouldn't think so, would you? But we've found that animal flesh is like a drug to revenants—it leaves them addicted, needing greater and greater quantities to satisfy the craving. Thus, the no-flesh diet."

For a moment, a red light lit the depths of his eyes, but it faded quickly. "Er . . . yes, point taken," he said solemnly. "Perhaps we can do the sit-in somewhere less likely to lead to a fall. A park? Hyde Park?"

"That sounds perfect."

"Yes. I will do that. Thank you, Ysabelle—that was an excellent suggestion. You will help with the sit-in, naturally?"

I smiled. "I'll do my best. If you have any problems, feel free to contact me."

"Very well." With a brisk nod, Tim gathered the orientation and welcome packets I'd given him. "I'd like to get started on it right away, but I suppose I should look up my wife and see what she's done to the house in the six months since I died. Knowing her, she's run amok with gingham or some other hideous scheme."

"Your family was notified last week about your resurrection, so they should be ready to greet you," I said, getting up to show him out. "If you have any questions or problems, please don't hesitate to call. My number is on the card."

He nodded and said good-bye.

I waved him out, then hurried to Noelle's door, knocking before opening it. "How did the infestation go?"

She looked up from her laptop. "Hmm? Oh, it went well, although there were a few more coblyn than I expected. But given Salvaticus, understandable. Speaking of that, how are you holding up? I know this can't be an easy time for you."

I sighed and rubbed my neck for a moment. "I'm tired, but I think my head is still above water. This is so different from anything I've experienced as a counselor, I'm a bit overwhelmed."

"It's bound to be. How many zombies do you normally have to deal with?"

I rubbed the back of my neck again, and wished for a couple of aspirins. "Usually fewer than five a year are raised by intervention."

"Intervention? You make it sound like revenants are drugs users."

I smiled. "Intervention in this case means someone petitions a being with the power to raise the dead. It's not an easy process. Because Salvaticus is traditionally the time of rebirth, the Society says we can expect more than three hundred new revenants over the next few days. Thank goodness this only happens every five hundred years. All the counselors are working around the clock to cope with the influx. Speaking of which, if my clients are playing poker in the hall, I'd best see to them before the neighbors start to complain about naked revenants. Sally?" I poked my head out into the flat's hall.

"*Oui? Vous* called?"

"Can you show in the next person? And please—watch your language. Some of these people have been dead for over a hundred years, and they're bound to be scandalized by any cursing."

My erstwhile spirit guide snorted and rolled her eyes as she drifted toward the front door. "*Années du* hundred *est rien. Moi, je* will be *cent soixante-douze* next March."

"And you don't look a day over one hundred and fifty," I said. "Please give the client the welcome packet, and tell him or her I'll be right there. I need to talk to Noelle first."

"It will have to be quick," Noelle said, glancing at the clock and saving her file. "I'm on duty tonight in the Tower of London's portal. It's been spewing out huge numbers of imps the last few nights, and the Tower's regular Guardian is too overwhelmed to cope with all the crossovers."

I frowned. "Salvaticus is the time of rebirth for revenants. Why would that make the imps come into our world?"

"Lots of reasons," Noelle said, snatching up her bag of tools and a small purse. "It's the week before Vexamen, the time of upheaval in Abaddon when demon lords struggle with one another for surpremacy. Those battles generate an excess amount of dark power, so the imps and other beings use that to access portals that would normally be beyond their abilities. And speaking of that, I wanted to remind you to be especially careful when you go out."

"Me?" I watched as she crossed over to her bedroom window and drew a protection ward on it, then followed when she marched out and repeated the process on all the windows in the flat. "What are you doing? I thought you warded the flat every weekend."

"Those are normal household protection wards. These are different—these will keep any being of dark powers out. They don't last as long as the others. I'm drawing them because you're at risk right now."

She turned to face me as Sally showed a middle-aged woman into the sitting room. I told the woman I'd be with her in a minute.

"What are you talking about?" I asked Noelle in a low voice. "Why am *I* at risk? It's not like I'm a sex bunny or anything like that."

"You're sex bunny enough to capture five husbands," Noelle said with a laugh.

I thinned my lips. "They weren't captured. They were all very nice men, considerate and thoughtful, if a bit . . . well, that's not a discussion for today."

"That's not the danger I was talking about, but you know full well you're attractive enough. *You're* not cursed with red hair and freckles."

I smiled. Noelle's hair and fair skin were the bane of her existence. "Oh, you're not going to tell me that men don't like red hair, because I know that's not true. You have lots of boyfriends."

"Perhaps, but there was only one who really mattered." She stopped next to a desk, her face drawn.

I put an arm around her. I had been in the country visiting a relative when she had met, been madly attracted to, and ultimately rejected by a mysterious man about whom she was oddly reticent to speak. "I'm sorry, Belle—I don't mean to be a wet blanket about this, but it . . . well, it still hurts."

"Men are scum," I said sympathetically. "Most, that is. Certainly the one who dumped you is."

"He didn't dump me so much as reject what I had to offer him," she said with a sad little sigh. "I just don't know how he could do that. It doesn't seem possible—it was against all the rules—but he did."

I murmured platitudes, feeling her pain. "I know it's hard now. It's only been, what, seven months? But in time, you'll realize that this man was not meant for you."

"That's just the problem—he *was* meant for me," she said, turning away. "He was . . . oh, what does it matter? He refused me, and that was the end of it."

"Then more fool him. You are charming, attractive, smart, and a wonderful person. And for the record, I quite like your red hair and freckles."

She laughed and gave me a hug. "And I like your dark hair and gray eyes, but that's beside the point. We're quite a pair, aren't we?"

"I still don't see what any of this has to do with Salvaticus."

"Then you're being unusually obtuse. You must know that

your double soul presents an extreme temptation to any servants of demon lords who are about."

My smile faded. I'd never been too comfortable with my unusual status.

"Anyone with my handicap will be a target," I said, crossing my arms and looking out the window at the rainy London morning. A thin drizzle spotted the window and made the street gleam damply, casting a gloom over the day that had me shivering slightly.

"Oh, for heaven's sake, you aren't handicapped. You're unique! There aren't that many of you around, are there?" she asked, her head tipped to the side as she continued to study me, evidently cheered out of her own glums by my moodiness.

I shifted restlessly, uncomfortable with such close scrutiny.

"That wasn't a condemnation, you know," she said softly, then tsked when the sitting room clock chimed. "Bloody hell, I'm late. Just watch yourself. Stay in and don't go out for the next few days just to be sure."

She was off to the front door, snatching up her coat and umbrella en route.

"I can't stay in—I have to go tutor a new child this afternoon who was sent down from his school."

"Cancel."

"I can't! I need the money. I'm tired of borrowing from you just to pay for groceries and things."

She paused at the door to make a face. "Why you continue to spend every spare minute of your time with that Society when they don't pay you—"

"You know why I volunteer with them. They need me. It's not their fault they don't have the budget to pay their counselors. I was lucky to get this tutoring job, so I'm not going to cancel and risk losing the only source of income I have."

She touched a blue and green tapestry that hung on the hall wall. "You could always sell some hangings."

I wrapped my arms around my waist, a little prick of pain

burning deep within me. "I've sold my loom. I've sold all my wools and other equipment. I've sold everything I could, but that piece is the only thing I have left of myself. I can't sell it, I just can't."

Noelle smiled. "I'm not asking you to, Belle. I know how much this means to you. Don't worry about money—we'll get by somehow. I can always take on some extra work if need be. Just stay here and take care of your zombies."

"Revenants," I said automatically as she slipped out the door, her red curls bobbing madly.

Worry held me in its ever-present grip, tightening across my chest until every breath was an effort to take. Noelle might be willing to do my share as well as hers, but that was a situation I couldn't tolerate. Despite her warning about being a target of the dark powers, I had to go to the tutoring job. A girl's pride could only take so many blows.

"*Vous est* coming?" Sally asked, poking her head through the door. I rubbed the goose bumps on my arms that remained as Noelle's words echoed in my head. "*Qu'est-ce qu'il y a?* You look *tres* worried."

"Nothing's wrong, and yes, I'm coming. I'm not worried, it's just . . ." I rubbed my arms again, trying to disburse the somber feeling that had been left in the wake of Noelle's warning. "It's nothing. Just someone walking over my grave."

Sally pursed her lips but said nothing as I entered the sitting room. Considering the obvious, I counted that as a minor miracle.

Chapter Two

"Yip, yip!"

"Oh God, not more . . ." Followed by a dozen or so tiny yellow imps, I burst out of the tube station and ran like a maniac down the street, tossing apologies over my shoulder as I occasionally bumped into people on their way home. It was early evening, and the sodden sky did nothing to lighten the way as I raced down streets, cut through alleys, leaping over fences and rubbish bins in the manner of a hyperactive Olympic hurdler. "Pardon me. So sorry. My apologies, sir."

"*Belle! Vous êtes* banging my head *dans la* bottle of water!"

"I'm a little busy at the moment, Sally," I muttered through gritted teeth. Mindful of my spirit guide's head, I spun around the corner as carefully as possible, but ended up skidding on the wet pavement and slamming into a large figure that loomed up out of nowhere.

"Oooph," the man grunted as I collided with him, falling backward. Inside my purse, Sally yelled out copious curses in mangled French.

My arms flailed as I attempted to regain my balance, but it did no good. We fell in a tangled heap of arms and legs, my nose bumping his cheekbone, his warm lips pressed against mine. For a moment I lay stunned—both by the blow and the fact that I was inadvertently kissing a total stranger.

I opened my mouth to apologize, but his arms tightened around me. His lips moved, sending little zings of excitement down my body. For a moment, I could taste blood, but the second his tongue swirled across my lip, teasing me, *tasting* me, all thoughts flew out of my head.

He must have been eating a spicy sweet or chewing clove gum or something, because his mouth tasted of a heavenly ambrosia I couldn't begin to put into words. A distant part of my brain was shocked that I was lying on a stranger in the middle of a London street, surrounded by passersby as I kissed him with everything I was worth. But at that moment all I wanted was to enjoy the spicy sweetness his mouth offered.

His body stiffened. I had a momentary glimpse of gray-blue eyes flashing surprise beneath the black rim of a fedora before they narrowed and he spoke. "Beloved!"

The sound of his voice brought me back to reality. My cheeks flamed with embarassment as I squirmed out of his hold. I got to my feet and gathered my backpack from where it had fallen. "I'm so very sorry, sir. There's no excuse for my actions other than the ground was wet, and I'm being chased—"

"*Tabernak! Peut-être vous* would like to murder *moi?*"

The man leaped up with a grace I lacked, looking toward the voice issuing from my backpack.

"Sorry. It's a little confusing, isn't it? That's actually my spirit—" I started to explain, still red-cheeked at my uninhibited display. But at that moment, the imps found me.

"Yip, yip, yip," clamored the murderous little monsters (imps seldom have good on their minds) as they poured around the corner in a yellow wave of menace.

"Bloody hell!" I scanned the street quickly, searching for the best escape route, but before I could make a decision, the man shoved me toward the entrance to a narrow unlit alley.

"Down there. Quickly!" he ordered, turning to block the alley with his body. I hesitated a moment, unwilling to place my Good Samaritan in potential danger, worried that he could be harmed. "Run, you foolish woman. I won't be harmed."

I didn't wait for him to tell me twice. I ran, my arms outstretched in a blind attempt to avoid trash bins and boxes of refuse that hid in the darkness.

"*Belle! J'ai entendu le* voice *du* man. Who was it?"

"Sally, I really don't have time—ow! Damn it, this is ridiculous."

The tiny alley ran behind a row of connected buildings, allowing little light to intrude from the shops and streetlights. Judging by the smell of rodent droppings and urine, I gathered the alley was not the safe haven I had hoped it would be. I swore again as my shin connected with something hard and pointy, then turned back to see how my champion was doing, prepared to go to his rescue if he was being overwhelmed. All I could see was his silhouette in the entrance of the alley, bobbing and weaving as he beat off the imp attackers.

"*Vous avez arrêté?* Why?"

"Because the man may be in trouble."

"*Run!*" he yelled, spinning around toward me. "Turn left at the end of the alley."

His voice was strong and confident, not at all like that of someone who was about to be overwhelmed by imps.

"Do as he says," advised the muffled voice. "*Il retentit tres* Sexy Pants."

"I am doing it," I snapped, sprinting down the last half of the alley with only minor injuries to my abused shins. I burst out into the lights of the busy street, turned blindly, and raced straight into a demon.

Pain exploded through my head and shoulder. Sally shrieked, her high-pitched screams piercing the fog in my brain and the stench of demon smoke. Woozy, I realized the demon had instinctively thrown me off him, no doubt believing I was an attacker. The pain, along with the sharp, coppery taste of blood helped clear my head. It focused its attention on me.

"Demon! Demon! Demon!" Sally screamed from inside the backpack.

"You smell of revenants," the demon said, sniffing the air. Its eyes narrowed on me as I got painfully to my feet.

"I mean you no harm," I said slowly, showing my palms so the demon would know I was unarmed.

"Get away, Belle! Demon! *Zût alors!* It will have you!"

My gesture of good faith did little good. The demon snarled one word at me, a word that made my blood curdle. *"Tattu!"*

I leaped backward as it lunged at me. If only I hadn't taken the tube. The imps never would have found me, and I'd never have run into the delectably kissable man outside the alley, and he'd never have sent me careening (intentionally, or accidentally?) straight into the arms of one of the few beings who could do me damage.

I whirled around, about to sprint away in a desperate attempt to escape the demon, but at that moment the man I'd been kissing burst from the alley, flinging himself between the demon and me.

I didn't wait around to see whose side he was on—I ran. Judging by the demonic curses and screams that followed me, the man must have been an ally. When I stopped three blocks away in a small square, one hand on my side to ease a stitch as I gasped for air, there were no demon or imps in pursuit. No mysterious man in a dark hat with glittery blue eyes, either.

"Qu'est que going on? *Porquoi* have you stopped?"

For a moment, I was disappointed that the stranger—back in the savior role—hadn't followed me, but I quickly regathered my wits.

"Economy be damned," I said grimly, limping to the nearest taxi rank. "The streets aren't safe for someone like me."

"Vous said it, sister."

"Tell me you're the tutor."

"I'm the tutor."

"Oh, thank God." The woman who opened the glossy black door of the three-story town house yanked me inside without any ceremony. She looked to be in her mid-twenties, and bore a frazzled, wild glint in her eyes. "Ew! What is that?" she asked, eying the paper bag I carried.

"I'm so sorry. It was an imp who got a little too personal with my leg. You know how they are—they'll mount anything that moves."

"Imps," the woman said, her eyes round with horror.

"*Il était seulement* one imp." I gave the backpack a little shake to remind Sally that I didn't want her speaking until I'd had the chance to check out my new employers. Not everyone is thrilled to see a tutor who has a spirit guide following her everywhere.

The woman's eyes widened even more at the words emerging from my backpack.

"Ignore that," I said.

"Yes, I think I'd better," she answered, her face tight. She said nothing more about either my unsavory package or my talking backpack, simply pulling me inside and slamming the door behind me. She frowned a moment, opened the door again, and dashed out to where the taxi driver was attempting to merge back into traffic.

"Save me from having to order one," she said breathlessly as she returned. She stopped in front of me, running an agitated hand through her hair. "What's taken you so long? I thought you'd never come."

I glanced at my watch. If she didn't appreciate hearing about the imp who had been hiding in the taxi, I doubted she'd care to hear of the demon I'd run into earlier. "I take it you're Mrs. Tomas? I apologize for being late, but it is only five minutes past my appointment time—"

"It doesn't matter, you're here now," the woman said, grabbing a raincoat from a nearby chair. I looked around the small entrance and noted the dark paneling on the walls, marble tile, and sparse but elegant furnishings. I had been told by the private tutoring agency I worked through that the child I was being assigned had been sent down from an exclusive boarding school. Coupled with what I could see of the house, I assumed the family must be pretty financially comfortable. "I don't know where he is right now, and frankly, I don't care. He's probably dismembering a cat or planning some evil crime against nature or plotting to overthrow the government. I don't know and I don't care! He's your problem now. I've had all I can take!"

"Erm . . ." *He,* I took it, referred to my pupil. What a very odd response this woman had toward her own son. She grabbed two large bags and her purse before turning to face me again. "You're Damian's mother?"

"Goddess, no!" The woman actually shuddered as she spoke.

"Ah. Then you must be the nanny. I was told there would be a new nanny. I'm Ysabelle Raleigh."

"*Was.*"

"Pardon?"

"I *was* the nanny. They hired me yesterday, but I hereby quit. I don't care how many bonuses they pay me to stay with him while they're gone, it's not worth living with that little monster."

A loud crash sounded from the floor above, startling me into an exclamation of surprise, but the agitated woman in front of me didn't even blink an eye. "Tell them they can send my wages to me. They have the address."

"I'm sorry," I said, completely lost. "I don't seem to follow you. You're the nanny but you're quitting?"

"Yes. You're here now. I didn't leave him until you came—you can tell them that. But he's your problem now!"

"Ce qui est celui?"

We both ignored my backpack. "My problem? I hardly see—"

"That's part of it, don't you understand?" She grabbed my arm in a tight grip, her eyes wild. Outside, the taxi driver tapped on the horn. "Everything looks all right, but it's not. Not any of it. And if you can't see that before it's too late, then all will be lost."

Before I could ask for clarification, the nanny grabbed her bags and hauled them out to the taxi driver. "Don't go anywhere, I'll be right back," she told him.

I waited until she returned for the last of her things. "I'm sorry, there seems to be some confusion. I'm not here for the nanny job. I'm just here to tutor—" I dug out the employment card. "Damian Tomas, male child, age ten."

The woman paused dramatically in the doorway. "If you take my advice, you'll clear out right now. The monster can take care of himself."

"Monster?" asked a muffled voice. "*Qui est le* monster?"

I desperately clung to shreds of hope that it was all a big misunderstanding, but sneaky little tendrils of dread kept tugging at me. "What about his parents?"

"Got away while they could. Smart people." She grabbed a cloth bag and a cardboard box, sending a glance of loathing at the ceiling before pinning me back with a look that had the hairs on the back of my neck standing on end. "Be afraid, tutor. Be very afraid. Guard your soul."

My mouth opened in surprise, but before I could form a coherent sentence, she shoved her things at the taxi driver and got into the black car, slamming the door behind her.

"The hell!" Sally said.

I watched the nanny leave, slowly turning to look at the stairs behind me. "I don't know about you, but I'm a bit worried."

"*Une* bit is all?"

"Well . . . all right, more than a bit. What could be so wrong with a child that he drove away his nanny in less than a day?"

"*Merde!*" Sally swore. "*Il est temps pour vous* to get away! *Cette* minute! But first take me *hors de* backpack."

"I'm not taking you out until I know it's all right—"

A rhythmic pounding started upstairs, interrupting both my sentence and my thoughts.

"*Allez, allez!*" Sally urged, the backpack beginning to twitch.

I squared my shoulders. "You know there's not a lot that can scare me." Brave words considering the feeling of dread that permeated my bones, leaving me with the unwavering suspicion that I had just gotten myself into a situation way over my head. I marched to the bottom of the stairs. "Hello? Is someone there? My name is Ysabelle. I'm the tutor."

The pounding stopped. A hushed, expectant feeling settled over the house.

"*Ce n'est pas* normal."

"Hush." I took a deep breath. "There's nothing to fear from a small child, not even one who frightens nannies."

Sally snorted. I set down the backpack and started up the stairs. Before I got halfway, a head poked around the corner and looked down at me.

"Hello. I'm Ysabelle. You must be Damian." I released a breath I hadn't realized I was holding. I don't know what I had been expecting, but the boy in front of me looked perfectly normal. Dark blue eyes watched me from beneath two thick slashes of eyebrows. He held a hammer in one hand, a small can in another. "It's a pleasure to meet you. Are you working on some home-repair project?"

As I rounded the landing and walked up the last few stairs, Damian frowned. "Where's Abby?"

"Is that your nanny?"

"I'm too old to have a nanny," he said, scorn dripping from his words. He had a slight accent that sounded vaguely Germanic to my ears. "She was here to watch the house while my dad and Nell are away."

"Nell being your . . . stepmother?" I guessed.

He nodded, turning to stride down the dark upper hall. I followed, looking around for signs that the boy had been engaged in nefarious acts, but there was nothing I could see. From what I could glimpse through the partly opened doors, the upper floor contained only bedrooms. None of them held dismembered cats, evidence of crimes, or mechanisms to overthrow the government. Abby the ex-nanny must have been of a high-strung personality not at all suited to the care of a child.

"She smells."

"Pardon?" I stopped in the doorway to the room Damian entered. I judged by the clothing strewn on the floor, the TV on but blessedly silent, and the number of electronic toys and game machines that this was his room. Two windows looked down on the square outside, but Damian had nailed a couple of dirty planks across one window, shutting out all light. He hefted a flat piece of board, grunting a little before glancing over his shoulder at me. "Nell. She smells. Are you going to stand there or help me?"

Autocratic little . . . I stopped before I could even think the word, and reminded myself that I had promised the tutoring agency I was good with children. "Perhaps you'd like to tell me why you're boarding up your windows?"

"Because—" He plucked a nail from the can he'd set on a small desk and wrestled the board into place. At another arrogant glance, I obligingly held up one corner of the board so he could nail it into place across the window. "Sebastian is coming."

"He is? Does he always come in through the windows?" I relaxed. Why didn't the agency tell me the boy was special-needs? No doubt the nanny had been unable or unwilling to deal with a child who had a different way of looking at life, but that was nothing new to me.

Damian shot me another look filled with scorn. "He can't use the door. Nell warded it. And the windows on the lower floor, but she didn't do the upper ones."

"I see. Who exactly is Sebastian?"

"He's my dad's enemy. He tried to kill Nell and Papa. Now he's coming for me."

"He's coming for you?" I added paranoia to my list of qualities most evident about Damian.

"Yes."

"How do you know that?"

"He said so." Damian stood back and admired the wood he'd nailed across his windows for a moment. He nodded, then gathered his tools and headed for the next room.

For someone riddled with paranoia, he seemed oddly unconcerned. I couldn't help wondering whether this was an attention-getting device, but that wasn't my major concern at the moment.

"Is there anyone else here?" I asked as he proceeded to nail a board across another window. "A . . . a housekeeper? Or sitter? Anyone?"

"Just Abby, but she's left. I'm glad. She didn't believe Sebastian was coming. She said I was . . ." He paused a moment to recall the word. ". . . delusional."

"Hmm. Well, here's the problem—I'm a tutor, not a nanny. I have my own home to go to, and other work I must do, so I can't stay here to take care of you."

"I can take care of myself," Damian said matter-of-factly. He nailed up another board.

"I'm sure you can. Regardless, I believe it would be best if I spoke with your parents." I sat on the edge of the bed, next to a cordless phone. "Do you have their number?"

"My mum is on a cruise. You can't talk to her unless she calls. My dad and Nell are in Heidelberg. But there's no phone because they're building a new house."

It took some doing, but after fifteen or so minutes, Damian was persuaded to hand over a slip of paper with his father's mobile phone number on it. Two minutes after that, I found myself talking to a pleasant American woman who identified herself as Damian's stepmother.

"I'm sorry, but I just can't stay," I said after explaining what happened. "I have many other clients, and although Damian seems like a delightful child"—Damian huffed and puffed past me hauling a handful of cobwebby two-by-fours from the basement, shooting indignant looks at my lack of helpfulness—"I simply cannot put it all aside to take on a nanny position."

"I wouldn't ask you to do so permanently," said the woman named Nell, a distinct note of pleading in her voice. "But we would be so very grateful if you could stay with Damian overnight. Just overnight. I will call the agency right away, but I know for a fact they won't be able to send someone out until tomorrow morning, and we can't possibly get away until after that. I realize this is a great deal to ask you, but if you could see your way clear to just staying with Damian until morning, we would be happy to pay you a bonus on top of your regular fee."

I bit my lip, swayed against my will by the word *bonus*. "I hate to appear mercenary, but I'm a bit tight right now financially, so it really does matter when I ask how much this bonus would be."

Nell was silent for a moment. "How does a hundred pounds sound?"

It sounded like heaven, but I had enough presence of mind not to blurt that out. Evidently Nell took my momentary silence as disapproval, because she quickly added, "I'll make it two hundred if you can stay until the new nanny arrives."

My hesitation wasn't due to greed. I quickly ran over a mental list of everything that I needed to do in the next twenty-four hours. "I will agree if you don't mind my clients coming here to see me."

"Your clients?"

"I'm a counselor," I answered.

"Oh. Occupational? Emotional?"

"Sort of a cross between the two. I counsel people who've undergone a major change in their life and need a little help to get going again. I have three appointments tonight, and a handful more in the morning."

"Ah, I see. Well, so long as no one unbalanced or dangerous is brought to the house, I don't see any objection. Thank you so much for doing this, Ysabelle. Adrian will be relieved to know his son is in such capable hands."

The son in question chose that moment to stalk by me with a fistful of kitchen knives.

"Erm . . . yes."

After a few basic instructions on where things were located in the house, and promises that a new nanny would be on the doorstep bright and early, Nell hung up. "Anything else you need, Damian will help you. He's very precocious," she said before she disconnected.

Precocious was one word for it. I promised to call if there were any problems, after which I set the phone in its cradle and watched with interest as Damian bustled around the room arranging knives, electrical tape, and more wood.

"Your backpack is talking."

"Hmm? Oh. Erm . . ." My wits, somewhat shaken with the events of the last half hour, attempted to pull together an explanation of why a spirit was in my backpack. "Damian, have you ever wondered what happens to people after they pass on?"

He shrugged. "Not really."

"Ah. Sometimes people who pass on unexpectedly are a bit . . . well, confused is as good a word as any. Many of them don't realize that they're dead. Some do, but they might remain behind in spirit form for other reasons—there's something important that needs to be done, amends to be made, revenge, that sort of thing. What remains of those people after their bodies fade are often called ghosts or spirits—"

"Sally speaks horrible French."

I did a quick mental double-take, upping my estimation of Damian a smidgen. "Ah. You chatted with her?"

"She asked me to let her out." His eyes narrowed for a minute before he dismissed me and turned back to his work. "I figured you had her trapped in there on purpose, so I didn't."

"Thank you, but she's not actually trapped . . . One second, I'll let her out and see if I can explain a bit."

It took a few minutes to smooth Sally's ruffled feathers, but at last she settled down enough to listen to me while I told her of our change of plans.

"What about *votre* clients *du* zombies that are *programmé ce soir?*"

I shot a glance at Damian, but he didn't seem to be listening, instead preferring to pound planks over the window. "I'll just have to see them here instead. There are only three more tonight, aren't there?"

She nodded.

"Excellent. I'll just deal with them and send them on their way. That should be the end of it."

Sally had a few choice things to say about the change of

plans, but I pointed out to her that we needed money to live. By the time I was finished with her, Damian had used the electrical tape to attach a couple of knives to each window. Sally took one look at the knives and headed for safer ground. "*Je* go leave *une petite* note on our door for *les* zombie appointments."

"Revenant appointments." I waited until Sally left for our flat before saying to the industrious boy in front of me, "Um . . . Damian . . ."

"Just in case," he said, not waiting for me to finish my question.

A few minutes of close scrutiny of his handiwork made it clear that Damian was not a stupid child. He handled the knives carefully, respectful of their ability to cause injury. I debated making him take the potentially lethal booby traps down, but decided that so long as he was not harmed—and did not harm anyone else—the rest was an issue for his parents or his nanny.

"I see. As fascinating as that is, I'm here to give you lessons, and even though your stepmother has asked me to spend the night here just to make sure all is well, I think we should proceed with the original plan and take a few lessons in English and history."

"I'm busy right now," Damian answered, not even looking at me as he went into a room made dark by more boarded-up windows. He selected two skinning knives and arranged them on each side of the window. "Why do you have a spirit guide?"

"She . . . er . . . was a bit of a gift. And just so you know, attempting to distract me isn't going to work. There are many other things I would like to be doing at this moment as well, but tutoring is what I'm being paid to do, and do it I will."

"Protecting us from Sebastian is more important than lessons," he said with a black-browed scowl in my direction. "My dad would want me to save your life over learning some stupid dates and writing compositions."

"I don't even know this Sebastian person," I pointed out. "Why do you think he would pose a risk to *me?*"

The look the boy gave me was rife with irritation. "You've got a double soul."

I swear, my mouth hung open for a moment at his statement. "I . . . I don't know what you're talking about. People don't have two souls," I said slowly, a chill running down my arms. How on earth could a mere child see my handicap? "Everyone is granted one soul only when they are born."

Damian shrugged and said nothing.

"What does Sebastian have to do with souls?" I couldn't keep myself from asking. "Is he a demon?"

"No. He's a Dark One." He looked up and grinned, two pointed canines clearly visible despite the gloom. "Like my dad and me."

I took a couple of steps back, a hand at my heart. I'd heard of Dark Ones—vampires, tainted by the dark powers, parasites who preyed on the lives of mortals—but I'd never seen one in person.

"I think . . . I don't know . . . I think I need a little air," I said, stumbling backward as my words jumbled together. Blindly, I made my escape, clutching the banister as I ran downstairs, aware now what Abby had found so wrong with Damian.

I wanted to run away, to go home and hide, to forget I'd ever been here, but as I stood with my hand on the front doorknob just about to bolt, my conscience took that moment to kick in and remind me that although Damian might be a vampire—*vampire!*—he was also a child. I couldn't just leave a ten-year-old alone.

"I'm hungry." Damian's voice drifted downstairs. "Do you have any blood?"

A flight instinct I didn't know I possessed kicked in. I yanked the door open, a survival instinct overriding my better sense into running. But a dark shape looming in the doorway had me shrieking instead, stepping backward in horror as a familiar man—tall, built rather solidly, and covered in blood—staggered through the door.

"You, woman, give me the ring!" he demanded in an authoritative voice that was immediately contradicted when his eyes rolled up and he collapsed at my feet.

I stared down at the man in shock, a thousand questions racing through my mind. What on earth was the kissable Good Samaritan from the alley doing here? Had he followed me? Was he a stalker rather than a lifesaver? How could anyone who kissed the way he did have harm on his mind? And what on earth was he babbling about? "What ring? Who are you? What did you have to do with those demons? God's mercy, you're bleeding! Are you all right? Should I call the paramedics?"

"Oooh," Damian's voice said from where he stood on the stairs, looking down at the scene before him. "You let Sebastian in. That isn't good. Now he'll try to kill us."

Chapter Three

"Who are you?" The voice was as rough and low as I remembered. "You are not the charmer. You cannot be. What are you doing in this house?"

Sebastian was bound to a chair, held by a thin nylon laundry line Damian had found in the basement. Before I could answer, Sally, only just returned from a quick trip to my flat, gasped and floated over until she was directly in front of him. "*Elle est* very charming! *Vous êtes tres* rude!"

"He said charmer, not charming," I said slowly, racking my brain to dig out information on charmers. Fleeting thoughts skittered away as I was swamped with the memory of Sebastian's mouth on mine.

"So?" Sally continued to stand with her hands on her hips, glaring at Sebastian. He glared right back at her.

"A charmer is someone who can unmake curses," he said, turning his gaze to me. I felt it as if it were a physical touch.

"That's right—they lift curses and wards and things. You are quite correct; I am not a charmer. My name is Ysabelle Raleigh. I am tutoring Damian. I take it you are Sebastian?"

"Yes. Where is Adrian?" His brows pulled together as he looked down at himself, noticing that his arms had been tied behind him. When he looked back up to me, his gray-blue eyes were flashing with indigation and just a smidgen of disbelief. "You think to hold me prisoner?"

Sally's form shimmered indignantly. "*Oui, vous êtes dérangé* man! And there you'll stay *jusqu'à ce que vous expliquiez* why you're attacking *pauvre* Belle!"

Sebastian's eyes narrowed at her for a moment. "You are aware, are you not, that you are not speaking actual French?"

"*Le* gasp!" Sally said, following word by deed and gasping in a thoroughly shocked manner. "*Je suis* too!"

"No, you are not. You are mangling a perfectly nice language—"

"*Zût alors!*" she interrupted, shaking an ethereal fist in his face. "*Je frapperai vous* on the nose—"

"All right, that's enough, you two." I gave my spirit guide a very stern look. She bristled, her eyes flashing. "Sally, please leave us alone."

"Like *enfer* I will! You are not safe—"

I shooed her toward the door. "Don't be silly. He's bound quite tightly, and if I need any help, I'll yell for you."

"*Mais—*" She shot both of us a shared indignant look as I shoved her through the door.

"I'm sorry about that," I said, giving Sebastian a wide berth as I returned to the desk I'd been leaning against. "She's a bit ecentric."

One of his eyebrows rose. "An understatement, but one I am willing to let go in order to deal with more important issues."

"Yes . . . your injuries seem to be healing. I take it you received them fighting the demon? Why did you do it?" I asked, desperate to distract myself from the strange attraction.

Damian and I had half dragged, half carried the unconscious Sebastian into the library, a room filled with comfortable leather chairs and several bookcases, all dominated by a large rosewood desk. As my aching arms attested to, he was a big man—imposing, but not fat—with hair the color of rich honey, his eyes a stormy grayish blue. Despite his arrogance, my fingers itched to run along the stubborn line of his jaw, to feel his touseled hair, to gently brush the width of those broad shoulders, tracing the solid planes of his chest down to that flat belly, and still farther below to where tight jeans accented masculine attributes. My lips positively burned with sensual delight at the thought of kissing him again.

"I disabled the demon . . . after a bit of a fight. What were you thinking, running straight into it?"

"I was running down the alley because you told me to."

He had the audacity to look annoyed. "I told you to turn left. You would have been safe if you'd done so."

"Moot point," I said with a smile. "I am . . . erm . . . sorry about running into you. And the . . . er . . . kissing. I'm not normally so forward."

He frowned. "That also is a moot point. Where is Adrian and the charmer? Why have you tied me to this chair?"

"Mr. and Mrs. Tomas are in Germany at the moment. As for the bonds—I'm sorry, but I felt it prudent given the nature of your arrival and Damian's avowal that you've come to destroy him."

"I have," Sebastian said simply, pulling uselessly at the ropes. Because of my weaving experience, I could tie a quality knot. "Germany. I should have known. Very well, we will go to Germany once you give me the ring. You will release me now and bring it to me."

I rested my hip against the edge of the desk, considering the man before me. "We? We will go to Germany? We as in you and who, exactly?"

"You try my patience, Beloved. You know full well I am referring to you. Now cease these games and release me. I have limited time to destroy Adrian, and we must Join as soon as possible."

"Hold on," I said, raising a hand to stop him. "Back up a moment—you expect me to go to Germany with you?"

"Of course. You will go wherever I go."

"Are you insane?" I couldn't help it, I goggled at him for a moment. "I don't know you! Wait—is this because I kissed you back?"

The look in his eyes was almost insulting. "Why do you pretend ignorance? I am a patient man, but you are pushing my limits. Release me!"

"Not on your life. This is about that kiss, isn't it? You think you're going to take me away to Germany just because I kissed you? Once? God's blood, what do you do with the women you sleep with—marry them?"

"I will marry you, yes. Now cease with this useless conversation and release me."

I shook my head. "I'm going to call in some professional help. Honestly, I think you must have bumped your head on the pavement when we fell. You're not making any sense—"

He swore in French, and his muscles bunched for a moment before the rope exploded around him. One second he was sitting, the next he was before me, his hands hard on my hips as he yanked me up against him. "We do not have time for these games. Your presence complicates matters somewhat, but we will overcome the obstacles you present. The first task at hand is to complete the Joining. Remove your clothing."

"What?" I shrieked, trying desperately not to melt against him.

"We must make love to complete the Joining. We will do that first, then retrieve the ring."

His body was hard against me, hard and aggressive and overwhelming to my senses, but it was an oddly exciting feeling, not at all the frightening one I'd expected. He was a vampire, I desperately reminded myself. A cold, heartless parasite who preyed on humans.

We prefer the term Dark One, actually, he said. With a start I realized he was speaking directly into my head. *And I assure you I am anything but cold and heartless. Right at this moment, I am very, very hot.*

My eyes widened as his head dipped toward mine, freezing as his gaze narrowed for a second on me. I had the sensation that he was seeing deep into my soul, baring all my secrets. I knew then that he'd noticed my handicap, and I turned slightly to avoid his piercing gaze. I felt like a succulent bit of prey watched by a dangerous predator—a feeling I did not enjoy, no matter how many tingles of excitement rippled down my body.

His voice, which had been deep and forceful, softened. "You do not know what I am talking about, do you?"

"No, I don't. All I know is that you mean Damian and me harm—"

"Beloved, I could never hurt you," he said, his thumb sweeping along my lower lip, teasing me until I turned back to look into those all-seeing eyes.

"You are a vampire. Hurt is what you do best, isn't it?" For some reason, I felt it necessary to remind my errant body that this man was not for me.

"I am as you see me. And you are—"

"I am quite well aware of my handicap, thank you," I interrupted, looking down, trying to control my breathing. Being pressed up against him was proving to be an overwhelming experience, one my body wanted to explore more fully.

"Handicap?" His heavy dark honey brows pulled together. "You consider having a double soul a handicap?"

"We are not here to discuss me," I said sternly, trying my best to ignore the bizarre attraction. It had been too long since I had been married, that's all. My hormones were simply kicking in and focusing on the nearest male body they could find.

"On the contrary, at this moment I can think of nothing more I wish to discuss." His gaze flickered over to the clock on the mantel. He sighed. "But I do not have time to indulge myself. Very well, since you are not aware of what has transpired in the last hour, I will give you a summary. You are a *tattu,* bearer of a double soul, and my Beloved, the one woman who can redeem my soul and save me from millenia of anguished existence. I knew that the moment we exchanged blood."

"Exchanged blood?" I asked, my head whirling. "When did we exchange blood? I kissed you, that's all! And, for the record, you started it by licking my lip!"

"Your lip was cut when you landed on me. I bit my tongue when I was knocked backward. We exchanged blood when we kissed. And now we must complete the other seven steps of Joining for you to be safe from the demon that will be pounding on the door at any moment. Once that is completed, I will be able to protect you. Until that time, you are vulnerable."

I touched my lip. It was sensitive, still tingling from Sebastian's kiss, and in one spot, slightly tender from our collision. I shook my head again, unable to digest it all. "Even assuming that I am your soul-saving person, why do you think that demon will be coming to Adrian's house?"

"He will follow your scent just as I did," he answered matter-of-factly.

I wanted to bristle at the idea that I smelled so strongly people could track me all over London, but the heated look in his eyes generated an answering heat that pooled deep within me, and left no doubt in my mind that whatever it was I smelled like, he did not find it offensive.

"You are *tattu*, a great prize for the demon's master. Do you believe it will not do everything it can to find you and take you to Abaddon?"

I shivered, leaning into him for a moment. I had just met this man, this vampire, but already I felt safe with him. It was as if an empty part of me was suddenly filled with life. "I . . . I don't know what to believe. This is all going too fast for me."

"I am sorry," he said, his eyes filled with regret. "I would do this differently if I could, but, Beloved, we have no time. We must Join now so I can protect you. It is my duty. I do not wish to frighten you, or force you into something you are not ready for, but you must believe me. We have no time for wooing."

His lips brushed mine, gently teasing the edges of my mouth until I sighed and started kissing him back. The world had gone mad, everything I knew was being turned on its head, but damn if I didn't care.

"We have completed several of the steps," he murmured into my mouth, his tongue flicking against my lips. I moaned and sucked his bottom lip, shamelessly pressing myself against him. "But we must exchange fluids once again for the Joining to be complete."

"I'm not going to make love to you," I whispered just before I deepened the kiss, tasting his mouth, twining my tongue around his.

"You must," he groaned, pulling my hips tight against his. I had no doubt that he was as aroused as I was, but even though I was giving in to this unexplained attraction, I wasn't stupid.

I pulled my mouth from his. "I have been married five times, Sebastian. I'm no stranger to either men or lovemaking. But I do not indulge in casual sex, no matter how . . . metaphysical the relationship is. There seems to be something between us that I wouldn't mind exploring further, but I am not sleeping with you."

Your souls are at risk, he said, nibbling my lower lip. My knees buckled, leaving me swooning in his arms, my head spinning with the scent and taste and feel of him against me.

Do you think they have never been so in the past? I slid my hands under his shirt and let my fingers dance across his back. I wanted to touch him, all of him, but I knew one of us had to keep some control, and clearly Sebastian was not going to be that person. I confined myself to stroking the planes of his back as he kissed me, allowing him to explore my mouth.

This is Salvaticus, he reminded me, his tongue dancing against mine. *For a week, all will be chaos, but even when Salvaticus is over and Vexamen upon us, the demon will not forget you. You will be in danger from here to the end of your days if you do not Join with me.*

"I can take care of myself," I mumbled against his mouth as we came up for air. "I always have."

"That was before you were marked by a demon. No, Beloved, the only answer is for us to Join. *Now.*" Hot kisses burned my neck as he found a spot that sent shivers of absolute pleasure down my back.

"Can you explain . . . oh, dear God, yes, right there . . . can you explain just how this Joining is going to save my souls? As far as I can tell, it's just some sort of emotional commitment. I don't see how that will help protect me from a demon or its lord."

Unbidden, my hands skimmed around to his sides, sculpting the long, sweeping lines of his torso. He nipped my neck when I found a pert nipple that was all but begging for attention. "A Beloved is the mortal woman who redeems a Dark One's soul. In return, he is bound to her, and protects her at all costs."

"You don't have a soul?" I pulled back enough to peer into his eyes. They glittered hot with desire, but I didn't see anything in them to indicate he was soulless. There was no sick feeling of dread emanating from him, as was common in a creature of the dark. The only feelings I got from him were desire, need, want, and an overwhelming sadness that pulled at my heart. "You don't look like a demon."

"I am not a demon. Dark Ones are cursed to remain soulless until their Beloveds regain it for them, but we are not demonic."

His eyes, dark navy-gray, regarded me as I tried to sort through what he'd told me. "You seriously believe I can regain your soul for you?"

"I know you can. It follows the Joining."

A little burst of pain zinged through me at the realization that I was means to an end for him. I was certain that the whole business with him protecting me from a demon was simply a little sugar-coating over the more important issue of his soul. Regardless of all that, I was shaking my head even before he finished the sentence. "I can't be your Beloved."

"You are."

"No." I pushed back on his chest. To my surprise, he released me. My breath came hard and rough, my heart beating wildly as I tried to regain composure. "I'm sorry, Sebastian. I realize that I look like a *get your soul back free* card, but there's a big point you are missing."

He watched me for a moment. "That is not an issue. You are my Beloved. I feel it. I tasted it in your blood. I know it in my heart."

I said nothing for a few minutes while I tried to sort through my tangled thoughts. If what he said was true, then I had very little time to make a decision that would change the path of my life. I hated feeling pressured into doing anything, and here I was being asked to commit myself body and soul to a man—a *vampire*—I'd just met. Could I do it? Did I even want to try? He said my handicap made no matter in the issue of Belovedness, but did he truly know that? What if we tried and it failed? What if he were just using me, manipulating me into giving him what he wanted without regards to the future? Did I really have any alternatives? Salvaticus would be over soon . . . but somehow, I knew that he spoke the truth. The demon had seen me for what I was, and it would move heaven and earth to return to its master with me as a prize. The man before me held the key to my salvation, just as I did for him.

Sebastian said nothing as I wrestled with my thoughts, simply holding me in a loose embrace, his eyes flashing bluish gray lights that mesmerized me.

"Very well, I will Join with you," I said finally. He needed a soul, and I could redeem it for him. I would do it his way because the alternative was unthinkable.

I didn't want to die. Not again.

Chapter Four

"What . . . er . . . do we have to say something?" I asked, more than a little nervous now that I'd agreed to bind myself to the man whose mere physical presence filled me with a strange excited happiness. "Is there something I need to swear to? Or is it like a ceremony?"

"There are seven steps to Joining," he said solemnly. "The first two are marking and protection from afar."

"The demon and the mind-talking," I said, recalling his soft voice in my head urging me down the alley. I hadn't thought anything of it at the time, but I recognized it now for what it was.

"Yes. The third and fourth steps involve the first exchange of bodily fluids, and entrusting the Beloved with the truth."

"That would be the kiss and . . . well, I guess telling me who you are."

He nodded. "The fifth step is the second exchange."

"I assume that"—I waved a hand to indicate the necking session in which we'd just indulged—"qualifies?"

"It does. The sixth step is for the Beloved to overcome the darkness within the Dark One."

"Oh." I thought for a few seconds, frowning as I ran over our conversation. "I'm afraid I don't quite see where we've done that."

"That's because you haven't promised yet to assist me in bringing down the Betrayer."

"Who?"

"Adrian the Betrayer. The man who sold me to Asmodeus."

I gawked at him for a second or two. "He *sold* you to a demon lord?"

"Yes." Sebastian's eyes grew as pale as a foggy dawn. "That is why I seek revenge against him and his family. I swore my vengeance as Asmodeus drained my blood away. Nothing but death will satisfy such a betrayal."

The urge to take him in my arms and comfort him, to lighten the darkness visible in his eyes, was almost overwhelming, but before I could act upon it, the door opened.

"Sally told me to make sure Sebastian doesn't try to do something bad to you," Damian said, marching into the room with a pugnacious set to his jaw.

Sebastian's entire body tensed. I put a warning hand on his arm. "Damian, we're having a bit of an adult conversation. Sebastian isn't going to do anything bad, so you can go back and tell Sally—"

"She also said to tell you that there's a demon outside the house demanding to see you. And a bunch of imps. She said she's called Noelle already, too."

I closed my eyes for a moment and wished for the sane, normal life I had when I woke up that morning.

"There are also five zombies outside with big signs, saying they need to talk to you about being kicked out of Hyde Park."

All right, maybe my life wasn't so normal. Still, it had been better earlier in the day. . . .

"To delay any longer is folly," Sebastian said, turning to me. "The demon is here. He will fight to gain control over you. We must Join now."

Damian wrinkled up his nose at us. "Ew. Joining. That means you're going to kiss her. That's gross."

I sighed at the boy. "Would you please tell Sally that we'll be right out, and tell Tim and his fellow sit-in revenants that I will be happy to talk to them as soon as I can. When did Sally say Noelle will be here?"

"She said she caught her on the tube, and it would only

take a couple of minutes. Who's Noelle?" he asked as I gave him a gentle push toward the door.

"Our roommate who is also a Guardian."

Sebastian jerked, as if he was startled by something. I shot him a curious glance, but his face was blank.

"Oh. That's good?"

"Yes, very good. If there is a demon to control, Noelle is the best person to have around. Go on now. We'll be right out."

Sebastian ground his teeth as he watched the boy slowly walk to the door, his body tense and poised to strike. "We must leave now, Beloved. We must Join and leave this house."

I touched his cheek, wondering how he could live through such atrocities and still show so much control. "How did you survive?"

His eyes flickered toward me. "Christian, more of a blood brother than a friend, helped me track down the Betrayer." Sebastian's expression darkened until his beautiful face was a vision of stark vengeance. The sight of it chilled me with frozen dread. I had seen such a look once before . . . and now to see it on the face of the man to whom I had just promised to bind myself was unbearable. "He later turned on me, throwing in his lot with the Betrayer."

"Papa isn't a betrayer," Damian said abruptly, standing at the door. His scowl was almost as fierce as Sebastian's. "He had to do what he did. Nell said he's a brave man because he let everyone think he was bad so he could save people."

"The charmer is deluded," Sebastian snapped, turning back to me. "Christian claimed the Betrayer was saving others by sacrificing me, but I know it was not so. Christian forswore me to distract me from my plan."

"Uncle Christian would never do that," Damian muttered, glowering at us both. "He knows Papa wouldn't do anything bad like you say he would."

"No? The Betrayer skewered me to the wall with a knife in the neck, nearly severing my head. But perhaps you do not call a near decapitation 'bad.'" Sebastian took a step toward

Damian, pulling down the neckline of his black sweater to expose a faint, ragged white line. I tightened my grip on his arm and gently touched the scar.

"No," I said simply.

Sebastian misunderstood me. "I will not ask you to participate in the actual killing of the Betrayer—that act is one I must do myself. But you understand now why I must seek justice for the crimes committed against me. We have delayed too long; we must leave now. We will go to Paris first—"

"No," I repeated, rubbing my arms against the chill that seemed to leech out from within me. "I understand what you've gone through. But I will not help you if you insist on this path of revenge."

Disbelief filled his eyes. "You will not—"

"No," I said again, lifting my chin so he could better see my determination. "If you wish for me to Join with you, you must first swear to me that you will release your oath of vengeance against Adrian and his family. I will not lift one finger to help you otherwise."

He swore softly to himself. "Why would you deny me what is mine? Do you not think I have every right to exact revenge for the betrayal?"

"I think you have a right to be hurt, yes. Angry, absolutely. Changed by your experience—without a doubt. But I have seen firsthand what revenge against another can do, and I will have no part in it. So make your choice, Sebastian—either you have a soul and a Beloved, or you can have revenge against someone who is probably just as much a victim as you were."

"Papa was cursed by Asmodeus," Damian chipped in. "He didn't have a choice. He had to do what Asmodeus told him to do because his papa gave him away."

Sebastian growled something rude in French. I gave Damian a narrow-eyed look of warning and made a shooing gesture. With head held high, he nodded, and reluctantly left the room.

I knew the second the door closed Sebastian would start

in on me about my demand that he give up his plans of vengeance, but I haven't survived as long as I have without learning how to deal with men.

"I think you're incredibly brave," I told him as he turned toward me, clearly about to lecture me.

"Ysabelle—" He stopped, frowning. "You do?"

I smiled to myself. Nothing distracts a man like a bit of flattery, especially when it's sincere. "Yes, as a matter of fact, I do. You had to be incredibly brave to survive being in the control of a demon lord and an attack that could have severed your head. I also think you're intelligent, charming, and . . . well . . . sexy as hell, to be honest."

He stood in front of me, his toes touching mine. I held his piercing gaze, happy to let him see in my eyes that I meant exactly what I said.

That puzzled him. His frown deepened. "Then why did you just threaten to leave me unless I did what you wanted?"

"I told you why—I've seen the effect of the sort of vengeance that you plan, and frankly—"

"Belle!" Sally swept through the door, her hands on her hips. "*Le* demon *est à la porte!* And *il vous* wants *parler!*"

"Yes, I know. Damian told me."

"Ysabelle?" A man's voice sounded muffled on the other side of the door. "Tim McMann here. I'm sorry to bother you here, but you did say to come to you with problems. Might I have a word about the sit-in? We seem to have a spot of trouble with one of the participants."

"What sort of trouble?" I asked, momentarily distracted from the grave decision Sebastian was demanding of me.

"It seems William here inadvertently ate two squirrels and a small ferret en route. He's fully willing to participate in the sit-in, but the others were wondering if that's quite proper since we are espousing the nonflesh lifestyle."

"They were very small squirrels," another man said with obvious distress, clearly the William in question. "Tasty, but not much meat on them. I'm still hungry, in fact. Anyone want to pop into the McDonald's for a quick bite?"

I sighed and hung my head for the count of five, wishing once again that I could rewind the day and start it all over.

"Ysabelle?" Tim shouted.

"I'll be right there. Don't let him eat any more meat."

"I can stop any time I want," William yelled through the door. "I'm just a bit peckish right now. Here, Jack, you doing anything with that arm?"

A squawk followed, presumably from the man named Jack. I rubbed my forehead and wondered how hard it would be to fall into a little coma.

"Ysabelle? We really could use your help out here. William just bit Estabon and Jamal when they pulled him off Jack. I believe he's frothing at the mouth. Surely there's something we can do to save him?"

"Brainnsssss," came the reply from the now thoroughly meat-poisoned William. I sighed again. I hated to lose a client to meat.

"Pull yourself together, man!" Tim bellowed. A sharp thwacking noise followed, as if the sit-in members were beating William on the head with their signs. "That's the very stereotype we're protesting against! Remember what we're standing for! Ysabelle!"

"Tie him up if you need to, but don't get within range of his teeth. Sally will show you where there's rope," I answered, turning back to face Sebastian.

The look of disbelief on his face was priceless. Sally rolled her eyes.

"Is Noelle on her way?" I asked her.

"*Oui.* She's coming *ici bientôt,* just a tube stop away. But—"

"Beloved, we must go now," Sebastian said. He grabbed my hand and pulled me toward a door at the opposite end of the room. "We do not have time to delay any longer."

"Just a moment, Sebastian. I'm not moving until we get a few things straightened out."

"Belle! *Le* demon!" Sally shouted, her hands gesticulating wildly.

"Yes, I know, but this should only take a couple of minutes. Until Sebastian and I have an understanding—"

A huge crash rocked the house.

"*Là, vous* see?" Sally's voice was complacent as both Sebastian and I ran for the door. "*Le* demon has blown up the house! *J'* hope that *vous êtes* happy."

"Bloody hell . . ." I beat Sebastian to the doorway, but he grabbed my arm and pulled me behind him as he raced out into the hallway. The sharp, stinging smell of explosive powder filled the air, making my eyes stream and clogging my throat. I coughed, peering through weeping eyes at the destruction. The remains of the front door hung drunkenly open, attached only by one bent and damaged hinge. The small couch and end table that sat at the far end were covered in bits of wood and plaster, and part of something I hesitantly identified as a revenant. Tim and the others emerged from under the remains of a large potted palm that had exploded.

"Brainsssssss," came the eerie wail from the bits of revenant on the destroyed couch.

Sally picked up an unattached leg and floated her way across the debris to where the still animated upper half of William sat. "Is this yours?"

"Oooh. That looks lovely. If you could set it just here next to me . . ."

Sally was about to give the revenant his leg, but heeded the look in my eye and retreated to a corner with it instead.

Damian, crouched at the top of the stairs, peered over the rail at me, his dark hair powdered gray, but he appeared otherwise unhurt.

"Are you all right?" I asked him.

He nodded, then pointed to the gaping hole that was now the doorway. Sebastian and I turned to look.

"*Tattu!*"

The demon I'd surprised earlier stood in the doorway, its eyes glowing with hate.

"Oh, crap," Sally said, brandishing the leg as if it was a weapon. "It's *ici*."

Sebastian moved to block the demon's view of me. I stared at the back of his neck for a second, amused but touched by his protective attitude. I'd barely met the man, and already he was acting like . . . well, like a doting husband. I couldn't help wondering . . .

"*Tattu!* Come with me and I will not harm the Dark Ones."

"Who is this now?" Tim asked, giving the demon a haughty look. "Is he holding us hostage? Are we in a hostage situation? Will he adhere to the proper rules governing treatment of hostages? Shall we designate one of us as a negotiator?"

I sighed and moved to Sebastian's side to confront the demon. Sebastian stood absolutely still, his eyes the color of bleached granite, his muscles tense. I slid my hand into his, not sure whether it was to restrain him from hasty actions or to comfort myself. His fingers tightened around mine, sending a little wave of warmth up my arm.

"This woman is my Beloved," Sebastian told the demon, his body language screaming that he was not about to take anything from anyone. "You will leave now."

"Beloved?" The demon's gaze turned to me. My skin crawled as it examined me, leaving me feeling tainted and foul.

A wave of imps washed up and over the demon's feet, collecting in a pool on the hallway floor before him. They yip-yipped aggressively, hopping up and down and shaking their little fists at us until Sebastian cast a glance at them. One look from him had them scampering back to the safety of the doorway.

"Imps," said William's remains. "I could go for a nice imp fry right about now."

You're a handy guy to have around, I told Sebastian.

In more ways than you can imagine, he answered, and for

one brilliant moment, my head was flooded with the most erotic images, thoughts and desires and urges that all involved me. My knees almost buckled at the things Sebastian wanted to do to me. The images were gone in a second, leaving me to wish we were alone so I could investigate futher some of the arousing thoughts he'd had. A snarl from the demon returned my attention to the moment at hand.

"The *tattu* is not your Beloved," the demon sneered at Sebastian. "You have not Joined. She belongs to my master. I will take her now, and there is nothing you can do to stop me."

"Can I have my leg back, please?"

Beloved, we must Join now. It is the only way I can protect you.

"*Vous et ce qui* army?" Sally floated over to stand in front of me, her arms crossed over her chest (she'd given William's leg to Tim). My heart warmed at her brave—but completely useless—attempt to protect me.

Ysabelle, we do not have a choice. We must Join before the demon attacks. Without help, I can disable it only for a short time. It will no doubt return with minions and other demons. Sebastian's voice was rich with regret that he was forcing a decision on me, but there was a faint echo of satisfaction that had me wondering again.

The demon walked right through Sally and stopped a few feet in front of Sebastian. It smiled. The lights in the chandelier near the stairs exploded, tiny bits of glass raining down on the floor behind us.

"Here now! Broken glass can be very dangerous!" Tim protested, taking a firm grip on William's leg as he started forward. He immediately beat a retreat when the demon turned its eyes on him. "Er . . . sorry for interrupting. Continue."

"Do not delude yourselves," the demon said. "You cannot stop me. I will have the *tattu*. Will you be destroyed as well, Dark One?"

Sebastian snarled something that was anatomically impossible (even for a demon), his muscles bunched as he was about to strike. A movement behind the demon, a dark shape faintly visible in the streetlight, caught my attention. Sebastian must have seen it as well, for his fingers loosened their painful grip on mine.

Ysabelle, this does not change anything. The demon will return, with reinforcements. We must Join!

"Just the foot would do. Surely you could spare me one little foot?" William pleaded with Tim.

I heaved yet another sigh, knowing in my heart that what Sebastian said was true. Now that the demon had found me, there was no way it was going to let me go. I knew even without asking that anywhere I went, it would find me, just as it found me in the middle of London.

"A couple of toes? Just to tide me over?"

I had no choice. I could either save myself and Sebastian, or I could damn us both by trying to avoid the inevitable. Sebastian's thumb stroked over my hand for two heartbeats while I wrestled with my thoughts.

What about Adrian and Damian?

Pain lashed through him, mingling with his anger and regret and need for justice. I held my breath, knowing if he made a choice I could not condone, we were both doomed. *I will do as you demand,* he said at last, the agreement costing him much. *I will forfeit my right to revenge myself on them if you will Join with me.*

Relief filled me. *I am not going to make love to you. Especially not right here in front of everyone!* I thought at him indignantly.

That is the preferred method, but not the only one. Another exchange of body fluids would do.

Body fluids?

Blood. I wish things were different, Beloved.

I know. I smiled at him as the demon whirled around, finding itself face-to-face with a short, red-haired Guardian barely visible through the doorway.

"What—" The demon was cut off in midquestion.

Now, Beloved.

"Belle?" Sally asked, her brow puckered as Sebastian pulled me into an embrace. "What are you—*mon Dieu!* Not that!"

A disgusted "Ew!" drifted down the stairs as Sebastian's mouth descended upon mine, his lips starting a desire inside me that I doubted would ever be extinguished.

"Here, you, little boy. Fetch me that thigh I see peeking out from under the chair."

"You're gross," Damian told the remains of William.

Despite the confusion of everyone surrounding us, the demon who was now hanging upside down in the doorway screaming curses, the revenants, the imps, and Noelle dimly visible outside as she began banishing the demon, I kissed Sebastian back with every tangled, confused emotion I had, and prayed I was making the right choice.

His mouth trailed heat as he kissed a path to the base of my neck. *I wish this were different, Ysabelle. But it is right we do it.*

I said nothing as his teeth pierced my flesh, my body quivering with both the sensation of him taking life from me, and the images he was sharing with me, feelings of arousal and need, of a bone-deep satisfaction, and surprisingly, a strong sense of rightness that resonated within me. My body went up in flames as his mouth moved on my neck while he drank deeply, my breasts aching and straining against him, my hips rubbing in a suggestive manner, heat deep within my core flaring outward in a rush of ecstasy. Every inch of my flesh was sensitized to the point where I thought I would climax right then and there.

The demon screamed, causing the windows near the door to shatter. Sebastian pulled his mouth from my neck, his eyes almost ebony as he looked down at me. Without a word he kissed me again, his tongue painting the inside of my mouth with a familiar, sweet, spicy taste.

Drink, Beloved.

He'd nipped his tongue. As I suckled it, drunk on the heady sensation of taking from him what he'd taken from me,

I merged with him, almost crying out at the dark emptiness where his soul should have been.

I filled him with as much light as I could give, dimly aware of Noelle as she yelled the words of banishment above the clamor of the revenants and imps. Sally sputtered around us helplessly, trying to gain my attention, but that was focused solely on the man I held in my arms, the man to whom I had just bound myself body and soul.

"Well, that's done." Noelle's perky voice drifted across the hallway to us as she dusted off her hands and entered the house. "Nasty fellow. We're going to have some trouble there, Belle, now that he's seen you. Hello, Tim, nice to see you again. Did one of you explode? I found a knee out on the walkway. We'll have to . . . oh my God. Sebastian?"

I pulled away from Sebastian. His eyes were clouded as he turned to face my roommate.

"Good evening, Noelle. You look well."

"You know each other?" I asked, looking from her to the man who still held me close to his side.

"I should say so," Noelle said, giving me an unreadable look. "I'm his Beloved."

Chapter Five

"You *lied* to me!"

"I do not lie."

"You told me I was your Beloved!" It's difficult to put indignation, betrayal, hurt feelings, and a healthy dollop of menace into a whisper, but I gave it my best shot.

I'd quickly discovered that Sebastian's eyes were a barometer to his mood. Dark midnight gray indicated sexual arousal. The lighter his eyes turned, the less happy he was. Right now they were a pale bluish granite. "You *are* my Beloved."

"Don't you dare lighten your eyes at me," I warned. "You have no right to be angry here. I'm the victim. I'm the one you used."

Noelle, who had been standing in the middle of the hall, moved over to join our whispered conversation. The revenants were busily blockading the gaping hole where the door used to be, while Sally had been sent to double-check that all the windows on the ground floor had been warded against possible imp or demon infiltration. Damian sat on the stairs, his chin in his hands, watching everything with bright, interested eyes. The remains of William were propped up against the wall next to him, alternating between offering the revenants advice on how to use the couch to block the doorway, and pleading for just a bit of flesh to appease his hunger.

"I'm not quite sure I understand this," Noelle said slowly as she looked from me to Sebastian. "He told you that you were his Beloved?"

"Yes," I said, glaring at the man in question. He crossed his arms and tightened his jaw, as if he were going to stand there until doomsday before he spoke another word. "I believed him. I Joined with him—oh, I can't believe I fell for that old 'You're my Beloved, save my soul' line! What a fool I've been."

To my surprise, Noelle exploded in anger . . . at me. "How could you do this to me, Belle? How could you betray me like that? I thought you were a friend! I never thought you would stab me in the back!"

"Wait a second," I answered, holding up a pacifying hand. "How could I do what? I had no idea that you were anyone's Beloved, let alone his!"

She gaped at me in disbelief. "I cannot believe you can deny that just this morning I was baring my broken heart to you."

It took a second for me to put the pieces together. I blamed my sorry mental state on Sebastian. "The man who dumped you was Sebastian?"

"Of course it was!"

I turned my attention to him. "You *dated* my roommate?"

His jaw tightened. "I refuse to be drawn into this argument. You are my Beloved. We are Joined. You belong to me now, and nothing and no one can sunder that."

"She is not your Beloved, I am," Noelle said, socking Sebastian on the arm. I knew just how she felt. "You admitted as much the last time we went out."

"You have two Beloveds?" I asked. "Is such a thing possible?"

"I have only one. You are she," he answered, with a particularly obstinate set to his jaw.

"You can say that as much as you like—it won't change the facts," Noelle whispered fiercely. "I know the truth."

Sebastian had evidently had enough. He grabbed me by the wrist and started pulling me toward the door. "It is a waste of time to stand here and argue. We must leave this house immediately. I must move Ysabelle to a safe area before

I contact the demon who is no doubt rallying an army to take her."

My heart felt like a lead weight, thumping painfully in my chest. My mind was numb with disbelief and confusion. I'd felt the emotions inside Sebastian—he truly believed we belonged together. But how could that be if Noelle was his Beloved? And how could I stay with him when I knew how heartbroken she was over his refusal? "I'm sorry, Sebastian, but I'm not going anywhere with you until we get this sorted out."

"There's nothing to sort out!" he bellowed, causing everyone in the hall to stop what they were doing. "You are my Beloved! You hold the key to my salvation. We are Joined! Previous relationships are not relevant here!"

"*Qu'est-ce fiche* he say?" Sally stopped in the center of the hall. "Noelle is his Beloved, *aussi?*"

"Please, Sally, not now," I said absently, trying to make sense of the confusion.

"Evidently the Dark One used to date the Guardian," William's remains said with a sickening cheerfulness. "This is as good as a telly show, eh, lad? Wish I had a little something to eat while we watch. Do you . . . eh . . . need all ten of those fingers?"

Damian scooted down to a different stair.

"*La la,*" Sally said, looking at Sebastian. "*Il doit être* Mr. Sexy Pants to have *deux* Beloveds."

"Prove it," Noelle said to Sebastian, ignoring everyone else as she confronted him. She straightened her jacket and gave him a quelling look.

"Prove what?" I asked, torn by the conviction that Sebastian spoke the truth.

"If she's your Beloved," she said, "and you Joined, then where's your soul?"

I looked at him, remembering the dark, tormented emptiness inside him. *You didn't get your soul back?*

He hesitated a few moments before answering. *It may take some time before I have it.*

I closed my eyes against the pain that swamped me at the unspoken acknowledgment. *She's your real Beloved, isn't she?*

No. She is a Beloved, but not mine. In all senses of the word but one, you are my Beloved. Can you not feel how we complete each other? You bring me light, Ysabelle. You stir feelings in me I never imagined existed. I want to protect you, to keep you safe. I wish to spend the remainder of my life discovering all there is to know about you. I have known you less than an hour, but already you have become vital to me. Only a Beloved could bind me to her in such a way. You complete me. We are one now, and nothing Noelle or anyone else says can change that.

I stood with my arms wrapped around myself, sorrow stinging behind my eyelids. Sebastian didn't try to touch me, just stood watching me, his mind open to mine, willing me to merge with him to read the truth for myself. I allowed my mind to fuse with his, rocked by the powerful emotions he held in check. He didn't lie—he was thoroughly convinced that we were meant to be together, that my very presence brought him immeasurable pleasure.

How on earth could I resist a man who so completely believed the sun rose and set on my word?

How could I betray the one friend who had stood by my side for so many years?

"What you're saying is that she's your Beloved in name, but I'm your Beloved in fact? Is such a thing possible?"

"Yes." With infinite gentleness, his thumb brushed away a tiny little tear that had crept from my eye. *Forgive me, Belle. I would have saved you this pain if I could.*

"So touching," Tim said quietly to another of the revenants. "Just like a chick flick."

"That it is," the revenant named Jack agreed. "Romantic."

"Romantic, my arse. I'm sitting here starving to death, and all you can do is yammer on about this drivel? Someone give me a bite to eat!" William's remains demanded.

Damian stood, picked up William's discarded leg, and walloped the half-a-revenant over the head with it.

You don't believe me? Sebastian asked.

Yes, I believe you. I couldn't disbelieve him—the regret he felt was so strong I didn't need to merge with him to feel it.

"Noelle?" Her stormy green eyes turned to me. "I have known you your entire life. Your mother gave you into my care when you became a Guardian, but I think we've become more than just roommates—you are my friend, and I love you. I would never hurt you. I know you and Sebastian had a less than amicable parting, but what I want to know now— what I *need* to know is what your feelings are for him. Are you . . . are you in love with him?"

"Well, it doesn't matter now what I feel, does it? You've gone and Joined with him. There's nothing left for me," she snapped, the words hurting me almost as much as the anger in her eyes.

"Noelle—"

"*Zut. Elle est tres* pissed," Sally said in a clearly audible undertone.

"Very," Tim said, nodding.

"I'm leaving now," Noelle said with icy dignity, gathering her bag of tools. She marched to the door, ruthlessly pulling down the barricade the revenants were building from bits of the door and part of the couch. "I am bound by the laws governing the Guardian's Guild to answer any summons you may make for help with a demon, but I would advise you to think twice before you call. I fear I would be quite, quite delayed in answering."

"Noelle, please, we can talk about this—"

She ignored my outstretched hand and marched out of the house, her back rigid.

I dropped my hand, pained by her actions but aware that I had hurt her deeply.

"She will understand in time," Sebastian told me, his fingers whispering across my cheek. "Do not feel guilty, Belle. You are innocent of any wrongdoing."

"*Où* the imps *sont allées?*" Sally asked, peering out into the darkness as the revenants rebuilt their barricade.

"They probably went back to Abaddon." With reluctance, I took a step back from Sebastian. I needed time to think things out, and I couldn't do that with him touching me, stirring feelings that had lain dormant for so long.

"That should hold it," Tim said as the men moved the last bit of hall furniture across the doorway. "We should be safe from those little yellow devils now."

"I could eat them, you know," the remains of William answered. "I'd be happy to do it. That would solve a big part of the problem, wouldn't it? I could probably put away a couple dozen braces of imps with no difficulty."

Sally frowned, looking up and down the street before coming back into the hall. "*Non. Les* imps don't just disappear, *hein?* They *doivent être* banished properly by *le* Guardian. *Ils ont disparu* somewhere else."

I frowned at her words, glancing through the part of the doorway visible around edges of the barricades. "They don't go off on their own? Then where did they go?"

A muffled crashing noise drifted up from beneath the floor. We all looked down.

"You checked the windows?" I asked Sally. "They were all warded?"

"Well . . . *oui.* So far as I know. *Je ne* quite sure what a ward looks like. . . ."

Sebastian swore.

"What's down in the basement?" I looked at Damian.

"It matters not. Beloved, we must leave now." Sebastian grabbed my hand and tried to haul me toward the door.

"Nothing is down there," Damian answered, shrugging. "A few broken crates, the furnace, a wine rack with no wine in it, and one of those big old-fashioned radios that Papa says everyone used to listen to."

Sebastian's gaze met mine. "Furnace?" I asked him.

"Pilot light," he answered, and without another word, snatched the back of Damian's shirt with one hand and my arm with another, kicking aside the barricade before shoving us both through the doorway. "Run!" he ordered.

I grabbed Damian and ran down the steps to the street below, heartened to see the revenants and Sally spilling out of the house after us. Sebastian brought up the rear.

"Here, what about me?" wailed a voice from within the house.

"Oooh, we've left Will," Jack the revenant said, but the rest of his sentence was drowned out by a loud explosion. Sebastian hurled himself at me, knocking both Damian and me to the ground, covering us when a fireball exploded from the house, consuming everything in its path.

Chapter Six

"Damn the imps," Tim muttered, as behind us Sebastian's door closed. Ah, sanctuary.

I collapsed into the nearest chair, heedless of the soot that no doubt came off my charred clothing. "Amen to that."

"Mmrfm wbrbl mnplm." Damian, on his way to investigate the video-game equipment in the entertainment center also housing a flat-screen television, paused long enough to pull a faintly smoking object out of a plastic carrier bag. He set the remains of William's remains—now just a blackened head—on the coffee table, propping it up next to a bowl of seashells.

"Ta, lad," William's head said politely. "I'm a bit peckish . . . anyone not using all their fingers or toes?"

"Did we have to bring *that?*" Sebastian asked, glaring at William's head. William grinned back and blew a kiss.

"Tim felt it would be wrong to leave a sentient body . . . er . . . part of a body behind," I explained wearily. "I suppose I can see his point. Once a revenant, always a revenant, until the entire body is destroyed."

"That's right, and I've still got me old noggin," William said, nodding. Unfortunately, the act sent the head rolling across the table until it was lying upside down.

Damian shoved it aside to perch on the coffee table, a game controller in his hand.

"Ooh, Xbox 360 car racing!" William said. "Give us a turn, will you? I love this one."

Sebastian's look become more pointed as Damian set a

controller before William's head and positioned it so it could be manipulated by the revenant's mouth.

"I admit it's stretching the precepts set down by the Society a bit far, but his head is still sentient."

"Vroom!" William said. Sebastian pursed his lips.

"Okay, just barely, but it still seemed wrong to leave him behind just because the imps blew up the rest of his body."

"I'm done. Next!" Jack said as he emerged from the suite's guest bathroom. Although we'd all survived Damian's house exploding, we were all a bit singed about the edges and covered in soot and dirt.

"Ysabelle?" Tim asked.

I waved an exhausted hand. "I'll wait. You all go ahead."

"You may clean up in my bathroom while I have a word with you," Sebastian said, hauling me to my feet again. "The bedroom is through here."

"Dibs on *le* couch," said Sally as Tim kindly let her out of another carrier bag. "Oooh! *Très bon* hotel room, Sebastian! *Je l'aime.* Is there service *du* food *en la* room? *Je suis* starved."

"I have a few things I'd like to say to you, as well, but I'm not going into your bedroom," I told Sebastian, sitting back down.

He stood in front of me, his hands on his hips. *Why not?*

Because you'll just try to seduce me, and quite frankly, I'm not sure I could resist.

The rotter had the nerve to smile. It lit his eyes, sending little tremors of excitement through me. *We are Joined. We will be together until the end of our days. Your body belongs to me, and mine to you. There is nothing wrong with me seducing you now.*

"I'm sure that's what you think, but I still have a billion or so issues to work through over this whole Beloved thing," I said blandly, and refused to let him pull me out of the chair again.

"*Est ce le* bedroom? Oooh! Huge bed!" Sally drifted into the bedroom.

"Anything you have to say you can say to me here," I told

Sebastian as he continued to glare and send me thoughts that just about steamed my blood. "There's nothing you can't say in front of my friends."

"That's right," Tim said, emerging from the bathroom with a damp shirt but a clean face. "I feel we owe a lot to Ysabelle. Clearly you two are having some sort of relationship crisis, and we all want you to know that we're here to help you work it out."

The other revenants nodded. Sebastian said rude things in French under his breath.

"That's very sweet of you. I greatly appreciate the support, although I'm a bit concerned about your safety." I glanced at Sebastian. "How long do you think we have before the demon tracks me down again?"

Before I could brace myself, he grabbed my wrists and pulled me into his arms. *You are the single most irritatingly stubborn woman I have ever met.*

I kissed the tip of his nose. "Oddly enough, I was just about to say the same about you. How long do we have, do you think?"

He sighed, his hands stroking gently down my back. My body—against my better intentions—melted against him. "I would say an hour or less, depending on the resources the demon is able to utilize. If it searches for you on its own, longer. If it rallies an army, perhaps twenty minutes at best. I must find it before it does either."

"Find it? Why find it? It's going to be here soon enough," I pointed out.

"I must destroy it before it can find you again," he answered, striding to a desk upon which sat a black attaché case. He rifled through it and extracted a small burgundy notebook. I couldn't help watching him move, admiring the lines of his impressive body, the strength and controlled power that he seemed to bear so easily. His every movement was filled with an almost feline grace that warned of a ruthless, potent being behind the sophisticated exterior.

"How do you destroy a demon?" Tim asked, holding out a chair for Sally. She beamed at him.

I raised an eyebrow at Sebastian, waiting for his answer. He didn't look at me. "A Guardian can destroy demons."

Tim glanced at me. "That's the only way?"

"Not the only way, no. Talismans created for that purpose can also be used, but unfortunately, the one I was trying to locate has no doubt been destroyed in the fire that claimed the Betrayer's house."

"A talisman?"

The color in Sebastian's eyes faded. "Yes. A ring of power, actually. It was thin, rimmed with gold, made of horn."

"Oh, you're talking about that ring you mentioned when you staggered into the house. I don't know where it is."

"It was in the possession of the Betrayer. In the right hands, it was capable of the destruction of the demon lord and his minions." His hands tightened on the notebook. "But now it is destroyed."

"It's broken, but not destroyed," a voice piped up over the muted sound of electronic cars racing down virtual country roads.

We all turned to look at Damian.

"You've seen the ring?" I asked him.

He shrugged, his eyes still on the TV. Beside him, William's head grunted as it manipulated the controller with his mouth. "Yes. It broke when Nell saved Papa. He gave me the pieces, saying it was a souvenir."

The last hour and a half spent talking to fire officials made it clear that there was not going to be anything salvageable from the house. "Damian, I'm sorry—I thought you heard when the fire captain said that the fire destroyed everything in the house. Not even a magical ring could survive it."

"The ring isn't in the house," he said, his shoulders twitching as he manipulated his virtual car through a hairpin turn.

Sebastian all but pounced on the boy, grabbing him by both arms. "Where is the ring now, boy?"

"You're hurting me," Damian said, frowning.

Sebastian loosened his grip. We all watched breathlessly as Damian reached into his pocket and pulled out an assortment of grubby items. He picked carefully through bits of string, a couple of shiny rocks, a key, hard sweets, and assorted fluff to pluck out three items. He handed them to me. Everyone but Damian and William's head crowded around me to see the three thin bits of curved metal that lay across my palm. They looked more like a broken hoop earring than a ring. I touched one of the pieces. "This is a ring of power?"

Sebastian slumped down onto the love seat, his eyes closed for a moment. "It *was*."

"Hmm." The pieces of the ring lay cool on my hand. I touched them, pushing them into a rough circle, looking closely at the edges of the breaks. "This isn't gold. It's carmot."

"Carmot? What's that?" Jack the revenant asked, peering at the ring so closely his nose almost touched my hand.

"Have you ever heard of a man named Edward Kelley?" I asked Sebastian.

He frowned for a moment. "No."

"Really? Erm . . . how old are you?"

"Two hundred and seventeen," he said, looking non-plussed for a moment.

"Ah. That would explain it. Edward Kelley was a bit before your time —he was an alchemist during the reign of Elizabeth the First."

Sebastian's eyes narrowed on my hand. "That ring was reputed to have been created in the mid-sixteenth century."

I nodded. "Edward Kelley claimed to have found the tomb of a bishop in Wales that contained not only the basis for his tinctures, which would transmute base metals into gold, but also of a manuscript that explained the secrets of the manufacture of the tinctures. He was a fraud, of course, since the tinctures were not as he claimed, but he did contribute one true finding to science—carmot, the basis for which philosophers' stones were made, and, when treated properly, a yellow metal a thousand times more rare than mere gold. This ring was made of horn and carmot, not gold."

"Why do I suspect there is more to this than a rare substance?" Sebastian asked, his gaze steady on me.

I smiled, my fingers closing over the broken bits of ring. "Because you're a smart man. One of the reasons carmot was used for items of great importance like this ring is because of its restorative property."

"Restorative in what manner?"

My smile deepened as I whispered three words: *magis plana conligatio.*

Before I could open my hand, Sebastian was on his feet, his expression startled. I stood as well, turning over my hand as I opened my fingers. The pieces burned a bright reddish gold for a moment before subsiding into a more mundane horn ring edged in a gold-colored metal.

"You remade it," Sebastian said, touching the ring with the tip of his finger, as if he were worried it would break again. "But . . . how?"

"Anyone who knows about carmot knows how to restore it to its manufactured form," I said, and pressed the ring into his hand. My fingers touched the pulse of his wrist. "I am giving this to you now because I know you will not use it unwisely."

His gaze flickered to Damian, now thoroughly engrossed in the video game. "I made a vow to you, Beloved. I am a man of my word."

I touched his cheek, the anguish inside him so great it leeched into me. *I know you are. I could not have bound myself to you if you were anything but an honorable man. I'm just sorry that I couldn't give you back your soul.*

Do not worry, Beloved. I can exist without a soul—so long as I have you.

I didn't know what to say to that. Sebastian seemed to have no difficulty sharing his thoughts and feelings with me, blithely accepting his emotions rather than questioning how such a strong relationship could develop almost instantly. I couldn't deny that some pretty strong emotions were building within me on what seemed to be a minute-by-minute basis, but I was not yet ready to either confront or accept them. There were other issues to deal with first.

"That's amazing," Tim said, peeking over Sebastian's shoulder to see the ring. "You just pressed it together?"

"*Elle est la fille de* alchemist," Sally said, sashaying forward to look at the ring.

I frowned at her.

"You are? I didn't know they still had such things," Tim said.

"They don't. If the loo is free, I'll go clean up."

"Who exactly was Edward Kelley?" Sebastian asked, following me into the bathroom.

The revenants had left me a clean towel. I scrubbed my face and neck, wishing I had a change of clothes. "He was a liar and a thief, a man whose ears were cut off early in his career as a laywer because of fraud. He later turned his talent for prevarication to alchemy."

"But it wasn't all false, was it?" Sebastian fingered the ring. "This carmot seems legitimate enough."

"It is. Carmot is the one thing in Kelley's life that was real, only he didn't understand that until the end of his life."

"What happened to him?"

I rinsed out the now-soiled towel. "The common belief is that he died during an attempt to break out of a Bohemian prison."

"The common belief? What's the truth?"

"Mind if I use your brush? Thanks." I toweled my hair quickly to get any soot out of it, then applied Sebastian's brush to the unruly mess, studying myself in the mirror. What could Sebastian see in my face? My eyes? Did he see the truth, or had some inner sense prompted him to press the subject? "He lost a leg during the prison break attempt, but he survived. He lived in seclusion for several years more, a broken man who could never recapture the fleeting fame he acquired in his earlier years."

"I assume he had a family?" Sebastian's eyes were watchful. Damn him, he knew.

"That would be a reasonable assumption." I set down the brush and turned to face him. "He had two children by a

Gypsy woman: a son and a daughter. One was captured and burned at the stake for his sins. The other escaped and was not heard of or seen again."

"Fascinating," he said, but I could tell what was coming next, and I dreaded it. Offense was my only option.

"If your next question is going to be, 'Was his daughter named Ysabelle?' I will walk out of the room."

Three seconds passed. "Was his daughter named—"

I left the room. "Damian, I'm going to have to go out with Sebastian for a bit. You're perfectly safe here, but Sally will stay with you—"

"Oy!" Sally said at the same time Sebastian, emerging from the bathroom, announced that I would not be accompanying him.

"Why not?"

He slipped on his coat and tucked the ring into the pocket. *You do not seriously believe I would allow you to come within range of this demon's powers?*

I thought the whole point of us Joining was to keep me safe from the demon.

It was. And you are safer now that your souls are bound to me, but if the demon destroys me, you will be unprotected again.

I rolled my eyes. "Then you should stay here, and I'll use the ring to destroy it."

"That would be the height of foolishness."

I started to bristle at the implication, but common sense kicked in and reminded me that while I was many things, powerful enough to destroy a demon was not on the list.

"You will stay here with the others where you are safe. I will destroy this demon, and return to you as soon as I am able." He moved to the desk and flipped open an address book. "Then we'll alert the Guardian that Asmodeus will shortly be making an appearance."

"Asmodeus?" I asked, startled. "Isn't that the one who held you prisoner—"

"Yes," Sebastian said with a smile. At the sight of it, a burning memory coursed through me. "The demon belonged to Asmodeus. I have no doubt that by now, the demon has told its master of the existence of a *tattu* in London. By destroying the demon, I will draw Asmodeus himself out."

I said nothing, rubbing my arms against the sudden chill that gripped me. Sebastian was almost through the door when he paused and looked back at me.

Beloved? You are distressed. You burn with fever.

It's not a fever, and yes, I'm distressed. I understand why you wish to destroy Asmodeus, but I don't like the way thoughts of revenge consume you.

His eyes glittered, pale. I felt his curiousity, but all he asked was, *Why?*

The air left my lungs, making it diffcult for me to breathe. I rubbed my arms, reminding myself where I was, that there was no threat to me in this hotel room. Despite that, my flesh crawled. Black dots appeared before my eyes. I couldn't breathe, I couldn't think. I was trapped, immobile, a prisoner of my own mind. Panic mingled with dread, flooding me with its inky, blistering presence, consuming every bit of me until nothing was left but a charred shell.

Chapter Seven

Sebastian reached me before I hit the floor, shouldering aside the revenants and Sally as they asked questions about what was happening.

"I will see to her," Sebastian said to Sally as she ignored the closed door and followed us into his bedroom.

"She is my charge," Sally started to say, but Sebastian cut her off, waving her out of the room.

"She is mine now. I will let no harm befall her."

To my great surprise, Sally just looked at him for a few seconds, nodded, then left without even glancing toward me. I felt oddly bereft . . . for the space of time it took for Sebastian to lay me on the bed.

"Why did you not tell me, Beloved?" he asked, his fingers gently brushing a strand of hair back from my cheek.

I turned my face so I wouldn't have to see the pity in his eyes. He didn't like that, gently but irresolutely forcing me to meet his gaze.

"It was not your brother who was burned at the stake for his father's sins, was it?"

"No," I said, choking on the word, desperately pushing back the memories.

Sebastian slid behind me, cradling me against his chest. I fought the temptation for a moment, but he offered too much of a sanctuary to resist.

"I have not asked you how you became a *tattu* because I felt you would tell me when you trusted me," he said. I turned in his arms, holding him tight as I buried my head in his neck. Tears, hot and thick, squeezed out of my tightly shut eyes.

Desperate to escape my own torturous mind, I merged with him, falling into the blackness that filled him. "Do you wish now to tell me how that came about?"

Images flashed through my mind—a gray-haired man bent over a flame, muttering obscure alchemical spells as he poured one liquid into another; another gray-haired man, flinching as the first swore eternal vengeance for his betrayal; the flash and pomp of Elizabeth's court; the snow and sleet of endless icy winters in Prague; the smell of smoke as it curled up around me, stealing from me not only my breath, but my very life.

"Your father threatened another?" Sebastian's voice was soft and caressing, his presence calming the panic within me. I didn't want to answer his questions, didn't want to think back on that part of my life, but I knew I would have to sometime soon if I wanted him to understand me.

"Edward Kelley befriended a scholar named John Dee early in his life. Dee helped him with much of the alchemical work he later used to parlay favors and money from various monarchs and patrons. But Dee realized that Kelley was little more than a con artist and broke off relations with him. Kelley had some success with carmot, but never fully understood its properties, and soon Dee's fame eclipsed his. He swore vengeance, claiming Dee stole his ideas and his alchemical formulas, going so far as to invoke a curse on Dee."

Sebastian's hands stroked my back. I shuddered back the anguish that welled up inside me at the memories, taking a small shred of comfort that the soulless, tortured Sebastian was one of the few people walking the earth who shared with me the ability to survive such profound torment. It was a bond of sorts, a wordless bond, but one I felt to my very bones as he offered me acceptance and understanding.

"He went to Prague to gain help from a sympathetic Emperor Rudolph in bringing Dee's downfall, but things soured, as they always did for him. When he was imprisoned in Prague by Emperor Rudolph, I was arrested as his assistant. My younger brother had been smuggled out of the country by my deceased mother's relatives, but I was beyond their reach. I was tried and sentenced as being in league with the devil. They burned me at the stake for the mere fact that Edward Kelley was my father."

Pain at the memory choked me. Sebastian said nothing, but continued to stroke my back. I burrowed deeper against him, allowing his comfort to slowly dissipate the agony within.

"Why were you brought back as a *tattu?*" he asked softly.

I let go of the breath I hadn't been aware I was holding. "My mother's mother was a powerful woman in her family. She had Egyptian blood and was viewed as being a noble in a society that did not commonly have such distinctions. She petitioned an archangel, pointing out that as I retained my soul, I could not have been involved in my father's sin of bartering with a demon lord for the curse on Dee. It took time, but eventually the petition worked its way to a sympathetic Power. Two lifetimes after my grandmother submitted the petition for intervention, I was declared innocent by the Power and granted another life to replace the one that had been wrongly taken from me."

"And when you were reborn, you were given another soul."

"Yes." I sighed. "That was a clerical oversight, actually. A new clerk only skimmed the resurrection order. He evidently saw the words 'demon lord' and 'curse,' and assumed I was being pardoned for a crime, and granted me another during rebirth."

"A small repayment for your suffering," he murmured, his mouth close to my ear. I squirmed a little. Baring my history to him hadn't been nearly as painful as I had imagined it would be, leaving me more than a little aware of just how tightly our bodies were entwined.

"I cannot pleasure you now, my Beloved," his voice rumbled in my ear, sending breathly little shivers of excitement down my arms. "I must destroy the threats to your safety first."

I pushed myself away from him, glaring with every morsel of indigation I could rally. "Have you heard *nothing* I've said?"

"I have heard all you have spoken and read the words on your heart, as well." He caressed my lip with his finger. I jerked my head away.

"You stupid, arrogant, revenge-minded man!" I snarled, trying to escape his grip. "I will not go through this again. I will not suffer for yet another pigheaded male whose precious ego is more important than those he is bound to!"

"I do not do this for vengeance, Belle—"

"Like hell you don't!" Although my insides felt as fragile as cracked glass, I scrambled off him, furious that I was beginning to have feelings for someone who could be so indifferent to my concerns. I stormed to the door, fully intending to grab Damian and Sally and leave him forever.

Before I could so much as blink, Sebastian was in front of me, not only blocking the door, but holding me in a steely grip that was just this side of painful.

"You will listen to me, Beloved!"

"I've listened, and you're not saying anything different—"

He clamped me tight to his chest, holding me against him with arms that felt made of titanium or some other horribly unyielding metal. My face was squished into his shoulder, making it difficult to breathe.

"I am not doing this for revenge, Belle. You are my Beloved—I must protect you. If we do not wish to constantly look over our shoulders, waiting for Asmodeus to destroy one or both of us, then I must strike now, before he has had time to rally his forces."

"But—"

"No, it must be now. Salvaticus and Vexamen are times of unbalance in Abaddon—the demon lords are watching each other suspiciously to see who will emerge as premier prince. Their attention is divided, and it is one of the few times when they are vulnerable to attack. We have no choice. We must strike quickly."

What he said made sense to my brain, but my heart, oh, my poor heart flinched in horror at the thought of someone dear to me allowing revenge to rule him.

It does not rule me, Beloved. You do.

I gave a watery chuckle at that thought, unable to keep my body from melting into his. *You would do anything I told you to do, then?*

Anything so long as it would not put you in danger, yes.

I thought long and hard then. I listened to the slow beating of Sebastian's heart, drinking in the sight and feel and scent of him, holding them close to my heart as I considered the idea that was slowly taking form in my mind.

"Can you destroy this demon easily?"

"Using the ring you have reformed, yes."

"Do you think it has told Asmodeus about me?"

"Probably, but I doubt if he has had time to act on the information yet." Sebastian was curious about where my questions were leading, but held that in check while I worked my way through my concerns, issues, and the burgeoning idea.

"If you destroy the demon, but not Asmodeus, what will happen?"

"Asmodeus will eventually track you down, and either trick you into his power, or use me to force you to surrender your extra soul."

I thought about that for a bit, and came to a decision. "Very well, I've thought about it, and I've decided that you can destroy the demon if you like."

Laughter was rich in his voice. "How very gracious of you."

I pushed back against now gentle arms, and gave him a glare. "However, I don't want you to make an attempt on Asmodeus until I talk to the Society."

The laughter in his face and eyes faded. "Belle, I have explained to you why it is important that I strike now—"

I bit his chin. "Yes, you have, but I think we have another option. However, I must first consult one of the directors at the Revenant Society to make sure what I have in mind can be done."

Softly, his mind touched mine, his curiosity so great it made me smile. Not one for mind games, I'd normally satisfy his desire to know what I was thinking, but this was a situation I wasn't even sure was possible. *I'll tell you about it the minute I know if it's feasible,* I told him.

A war broke out within him, a desire to show confidence in me fighting with the need to protect and safeguard. The fact that he struggled so strongly touched my heart.

"I think I could very easily fall in love with you," I told him, pressing a quick kiss to his delectable lips.

His eyes darkened. "Was that meant to be a kiss? Or did you mistake me for your grandmother?"

"Hey now!" I frowned, searching his eyes. "I'll have you know that none of my husbands, not one single one of them, ever complained about my kissing skills."

"They do not matter," he said, his voice a low growl that turned my bones to jelly. I sagged against him as his mouth descended upon mine. "*I* do. Either you kiss me as I deserve, or you will not kiss me at all."

I opened my mouth to tell him what he could do with such an arrogant demand, but fell victim to my own folly when his lips took charge. His kiss was hard, hot, and absolutely unyielding. His body moved against me, his hands touching and stroking whatever he could reach, his hips urging mine into a rhythm of desire. But oh Lord, it was his mouth I couldn't resist, his lips and tongue demanding a response that I couldn't deny. By the time he broke the kiss, I was breathless, gasping for air, my mind filled with the taste and feel of him.

He looked down at me with a smug satisfaction that was wholly male. I tried to rally a morsel of dignity, a tiny shred of indignation over such a chauvinistic attitude, but my mind refused to cooperate.

"You are not to leave the suite. I will return as soon as I have destroyed the demon."

He kissed me once more, sending the few wits I desperately tried to gather flying. It wasn't until he left, tossing commands to the revenants over his shoulder, that I could put myself together enough to protest his order.

"*Vous ressemblez à vous avez été* pulled backward through *le* hedge *du* prickly," Sally said, drifting over to where I clutched the door frame to the living area. "*Vive Monsieur le Sexy Pants,* eh?"

"And how," I answered, touching my lips. They were hot and tingling, the spicy-sweet taste of Sebastian still burning on them. It matched the burn he'd started deep in me, embers of an emotion too fragile to face yet. I shook my head, wondering how he had become so much a part of me so quickly.

Sally watched me for a moment before softly asking, "*Vous l'aimez?*"

I pushed myself away from the door and went to the phone, glancing at the open notebook Sebastian had left. The name and number of a London Guardian was written in a bold hand. I flipped through the book, feeling both pleased and guilty that Noelle's name didn't appear. How could I take such pleasure in a man when it gave pain to my friend?

"Take a number and join the queue," I said, praying Noelle would forgive me for pushing her to the middle of a list of things I needed to do before all hell broke out.

"What now?" Tim asked, wandering over as I punched in a phone number. "Are you ordering dinner? I admit I'm a bit on the hungry side, and William there keeps nagging about fading away to nothing if he doesn't get some sustenance."

"I'll order some dinner for everyone—vegetarian dinner—before I leave," I told him, glancing at the clock. It wasn't too late for the one director I knew to be in the office.

"Leave?" Tim frowned. "Sebastian said that no one was to leave the suite except the Guardian you were going to call. He didn't mention anything about you going off on your own."

"It doesn't matter," I said, waving a hand as I waited for the director to pick up the phone. "You'll all be safe enough once I'm gone. I'm just going to the Society and back. Hello, River? Ysabelle Raleigh here. I wonder if you have a few minutes you could spare me. Fabulous. I'll be there in about twenty minutes, all right?"

I hung up, intending to give a few commands of my own, but when I turned to face everyone, I was met with a wall of unhappy faces.

"Erm . . ." I said, a bit surprised by the solidarity of a group of people who had so little in common. Everyone, from Damian clutching William's head by his hair, to Sally, who was supposed to support me in all that I did, stood in a line with their arms crossed over their chests, identical frowns on their faces. "I take it that plan doesn't meet with your satisfaction."

"Sebastian said no one was to leave," Tim repeated, a particularly obstinate look on his face.

"Yes, but—"

"He said the demon would grab you if you left," Damian added.

I raised an eyebrow at him. "Since when do you care what Sebastian says?"

The boy gave one of his shrugs. "Nell says we should give him a chance to get over what was done to him, so maybe he's not as bad as Papa said he was. He likes you."

I was touched by the approval inherent in his statement. "Does that mean you like me, as well?" I couldn't help asking, half teasing him.

His dark blue eyes considered me for a minute. Then just as I knew they would, his shoulders twitched in a careless shrug. "You don't stink like other Beloveds. I like *that*."

Sally snorted as I was put so soundly into my place.

"We shall be grateful for small favors, then," I told Damian, and considered the line of people bent on keeping me from my purpose. "I suppose a promise that I won't go anywhere but the Society headquarters and straight back wouldn't merit me parole?"

Six heads shook a negative answer (William appeared to be dozing despite being held up by his hair).

I sighed. "Very well, you can come with me then, although how we're all to fit into one taxi is beyond me."

There were a few halfhearted protests, but ten minutes later we emerged from the hotel onto the damp pavement outside the hotel, both William's head and Sally in their respective travel bags.

"Stop giving me that look," I told Tim in a quiet voice as the hotel doorman waved a taxi up to us. "I told you that I'm in no danger with all of you around. It's not as if the demon is going to spring out of nowhere and capture me."

Tim opened his mouth to reply, but I never heard the words he spoke. The demon that I'd seen earlier that day ripped open a hole in the fabric of being, wrapped both arms around me, and jerked me backward, away from reality as I knew it.

Chapter Eight

The voices were the first thing I noticed. They were oddly familiar.

"Is everyone here? Did we all make it?"

"I'm here, although I'm fair starving to death. Someone lend me a hand. Or a foot. A thigh or two wouldn't go amiss, either."

"*Je suis ici,* as well. *Zut alors! Qu'est-ce le* hell?"

"Papa says they prefer Abaddon to hell," a childish voice said. I recognized it immediately as Damian.

"Do you think Ysabelle is all right? She is very still."

That had to be Tim. I was warmed by the concern in his voice, but a bit puzzled by my eyelids' apparent inability to move. They felt as if lead weights had been anchored to them.

"Is she dead?" William's voice was shamelessly hopeful and not in the least bit muffled, which meant Damian must have taken him out of the carrier bag. "Dibs on her if she is."

"It would take a lot more than a demon yanking me through the fabric of existence to kill me," I answered without thinking. A moment later I sat bolt upright, staring around wildly as my memory returned. "The demon!"

"*Il a disparu* bye-bye *avec* my boot on its derierre," Sally told me, hovering over me with a worried look in her eyes. "*Vous* okay?"

"Yes, I'm fine." I got to my feet, feeling a bit dizzy by the experience of having been pulled through to who knew where. "Erm . . . would someone like to tell me why you're all here? I don't seem to remember the demon grabbing everyone, and the last I saw of you lot, you were about to get into a taxi."

"*Je vous* grabbed." Sally patted me carefully, as if looking for broken bones or injuries. "All right, *vous n'êtes pas blessé.*"

"Thank you for that checkup, Dr. Sally."

She sniffed and tossed her hair. "*C'est* my *travail,* if *vous* recall."

"For which I'm very grateful," I said, giving her a little hug. "Now that explains how Sally got here, but what of the rest of you?"

Damian adopted an innocent look that was wholly at odds with his character. "Sally had a hold of me when she grabbed you. I had William."

"When I saw them hauled away with you and the demon, we jumped in after you all." Tim beamed happily at me. It was on the tip of my tongue to tell him he had probably signed his death warrant, but I couldn't reward such an act of selflessness and bravery with a dire prediction.

"Where exactly are we?" I asked, looking around. We seemed to be in some sort of dimly lit cave alcove. Large outcroppings of rock obscured the view, but odd patterns of light danced high on the wall behind me. My stomach tightened as I moved to the entrance of the alcove, stepping clear of the rock.

Fire. There was fire everywhere. Not just little campfires, the sort I'd learned to act completely normal around . . . no, this cavern was filled with great pools of fire, burning from some unknown underground source. Snaking between the great, billowing flames, a stone walkway meandered to the far end of the cavern, where a plateau held what appeared to be an office, complete with desk, chairs, bookcases, and a couple of filing cabinets.

"Oh, God's mercy, we're in Abaddon," I said as my lungs began to struggle for air.

"No, although I suppose it's easy to see why you could imagine that."

I whirled around at the mild voice that spoke behind me, my hand already at my throat. The sight of the flames, the smell of the smoke, threatened to overwhelm me. Desperately, I fought to keep under control the panic that welled within me. "Who are you?"

"I am Simon," the demon said. It appeared in human form, that of a young man with a weak chin and blond goatee. The demon waved its hand toward the narrow path. "I am the steward to Asmodeus. I have never met a *tattu* before—it is a great honor to have you here."

"Where is here if not Abaddon?" I asked.

"This is my lord Asmodeus's home. He prefers this design to the mundane houses, but technically, we are within the boundaries of London."

"This is all just an illusion, then?" Tim asked, looking around the huge, smoke-filled cavern.

The demon hesitated a moment. "In a manner of speaking, yes. This location is actually in a house, but it has been altered to an appearance more pleasing to my lord."

"Damian, come stand by me," I said softly, holding out my hand for him.

Damian rolled his eyes, picked up William's head, and reluctantly joined me. I wrapped my arm around his shoulders, giving the demon a firm look to let it know I would defend the child at all costs.

"I wonder, what does demon taste like?" William's head asked no one in particular.

"Duck, I'm told," Simon answered, then gestured again toward the path. "If you please? Lord Asmodeus is most eager to meet you."

I glanced at the huge pits ablaze with the fires of hell, and shook my head. "Illusion or not, I'm staying right where I am."

Simon tipped its head to look at me. "Afraid of the fires, are you? That's not good. That's not good at all."

"How so?" I asked, one eye on the nearest conflagration. I

felt sick to my stomach at its nearness, my psyche shrieking to get out of there by any means possible, but I couldn't leave Damian and my friends.

"I believe I'll let my lord answer that. If you please?"

I took a deep breath. "You can tell Asmodeus that I'm not going anywhere, and if he wants to talk to me, he can just get his pox-riddled behind over here to—"

A noise unlike anything I've ever heard in this world or the next shook the cavern, echoing off the high stone walls, doubling and tripling on itself. The flame pits erupted in bonfires that nearly touched the ceiling, the fire and horrible scream almost enough to bring the entire structure down upon us. I pulled Damian behind me, trying to shield him as I backed up against the wall and prayed the glamour or whatever was being used to create this illusion was strong enough to protect the physical world from this nightmare.

Eventually, the noised died down, and the flames dropped to their normal level. My hands shook as I dusted off Damian, making sure he wasn't injured before turning to face the demonic steward.

Simon glanced nervously toward the distance corner of the cave. "I respectfully suggest you not anger my lord again. He does not take well to being told what to do."

"He can bite my shiny pink—"

Sally shut up with a look from me, but she muttered several rude threats in her odd mixture of English and mangled French. I examined my options quickly and decided that I really didn't have a choice.

"Fine. I will go speak to Asmodeus. But he must first release my friends." Sally, Tim, and Jack all protested, but I held up a hand to stop them, keeping my gaze firmly on Simon. "I will go just as soon as my friends are released, but not before."

I half expected another roar from the demon lord, but to my surprise, Simon smiled. "But, my good lady, your friends are not prisoners here. They may leave at any time."

"They may?" I blinked a couple of times, then glanced at

the fire pits. There had to be a trick somewhere. "Very well. You will escort them out. Once they are safely outside this building, I will see Asmodeus."

The demon gave me a look that said it was humoring me, but put two fingers in its mouth and blew a sharp whistle. A small demon in running shorts and a dirty T-shirt appeared before it. "Wassup?"

"These people . . . er . . . revenants, Dark One, and spirit need escorting outside. See to it."

The little demon looked curiously at me, its eyes opening wide when it noticed my double souls. Its lips pursed together, but before my friends could protest again, it ripped open the fabric of being, shoving them through it with one last look at me.

"How do I know they're safe?" I asked, immediately seeing the flaw in my hastily thought-up plan.

Simon rolled its eyes, and gently shoved me toward the path. "Asmodeus has no interest in them. Mind the lava."

"Lava. Such a quaint touch," I murmured as I stepped carefully over a thin trickle of molten rock, careful to stay as far away from the raging pits of fire as was possible. I am not ashamed to admit that there were two times on the journey across the cavern floor where I came close to turning tail and bolting, but each time Simon seemed to sense my rising panic, and stopped long enough for me to regain composure.

"Here we are, then, all safe and sound. Well . . . for the moment." Simon's smile as we crested the plateau was feeble even by demonic standards, and did nothing to promote a feeling of security. "My most gracious lord, the *tattu* is here."

For the most part, my life has been sheltered. I've seen monarchs and politicians rise to power and fall away into obscurity. Radicals, geniuses, madmen . . . they've all crossed my path at some time or other. But with very few exceptions (Sally being one of them), they have all been mortal. The Society has been a recent phenomenon, forming a shy fifty years ago, and although my work there has afforded me a chance to mingle with other immortal beings, I seldom do.

Asmodeus was the first demon lord I'd ever seen, and I had to admit that I was somewhat disappointed by the mundane appearance of the man who rose from behind a desk to greet me. He could be any fifty-something businessman crowded into the London tube, clutching a briefcase and a copy of a morning paper.

"If you like, I can adopt a more fearsome appearance," he told me, apparently reading my mind. "And no, I can't read your mind. That, to my great regret, has been a skill that has eluded me."

I blinked twice. "If you can't read minds, then how did you know what I was thinking?"

He reached out to touch my face. I took a step backward, out of his reach. Simon said something about attending to other business and slipped out a door built into the rock wall.

Asmodeus's hand fell. He propped one hip up on his desk, his arms crossed as he considered me. "I am quite adept at reading expressions, and your look of surprise at my mortal appearance presented no difficulty in interpreting. Do I frighten you?"

I swallowed hard, ignoring the urge to look behind me at the room filled with fire while wondering whether I could pull off a bald-faced lie. I've never been good at deceit, so I decided to go with honesty. "Very much so. What exactly do you believe you are going to do with me? I am a Beloved, bound to a Dark One."

"You are *tattu*," he said simply, falling silent for a moment.

I willed my body into quietude despite the horrible need to fidget . . . if not outright run away screaming at the top of my lungs.

"You have that rarest of things, a perfectly pure soul."

"I have two pure souls," I said, throwing caution to the wind.

"No, you have the soul you were originally born with and the second, which I assume was granted at a rebirth. The first is flawed; it is the second that I desire."

"You can't have it." I rallied enough inner strength to carry my trembling legs over to a chair, which I sat down upon in a sudden manner that belied my brave words. "It's mine. They both are, flawed or not. They're mine, and I have no intention of giving either up."

"Do you have any idea what a perfectly pure soul means to me?" he asked with deceptive mildness—deceptive but for the sudden light of unholy greed that shone in his eyes. Just meeting his gaze took a year or two off my life. I looked down at my hands, which were clutching each other. Chills ran down my back and legs, my stomach tightening into a leaden wad.

I shook my head.

"A soul affords me power. But a perfectly pure soul, one untainted by its bearer, can provide me with almost unlimited power. With a soul such as yours in my possession, my ascension to the throne of Abaddon is guaranteed."

My stomach roiled at the thought of my beautiful clean soul being soiled and ultimately destroyed in Asmodeus's attempt to become premier prince of hell.

"You can't have it," I said in a low voice, gripping the arms of the chair so hard my fingernails bent. "I will go back to the Akashic Plain before I allow you to destroy something so good."

He smiled, and for a second, I saw his true form. A red wave swept down over my vision, blinding me, stripping me of air and thought and, for a brief moment, the desire to live.

I never thought of you as a quitter, a soft voice said, imbuing me with feelings of being loved and cherished and valued above all things.

Sebastian?

I am here, Beloved. I will be with you momentarily. Do not allow Asmodeus to frighten you. I will not allow any harm to come to you.

Where have you been? Why haven't you talked to me? You left and I couldn't mind-talk with you.

Regret mingled with sorrow leeched into my brain. *I apol-*

ogize. I was indisposed. But now I am back, and together, we are more powerful than you can imagine. His mind brushed mine with an emotion that I couldn't mistake.

Do you always fall in love with women so quickly? I asked, half joking.

You are the only one, Belle.

Where are you?

Near. I will be with you in a few minutes.

I lifted my chin, and kept my gaze steady on Asmodeus. "I don't see that we have anything further to discuss. I have no intention of relinquishing my soul to you, and there is no way you can force me to do it."

He smiled again, but this time I was ready for it.

Good girl, Sebastian said, his thoughts full of approval. *You have been tempered. You can withstand this.*

"I hate to disappoint such faith, my dear, but time grows short." Asmodeus raised his voice. "Simon, bring in Orinel."

The door opened just enough for Simon to poke his face through the crack. "My lord, there has been a . . . an unforeseen event."

Asmodeus frowned. "Spare me your gibberish and summon Orinel and its prisoner to me."

If it were possible for a demon's face to grow pale, Simon's did. "Er . . . my lord . . ."

The door burst open at that moment, sending Simon flying into the room. He landed in a heap at my feet, but made no move to rise. I stood slowly as a man entered the room, moving as silently as a panther. A blond panther.

"Asmodeus. I would be lying if I said it was a pleasure to meet you again," Sebastian said, holding out a hand for me. I stepped over Simon's inert form and took his hand, his fingers tightening around mine. "Although I admit to looking forward to this moment for a very long time."

The demon lord frowned a second time. "Where is Orinel?"

"The demon has been destroyed." Sebastian lifted his hand to show the ring of power on his thumb. "I believe I took it by surprise, since it spent a good five minutes before I dispatched it telling me of your plan to capture me and use me to force Belle into compliance."

At the sight of the ring, a red light shone in Asmodeus's eyes, but it quickly faded into one of speculation.

"That ring was destroyed."

"It was remade."

Asmodeus nodded. "The folly of alchemists and their precious carmot. Very well, we are at an impasse. You have my ring of power, and I have your Beloved. How do you suggest we proceed?"

Sebastian released my hand and pulled me close to his side. "Belle and I will leave with the ring in our possession. You will be allowed to continue as you are, until such time as you attempt to harm either of us. At that point, I will use the ring to destroy you just as I have done your minion."

Is the ring powerful enough to destroy a demon lord?

In the right hands it is.

Asmodeus looked thoughtful for a moment. "That is not acceptable. I, however, have a solution to the situation. In exchange for your Beloved's extra soul, a soul, I might point out, she has no need or use for, I will swear an oath to never harm you or your families."

Sebastian was shaking his head even before the demon lord stopped talking.

I took a step away before Sebastian could refuse Asmodeus's ridiculous suggestion. Unless I did something, I knew the situation would deteriorate quickly.

"I just want to make sure I have this all straight in my mind," I said quickly. I backed up a couple of steps until my back was to the fiery hell pits. "You're not going to let us walk out of here unless I relinquish one of my souls, are you?"

Asmodeus pursed his lips. "No. Sebastian may hold the ring of power, and he may possess enough power to use it against me, but he would be destroyed in the attempt. You are his Beloved. He will not do anything to endanger you, including bringing his own life to an end."

I looked at Sebastian. The truth was in his eyes.

Do not listen to his lies. I have power enough to destroy him.

I know you do, I answered gently. But I also knew that Asmodeus spoke the truth . . . the attempt would end in Sebastian's destruction as well, and that I could not tolerate.

I looked at the cavern that yawned behind me, at the still-inert demon lying at the feet of the chair, at the man and the demon lord before me. A time had come that I suddenly felt as if I'd been waiting for all the years of my life. I prayed that what I was about to do would work. If it didn't . . . well, I'd been through that, as well.

"There is only one path open to me." My heart sang as I acknowledged the emotions that had been blossoming since I had first seen Sebastian. *I know you haven't asked me, and it's only been a short time that we've known each other, but somehow, I've fallen in love with you. I never thought I would willingly sacrifice myself for another, but you are more important than even my life.*

Belle—he started to say, but I held up a hand to stop him.

"A soul cannot be taken away by force," I said, my love for him all but bursting from me. "It must be freely given. Sebastian de Mercier, I do willingly cede unto you my soul. Bear it with all the love I have for you."

Sebastian knew at that moment what I was going to do. Asmodeus screamed as Sebastian leaped forward to me, but I stepped backward, off the stone plateau, down into the flames that called my name.

I love you beyond life itself, was my last thought to Sebastian before I was consumed by the fire.

Chapter Nine

Such a dramatic exit.

Oh, be quiet.

If I'd known you were capable of such acting, I would have suggested that you simply brazen your way out of the situation.

Such a funny man.

You had me believing you were sacrificing yourself.

I wasn't sure it would work. I didn't have time to talk to the director about whether a soul transfer could be conducted via a sacrifice.

Had I known of your plan, I wouldn't even have bothered to destroy Orinel. You could have acted him to a grave.

I reached behind Sebastian and pinched his delectable rear. *One more smart comment like that, and I'll regret thinking I was dying for you.*

Immediately, my head and heart were flooded with a wave of love so profound, it made my breath catch in my throat. *Beloved, nothing will ever approach the unselfish acts you conducted on my behalf. I know what it cost you to believe you were sacrificing your life for me, and I will spend eternity humbled by your show of love.*

That's a little more like it, I said, allowing him to see the smile in my mind. I couldn't resist a possessive little touch to Sebastian's shirt as Sally opened the door to the suite. *They're here. Behave yourself.*

I have promised to do so in front of the Betrayer. But once he has left, all bets, as they say, are off.

The accompanying growl in my head left me breathless and wishing that Damian's parents would hurry up and take him off our hands so I could fling myself shamelessly on Sebastian and allow him to pleasure me in all the many ways he had been imagining since I had woken up in his arms.

Those are only the tip of the iceberg, he said with a silent laugh, stiffening slightly as an auburn-haired man entered the room.

"Hullo, Papa," Damian said, glancing at Adrian and a woman I assumed was his wife. "Hullo, Nell."

"Don't bother getting up on our behalf," Adrian told his son in a dry tone.

I looked him over, wondering what sort of life he had led to be named the Betrayer.

You forbade me to dwell on it.

"Sebastian," Adrian said, turning to face us, giving Sebastian a little nod.

"Betrayer," Sebastian said, making a stiff nod of his own. I elbowed him. "Er . . . Adrian."

I smiled at the love of my life, filled almost to bursting with the joy he brought me.

Adrian's dark blue eyes, so like his son's, passed over me with curiosity. "I do not know what miracle Ysabelle has wrought to turn you from predator to protector, but Nell and I are grateful nonetheless that you have kept Damian from harm."

Adrian held out his hand. Sebastian's jaw worked, but the rest of him was frozen into a big, unyielding block. I nudged him again.

It wouldn't kill you to be polite, you know. He's offering you his hand, if not in friendship, then at least in peace.

He is the Betrayer—

Yes, I know, the one who handed you over to Asmodeus to be tortured, but you survived that just as I survived being burned at the stake. Twice. Tempered, remember? It's now time to move on, Sebastian. The present holds enough challenge—we can't live in the past.

Sebastian's struggle was evident on his normally stoic face.

I bit my lip to keep from smiling as he wrestled with the memories of the hell he survived with an understanding of what I was asking of him.

"You can do it," Adrian said, dimples flashing to life for a moment. "It's painful at first, but it gets easier. Or at least my wife keeps telling me."

"Honest to God, these men. You'd think asking them to behave in a civilized manner meant the end of the world," Nell said with a roll of her eyes as she walked over to Damian and told him to gather his things.

The boy's nose wrinkled when she stopped next to him. "You still smell," he told her.

"And you're still obnoxious," she responded with a ruffle to his hair that spoke of affection despite her words. "Get your things and we'll stop by the museum so you can say hi to the mummies."

I raised an eyebrow at Sebastian. He was still imitating a statue, staring down Adrian, whose hand was still extended. "Stop acting so stubborn," I hissed, nudging him with my hip.

"I can stand here as long as you can," Adrian said, humor lighting his eyes. "You might as well give in."

Sebastian ground his teeth, his hands fisted tightly at his sides.

You stubborn man. Don't you see that Adrian was forced to betray you by Asmodeus? If he didn't sacrifice you, who knows how many innocent people would have been killed? You wouldn't have wanted them to suffer in your stead, would you?

It took a few seconds for him to sigh heavily into my mind. *No. But—*

I leaned into him. *The sooner you shake his hand, the sooner they'll leave and I can reward your generous nature.*

You count too heavily on my ability to forgive, woman.

And you are adorable beyond words.

"Pax, then," Sebastian said, grabbing Adrian's hand and giving it a hearty handshake. He all but ran to open the door for them, sliding me a look that expressed both his annoyance at having to forgive Adrian and his intention to claim his reward.

Adrian laughed, but said nothing as he collected his family and herded them toward the door.

"Can we stop at a supermarket before we go to the museum?" Damian asked, handing his stepmother a bulging carrier bag. "Be careful, he's sleeping."

"A supermarket? I suppose so," Nell said, looking curiously at the bag.

"Good. Belle said I can keep William, although he's only to have vegetables and no meat at all."

"William?" Nell asked as she walked through the door. "Is William a hamster or something? I suppose we could handle a little pet, but nothing large . . ."

Sebastian closed the door just as she was peering into the bag. I held my breath for the count of five, expecting Nell to be pounding on the door asking what on earth we were doing giving the disembodied head of a revenant to her stepson, but for once, the Fates were with us.

"And now, my sweet Beloved, you will pay for forcing me to behave in a polite manner to the man who has so much of my blood on his hands."

Before I could protest—not that I intended to—Sebastian scooped me up and carried me into the bedroom in the best romantic hero tradition.

"You've been watching too many French movies," I told him with a kiss to the tip of his adorable nose. "No, Sebastian, seriously, we must talk."

"You may talk. I will feast."

"I can't possibly . . . wait." I pushed back on his chest until he put a few inches between us. "Are you hungry?"

His eyes went midnight gray. "I am hungry for you, sweet Belle."

The flood of images into my head had my toes curling in delight. "Oh, that all sounds lovely—I particularly like that third idea you had; was that whipped cream and strawberries?—

but what I meant was, are you *hungry* hungry? You know, for . . . er . . . lunch?" I tipped my head to the side and presented my neck.

Sebastian growled again, a sound that just about caused my blood to boil. His mouth was hot on my flesh, and I was tempted to throw morality and friendship to the wind and grab him, but fortunately, my errant companion chose that moment to check on me.

"*Les* zombies *sont partis aller* home, thank *Dieu*. How did—*sacre bleu* and all the saints! *Il* ravishing *vous?*"

"No, but—"

"Yes," Sebastian said, rolling off me and onto his feet. Sally's eyes widened as he stalked toward her, his hands on his shirt. With a short rending noise, he ripped the shirt off, two buttons flying right through her. "Yes, I'm ravishing her."

Sally looked in surprise at the buttons behind her, then back to the now bare-chested man approaching her. She backed up toward the door. "*Zût!*"

"Unless you wish to watch me make lengthy, passionate love to Belle, I would advise you to leave now," he told her, pausing to kick off his shoes.

Her eyes grew huge as he whipped off his belt.

I rolled over onto my side and admired the sight of the man I was bound to heart and soul . . . souls . . . as he did a striptease. It was funny how life worked out. I never in five hundred years would have imagined that I would fall in love with a vampire.

Dark One, a voice in my head corrected.

"Are you . . . you're not going to . . . Belle, he's not going to—holy *merde!*" Sally made an odd *eep*ing noise and disappeared through the door just as Sebastian's pants came off.

"You ought to be ashamed of yourself scaring her that way . . ." The words, which seemed to have no problem rolling off my tongue while I ogled Sebastian's backside, legs, and back, suddenly dried up when he turned around. "Holy *merde*, indeed."

Sebastian rolled his eyes as he strolled toward me. "I am

just a man, Beloved. There is nothing here out of the ordinary. Well, perhaps *extra*-ordinary, but nothing to make that much of a shocked face over."

"My other husbands—" I started to say.

"We will not discuss your previous husbands," he interrupted, his movements like a big cat stalking its prey.

My gaze wandered across an incredibly broad chest, down abs that were impressive without being too sculpted, ultimately following a dark honey trail of hair that led to an impressive male endowment. "Fair enough. But—"

"No. You are mine now, Belle, and you will have no other man. What passed before we Joined does not matter to us."

"But—"

He pounced on me before I could finish the sentence, pulling off my shoes, pants, shirt, and underthings so quickly, I didn't have time to do more than blink before I was naked. He rolled me over until I was on my back underneath him, my breasts, my thighs, my hidden female parts all tightening at the sensation of his flesh against mine. Erotic images filled my mind, images of what he wanted us to do together, sending my temperature up several degrees. He kissed me then, a long, thorough kiss that lazily explored my mouth, demanding I respond without holding anything back.

"Yes, it does," I said a few minutes later when I managed to pull my mouth from his, desperately trying to hang on to the few fragmented wits I had left. "At least, one thing does—Noelle."

He froze at the mention of her name.

"I'm sorry, Sebastian." I put my hands on both sides of his face, willing him to understand my somewhat tangled emotions. "I love you. I love you more than I've ever loved another person, but she is my friend, and she has a bond to you—"

"You are my Beloved, not her."

"But she—"

His eyes lightened as he pushed back a bit to glare down at me. "You bring me happiness. You brought light and love into my life, ended my torment, and gave me the most precious gift anyone has ever been given. How can you believe you are not my Beloved?"

"Well . . ." I tried to come up with convincing proof, but he was right. The one thing I hadn't thought I'd been able to do for him had worked out.

Perhaps it wasn't the traditional method of soul redemption, my love, but the result was just as successful. And I will be eternally grateful that I was blessed to find you.

The words, and emotions behind them, were enough to make me blush, but one thing still bothered me, one problem that we had yet to overcome.

"I am willing to accept that we were meant to be together. But Noelle is a friend, and we've hurt her. I must do something about that, or it will taint our relationship."

He was silent for a moment, his beautiful face reflecting the thoughts he shared with me. "We've proven beyond any doubt that she is not my Beloved. Thus we will help her find the man for whom she was meant."

I nibbled my lip. "She's never been one for blind dates, but honestly, I don't see much of an alternative. I just hope she understands that we will be doing everything in our power to help her, though."

"We will make her understand," he promised, his mouth descending to mine, gently tugging my lip from where I was still nibbling on it. *Whatever it takes, we will do. I do not like these feelings of guilt within you. They distract you from the proper adoration of me.*

Arrogant vampire, I answered, gasping when he found a ticklish spot behind my ear. *You never answered me. Are you hungry? For . . . blood?*

I didn't want him to know, but I was a bit squeamish about the whole blood-drinking aspect to our relationship. I'd never been one of those women who thought vampires were sexy . . . the thought of someone feeding off me was almost repugnant.

I will not feed, sweet Belle. You will provide life for me, but it will not be an act of feeding. You will give me life, and in return, I will worship you as a slave might.

I don't want a slave, I said, my body burning as his mouth kissed a hot path down to my breastbone. *I want a man.*

I am yours. His cheeks, roughened slightly with golden stubble, brushed against my left breast. At the gentle abrasion it suddenly became the most demanding part of my body.

"Oh," I gasped, waves of little shocks rolling down my body. Sebastian lifted his head long enough to send me a look so heated, it damn near set the bedding alight.

"I think we can do better than that," he growled, his mouth hovering over my suddenly insistent breast. Every muscle in my body was taut with anticipation, my breath so ragged it was a wonder I was getting any oxygen. When he took the tip of my breast in his mouth, I thought I would die. When he suckled that breast while gently tugging on my second nipple, I knew I was in heaven. And when he nuzzled the soft area on the underside of my breast, his teeth grazing the flesh for a second before piercing the skin, a white-hot pain dissolving into a feeling of profound pleasure that was multiplied by the joy he felt in taking life from me, I exploded into a nova of ecstacy.

This is not feeding, my Beloved. This is a celebration of life—of our lives together, today, next month, and a millenia from now. His voice was soft in my head, full of love and appreciation, and my heart swelled to know he was mine.

Always, he said, moving over me. I parted my legs, reveling in the purely physical pleasures to be found in the weight of him on me, of the sensation of my legs rubbing against him, of his chest hair teasing my already sensitive breasts. *You will always be mine.*

I bit his lip, sucking it into my mouth, and demanded that he do something about the tight ache he'd built up inside me. *I will hold you to that, Sebastian. Now stop tormenting me!*

His chuckle filled my mind when he entered me, the feeling of him gently pushing into my body a familiar pleasure, yet wholly different. I pulled my knees around his hips to accept more of him into me, digging my fingers into the muscles of his behind. His hips flexed as I twirled my tongue around his, drowning in the sensation of the taste, scent, and feel of him. He was everywhere, in my head, in my body, his mouth possessing mine until I broke free to breathe. His eyes were dark as night, but glowing with more love than I ever thought I'd see.

"I love you, my adorable zombie," he murmured against my neck.

"Revenant," I said on another gasp of pleasure as all my insides began to tighten even more. "I'm . . . a . . . rev . . . rev . . . oh, God's bones!"

My words trailed off into a high scream of absolute rapture as he surged hard into my body, his teeth deep in my flesh, the sensation of his approaching orgasm mingling with my own, as well as the sensation of him taking blood from me. My back arched as I clutched him, our bodies moving quickly in a rhythm that seemed to start in my heart.

God's blood, I had no idea it was going to be like this. Why didn't I meet you a century ago? I asked just before my being burst into a thousand little pieces of dazzling brilliance. Our souls, my own and the one I'd given him, touched, and for a moment, we were one glorious being as his orgasm claimed him, sweeping me along.

It seemed to take hours for me to finally come to my senses, but I'm sure it was just a matter of minutes. I was pleased to notice, as Sebastian rolled onto his back, taking me with him so I rested on his now damp chest, that he seemed to be having as much difficulty catching his breath as I did.

Smug vixen, he said, one hand caressing my behind in a gesture of love so sweet, it brought tears to my eyes. *What was that you were saying about your previous husbands?*

What husbands? I smiled into his head and let myself relax on the solid body beneath me, warm, contented, and for the first time in I don't remember how many centuries, truly happy.

Epilogue

"Noelle—"

"No! I don't want your help! You and . . . and . . . blood boy there can just go about your merry little way. I can find my own man, thank you." Noelle stalked over to the window in the flat, the same window I'd been looking for such a short time ago. Her body language bespoke anger, leaving my heart aching to know I had caused so much unhappiness.

"I have promised Belle that I would help you, and I will, regardless of your pride," Sebastian said calmly. His hand slid around my waist. I leaned into him, the feeling of him next to me giving me strength. "I will personally see to it that every unredeemed Dark One in Europe is brought before you, so that you might find the one for whom you were meant."

I assumed Noelle would bristle up at that, but to my surprise, the look in her eyes when she turned toward us was more cautiously speculative than angry. "You think another Dark One is the answer?"

"I do." Sebastian nodded. "You are a Beloved—there is no denying that. Since there is also no denial that Belle is *my* Beloved, we can only assume that the one for whom you are intended is still out there, waiting to find you."

It took a moment for the meaning of what they were talking about to sink in. "Wait one minute!" I pulled out of his embrace to stand in front of him, my hands on my hips. "Let me see if I have this correct . . . she's a Beloved, originally yours until you met me."

Noelle straightened her shoulders and tried to look huffy,

but sighed and slumped into a chair. "Oh, I give up. I'd like to be angry about this, I really would, but it's clear to me now what Sebastian meant all along. We just aren't compatible, and you two are."

"Well?" I asked Sebastian, nodding to Noelle to show her I'd heard her comment.

He looked momentarily disconcerted. "That is as good a summary as I believe can be made in a single sentence."

"In other words, you're saying Beloveds are not unique? That they can be passed along from Dark One to Dark One?" I poked him in the chest. He captured my hand, casting Noelle a long-suffering glance over my shoulder. It just made me want to poke him even harder.

A faint giggle escaped Noelle.

"It's not quite as stark as you stated, but in this instance, yes. Noelle was born a Beloved, but has yet to find the Dark One she was meant to redeem—"

I punched him on the arm. Hard. "You told me a Beloved was the one woman in the world who could save you. That is, one woman in the whole history of time who could bind herself body and soul to you, who would fulfill you, complete you and make you whole. And now you're saying that we're . . . *disposable*? I thought I was the only one for you!"

Noelle covered her mouth and pretended to cough, but I knew she was hiding her laughter. Sebastian made like he was going to pull me into another of his mind-meltingly wonderful embraces, but I held him off with an outraged glare.

"You are the only one for me, but since you bring it up, I would like to point out that you had five husbands before me. Five. Did you love them?"

"I . . . they . . . I was lonely. . . ." My teeth snapped shut over the protestations I wanted so badly to make, but damn it, Sebastian had a point, and he knew it.

"You see? You managed to have five husbands whom you loved, and yet you still love me to the exclusion of all else."

I grumbled to myself that I could change that if I really wanted.

"Add to which the fact that I don't love her," he said, pointing at Noelle. "I never have."

"You know how to make a girl feel so special," Noelle said, her lips twisting slightly.

Sebastian offered her an apologetic smile. "I meant no insult."

"Oh, none taken." She sighed again, then stood up and gave us a watered-down version of her usual cheery smile. "Men tell me all the time that they don't love me. It seems to be a frequent theme in my life. Very well, I give you two my blessing, not that you've asked for it in particular. I'm still a bit confused by this whole Beloved thing, but it's obvious to me how much in love you both are. I will hold you to your promise to find me a Dark One of my own, mind you, so don't think you're getting off easily."

"It will be our pleasure to help you," I said as Sebastian grabbed my wrist and started pulling me toward the door. "We won't rest until we've found the perfect man for you, one who is tender and witty and wholly deserving of your affection, not like this monstrous beast I seem to be stuck with."

Sebastian stopped in the doorway, raised one eyebrow, and growled deep in his throat.

My legs melted. *I just can't resist you when you do that,* I told him as he pulled me through the door into a blessedly empty hall.

That is the plan, my sweet little zombie, he said as I met him halfway in a kiss so hot, it came close to melting my shoes. *I'm so very glad it's working.*

Behind him, Sally appeared for a moment, smiled, then turned back into the flat. "Noelle! *Vous avez besoin de* a spirit guide *tres* groovy cool! Luckily, *je suis maintenant* available. Shall we talk about how *je peux aider* you be *tres jolie* Guardian?"

Gentlemen Prefer Voodoo

Angie Fox

Special thanks to intrepid readers Michelle McMurry and Julia Grace, who braved St. Louis Cemetery Number One as well as the back streets of New Orleans to take site pictures and answer lots of (rather odd) questions.

To Koren Cota and Sandie Grassino for the translations. Also to Jessa Slade for hanging out at RWA Nationals and brainstorming "the perfect word" to describe a rat. (Hey, these things are important.) You, my dear, are resplendent.

Chapter One

Amie could barely see her customer as the woman lurched toward the counter, arms loaded with a voodoo love spell kit, fat pink altar candles, a well-endowed Love Doll, a twelve-pack of Fire of Love incense, and "breath mints," the woman huffed. She dumped everything on the mosaic countertop and reached for the Altoids display, a nervous smile tickling her lips. "Not that I expect all of this to work right away."

Amie couldn't help laughing as she caught a supersize bottle of Heat Up the Bedroom linen mist before it rolled under an arrangement of Good Fortune charms. "You never know."

Her customer couldn't have been more than forty, with gorgeous green eyes, a warm, well-rounded face, and a lonely heart. Amie could see it as clearly as the glow-in-the-dark Find Your Lover charm at the top of the heap.

Well, Amie had just the thing.

She closed her eyes, blocking out the pink and green painted walls and loaded display tables.

Wind chimes at the back of the shop swung in circles. Their limbs, carved from bayou swamp trees, clacked together.

She let her magic well up inside her, vibrant and sweet. "Now." She reached across the counter and found the woman's hands. She braced herself as the power flowed through her. "You'll find what you need."

She squeezed once and let go. Once was all it took.

That's when the growling started.

It began as a low rumbling at the back of the shop and

continued until a thin line of smoke seeped from behind the Voodoo Wash Yourself Clean soap display.

"It's a faulty heater," Amie said, well aware that it was July. "Ignore it."

"Sure," the woman said, watching Amie pack her things in two overflowing bags. "Some of this is bound to work, right?"

"Voodoo can be very powerful," Amie said, "if you believe."

Amie smiled to herself as the door swung shut against the sweltering New Orleans heat.

Flower petals and grave dust sprinkled down from the spell bundle she'd hung from the vintage tin ceiling. Made from an old family recipe and wrapped in her lucky green scarf, it warded off evil spirits and helped cut down on shoplifting.

Amie scooted around the counter, her bracelets jangling as she smoothed back her thick black hair.

"Okay, you big, bad beast, you can come out now."

A red leathery creature the size of a swamp cat burst out from behind a display of bath fizzies. He resembled a small flying dinosaur. "By thunder and lightning and Papa Limba," he said with a thick Congo accent, blowing out a breath as a pink and white begonia threatened to land on the tip of his beak. "You are giving your magic away to people off the street?"

Isoke was small for a Kongamato. His wingspan was only about three feet. He had leathery skin, gorgeous blue eyelashes, and all the tact of a battering ram.

"You need to stay on your perch." At least while customers were in the store. "What if that poor woman had gone back for another Mango Mamma bath melt?"

"Go dunk your head in the Jiundu swamp. I am not here to be a ceiling decoration." He sniffed at his usual place, where he hung upside down near a display of rainbow-colored wind socks.

His eyes glowed yellow. "I am here to protect you," he said, flaunting two rows of razor-sharp teeth. "Maybe next time I will bite the woman. That will keep her from robbing you."

"My magic is freely given," Amie insisted, straightening the bath fizzie display. She might not mind grave dust on her floor—that had a purpose. But the rest of her shop was immaculate.

The dragon watched her with a guarded expression. "Amiele Fanchon D'Honore Baptiste, you waste your magic. It's bad juju. First, your mother and now you."

Amie's back stiffened at the insinuation. Her mother had lived fast, died young—and left Amie very much alone. Well, with one rather obnoxious exception.

"Your mother wasted her love magic on a legion of men. You give yours away to strangers. In three hundred and eighty-six years, I have never seen anything like it."

"You're being unfair." She refused to look at him. Instead, she busied herself rearranging a sagging display of gris-gris bags near the front of the shop. The bright red and yellow bundles contrasted against the hot pink walls and silver posters of Erzulie, the spirit of love, and Papa Ghede, lord of the erotic. "Mom gave her love magic away to men who didn't appreciate it," she said, with more than a twinge of regret. There had been many, many men.

"And she received none of it back," he replied, his voice low in his throat. "I watched her waste away. I'm not going to watch you too."

Amie fingered a Fall in Love bag before stuffing it back down with the rest. "Ah, but there is a difference. I am getting bits of magic back. You don't think I'm going to feel that woman's happiness? She might not know what I did, but every time someone is grateful, it filters home."

"Crumbs," Isoke declared. "You need a man, someone who will take your love magic and give his to you tenfold."

Amie's stomach dropped as she tidied an already perfect row of voodoo history books. "I've tried that."

She'd dated. None of the men fit the bill. New Orleans was a wild city, and she wasn't going to lash herself to some beer-guzzling party boy just to save a little magic.

"When? When did you last see a man?" the Kongamato prodded.

Amie opened her mouth to answer.

"A man you trusted with your love magic?"

Her smart answer died on her lips.

"Nine years." Her stomach twisted at the realization. *Nine years* since her last boyfriend. And, no, he hadn't returned her love magic. If her mother was any indication, men never did.

Isoke cocked his head. She felt his hot breath against her leg, even through her gauzy yellow skirt.

"Look, I'm fine the way I am. I don't want to worry about when some guy is going to call or how to act on a date or whether he's going to turn into a cretin if I sleep with him."

"Eeking out a life is not fine." Isoke huffed like a blast furnace.

"Stop it," Amie admonished, "you're going to singe the floor again." She couldn't keep throwing rugs everywhere. Her landlord was suspicious enough when he found the hot tub in her back storage room full of muddy water, sticks, and Spanish moss. You could take the Kongamato out of the swamp, but you couldn't take the swamp out of the Kongamato.

Just then, a group of giggling teenagers burst through the door. Isoke froze midsnarl while Amie went to help them. After they'd left, loaded down with passion fruit incense, Amie returned to her display. Isoke resumed his grumbling, his tail dragging along the floor.

"Stop it. You're messing up the grave dirt."

"Even your dirt is organized?"

"Yes." It had to lay where it fell. "What kind of Kongamato are you?"

"One who is about to lose his tail."

"Excuse me?"

"For three hundred and eighty-six years, I serve. I help the women of your family fulfill their destinies as women of voodoo. But with you? I get stressed. You do everything wrong. And when I stress, I molt."

She planted a hand on her hip. "So your tail is going to fall off if I don't go out with some rum-swilling boozehound?"

"Yes. I mean, no." His wide nostrils quivered. "You do not go out with a boozehound . . . you go out with a man!"

Amie rubbed her fingers along the bridge of her nose to tamp down the dull ache forming there.

Did she really have to discuss her dating life with her dead mother's mythical monster?

No. She didn't owe the Kongamato anything. Not after he blew flames out the upstairs window last week. Sure, he'd managed to lure a half dozen firemen into Amie's bedroom, but she'd had a devil of a time explaining how seven 911 callers had been mistaken about the fire.

Too bad for Amie, Kongamatos were as stubborn as they were loyal. "I worry about you," Isoke said, following her. "This is not natural. The women in your line—they are passionate."

"I am passionate," she said, fighting the urge to stuff him in a doggie carrier and mail him back to Zambia. "Look at this store. This is my passion." Couldn't he see what she'd done here?

She was damned proud of it.

Every detail was perfect. Everything was in its place.

His yellow eyes drilled into her. "The women in your line are women of action."

What did he want from her? "You know what? The women in my line are gone. Mom is gone. You have me now. This is how I am and I like it."

He studied her for a moment. "No. You are unhappy."

"I am happy!" she shouted.

"That's better," he said, utterly delighted as Amie clapped a hand over her mouth. She never yelled.

Amie waited to make sure nothing bad was going to come

out before she spoke. There was nothing wrong with being in control. "Okay, it's not that I wouldn't like a man in my life." Who wouldn't, right? "I'm just not going to settle for anything less than perfect."

Isoke growled.

"And no more firemen."

He rolled his eyes. *Drama queen.*

Amie selected a Love and Happiness candle from the shelf next to the organic bath oils and lit it. "See? Look. I'm starting already."

Isoke landed on the multicolored countertop next to the candle, clipping a wing on the cash register. "Eyak. This store was not made for Kongamato."

Amie managed a weak smile. "I didn't know I'd inherit you so soon."

"I could not save your mother, which means I will try doubly hard with you." He folded his wings like a bat. "Please, for the sake of my tail, you must consider it."

Amie ruffled the three stiff feathers on the top of his head. "For you, Isoke. I will try."

Nine years. The shop had been busy all afternoon and still she couldn't get it out of her mind.

She hadn't had a date in nine years. Amie closed her cash register and said good-bye to the young couple who had just purchased a fertility doll and an extra large bottle of sandalwood massage oil.

She had to think of something else. Her eyes settled on the poster of Papa Ghede, laughing and cavorting with his latest lover. Yeah, that didn't help.

Okay, so it had been a long time—too long—but Amie had been busy. She'd graduated college, opened her own shop, fixed up the apartment upstairs. The second floor had needed a lot of work. Her landlord had used it as storage. It still had the French-style mirrors on the ceiling from its glory days as a bordello. Okay, so Amie had left the mirrors. But she had done a lot to the place.

It's not like many people held down jobs and decorated their apartments *and* dated, right?

Oh hell. Maybe she did have a problem.

She glanced at the Kongamato settling in on his perch. He hung from the ceiling, folding his wings around him like a giant bat.

She hoped Isoke wasn't the type to gloat when he got his way.

True, she would never be able to bring herself to go out with any of the men she saw up and down Bourbon Street at all hours of the day and night. And she definitely didn't want a man like the kind her mother had dated. They might appear nice at first, but all of them were drunks, gamblers, or cheaters in the end.

Luckily for Amie, she knew another way.

She fingered her blue and silver beaded necklace, a Do Good charm she'd fashioned years ago. *My power is both a gift and an obligation. Let good works flow through me.* She'd been using her spells to help her customers find love. So why hadn't she used it on herself? Because men were brash and unpredictable.

But what if she could eliminate the risk?

She'd tried that once, with her last boyfriend. He'd been nice and safe, soft and accommodating, with an average build and eyes that focused on ESPN more than her. She'd composed entire grocery lists while they made love and more than once had been tempted to stop midcaress so she could make a quick note about the need for more bananas or bread. He'd never surprised her, never challenged her, and when he left, she hadn't cared.

While she was quite pleased that she hadn't been hurt like her mother, Amie also knew she'd wasted her time.

But if she could control things, perhaps she could welcome some passion into her life—without the pain. She could actually let herself feel, dream, give her love with absolutely no fear that he'd break her heart.

She could summon Mr. Right!

He'd know how to act, know how to dress, and know how to please her. He wouldn't complicate her life.

At last she'd have someone to spend her evenings with, to walk the French Quarter with, someone who might want to try out the mirrors over the bed. The mere thought of it sent heat pooling to her belly. Yes, the Kongamato had a point. Perhaps it was time to voodoo herself a valentine.

Amie locked the shop early that night, feeling nervous, as if she were heading out on a date. Ideally, the spell should be performed at sunset. Of course Amie knew better than anyone that love spells took time, and they only worked if a girl was ready to accept love into her life.

Was she ready?

Amie already loved her shop, and her life. But, yes, there had to be something more.

She turned off the metal, industrial-style VooDoo Works sign outside and punched in the alarm code. With the waning sun and soft security lights to guide her way, she gathered a single sheet of blank white paper and two quartz crystals from the Sale table. Then she ducked under the counter to find her odds-and-ends box.

She'd put together a selection of colorful jewelry-making kits a while back and had stashed the extra weaving thread . . . "Here," she said as her fingers located the red and black strands.

Amie swallowed her excitement as Isoke, bathed in shadows, stirred on his perch.

She hoped she could finish before he woke up to go hunting. If she was smart, she'd wait until after her Kongamato was gone for the evening. But Amie didn't know how long her courage would last.

Isoke sank back into his slumber, a bit of drool sizzling down onto the floor. She was never going to get her security deposit back at this rate. She slid a copper incense burner under him and fought the urge to straighten the three rumpled feathers that stuck out from the top of his head.

She eased into the back room of the shop, closing the EM-PLOYEES ONLY door behind her.

The cloying incense was stronger back here, mixed with the heady scent of beeswax altar candles. Isoke's hot tub hummed in the center. On two sides of the room, wooden shelves held boxes of merchandise while drying herbs hung along the third wall. In the very back, under a small stained-glass window, stood a humble wooden altar that had been her great-grandmother's. Amie touched the battered surface reverently as she laid out her spell ingredients and closed her eyes.

The air was thick and warm. She inhaled deeply, letting peace wash over her. To anyone else, this might have looked like a highly organized, if unusual, storage room, but to her, it was a special place. Here, she was surrounded by the things she loved.

The crickets had begun to chirp outside. Paired with the earthy bubbling of Isoke's hot tub swamp, Amie almost felt like she was back in her grandmother's old stilted house on the bayou.

Amie focused on the affection she felt for her mother, her grandmother, and all her ancestors. These women had passed along their power, their strength, their passion—their love.

Love.

Amie lit the fat red altar candles.

She relaxed, letting her mind take her where she needed to be. She saw her perfect man—cultured and refined. He was lean yet strong. He was passionate, determined. He wouldn't drink to excess, like her mother's men had. He wouldn't lie, cheat, steal. He wouldn't leave. No, he would wrap his strong arms around her and keep her safe. She could almost see him in her mind. Almost. It was as though he was barely out of reach.

Amie cracked open one eye. The spell would work better if she were naked. Amie wasn't particularly fond of stripping in her storage room. But if she was serious about finding the right kind of love—and she was . . .

She adjusted the altar candles, tested the weight of her crystals, her stomach twisting with indecision. She was stalling and she knew it.

Slowly, her fingers trailed down her sides and found the edge of her cami top. Her breath hitched as she drew it over her head. The bra soon followed, along with her flowing yellow skirt and her hot pink panties.

Amie ignored the cool breeze along her back as she ripped the paper, shredding it into two rough hearts. She placed them together and, her voice hoarse, chanted, "I call on Erzulie, loa of the heart; Papa Ghede, loa of passion; my ancestors, women whose blood boiled strong with the love of their men."

She now saw her ideal man clearly in her mind's eye. He had a small scar above one arched brow, dark brown hair clipped short and tight, and the most arresting blue eyes. Sharp recognition wound through Amie.

He seemed to be looking right at her.

She drew the crystal against her bare chest, the roughened stone teasing her smooth skin, sending shivers down the length of her body. Her nipples tightened. She could feel the vibrations in the gemstone as she lowered it over the paper hearts.

"Send to me . . ." She paused. *The man I just saw.* In her haste, she hadn't quite decided how to word her request.

She knew the more specific the better, but really, it wasn't about six-pack abs or a body that sent her pulse skittering.

She wanted someone she could love.

How hard was that?

Amie swallowed. "Send to me," she said, her voice husky, "the *perfect man* for me." She didn't care if he had that square jaw or that rugged look about him. She needed someone kind, loving, *hers*.

A man she could give her love magic to without being afraid.

Her stomach tingled at the thought.

Slowly, she wove the black and red threads into a homemade ring. All the while, she filled her mind with thoughts of love in its purest form—passion, giving, acceptance.

"The perfect man for me," she repeated, tying off the ring and slipping it onto her right ring finger. She was careful to blow out the candle in a single breath before gathering up the hearts.

The room was nearly dark, which meant the sun had almost slipped under the horizon. Good. Because Amie was naked and she still had to bury the torn hearts.

She hesitated at the back door. This was the French Quarter, but still, what would the neighbors think?

Do it fast.

Amie double-checked the key in the pocket of her skirt before throwing the whole thing over her shoulder. She slipped out into the back alley, squinching her nose at the smell of old beer and garbage.

Never mind. The spell was complete. The burial only sealed it.

Luckily she kept a flowerpot filled with consecrated earth for that very purpose. Now if she could only keep Mrs. Fontane down the way from filling it with geraniums. Amie reached past the roots of the plant and buried the torn hearts deep.

"Earth to earth. Dust to dust."

Now all she had to do was wait.

Chapter Two

Amie took a long, hot shower and changed into a simple white nightgown. She traded her contacts for glasses and eased onto the edge of her wide four-poster bed to comb out her hair. Amie loved her bedroom, with its gauzy white drapes and comfortable furnishings. Everything in here was well-used and loved.

She'd chosen the smallest of the three upstairs rooms as hers because it was the only one that faced the back of the house. She liked to forget she lived smack dab in the middle of Royale Street, in the heart of party central.

The old bordello's main boudoir had become Amie's living room—or given the bookshelves that lined every wall, her library. She'd converted the rest of the space into an efficient kitchen and eating area.

Amie smiled to herself as she slipped into bed. Perhaps before long, she'd have to set another place at her bright yellow kitchen table.

She'd just about drifted off to sleep with the latest Charlaine Harris novel when three distinct knocks echoed through the house.

"What the—?" She scrambled upright and managed to bump her glasses off the end of her nose and onto the floor.

The knocks sounded again.

"Isoke?" Amie slipped out of bed, using her toes to locate her glasses on the hardwood. Leave it to the dragon to be dramatic. It's not like she hadn't taught him how to disable the alarm.

Bam. Bam. Bam.

"Coming!" She shoved on her glasses and hurried for the back stairs. No telling what mythical monster fists could do to her back door.

Isoke claimed Kongamatos were bad with numbers. Well, if he couldn't memorize a simple alarm code, she had a good mind to install a perch outside.

Bam. Bam. Bam.

"Hold your tail," she said, flicking on the lights and punching the alarm code on the back door. "If you can't remember how to let yourself in the house or to stop leaving muddy Kongamato tracks on my floor *or dead mice in my shoes* or—"

Amie flung open the door and gasped.

A man stood on the slab of concrete that was her back porch. Not just any man, either. Broad shoulders, tousled dark hair, a strong jaw—the man from her vision.

His lips quirked in a smile and he gave her a heated look that would have melted her into a puddle on the floor, if she'd been susceptible to that sort of thing—which she was not.

He strode straight for her, cupped her face in his hands, and kissed her. The rush of sensation shocked her, poured through her. His mouth was hot and demanding.

So this was what sheer desire felt like.

His touch stirred something deep inside her, an urge she hadn't even known was there.

She couldn't talk, could barely think as he wound his fingers through her hair and urged her closer. Her body collided flush with his. Her skin tingled. She'd never felt anyone so strong and hard and *good*.

He groaned deep, his hands sliding down the exposed skin of her arms, leaving goose bumps in their wake. He smelled earthy and elemental. Real. And she was a powerful, sexy voodoo mambo. Wild pleasure shot through her as she wound her arms around his shoulders.

She wanted to feel him, connect with him. No man had ever affected her in such an intense and immediate way. She'd never let one get close enough.

But now here he was, the man from her vision, and he was

just as mind-blowingly perfect as she'd imagined. He slid his hands down to the small of her back, urging her closer, until she could feel him—every rock hard inch of him—against her.

It was the craziest thing she'd ever done. He was a complete stranger and yet he made her want to do things that she hadn't let herself think about in years.

He nipped at the sweet spot behind her ear, trailed scorching kisses down her neck. She gasped with pleasure. He must have just gotten up in the middle of the night and come straight to her. It was insane.

"What are we doing?" she asked on a moan.

His hands circled her waist as his lips touched her collarbone. "You are going to be the love of my life," he said, his voice husky, his Spanish accent pronounced as he turned his impossibly blue eyes up to her.

How could he even presume to know that? Amie traced her fingers over the faint scar above his right eye, exactly where she'd envisioned it. Unbelievable.

His eyes darkened as he stood and pulled her close. Her heart sped up. It all felt so right.

"My one true love," he murmured, drawing her in for a slow, sensual kiss.

Mmm . . . he could say what he wanted. She wouldn't argue. Not now, at least. For once, she could pretend to be in love. She ground against him. Or perhaps in serious lust.

He was merciless. She melted a little with every hot, hungry kiss until she was positively aching for him. She wound her fingers through his short dark hair. She gripped his muscled shoulders. She slid her hands down his back, past the sweat-slicked skin at his waist, to where his pants should have been.

If he'd been wearing pants. Amie gasped as her hands closed around his bare butt.

By Kalfu's gate! This Adonis of a man was as naked as the day he was born.

Amie broke the kiss, her eyes darting over his wide shoulders, down his well-built chest, past the narrow stretch of hair that began just below his belly button, to where she should not have been looking at all.

Heat shot through her. "I'm sorry," Amie said. Great juju, the door was still open. She slammed it behind him, averting her eyes as he strolled past her into the storage room. The space suddenly seemed quite a bit smaller.

He didn't seem to be bothered at all by his complete lack of clothing. As she watched his firm backside, Amie had to admit her mystery man had a lot to be proud of.

Amie shoved her hair out of her eyes and adjusted her glasses. He was going to turn around again. She had to get it together.

She scanned his handsome face, strong chest, flat abs—oh my! She wasn't going there again.

"Forgive me," he said, noticing where her eyes had gone. The man was impossibly tall. "I've never appeared naked at a woman's door." He ran a hand down his chest. "Or naked anywhere, for that matter."

Amie tried to avert her eyes, but it didn't work. She hadn't seen anything like that in a long time. Ever, in fact.

She felt the color rise to her face. "How about we find you something to wear?" she said, reaching for the first thing she could get her hands around—a silk wall hanging of *le grand zombie*, a very powerful snake spirit.

He wrapped the green and gold cloth around his waist like a towel. Amie wished she could close her eyes. If anything, the fabric accented his hard, stiff . . .

"Much better," he said, double-checking the knot.

If he only knew.

She'd asked for moonlight walks through the French Quarter, not *this*.

"Why on earth were you—"

"Naked?" he asked. "Not the best circumstances, I admit." He drew her into his arms. Her heart fluttered as she leaned against the full length of him and let him brush his lips over hers. "Still, when you think about it logically, you cannot expect clothes to survive almost two hundred years."

Amie's gut dropped.

He frowned as she escaped his embrace. "Are you all right?"

She took two steps back, thought about it, and took two more. "By Ghede." She wiped at the cold sweat on her brow. Her mouth felt dry. Amie took a deep breath and asked the question she really, really didn't want the answer to. "Where did you come from?"

"You called me," he said, as if that explained everything.

Dread slicked down her back. She'd asked for her perfect man. She didn't *call* anyone from anywhere. In fact, she was hoping she'd meet a cute guy in church or maybe over a beignet at Café Du Monde.

"I'll ask you one more time," she said, as calmly as she could manage. "Where did you come from?"

He took a step toward her. "St. Louis Cemetery Number One."

She froze on the spot. "Oh no." She blinked hard. "You're," she forced herself to say it, "dead."

He stood inches away from her, dark, brooding, and sexy as hell. "Not anymore."

Her heart sped up. By Papa Legba, what had she done?

This was unnatural. This was wrong. She'd misused her magic in the worst possible way. How could she be so irresponsible?

"Thank you," he said, touching her cheek. "You do not know how long I have waited for a second chance."

Amie knew she was gawking, but she couldn't help it.

She'd spent her life promising herself she'd never repeat her mother's mistakes. She'd never date men who gambled her money away, who lied, who cheated. No. Her man would be different.

And he was.

He was a zombie.

Chapter Three

He brushed her hair out of her eyes. "It's okay, Amie. It's not every day you meet your ideal lover. This is overwhelming for me too." He leaned down to kiss her.

"Stop it," she croaked. He wasn't her better half. He was a mistake. And how did he know her name? Of course, she'd called him. She'd asked for him. She'd practically given him her cosmic Social Security number. *Think. I need to think.*

He stepped back, giving her space. "I could use a bath." He brushed at his muscled arms. "Grave dust." He caught her gaze and held it. "Or once you calm down, perhaps we can take one together."

"Oh no," Amie stammered, "out of the question." She wasn't letting this man take one more step into her shop or her house, much less into her bathtub.

She already felt like he'd undressed her with his eyes.

"Do not worry. I will marry you first, if that is what you desire."

Amie crossed her arms over her chest. He had to be kidding. This man wasn't going to walk her down the aisle. He was going back to his grave.

Then she was going to take a long, cold shower and never date again.

While she was mentally reprogramming her life, he slipped past her into the shop.

"Stop," she ordered as he clanged into the bowl she'd set down to catch Isoke's drool.

Amie flipped on the lights to find her Spanish zombie inspecting her colorful display of gris-gris bags.

"Hands off," Amie said.

"Of course." He nodded, looking at her as if she was the one in the towel.

Amie wrinkled her nose at the smell of singed . . . floor. The Kongamato drool!

With one eye on the zombie, she rushed to the counter for a rag. She could feel his eyes on her.

"Can you wait in the storage room?" she asked, her rag smoking as she sopped up the mess he'd made.

"There's no need. I'm much more comfortable in here," he said, touching off a set of wind chimes. "I find your store utterly fascinating. Very well done, *mi corazon*. Beautiful and colorful, just like you." His fingers closed around a glass bottle with a bejeweled skeleton label. "Florida water," he said, turning the bottle sideways and watching the shaved orange rinds—her family's special ingredient—float through the liquid.

"Give me that." She dropped the rag and shoved the bottle under her arm. "And I'm not your love," she said, retrieving the rag with two fingers and depositing it in the trash. Why had she ever thought she needed a man in her life? "This is a big mistake."

Huge.

Her grandmother had told stories of voodoo mambos calling zombies, mostly to work in the fields at harvest. One particularly powerful voodoo queen asked for a bodyguard and gained a mobster with a price on his head. Little Mickey was killed (again) as soon as he set foot in New Orleans. It was considered gutsy to call a zombie. Rarer if one came, and even though zombies looked—and acted—like their human selves, to her knowledge no one had ever tried to date one.

Zombies lingered until they'd completed their task, and then they returned to their graves.

Well, she didn't want this love zombie to do anything for her—or to her. She had to put him back and end this mess.

What she needed was a zombie neutralizing spell.

She'd have to look it up, but right off the bat, she knew she needed Florida water. She glanced at the bottle under her arm. Check. She'd need a pair of black candles . . .

Amie took two candles from the display next to the counter. While he browsed the books for sale, she grabbed a hemp bag off the hook behind the counter, tossing the ingredients inside.

She'd need grave dust. She looked her zombie up and down, from his strong jaw to his wide toes. "I think we have that covered."

"Ah, *The Complete Illustrated Kama Sutra*." The blue of his eyes deepened as he gave her a smoky look.

Desire tangled in her stomach. She ignored it because, well, it was just plain ridiculous. The kiss was amazing, before she knew what he was, but she certainly hadn't asked for this. Amie stomped up to him with her hand out. "Give it back."

He grinned. "The spine is creased." He flipped through the pages. "Right here. Do you look at this book sometimes?"

The next time Isoke had any great ideas about finding her a man, she'd tie his beak shut with a fire hose.

He examined the Moon position. "Now that looks interesting," he said, his fingers splayed wide over a couple having a lot more fun that Amie ever had. She felt the heat rise to her cheeks.

"Stop it. We're not doing the Kama Sutra. We're not going to fall in love. I don't even know you."

"You will be my true love," he said, as if he was informing her of the weather or how the Hornets had played the night before. "I can prove it."

"How?" Amie asked, not sure she wanted to know.

He closed the book and placed it back on the shelf, seeming to forget about the Moon, the Lotus, and the rest of the positions *she* couldn't quite get out of her head. "Come. You will go with me back to my grave." He took her hands in his and kissed her on the top of the head.

Amie yanked her hands back and wiped them on her nightgown, ignoring his frown. His touch would have felt good, if she hadn't known what he was.

"You know what?" Amie said, as she let a plan of her own

take shape. "That's a good idea. Let's go see where you were buried." She really didn't want to put him back to earth right here in the storage room. There was the matter of the body. She couldn't just carry it down Canal Street and back to the cemetery. But if she could follow him back to his grave, it would be like zombie express delivery.

His face lit up. "Fantastic. No one has visited my grave since the Roosevelt administration."

"But you have to wait right here while I get ready, okay?"

"Absolutely, my dear." He resumed his assault on her bookcase, one hand at his waist holding his silk wrapper closed.

She paused on the bottom step. "I'll also find you something to wear."

Amie almost asked him what he wanted to show her at his grave, but stopped herself. She didn't want to be any more involved in his undead life than she had to be. Besides, she'd put him down as soon as they arrived. "Be back soon," she said, taking the steep stairs as fast as she could manage.

"During that time, do you mind if I remove a few geraniums from the pot outside? We'll be passing my grandmother's vault on the way in."

"Knock yourself out," Amie called. She'd prefer her zombie outside anyway.

Amie dashed into the library and found her spell book. She flopped it on the kitchen table. "Zombie . . . zombie care, zombie feeding, zombie summoning . . .

On rare occasions, zombies can be called with a spell in order to assist with a task.

Ah, so that's what her love life had come down to. Great. Evidently, his task had been to kiss her silly.

A zombie will deteriorate and die again once it has fulfilled its purpose or once the voodoo mambo no longer requires its services.

Well, Amie didn't require his services. And she certainly wasn't going to let him fulfill his purpose—not if he thought it meant marrying her.

She flipped through the book again and pressed her finger to a final entry, "zombie termination." She made a mental list of the ingredients she needed before shoving the book in her bag. Digging through her kitchen drawers, she found a flashlight and a box of matches.

Amie caught her reflection in the hand decorated mirror above her kitchen sink. Her black hair frizzed about her face and her eyes were wide with shock.

"If you get out of this," she told herself, "you will never wish for another date. Because *this* is what happens." Men were trouble every time.

And undead men were worse.

Amie blew out a breath. She didn't have time to be feeling sorry for herself.

In less than a minute, she'd changed into a long orange skirt and a yellow top. She pulled on her barely used tennis shoes, grabbed him a pair of sweat pants, and headed down for the shop.

"Hi."

"Ga!" She clutched her chest and pitched forward. She fell the last three steps and directly into his arms. He was warm, strong.

She lurched away. "What are you doing? You were supposed to be outside." He didn't feel dead. She remembered what it felt like to have his arms wrapped around her. And his kiss had been downright electrifying. Didn't matter. He was dead.

He eased a lock of hair behind her ear. "Here I am, bursting into your home, ready to marry you tomorrow." He raised a brow. "Or tonight if you know a priest." When she couldn't quite move her mouth to respond, he continued. "It occurred to me that we haven't been properly introduced."

Every cell in her body screamed for her to close the distance between them. Feeling his arms around her reminded her too much of how it had felt when he kissed her. That's what she got for making him her first kiss in nine years. Damn the man.

He was clearly *wrong* in more ways than one. She refused to marry a dead man, or kiss him again. She didn't even want to talk to him.

Amie took a deep breath. She made a mistake and she'd fix it. He was going back into the ground.

"I don't need to know your name," she said, inching past his massive form and plucking an extra cleaning rag from under the counter. She'd be glad to have it if things got messy.

"My name is Dante Montenegro," he said, bowing slightly, his accent even more pronounced.

Okay, well good. At least she knew what grave they needed to find.

"Put these on." She handed him a pair of her largest sweatpants, the kind with the string tie.

He held them up. "Canary yellow?"

"Deal with it."

He ignored her sarcasm like the gentleman he was. "Actually, I used to own a pair of breeches in this very shade."

His civility was making her uncomfortable. "Okay, well just put them on," she said, turning away. She did not need to see him undressed again. Plus, she needed one more thing from the shop.

She had to find something of hers that she could burn, dust to dust, ashes to ashes. It should be small, so she could carry it. It had to have been in the presence of magic. "Preferably something I've owned for years," she said to herself, as the perfect sacrifice came to mind. She hated to lose the Lisa Simpson keychain she had looped over the corner of her register, but desperate times called for desperate measures.

Amie stuffed the keychain into her bag.

Let's see, she had candles, water, Lisa Simpson, grave dust, a zombie. She glanced back at the man behind her. She'd give him one thing—he was the Don Juan of the zombie world.

She shook her head. It didn't matter. He didn't belong here.

"After you," he said, as she led them out into the night.

Chapter Four

Laughter and conversation from the party crowd erupted in waves on the other side of the wall of buildings as Amie and her zombie hurried down the alley that led to Canal Street. For the first time in her life, Amie wished she could be one of them, instead of running side by side with a dead Romeo through the back streets of New Orleans.

How had she gotten herself into this?

He actually believed he was going to marry her.

If he thought he was going to convince her based on something they'd find in a cemetery at one in the morning, he was even crazier than she'd imagined. No true love of hers would act this way.

This little trip through la-la land was her penance for thinking, believing, *dreaming* she could step out of her normal life and expect more than she had any right to expect. Hadn't her mother taught her that? Her grandmother? The women of her line were destined to be alone. She had to stop listening to bossy red monsters and start behaving like a proper voodoo mambo.

Sweat trickled down her back. There was no escaping the humid heat of New Orleans, even after midnight.

Amie felt a familiar tug as the white stone walls of the graveyard came into view. Her calling as a voodoo mambo gave her a certain kinship with the dead. It was part of the job. Still, she didn't like the way the ingredients in her bag began to stir.

St. Louis Cemetery Number One used to be located at the outskirts of the city, which now meant the edge of the French

Quarter. The cemetery closed at dusk to keep vandals and criminals at bay. Visitors were often robbed in broad daylight. Drug deals went down day and night. Tourists were always encouraged to visit in groups.

More than one hundred thousand former New Orleans residents rested inside those walls. Most had been buried in the eighteenth and nineteenth centuries. Entire extended families shared mausoleums separated by narrow pathways. Many of the dead had practiced voodoo. Their power called to her. She'd have to put her zombie down quietly and get the heck out.

Amie kept a hand on her bag as she followed the zombie down the deserted sidewalk past the front entrance, with its tall gate topped by a simple wrought-iron cross. She stiffened as they passed the crumbling tombs inside. A red spiral of energy curled from one of the graves closest to her, the filmy tendril reaching for her.

She'd never seen a red apparition before. Her breath hitched. She really didn't want to learn anything new tonight.

"This way," he said, leading her to an area at the north edge where the streetlights were widely spaced and foot traffic was nonexistent. He mounted the thick white stone wall like a Marine and reached down for her.

"Oh no," she said, refusing his outstretched hand. While Amie was all for getting inside, she was even more interested in having a way out. "Can't we find a back gate or something?"

"Do not argue, my love," he said, his face obscured by shadows as he reached for her again. "This is the quickest."

"I'm not your love." She took a step backward. "And you can't possibly expect me to—*eek!*" He caught her by the wrists and vaulted her up onto the top of the wall.

She pushed against his chest, but it was like fighting with a boulder. "Listen, Tarzan. I don't know what century you're from, but—"

"I told you, I don't like to argue." He wrapped an arm

around her waist as they thundered to the ground. She felt the impact vibrate through his body as her toes scraped the rocky path on the other side of the wall.

She shoved away from him. This time, he let her. "You could have killed me!" she hissed. She could have broken her neck or smashed her head in or—

He shot her a withering look. "Death is *not* something to speak of lightly," he said in a coarse whisper. "Now come. We are not alone."

Lovely, just lovely.

Amie glanced back at the eight-foot-high wall. Last night, she'd been snuggled in bed with a book. Tonight, she was in a haunted cemetery with no way out and a dead guy telling her what to do.

Once they left the shadows of the trees, the moon lit their path. She followed him, cursing at his round, firm backside as he wound through mausoleums of all shapes and sizes. The place smelled like mold and concrete and New Orleans heat. Wrought-iron gates with thick spikes hugged some of the white stone vaults, while others lay neglected, their plaster falling away to expose redbrick skeletons. Still others had sunk into the ground, their inscriptions worn and barely visible as earth swallowed them whole.

Amie paused as she heard men's voices a few rows away. They sounded tense and angry. Wonderful. Amie cringed. She just hoped they were grave robbers instead of muggers. Either way, she didn't want to run into them.

The zombie touched a hand to her shoulder and silently bid her to continue. Amie nodded. They needed to keep moving.

The cemetery was alive. She caught another wisp spiraling skyward, like a paranormal spotlight. It was a fine time to be trapped.

She held her bag to her side, wishing she was hauling around a ferret instead of restless spell ingredients. The zombie moved silently ahead of her, like a bloodhound on a scent.

That was another problem. After she put him back to ground, what was she going to do? Avoid the muggers and the apparitions until the gates opened in the morning? She certainly couldn't scale the wall.

"Stop." He reached behind him to steady her.

"What?" she rasped, trying to keep her Maglite from clanking against the bottle of Florida water.

"Dominga Deloroso El Montenegro," he said, bowing his head before a squat white vault. The plaster had crumbled away around the arched top, revealing brick and a small cropping of weeds.

Right, his grandmother.

He placed the geraniums on the uneven pavement at the front of the tomb. "*Que oró por mi segunda oportunidad*," he said, "*y ahora está aquí.*"

Amie fidgeted. He'd said something about second chances. Written Spanish she could do. Hearing it out loud could be tough. And she didn't like to think of him having a grandma.

She studied the other names etched into the gray stone and stiffened as she read the curling inscription dedicated to the memory of DANTE MONTENEGRO 1779–1811. *EL HOMBRE ADORO DEMASIADO.*

He loved too much?

He'd also died too young. Well, she'd known that already. Her stomach quivered. Seeing it in stone made it real.

"Now I will show you," he said. "You see?" He touched a circular area on the front of his tomb where some of the rock had been chipped away. "It is a symbol of the sun. Placed here when I decided to wait for voodoo to bring me back. You etched it deeper when you brought me back tonight."

She'd never heard of anything like it. Of course, she didn't know any zombie raisers. Amie squinted at the crude carving. It looked more like a squashed bug than a sun. "You think I'm going to fall in love with you because of a defaced piece of rock?"

He flinched as if he'd been slapped. "This is proof."

"Not in my world."

"You want more proof?" He turned back to the tomb and placed his hands on either side of the stone marker. "Fine. I will go get it."

Amie's jaw slackened as he lifted the stone away, opening the grave. She wasn't going to ask. She just stared at the gaping hole that led into the crypt.

She wrapped her arms around her as an unwelcome chill seeped through her. She'd called up a man from the dead. Amie could never have imagined she'd had that kind of power. She was shocked. She was awed.

And she was scared to death.

If her ancestors could only see her now.

Amie's fingernails dug into her arms. *Please help me fix this.*

A cloud moved over the moon and the cemetery plunged into even deeper darkness. She fought to ignore the churning in her stomach and was almost glad for the shadows as the zombie crawled back inside his grave.

Scraping sounds echoed from inside the vault as Amie set her bag on the concrete path and unloaded her supplies. *This will all be over soon.*

Please let this be over soon.

Everything was too dark and too scary and too . . . dead.

She had to make this right.

Amie quickly lit the black candles and rubbed their sides with the grave dust he'd left on her arms when he touched her. She sprinkled Florida water over everything.

"How's it going?" she asked in a rough whisper, forcing her voice to remain even. She needed to focus her power, but she'd have a hard time concentrating knowing the zombie could pop out of his grave at any moment.

A frustrated sigh echoed from the tomb. "I'm having trouble finding it. It's dark. There are many fragile things on all sides."

Yeah, like bones.

Amie adjusted her candles, one in front of her and one

behind. Their flames created twin oases of orange light. If she did this right, he'd be just another pile of bones.

She closed her eyes and focused her power.

Earth to earth. Dust to dust.

She felt her life force well up inside of her. Amie took her Lisa Simpson keychain and held it over the flame in front of her, watching the plastic smoke and curl.

"I give of my magic," she whispered. "I give of myself. To let this man go back to ground."

Amie removed the ring she'd woven and dug her fingers into it, separating the black and red strands.

"We are not connected. We are not bound. As it began, so does it end."

She felt the power stir inside her.

She stood slowly.

She almost had him.

Amie approached him from behind, her fingers burrowing into the pocket of her skirt for the two dirty paper hearts she had unearthed from the planter outside her door. She ripped them in half and sprinkled them over the only part of him she could see—a muscular calf and a very large foot. The magic shot off orange sparks where it touched him.

Such a waste, she thought as she willed him back down, into the ground, to the earth.

"Ow!" He banged against something inside the tomb and came out rubbing his head. He brushed the torn hearts away like they were fireplace embers.

"What is this?" He saw her supplies and his eyes went narrow. "Are you trying to kill me?"

Amie's breath hitched. She really didn't want to watch this—watch him turn from a fine man to dust and bones. Her heart tugged.

In his own deluded way, the creature had loved her.

She held her breath. Waiting for the collapse. This was her doing. Her mistake. She owed it to him to watch him go back to ground. As if forcing her to witness what she'd done, the moon chose that moment to emerge from behind the cloud. It shone full once more on the man Amie had condemned.

Amie waited for the end.

And waited . . .

And waited.

Instead of crumbling to powder, he straightened and stood over her, looking gorgeous and unkempt with a smudge of dirt along his cheek.

Amie stared at him.

Damn the man. He should have been dead. She couldn't mess this up too. She chewed her lip as she ran through her spell in her mind. She'd done it correctly.

So why was he still here?

"I ask you again"—he took a powerful step toward her—"my love." He ground out each word as she took three steps back, scattering her candles across the pavement, "Are you trying to kill me?"

Amie froze. She dug her fingernails into her palms as dread blanketed her. She was trapped. In a cemetery. With the undead. A second later, she snapped.

It was too overwhelming, too intimidating, and frankly—too absurd. "Of course I tried to kill you," she said, her voice an octave higher than it should have been. "What am I saying? I'm not killing you. You're already dead! You see your name on that tombstone? I do. Dante Montenegro. Dead."

He gave a mirthless laugh. "What does that have to do with anything?"

He had to be kidding. "It has everything to do with—everything. I can't marry a dead man."

"Ah!" he said, the twinkle back in his eye. "Every couple has issues they need to work out."

"Work out?" Amie stammered. "No." Out of the question.

He leaned against his tombstone, clearly amused.

Anger rocketed through her. "Oh is this fun for you? Well, this is not fun. This is wrong. This is unnatural. You are deceased, demised, buried for goodness sake!"

The zombie hitched his thumbs under the waistband of his borrowed pants. "Not anymore."

Of all the cocky... "That is completely beside the point."

"Your bag is on fire."

"Ohhh!" Amie rushed to where one of the scattered candles had ignited her mother's hemp sack. She stomped out the blaze.

If he thought this was the end of their conversation, then maybe he'd been reanimated without a brain.

"Don't you understand?" she said, refusing to even spare a glance at the smoldering remains of the bag. "This is one giant horrible mistake. I'm not kissing you. I'm not picturing you naked." Where had that come from? Never mind. Amie plowed forward. "I'm not marrying you, so you might as well admit that your usefulness has ended and you can rest in peace."

Fury rolled off him in waves. "You called me," he said, as the night breeze scattered the torn hearts down the narrow path. "You burned a resurrection symbol into my grave."

"I didn't know," she said, her hope for an easy answer spinning into oblivion with those hearts. Even if she chased them down, she'd never be able to recover enough pieces to perform the spell again.

What would it matter anyway? It hadn't worked. Everything in her tidy little world was hopelessly, horribly out of control. And here he stood, all gorgeous and dead, expecting her to accept that. She just couldn't do it. She raised her chin. "I thought I wanted you, but obviously not *you*."

He stalked up to her, close enough to kiss. "Listen, sweetheart. It's not my problem that you don't know what you want."

He strode past her and took the last lit candle.

"Hey! Give that back!"

"Come and get it, darling," he said, ducking back into the tomb.

Amie wanted to bang her own head against the nearest

vault. What kind of a zombie-killing fiancée was she if the zombie started taking her spell ingredients? And she couldn't imagine what she was going to do now that her spell hadn't worked. Now that he knew she wanted to kill him. She'd have to find another way to put him down and, frankly, that might be tough.

He eased back out of the grave, looking triumphant, a gold wedding ring in hand.

"You're married?" she gaped. She shouldn't have felt betrayed, but she did.

"I was." He placed the candle on the ground and made a move to slip the ring onto his finger. "Now look. It will not fit anymore."

The ring seemed to resist as he drew it over his finger. It stopped less than an inch down, refusing to go farther.

What did that have to do with anything? "Maybe your knuckles swelled."

Anger flashed across his face. "No. I can no longer wear this because I have found my one true love," he said, gripping the ring between two fingers, holding the shimmering gold band between them. "That is you. Why do you find this so hard to accept?"

"Oh, I don't know. Because it's impossible?"

He looked mad enough to spit. "It is true!"

"So you say."

"So I know! I feel this with every breath in my body and I will not stop until you understand what it is you mean to me."

Amie's gaze drifted down the path. She had to pick the determined zombie. "How did I get into this?"

"Quiet." He stiffened, his eyes fixed out into the night. "Do you hear that?"

Amie strained her ears. Yes. She heard a definite crunching coming from the graves to the left. This was too much. She'd better not have called up a whole army of lovers. How would she explain a harem to poor Isoke? He'd lose his tail and his top feathers too.

Amie crouched closer to Dante's grave. If only it were a hoard of zombies. Then she would have been safe. As it was, her breath quickened as she saw two scarlet shadows fall across the path in front of her.

Oh no.

Her heart skittered. She'd heard of this—residual ghosts called up by voodoo magic. But she'd kept her magic contained.

Until it had escaped down the path.

Holy hoodoo.

How could she have been so careless?

"This is my fault," she said under her breath, warning him. She didn't know what was coming, but it couldn't be good.

He stood next to his grave, waiting. "I know."

She glanced at the long, dark path behind her. It would feel so good to run. The kicker was, there was nowhere to go. Besides, she had to fix her mistakes. She glanced at the zombie. Okay, she'd fix the most recent mistake.

Gripping her bottle of Florida water, she crouched low. One hand curled around the moldering brick tomb. Her heart beating low in her chest as the red shadows grew longer.

They were going to find her. She stiffened, unscrewing the bottle with shaking fingers.

By *Papa Ghede*! She gasped as a pair of thugs stepped out onto the path in front of them. Their eyes glowed red with possession.

A chill ran though Amie. She's seen the dead possess the living during voodoo rituals. The chwals she knew only allowed themselves to be taken by clean spirits. These men hadn't done as well.

"I believe these are the men we heard before," Dante said under his breath.

They moved like predators, and they were armed.

"What do they want?" Amie stammered.

Dante hesitated. "You."

As they drew closer, she could see their gang colors and

the fiery burning of their eyes. The one on the left snarled, his face a mass of anger and hate.

This was her fault. She'd never learned about death magic. She didn't know what could happen if it escaped. She'd been too rash in coming here.

Amie's fingers tightened around her blessed water. They were looking straight at her.

She could exorcise the spirits if only she had a bottle of 151 proof rum and a live chicken. Without them? She'd have to do the best she could. Amie poured her Florida water onto a patch of dirt, rubbing her fingers frantically into the mud.

"I command you to the earth," she said, low in her throat. *Focus your power.* She dug harder. "I command you to the earth."

The one on the right laughed. It was a hollow, menacing sound. He turned the barrel of his gun toward her. As if the world had slowed to contain only that moment, she watched the thug's trigger finger squeeze tight.

Dante slammed into her as the shot cracked the night, ringing in her ears. Her cheek hit the ground as she watched blood splash onto the white gravel in front of her.

"Oh my god." She clutched at the path.

The zombie leapt for the first mugger, knocking the gun from his hand.

Amie scrambled for the gun as her zombie barreled for the second man. Dante kicked the gun out of his hands and crashed into a crumbling brick vault. The second gun skittered into the night as Amie closed her hands around the first.

"Freeze," Amie commanded, aiming the weapon at the men. "Now get out or I'm going to send you straight to hell."

The thugs spasmed as the spirits roiled out of their bodies. Their eyes rolled up into their heads. Two red masses shot into the night before the men crumpled to the ground.

Dante climbed to his feet and put his fingers to the neck of the closest man. "He's out cold."

Heart hammering, Amie hunched next to the other man

and lifted his eyelid. The pupils were clear. He'd have a massive headache, but he should be awake by the time the first tour group rolled through in the morning.

"Come." Dante reached a hand down to her. His wide shoulders shook with tension and his left arm was a bloody mess.

"Oh my god."

He ignored her. "We have to go."

Amie laid the gun on the path next to her and grasped the neck of the bottle. It was mostly rubbing alcohol anyway. But it had been smashed on the ground. She used the broken edge to rip a strip of cloth from the bottom of her skirt. She closed her eyes for a moment, fighting the fabric. When she had enough, she wadded it into a bandage and touched it to his arm.

"Ow!" He jerked back.

"Calm down," she said, her own pulse racing as she wiped the blood. "Hold this on there. We can clean it out at my house."

He gave her a long look. "As long as you promise not to try to kill me."

She rolled her eyes as if she hadn't been trying to do that very thing a few moments ago.

Only before, he wasn't quite human. Now, she didn't know.

By Gedhe, this was such a mess.

Amie watched Dante seal the guns in his vault and grab the ring. Who was this man who had burst into her life, kissed her silly, and brought her here?

Is that what he was?

A man?

She didn't quite believe it. In fact, this entire night had been one big surprise after another.

"Dante," she said, watching him startle as she called him by name for the first time, "let's get out of here."

Chapter Five

His upper arm howled in protest, but Dante didn't care. Pain meant he was alive. As for her attempt to kill him, he'd deal with that soon enough.

She dialed in the alarm code at the back of her building. Amie moved with liquid grace, strong yet undeniably feminine. She was all curves and substance, with large almond-shaped eyes and a lush mouth. But what he really liked was her squared-off chin. It was bold, defiant. Too bad she'd grown from delectable to downright infuriating. She seemed to sense his anger as she opened the door to the storage room.

"Hell-o!" A Kongamato lounged in what looked to be a pit of mud and sticks.

Amie cringed. "Dante, this is Isoke."

If she was counting on the creature to save her, she was sadly mistaken.

Dante bowed toward the Kongamato. The beast was positively beaming.

"Isoke, this is Dante."

He showed a double row of teeth. "Charmed, *rafiki*. She is quite a catch, no?"

She would be, once she understood what was happening. Dante ran a hand down Amie's back, pleased at the way she stiffened. She might fear him, but she still wanted him.

Isoke launched himself out of the tub, sending sticks and pieces of moss flying. "Would you care for a soak? I was just going to go for a cool-down swim in the Mississippi." He waggled his brows at them like a proud uncle as he shook a wet leaf from between his toes. "This mud is good for your pores, no? And very romantic."

"We have to go," Amie said, leading Dante through the door to the shop.

"Have fun, kids!" Isoke called. "And just so you know, I will not be leaving gifts in your shoes if you are busy making love!"

She seemed embarrassed. "I'm sorry. He's just . . ."

"A Kongamato." Dante had seen voodoo mambos in the cemetery.

"Right," Amie said, avoiding his gaze. They were back to being polite. It would not do.

"This way," she said, leading him upstairs to her apartment.

Her living space was as colorful as her shop and stacked with books and various homemade oddities. Yet instinct told him there was more to this woman than she'd revealed.

He would get to the bottom of it.

She led him into a small bathroom off of the library and flipped on the bright overhead light.

Amie gasped when she saw his injury clearly for the first time. "I'm so sorry."

The wound was ugly, his olive skin ripped and torn.

He shrugged and immediately regretted the move as hot fire shot down his arm.

There didn't seem to be any major damage, but there was a lot of blood. Her fault, but he wouldn't get into that right now. Her knee bumped against his leg. This was the closest she stood to him—voluntarily—since she'd kissed him.

"I'll fix it," she said, earnestly.

Dante held his temper as he watched Amie wrestle with an impossible number of tubes and jars in a miniscule cabinet over the pedestal sink. That's not to say anything was out of place. If he wasn't mistaken, the items were actually lined up by size. He just didn't understand why a woman would need that many.

Some things never changed.

He turned her to face him. "Forget the bandages. We need to talk."

She seemed wary, afraid. It was ridiculous.

He'd proved to her tonight that she was his one true love. He'd shown her the mark on his tomb. He'd been unable to wear the wedding ring his former wife had given him. Despite that, Amie had rejected him outright.

She might have reacted with shock at first, then joy and absolute glee, as any woman would. But outright denial? He never would have imagined it.

What more proof did this modern woman need?

Her gaze fell on his arm. "I agree. We need to talk. But not with you looking like that."

"Amie," he warned.

She turned back to the medicine cabinet.

His fists clenched and his shoulder burned. He wanted to be a gentleman, but, "I am done with excuses."

Amie was supposed to be his one true love—a once-in-a-lifetime connection—a woman who could call him back from the grave and give him a second chance at love and at life.

She was passionate. Her kiss at the door had proven that. His body tightened just thinking about it.

So why was she fighting?

It was insulting as hell. "Why did you call me?" Why put him through this for nothing?

She didn't answer. Her lips pursed as she selected bandages and clanked through the bottles in the medicine cabinet—as if that was the most important thing they had to deal with.

Damn it to hell, he wouldn't be cast aside.

He reached for her, ignoring her squeak of surprise as he took her by the waist and slapped her down on the edge of the sink.

"Ow!" she protested.

"It does not hurt." He brushed his fingertips along the trembling at her collarbone. *"Mi corazon."*

Her breath quickened. She tried to buck off, her thick hair falling over one eye. "Don't you manhandle me."

Hands on her hips, he pulled her up against him so that she was forced to see him. "Then don't play games with me."

She drew a careful breath, her fingers absently tracing the velvety soft skin he'd just touched.

He'd have a conversation with her if it killed him. What he hadn't counted on was the lick of desire that slid down his spine.

He pushed closer, just to test her and watched the rosy flush creep up her cheeks. "I'll ask again," he ground out. "Why did you call me?"

She touched her lips together nervously.

Madre de dios. His whole future hung in the balance and this woman, this savior of his couldn't even answer a simple question.

She chewed at her delectable lower lip, her eyes wide, her hair damp around her face. "Look," she said, "I made a mistake."

No. "That kind of power doesn't come from accident. You did this on purpose."

At first he had been amused that she could be so powerful that she could call him and not understand what it meant. But if she didn't want him anymore, that was downright terrifying.

"Why do you care?" she demanded.

Damn it to hell. "Because it's not supposed to be this way. Not for me."

Dante had never been an overly patient man, but he'd haunted the cemetery for two hundred years. The one thing that had kept him going was the one in a million shot that someone would call him back and give him another chance.

Tears filled her eyes. "Just let me fix you."

He stepped back. "I am afraid that is impossible."

Dante sat on the edge of her tub, his head in his hands. He had to make her understand.

She leaned over him, her yellow sleeve brushing his cheek, her nose red. "This won't hurt a bit," she said, right before she poured molten lava down his arm. He cringed.

She sniffed and wiped at her eyes. "It's iodine," she explained, dabbing at him again with the cotton ball. "It'll help, I promise." She swallowed. "I was actually hoping you'd be healed by now."

"And why was that?" He asked, teeth gritted.

"Well, you're . . ." She paused, obviously trying to think of a polite way to say what he probably didn't want to hear. "Undead. Or should I say reanimated?"

He planted his hands on his knees and felt a drop of sweat slide down his back as she resumed her assault. "I regret to inform you that while I may be reconstituted, as it may. I have always been, and I remain, a mortal man." All the pity. "I can age and I can certainly die."

Her lips parted slightly.

The hollow feeling in his gut grew.

Dante didn't know how much time he had, but if Amie didn't offer him more of her magic, freely and completely, their bond would wear away. Then he'd be truly and forever dead.

He couldn't let that happen.

"Put those things down," he said, taking the cotton and the iodine from her and placing them behind him in the tub. "Now," he said, standing, "I will show you just how alive I am." He held out his hand to her.

Amie hesitated. He could see the wild pulse at her neck, hear her shallow breathing. The air in the small room had grown quite warm. Slowly, he reached for her hand. She swallowed hard as he drew her closer and placed her hand over his beating heart.

She exhaled as they both felt his heart pound against his chest.

He took her other hand and touched it to his lips. "I am human. Just like you."

She blinked once, twice. Confusion trickled across her features. "But back in the cemetery, you went after those possessed men unarmed."

"Yes," he said. He'd do it again.

She lingered on his arm. "You mean, if this had hit you in the chest, you would have died?" Realization dawned in her. "You almost died for me? Why?"

He felt the corners of his mouth tug as he returned his tired and battered body to the edge of the tub. "I didn't want to watch you die."

She sat down next to him. "Nobody ever stood up for me like that."

He closed his hand over hers. "I'm sorry to hear that," he said. And he meant it.

Why today's women did everything on their own was beyond him. In his day, most came from large, extended families. They spent lifetimes building large networks of friends. People helped one another.

It was one of the things he'd missed most of all, haunting the cemetery alone after his family had passed on.

"The bleeding isn't stopping," she said, worried.

"No," he said. He couldn't fully heal himself. Not until she could open herself up and give him a little of the magic she'd used to call him, the magic he needed to survive.

Still, she was wary of him. He'd have to proceed carefully.

He watched as she wound a thick white bandage around his arm.

What had his grandmother always said? Patience. Small steps. He'd never been good at that. Dante drew his fingers slowly over Amie's as she secured the bandage with medical tape. Perhaps he'd learned to temper himself over the past two centuries. He'd gotten her talking, which was no small thing.

And perhaps she understood him a little better too.

Life was precious. He knew that now.

Now all he had to do was convince her.

Tomorrow, he thought, as he moved to her library and sank into a soft recliner. He'd do it. Somehow, he'd convince her he deserved a second chance at life.

And perhaps he'd show her a thing or two about living as well.

Chapter Six

For the first time, Amie regretted the mirrors on her ceiling. They used to be fun and funky. Now all she could do was stare at herself lying in bed amid an immense pile of books she'd dragged in from her library.

Past the sleeping zombie.

At least someone was getting some rest. It was five in the morning—nearly dawn. Amie stared at her reflection. Her hair frizzed at odd angles, her eyelids had puffed to twice the normal size, and she had a line down the side of her face from falling asleep on top of a hardback collector's edition of *Out of the Darkness: The Ethnobiology of the Modern Zombie*.

She looked like hell. And why not? She'd certainly put herself through it in the last five hours. Five hours? Is that all it took to ruin a life?

The past night had been a disaster.

Well, except for that kiss. And the strong beat of his heart on the palm of her hand. The gesture had been oddly comforting. It made her feel safe, which was ridiculous.

Dante was dangerous, unpredictable. She shouldn't like it. Men like him were nothing but trouble.

She wriggled at the memory of Dante—all of him—as he pulled her flush against him and kissed her senseless. Well, there was nothing wrong with having a moment or two. She couldn't deny that she enjoyed his touch. She just needed to keep things in perspective. The only difference between this and her mother's failed attempts at love was that Amie *knew* Dante was going to leave.

*A zombie will deteriorate and die again once it has fulfilled
its purpose or once the voodoo mambo no longer requires
its services.*

She refused to let him hurt her on the way out.

Amie rubbed her eyes, red and gritty from lack of sleep.
Why hadn't she gotten a zombie who would clean her shop?
Or keep Isoke from chasing alligators? But no. She'd called up
a man who wanted to make her fall in love with him. Amie
tensed as she heard him moan in his sleep. She could almost
see him stretched out shirtless on her green La-Z-Boy. Part of
her couldn't believe a man like that wanted her. Zombies
wouldn't come unless they were called to do something they
wanted to do.

She rolled over into the pillow. Bosou! What was she
thinking?

This time yesterday, she'd been totally in control. Oh for
the days of all work and no play, when men were boring and
life made sense.

What she'd discovered reading through her research
books, well, she still couldn't believe it. Amie rolled to her
side and reached for a thick red book with a broken spine.
She'd snapped the binding when she threw it off the bed car-
lier this morning. She brushed through its crushed opening
pages. Her fault, when she'd fisted them out of sheer astonishment. She opened the book to the place she didn't really
want to see again. Still, she had to look. It was like a shocking
accident—she couldn't look away.

*A love spell can only be used to call a zombie if said zombie
is the voodoo practitioner's one true love.*

Ridiculous.

Laughable.

If she didn't have the niggling suspicion that it could be
true.

"Oh god, oh god, oh god . . ." She shoved the book off the bed and watched it land in a heap on the floor.

He couldn't be. He just couldn't. Dante was temporary. He was leaving. He was all wrong.

And Amie was always right.

Dante needed another cup of coffee. Hell, he needed another pot. His head swam as he braced one hand on Amie's living room window and watched the sun rise over Royale Street.

He was not going back into that kitchen.

The Good Girl's Guide to Love Magik lay open on the flowered tablecloth, right where he'd left it. The thick tome was pink, which made it worse.

Besides, he didn't need to look at the starred, underlined entry to know what it said.

A love spell will bind for a maximum of three days and nights. If love magik is not exchanged during that time, the spell will be broken.

She'd made it clear she didn't want him. She had no desire to fall in love with him. Now he had three days to convince her. It wasn't enough time. Hell, he'd been engaged to his late wife for six months and he hadn't known she didn't care until he found her in bed with their neighbor.

Maybe he just hadn't wanted to see the truth.

Dante swiped at the blood trickling down his arm. He'd need to find a new bandage. The wound throbbed, refusing to heal.

It wouldn't get better without her love magic. He didn't have the ability to heal himself. Not until the spell was permanent.

Did he even want that anymore?

He watched a few industrious shopkeepers hose off the streets in front of their stores. His former wife, Sophia, had married him out of duty. Their fathers ran a shipping business together. Sure, she'd been attracted to him. At least, she had been at first. But like the feathered hats she collected, Dante was one more object to be had, one more conquest. At least she'd admitted it.

While she'd been pleading with him not to shoot her lover.

He felt the stab in his gut as if it were yesterday.

The kicker was—he'd loved her. Now she was dead and he might be—again—sooner rather than later.

Dante rubbed his chin, feeling the start of a beard and gave a small chuckle. He hadn't had to shave in one hundred and ninety-eight years.

Now he had another chance at life. Dante opened the window and let morning filter into the room—birds chirping, the smell of sunshine and fresh cut grass, shopkeepers laughing and calling to one another. He stood for a moment and just listened. He'd enjoy the little things while they lasted.

Dante glanced behind him at Amie's closed door. He'd take one day at a time, because right now, his one true love didn't seem to know what she wanted and he was running out of time.

He sighed.

Well, he'd rather be dead than have another woman pledge herself to him out of obligation. His feet moved on their own until he stood outside her green painted door. He detected a trace of her honeysuckle perfume and placed a hand on the smooth wood. If Amie didn't want him, he'd leave. But first, he'd do his damnedest to show her just why she'd brought him back.

Amie rolled over and stretched. Mmm . . . something was baking. She detected the heavenly aroma of cinnamon and bananas, along with fresh brewed coffee. Her house never smelled like this. She certainly didn't cook.

She cracked her eyes open. She couldn't believe she'd actually fallen asleep. Sunlight streamed in from her window. Delivery trucks rumbled down the alley. Then she heard Dante singing low and deep.

Yawning, she extricated a book out from under her cheek and rubbed at her face.

She'd give it to him. The man had an amazing voice. She sat up slowly as the cobwebs cleared from her head.

For a moment, she thought she recognized the song. "I Can't Help Falling in Love with You," only different.

Plaisir d'amour ne dure qu'un moment.

A haunting melody.

Chagrin d'amour dure toute la vie.

He sounded like a Spanish Elvis. And from the sound of it, he was in her tub.

She pushed her way through the books, to where her bedside clock lay facedown. She lifted it enough to look at the big, red numbers. It was only nine in the morning. She let go of the clock and it tumbled down, face-first again. According to her books, zombies had to sleep at least twelve hours a night. Just who did he think he was?

J'ai tout quitté pour l'ingrate Celeste.

Elle me quitte et prend un autre aimant.

Water splashed in her tub as he hit a low note. She lurched out of bed and made her way to the kitchen.

Coffee gurgled on the stove. He'd used her grandma's ancient pot instead of the plug-in KitchenAid on her counter. To each his own. She opened the oven and peeked at the bubbling dough inside. He could cook too. It figured.

Wouldn't it be nice if her life was really like this? Waking up to a hot breakfast and a hot man.

It was such a tease.

Amie pulled an I BRAKE FOR UNICORNS mug from above the sink and sampled the brew. She closed her eyes at the rich flavor with just a hint of vanilla.

She scanned her countertops for the package he'd used. She hadn't bought any vanilla coffee.

Her fingers tightened on her cup when she saw one of her

spell books open on the kitchen table. He'd been doing some research of his own.

It was the pink love magic book, one of her mother's. Amie groaned. She hadn't had time to go through all of her mom's books yet. This one was well used. It figured her mom would resort to voodoo.

And now Amie had too.

Terrific. Just like Mom.

She sighed. Well, at least she wasn't taking any strange men to bed. She dragged a hand across her face. She was just letting them in her tub.

Water splashed as he got out. She heard the towel bar clank. As if she needed him in her kitchen too. She topped off her coffee.

Fingers shaking, Amie rubbed at her temples and told herself she had about two minutes to get it together.

She was wrong.

The bathroom door swung open. "Ah! You are awake."

Water droplets beaded at his shoulders as he strolled through her front room with a towel wrapped around his waist, a fresh bandage white against his skin. His short black hair stood at spiky angles, which only accented the sharp planes of his face.

Amie straightened, felt her toes curl.

She took a quick swallow of coffee, just to do something—anything. "Of course I'm awake," she said, telling herself the heat in her belly was, in fact, from the coffee. "The real question is why are you awake?"

"Community Coffee Dark Roast," he said, as he pulled a HOUSE OF BLUES mug from the sink and poured himself another helping. "I find myself acting like a complete zombie before my first cup."

"That's not funny," she said, momentarily distracted by a water droplet that slid down his perfect back and settled under the towel.

"Breakfast?" he asked, using one of her grandma's woven pot holders to pull a tray of banana fritters out of the oven.

They looked like a cross between a doughnut and a pancake. "You made these?"

He sprinkled a plate with powdered sugar and set it in front of her. "I watched Cook do it many times. Then I merely dreamed about them for twenty decades."

Amie bit into a warm, doughy fritter and almost had an orgasm.

They ate in silence. It was almost too domestic. Amie squirmed in her seat. She had no business wanting this.

She welcomed the distraction of gathering up the plates and insisting he take the last cup of coffee.

"Now that we have eaten, there is something we need to discuss." He leaned against her yellow countertop and took a long sip from his mug, eyeing her as he did it. "You used a love spell to call me from the grave."

"Yes," she said, folding her hands in front of her, "but I didn't call *you* necessarily."

Amie fought back a sliver of guilt. Who was she kidding? She did call him. She saw him in her mind's eye. He'd responded voluntarily because he could love her back. Now, here he was, her perfect man.

And if he could somehow touch her that deep, then having him and losing him would be worse than all of her mom's heartbreak put together.

She just wasn't ready.

She didn't think she'd ever be ready.

To her relief, he let it go.

"Give me three days," he said.

"Excuse me?" He couldn't be serious. She didn't know if she could ever open herself up to the kind of hurt she might find in a real relationship, but, rushing certainly wouldn't help. "Three days? I can't decide anything in three days." It had taken her longer than that to pick out her kitchen curtains. "Besides, I have a life. I have a shop to run."

Dante set his mug on the counter behind him. "Yes, but is this the life you want?" he asked, walking straight for her.

"Yes." Mostly. How could he look confident and inviting when what he was asking was absurd? "You don't understand."

He took Amie's hands in his. They were warm and strong. She could feel the heat radiating off him, calling to her. It traveled from where he still held her hands, up her arms, to her shoulders. It was both exciting and nerve-racking. She wanted to run, but she knew it would kill her to destroy this moment. So she didn't. She waited. He leaned down to her, his face inches from hers.

Was he going to kiss her again?

Would she let him?

"Let me court you," he said, a breath from her ear.

She wet her lips. "For real?" she asked, warmth settling in a place she'd rather not think about. She liked it when men opened doors for her, but to be courted? By an eighteenth-century gentleman? In a towel?

The man needed to start wearing more clothes.

His hands traveled up her arms, burning a path to her shoulders. "*Sí.* If it is right, three days will be enough," he said, his expression intense, earnest. "If it is not, I will accept that."

She searched his face, his blue eyes so electric and sincere. "Will you really?" She was suddenly disappointed that it could be over so soon.

"I will leave," he said solemnly.

"Knowing that it took me more than three days to decide if I even wanted to go out with my last boyfriend?" she said, giving fair warning.

The lines around his eyes crinkled as he gave her a tight smile. "Yes."

Interesting. She'd had him pegged as the stubborn type. Unless he had a plan he wasn't telling her about. "Why do you want to do this?"

He touched his fingers to her chin, rubbing his thumb back and forth on the soft patch of skin below her lips. Heat curled through her. "Believe me, *querida*, I have waited two hundred years for you." He brushed his lips against her forehead. "You called me back. Now I will show you why."

"I already know why." She'd been weak. She'd been lonely, and only too human.

If she wasn't careful, it was going to hurt something terrible when he left.

She forced herself to stand tall, ignoring the insane desire to touch him back.

"Let me court you." His lips brushed her cheek.

She broke away from him. "Look, I'm not an eighteenth-century miss. I don't expect love poems and flattery. I know better than to think roses cure everything. I'd think you were crazy if you threw your jacket over a puddle or expected me to simper around while you do manly things. I have a mind of my own, a successful business, a *life*, for goodness sake, and I'm not going to fall in love and make a lifetime commitment because somebody says I should."

"Are you finished?" he asked.

She lifted her chin. "Yes."

His head dipped toward hers. "Three days," he whispered in her ear.

She knew she shouldn't want it, but she did.

Amie wet her lips. What harm could come in three days? If she knew she couldn't have him past that, then she wouldn't expect more. He would be fulfilling his purpose, hopefully with more fritters and coffee, and then she'd be free of him. Better yet, she could relax and have fun, with no strings attached. This could be safe if she watched herself.

It would certainly be exciting.

"Okay." She shivered. "Three days."

Heaven help her.

Chapter Seven

Amie stuffed her feet into her white Keds, thankful that Isoke hadn't left her any gifts last night.

She hoped the Kongamato hadn't given Dante too much trouble. She'd sent him downstairs with directions to her friend Oliver's store, and asked him to find something to wear. She hoped that something included a shirt. She didn't need to be drooling over Dante all day. Control was key.

Besides, Oliver owed her. She'd used her magic to find him a man, and a decent three-year lease on a building down the street.

When Amie hopped out into her living room, tugging on the back of her sneaker, she realized her friend had failed her in the worst possible way. Dante sat at her kitchen table with the newspaper spread out in front of him, sipping coffee and looking better than he did half-naked.

He wore a black T-shirt that should have been modest. Instead, it hugged his chest and arms in all the right places. And if that wasn't bad, he'd chosen a pair of tan cargo shorts that made him look relaxed and sexy as hell. A pair of black flip-flops completed the outfit.

Damn Oliver.

"Are you ready?" Dante said, easing back from the table.

Would she ever be?

He'd even cleaned her kitchen.

Enjoy it while it lasts.

"What's the plan?" she asked just to have something to say. He was looking at her as if he'd like a repeat of what they'd done when they'd met.

Amie straightened. *Get it together.* She'd be in trouble if she couldn't maintain her focus.

He approached her, athletic and strong. "No plan," he said, easing an arm around her as he led them to the door.

"That's right," she said. "You're probably not familiar with the city anymore." He smelled like Ivory soap and pure man. *Three days*, she reminded herself. One foot in front of the other. Shoulders back. And no drooling.

Of course Isoke had left them love and fertility presents on the stairs.

"Your dragon works fast," Dante said, navigating her past a series of mud-coated rocks and hairballs. "I had these cleaned up a half hour ago."

"You should have seen what he did for my birthday."

Amie tamped down the urge to clean before they left. It wouldn't help, not if the Kongamato was determined to bring them his brand of luck.

But love charms didn't work on the unwilling, and Amie knew her limits. Whatever she had going on with Dante would end in three days.

She leaned against her zombie as he lifted her over a particularly tricky spot.

Isoke would say she was settling for crumbs again, but he wasn't the one who had to bear responsibility when things got out of control—and they would if she wasn't careful.

Lasting love didn't happen to the women in her family. Wishing for it would only make her end up like her mom.

Much to Amie's relief, she and Dante escaped VooDoo Works without Isoke trying to help them further. She kept the CLOSED sign in the front window of the store, feeling strange and, for the first time in a long time, free.

The sunshine warmed her face as they strolled past the people and shops that crowded Royale Street. Two- and three-story buildings lined the way, topped with wrought-iron balconies and rich with flowering plants and vines. Amie breathed deep. Mmm . . . jasmine and roasted almonds.

And dead rat?

The acrid odor touched Amie's nose a second before she spotted a red Kongamato tail disappear into The New Orleans House of Wax.

A muddy brown rat flew out of the door behind him, very dead and sporting a necklace of white Life Savers breath mints.

"Isoke!" she hissed, as the rat skittered across the pavement.

She zigzagged around the festooned rodent as she barreled through the door.

What was he thinking?

No Kongamato went out during the day. Isoke would be seen. She didn't want him hunted, hounded . . . or worse.

Amie closed the door of the wax museum and almost tripped over the stack of free tabloid newspapers and coupon books at the front. She breathed a sigh of relief as she spied Isoke in the front entryway, posed next to a life-sized statue of voodoo queen Marie Laveau. The Kongamato's teeth shone in rows of white and his face and body contorted into a giant snarl.

"What are you doing?" Amie hissed, glancing around the small front room.

Isoke dropped the pose. "I am helping you fall in love. Did you get my rat?"

Amie squinched her nose. "Yes," she said, peeking out the door. "Dante is cleaning it up right now."

Isoke brightened. "Good. Lots of love magic in that one. And breath mints! You know, for before you kiss."

"Stop it. Go home now. You know this is against the rules."

A teenager in a House of Wax polo shirt stepped out from the main lobby. "Can I help you?"

Amie jumped. "Err . . ." She eyed Isoke, who had fallen down dead dragon-style at Marie Laveau's feet.

"Ticket sales are this way," the girl continued.

Isoke refused to budge, except the edges of Isoke's mouth seemed to tip into the start of a smile.

Amie hesitated. What was she supposed to say? I can't leave without my bullheaded-pain-in-the-neck-better-go-home-if-he-knows-what-is-good-for-him Kongamato?

And now she couldn't even look at him because she sure as heck didn't want the ticket girl noticing anything.

"You behave," she said to the Marie Laveau statue before turning on her heel and leaving the Kongamato to obey—or not.

Outside, Dante leaned against a streetlamp as if nothing had happened.

"I told him to go home," Amie said.

"You think he will?"

"No," she said, glancing back, "but he's also going to keep hiding in plain sight until we leave."

"Then come," Dante said, offering his arm, "let's oblige the little monster. Isoke must handle things his own way."

That's what worried her.

Amie fought the urge to glance backward as she and Dante continued down Royale Street.

She wished she knew more about her own city. Truth was, she didn't leave the neighborhood much. "I can suggest a few things to do," she said, enjoying the tingle of excitement as she leaned against his hard frame. They did need a plan.

"No," he said, his fingers lingering at the top of her pink silk skirt. She sucked in a breath as he found the warm skin just above her waist.

"We could go to the information office," she said quickly.

"No." His fingers drew lazy circles on her skin.

"Tour guide?" she suggested, ending in a squeak.

Rat or no rat—in a minute, she was going to have to drag him behind Ed's Oyster Stand or run like hell.

He laughed at that, delighted. "No." He took her hands in his, not bothered at all by the people who had to walk around them. It was as if he was carving out a little piece of New Orleans just for them. "I think we will do quite well on our own. Relax."

"I'm relaxed," she said too quickly.

He wrapped an arm around her and they began walking again. "Why is it so hard for you to simply let things come?"

"I don't know. I'm a modern woman." She trailed one hand over a sculpted guitar outside Manny's Jazz Club. "Besides, what's so wrong about knowing what I want?"

It was certainly keeping her out of trouble today.

They wandered past vendors and street musicians and mimes. They made it to St. Louis Cathedral, where his youngest sister had married, and to the spot just to the right of it where the wedding party had fled after guests pelted a beehive with rice meant for the bride and groom.

"You have to understand the dresses back then," Dante said, holding his hands wide.

"I have some idea," Amie said, trying not to laugh.

"For a moment, we believed a bee had gotten up there. I wasn't going to check and my sisters were scattered everywhere. I looked over to Antonio," he said.

"Another brother?" she asked.

"The groom," he corrected.

Amie gasped. "He didn't."

"He escorted her directly behind that wide oak for a quick inspection."

Amie gave an exaggerated gasp. "The morals of the eighteenth century."

"Scandalous," he agreed.

Danted leaned in to kiss her and Amie was about to close her eyes when the tree above them shook. A giant black rat hit every branch on the way down and thwumped at their feet.

"Isoke!" she shrieked.

Then she noticed the gold band tied to the rodent's tail.

"My apologies." Isoke flapped his wings as he settled on a high branch. "I saw you heading for the church and wanted you to be ready!"

Amie opened her mouth for the lecture of the century when Dante touched her arm. "Don't."

A crowd had begun to gather, murmuring questions.

Two boys rushed up. "It's a rat!" they yelled, to a chorus of *eeews*!

Amie kicked the rat's tail until the ring came loose and Dante—bless him—pocketed it. No telling where Isoke had found the gold band, but he *would* return it.

"Come on." Amie grabbed Dante's hand and dragged him over to Café du Monde, muttering, "The little beast is going to get himself captured." Or killed. And dang it, she really would have enjoyed that kiss.

"Let him be," Dante said, pulling back a chair for her. "Maybe he'll give up."

He didn't know Isoke.

At least the crowd hadn't noticed the red Kongamato waving to Amie and Dante from the high branches of the ancient oak.

Amie introduced Dante to caffe lattes as they watched the small mob disperse.

"I swear that monster has nine lives."

Dante's gaze slid over her, warm and sensuous. "Let's just hope I only need two."

Afterward, they kept an eye out for rats bearing gifts as they wandered to the Farmers Market. There Dante completely lost his mind over the variety and flavors of hot sauce. Amie bought him a bottle of Gib's Bottled Hell and he rewarded her with an utterly blissful shrimp jambalaya upon their return home.

She pushed back from the yellow table, unable to eat another bite. "Amazing."

Dante leaned over her to take her bowl. "Don't thank *me*." He nodded to a book open on the countertop. Smiling crawdads holding forks and knives danced over the cover of *The Rajun Cajun: Recipes from New Orleans*. It had been a gift from Oliver. Naturally, she'd never cracked it open.

Dante rinsed the bowls and poured himself another cup of coffee—his third since they'd returned. Then he leaned against the counter and smiled for no reason at all.

It made no sense, but she found herself smiling too.

She could almost excuse the last twenty-four hours as something that had been done to her. He'd showed up at her door. He'd suggested a date. He'd asked permission to court her. She flushed, remembering the purple cone flower he'd picked for her from a stray plant along the way. She'd tucked it behind her ear and felt every inch the lady.

Maybe it was time for her to do something back. She'd been thinking about kissing him all day and now was her chance. Amie stood.

"*Querida?*" he asked, setting aside his coffee mug.

Amie drew close to him. Their first kiss had been mind-numbingly intense. She'd waited, expected him to kiss her again today. He'd held her hand, touched her side, laughed close. But he'd never taken the next step. She couldn't believe she was actually going to be the one to make a move.

He was so beautiful, so alive. After her dull dating history and nine dry years, she'd earned this. Amie practically sighed in anticipation. She knew just what she needed—and just how much she was willing to give.

Amie slid her arms around Dante's neck, warm and strong. "Thank you," she said. "This has been a wonderful day."

She raised her lips to the long column of his throat and was delighted when he let out a soft groan. She licked his ear and he shuddered. She touched her lips to his and he pulled away.

"Amie, wait," he whispered against her.

"It's just a kiss," she said, nuzzling him. A small thing, really.

They'd done it before. They'd almost done it this afternoon. Nothing had changed.

"You don't mean it," he said quietly.

"Yes, I do," she coaxed, nibbling at his lower lip.

He gathered her into his arms. "No," he said, touching his forehead to hers. "You don't."

She could feel him—all of him—pressed full against her. He wanted this.

Dante rubbed his hand along her back. She could feel the

tension in him, and the longing. "It has to be real. This either means you want me," he said, "that you're willing to at least try to love me. Or it doesn't. You tell me which."

"Dante," she protested. This was a big step for her, to go out with a man who wasn't safe. Besides, what did he expect? He was leaving soon. "I'm out on a limb here as it is."

He brought his hands to her waist and held her there. "I don't want you out on a branch. I need you to jump."

She drew back, hurt. "You know I can't do that." This was her first date in nine years. She'd closed her shop. She'd shared the whole day with him. She'd dodged rats bearing gifts. She'd told him what to expect from the start. This had to be enough.

Amie saw the pain in his eyes. "I will not settle for less than the real thing," he said. "Not this time."

"You've got to be kidding." She'd just tried to give him more than she'd given anybody and he somehow needed more? "What do you want from me?"

He gave her a penetrating look as his hands snaked up her back, leaving ribbons of pleasure in their wake. "You know."

Love magic. Amie closed her eyes. She couldn't imagine what it would be like to share love magic with a man like him. It would be passionate, explosive. It could eat her alive and leave her with nothing.

She shook her head. "I'm sorry." She couldn't do it. She couldn't risk it. Not in a million years.

Chapter Eight

Dante was still hard as a rock when he woke up twelve hours later. His shoulder throbbed. Well, what else was new? He pushed the thought aside and cranked the La-Z-Boy to a sitting position.

Amie was in the kitchen with a fresh pot of coffee, French roast if he wasn't mistaken. Dante planted his feet on the floor. The cargo shorts dug into his waist. He stood and let them fall naturally. They'd been uncomfortable as hell to sleep in, but he'd been too tired take them off.

The fatigue had come on quickly last night, and he'd slept in today. The spell was wearing off. He'd better make today count.

He could hear Amie in there talking to herself. The woman was trouble—more so than he'd imagined.

Dante ran a hand through his hair. It had all seemed so simple. A powerful woman, truly meant for him would seek him out. He'd have a new life and a new love at the same time.

At last—someone who could love him back.

Now he had Amie, who could be that woman if she gave herself half a chance. Instead, she wanted to give him scraps of herself. Well, he wouldn't do it.

Dante tucked his shirt into his shorts, his gaze settling on the wedding ring he'd left on the top shelf of her bookcase. Amie needed to decide what she wanted. He'd already married one woman who didn't care enough. He'd rather die than go through that again.

"Latte?" she asked, as he made his way into the kitchen.

Amie wore an orange sheath dress that accented her curves—and her breasts. For a moment, he lingered only on her. Then he saw she'd been busy while he slept.

The woman had not only bought a cappuccino maker, she'd laid out jeans and a dark green button-down shirt over one of the kitchen chairs.

"Thanks," he said. He would have been embarrassed if he'd let himself think on it too long. He couldn't remember anyone, save his mother, buying gifts for him.

He leaned against the counter and watched her make foam.

She gave him a sideways glance. "Four cups a day keeps the zombie away."

"Then I'd better stick to three," he said, as Amie handed him a fresh latte.

He took a long sip, savoring the sweet warmth. He took her delicate hand in his and squeezed it.

If he did die again and if he had to go away for good this time, he'd know he had this moment.

"Come on," she said, "let's try to get out before Isoke wakes up."

Dante showered and dressed before they headed downstairs.

Amie's shoulders dropped slightly when she saw the empty perch at the back of the store.

Dante touched the top of her arm. "I'm sure Isoke is fine."

Amie sighed. "I just wish we knew where he was."

Dante opened the door for her, as had become their habit, and Amie hadn't even hesitated today when she left the CLOSED sign on the door of the shop.

"Why VooDoo Works?" he asked, admiring the display of love charms in the window.

She glanced at the industrial sign that she'd commissioned. "Because it does." She laughed. "Sure the spirits can be unpredictable, but the everyday practice of voodoo is really quite practical."

"You're kidding me, right?" he said as grave dust wafted down on the other side of the door.

"Well, you can't always predict exactly what results you're going to get," she explained, slipping her hand into his, "but you usually get what you truly need."

Indeed.

Amie got her wish when they boarded the St. Charles Steetcar and spotted a Kongamato roof ornament. Dante could hear the beast's claws clattering against the tin roof the entire way from Canal Street and into the Garden District. Dante pointed to a corner of Audubon, which was packed with neat, modern homes. "I used to live right about there."

She leaned against him. "Do you miss it?"

"No," he said, surprised. Rather, Dante found the new houses most intriguing with their wraparound porches and big yards, perfect for raising a family. His old life was dead and gone. Amie was his future. "Although," he said, drawing close, and breathing in her honeysuckle perfume, "I do miss the crawfish."

Amie wrinkled her nose. "I never cared for them. Too ugly."

"Well, you would have loved our crawfish. We used to catch them in the freshwater stream out back. The most handsome crustaceans you'd ever meet."

"I am a sucker for a handsome face," she said, fighting a smile and not succeeding.

They reached the end of the line—twice. Each time, the streetcar tracks ended, the driver would flip the shiny wood bench seats in the opposite direction. They'd pay a dollar twenty-five and continue on their way.

Dante laughed out loud when she described the young girl who'd bought a love potion for her two turtles.

"I didn't have the heart to tell her she had two boy turtles."

"Well what's wrong with that?" he asked.

"She wanted babies."

"Ah," he said, delighting in it. "I can see where that could be a challenge."

She grinned up at him, radiant.

For the first time, Amie understood just why her mother could want a relationship like this. She couldn't remember a time when she felt so good. Dante brought out the best in her. It was invigorating and electrifying, and addicting if she wasn't careful. Luckily, Amie was always careful.

He toyed with a curl of hair at her shoulder. "Speaking of creatures, tell me about Isoke."

She gave him a sideways glance. "He's a pain in the rear, that's for sure."

"Watch it," she heard from the roof.

"And he has supersonic Kongamato hearing."

His claws dug through the metal roof. "Aye mambo! They have spotted me!"

Amie clutched the edge of the window as Isoke shot up into the sky.

"By Ghede's ghost!"

"At least he's gotten away," Dante said, as a confused group of tourists ranted to a nearby police officer and pointed toward the empty blue sky.

Amie leaned back against the bench in relief. "He'd better behave." She'd grown more accustomed to that Kongamato than she'd like to admit. He was, in essence, the last of her family.

"I've only had him since the holidays," she said. "He came to live with me after my mother passed."

"Is your father still with you?" Dante asked.

Amie gave a brittle laugh. "My mom didn't even know who my dad was. She wasn't what you call picky." She paused, swaying against him as the streetcar rattled over the tracks. He waited, as if he understood she needed time to gather her thoughts. He really was a gentleman.

She took a deep breath and let it out. "Mom dated. A lot." Amie frowned hard, remembering. "If she didn't go for a loser, she went for a drunk. If they weren't stealing our grocery money, they were cheating on her. Every one of them crushed her on the way out the door."

It had hurt so bad to watch it happen, over and over again. Every time her mother wept, Amie lost a piece of herself too.

Dante watched her carefully. "And you were afraid of dating men like that."

"Of course not," she said, shaking off his concern. "I'd never do that to myself." She let out a small sigh. "If you'd have seen how she looked when one of them left—like he'd ripped out a part of her."

Dante drew her into the crook of his arm. "Love can hurt immeasurably."

"I know," she said, letting her head rest against his shoulder. She had watched her mom give until she had nothing left. "I still can't believe she's gone."

Dante nodded and held her closer. Here he'd been trying to get her to understand him, when he'd also needed to learn about her. He kissed Amie on top of the head. A small gesture, meant for comfort and nothing more. Still, she pulled away from him, her eyes red around the edges.

"I'm certainly not going to go through that."

He fought the urge to close the distance between them. "I see."

She shook her head. "I'm sorry, Dante. I know you think you love me and that we're supposed to be together, but I'm not the kind of girl who falls in love. It's just not in me." She wiped at her eyes, but not before he saw the start of a tear. "I'm sorry."

"I am too," he said, as the full weight of her declaration settled around him. She could never love him. It would be the end of him. He should have been angry. He wanted to be the kind of man to take that love from her. She called him. She owed it to him. But he didn't. Dante would not demand what she couldn't give, what she couldn't understand.

"You'll have another chance," she said, her back against the hard bench, looking out the window as he settled his arm on the seat back behind her.

He didn't respond. He didn't want her pity, or any half-hearted attempts at love.

They rattled down Carrollton, past the restaurants, old houses, and a small cemetery.

There was so much left to say, but still it startled him when she spoke. "You were a ghost for two hundred years."

Dante nodded, knowing it would be personal. They were beyond the polite stage.

She watched him for a few seconds. "Why did you stay? Did you have a bad life?"

He spied an older couple cuddling on one of the balconies overlooking the street. "Bad? No. Just incomplete."

She tilted her head toward him. "How so?"

Dante looked away from her, out into traffic. Perhaps sharing secrets wasn't such a wise idea.

"What was your wife's name?" She touched his arm.

He didn't respond. After two hundred years, it still hurt to think about it. This was going to be harder than he'd thought.

"Did she have something to do with your death?"

"No," he said much too quickly.

"I think she did," Amie said quietly.

The kicker was, she was right. He'd eat his eyeballs before he'd admit it to her, but he wouldn't be riding down Carrollton Street with a voodoo mambo if it weren't for his former wife.

Sophia. Beautiful, treacherous Sophia.

Everyone in his large family had found someone to love them—his five sisters, his parents, his grandparents. Going to a family gathering could be downright depressing.

You'll find someone.

She's out there.

Yes, Sophia had been out there. But she never loved him back.

He followed Amie's gaze to where he'd been absently stroking his ring finger. Damn.

"Did you get shot for her too?" Her expression darkened. "You did. I can see the blue in your aura."

"I didn't know voodoo mambos believed in that."

"I do."

Well hadn't he hit the jackpot?

"Yes, I was shot," he ground out.

She closed her hand over his. "Why?"

If she really wanted to hear, he'd tell her. Maybe then she'd be sorry she asked.

He took a deep breath and let it out. "I loved my wife with all my heart," he said. "Alas, she did not feel the same."

"You can't possibly know—"

"I found her in bed with another man."

"Oh."

Dante gritted his teeth at the reminder. "I challenged that man, as we did back then. He shot me here," he said, running his finger over the puckered scar above his right eye. "I was dead. She married him."

"I'm sorry," Amie said on an exhale.

He didn't want her sympathy.

The past was the past. Sophie had moved on a long time ago. She'd joined her lover in the afterlife.

Dante looked down at Amie, glad to see the sympathy gone from her eyes.

"And you never left."

"No." It would be hard to spend eternity as the odd man out. He smiled to himself. He'd met Marie Laveau in the cemetery. She understood him. He told her how he wanted, *needed* a second chance. That's when she told him about zombies. She'd said he had to be chosen to come back. That there would be much love behind that calling.

He had to believe that.

"You waited all that time?" He could see her surprise. Strange. Who wouldn't wait for real love?

"I couldn't leave if there was a chance," he said. "I still can't."

He leaned down and kissed her. A soft taste, simple and pure. A kiss worthy of her. She sighed against him and deepened their kiss. He touched the back of her neck and drew her closer. She was trembling as he pulled away.

"I don't know what to say," she whispered.

"*Mi corazon.*" He wrapped his uninjured arm around her even tighter, letting her bump against him as the streetcar rattled down the tracks.

He supposed neither of them had a reason to trust. But since when was love reasonable?

Dante smiled down at her. She felt good against him, solid. "My family would have loved you."

Pleasure soaked her voice. "You really think so?"

"Without a doubt." He certainly did. Dante turned to look at the gates of Tulane University.

He loved her.

There was no sense fighting it. It was only natural. Love magic had called him to her.

His chest tightened. He only hoped he hadn't fallen for another woman who couldn't love him back. At least this time, he didn't have to stay.

"Dante?" She looked up at him with those big brown eyes.

"Yes," he said, careful to mask his emotions.

"Let's ride again."

That evening, as they reached the bluffs overlooking the Mississippi River, Dante let himself tumble to the soft ground. He could feel himself tiring quicker than before. The spell was wearing thin.

He lay in the grass with his arm around her, watching the endless flow of the river. He knew she feared loss. He did too. There was nothing so awful as to lose the one you love. But that did not mean she should stop feeling. If she did that, she would be as dead as he once was.

Dante refused to let her hide.

He touched her at the waist, his lips skimming hers. "Do

you think there is a chance, however remote, that you can love me?"

She drew back, her fingers tracing the outline of his face. "Can't this be enough?"

He felt the energy drain from him. She looked at him imploringly as he felt his hand twitch against her waist.

More than anything, love had to be a choice. "If that is all you can give, then it will have to be enough."

He kissed her and drew her to her feet in the soft grass. The night had cooled somewhat and a slight breeze had found her hair. He closed his eyes at the sensation of her pressed up against him. "Let's go home."

"Mmmm . . . yes," she said, hands trailing down his back. "And this time, don't worry."

A riverboat horn sounded in the distance.

"No?" he asked, nipping her lips.

She gave him one last kiss and then snuggled against his chest. "I won't lead you on," she said. "I promise."

He nodded, even though a part of him had just split in half.

Hadn't he said he wanted all of her or nothing at all?

Fatigue crept up on him with bone-wearying tendrils.

Tomorrow would be enough, he told himself.

He only hoped he was right.

Chapter Nine

He was worse by the time they arrived home. She'd seen signs of it all day. His hand would shake slightly as he held her. His eye would twitch, but then be fine. Dante had ignored it, or maybe he didn't realize what was happening. Amie was worried.

"I think I can help you," she said, reaching for her zombie reference guides as he sank, bone weary, into the La-Z-Boy.

He leaned back, his profile clean and strong, even as he began to lose his grip on life. "What I need isn't in a book," he said, his eyes widening slightly as he held his hand out in front of him. His pinkie and the two fingers next to it had begun to twitch.

"Um hmm, and who's the voodoo mamb—" She gasped. His left foot had begun to jerk uncontrollably. Amie gripped the book tightly. This was worse than she thought.

Dante followed her gaze before leaning his head back, spent.

He was being far too calm about this. "What? Have you seen this happen before?"

"Once," he said, not looking at her, "about seventy years ago."

"And?" She didn't have time for him to hold back on this.

"It didn't end well."

Her stomach tightened.

"I'm not going to lose you," she told him, and herself.

She grabbed two more books off the shelf and plopped down on the floor. The answer had to be here . . . somewhere.

She scrambled through the index of the first book, her mind racing until she forced herself to take a step back and focus. *Think.* So the spell was wearing off. She could fix this.

Amie reached back to the bookshelf. Heart pounding, she dumped all of her zombie books on the floor around her. She brought him here. She could keep him here.

Seven books later, her head was pounding. Worse, she still wasn't any closer to a solution. None of her spell books talked about reanimating an already animated zombie. It was as if she was missing a crucial step.

"Where's the pink book?" she asked. The entire left half of his body twitched uncontrollably. Could he even hear her anymore? She forced her voice to remain even. "You know. The one you had out on the table yesterday. My mom's pink book."

"With the cookbooks," he mumbled, not even opening his eyes.

Well, no wonder she hadn't seen it. She hurried into the kitchen and found it next to her mother's old *Betty Crocker Homemaker's Guide.*

She turned back to find him trying to stand.

"Dante!" She rushed to him.

He reached out to her for a moment, before his entire arm dropped lifelessly to his side.

"Just . . . hang on." She helped him back into the chair. Blood soaked through the bandage on his arm. "You need another one," she said, thankful to focus on something as mundane as a gunshot wound.

As for the rest, Amie didn't know what she was going to do.

She'd just gotten Dante back into the chair when she heard the alarm beeping downstairs.

Isoke!

The alarm gave a low *bong* sound as it rejected whatever code he'd dialed in. Typical. Still, her heart lightened. She'd welcome Isoke and a dozen dead rats if he could just tell her what was wrong with Dante. The Kongamato may not know how to string a set of numbers together, but he had eight generations' worth of practical voodoo.

Amie she rushed downstairs, dashed through her shop and threw open the storage room door.

"Yak!" Isoke jumped backward and stumbled into a flowerpot. His beak flew open and he dropped the large black rat he'd been carrying. "*Kipofu!* You have ruined the surprise."

Amie let out a shriek as the rodent ran straight for her. "Get it out of here!" Luckily, the rat seemed to know where he was going. It dashed under the Kongamato's spread feet and out into the night.

"Quickly," Amie said, ushering him inside.

The Kongamato flapped his wings as he maneuvered sideways through the door. "What's the rush?" Isoke grumbled, folding his wings and waddling past Amie. "I'm ignoring all of my instincts letting that resplendent creature go."

She closed the door behind him. "It's not important right now. I need your help."

Worry clouded his features as he read the look on her face. "What have you done?"

Amie chewed her lip. Would he even want her to see Dante if he knew the truth? She'd hate to see Isoke if he was trying to *discourage* a romance. "I called up a zombie," she admitted.

There. She said it. She was a failure as a voodoo mambo and as a human being. She'd called a man from the dead and if she wasn't careful, she was going to kill him again.

Isoke's mouth dropped open, showing a double row of razor sharp teeth. In the strangled silence, two red scales pinged to the floor.

Oh no. The last thing she needed was trouble with the Kongamato. "Are you alright?"

The feathers on the top of his head shook, along with the rest of him. "Have you been smoking *mlima* leaves?" he barked. "Of course I am not alright. I leave you with a nice healthy man and you call up a zombie."

Amie took a breath. "The nice man is the zombie," she confessed.

The Kongamato looked puzzled for a moment, then broke into a grin. "Ah! Well, why didn't you say so? This is fine." He puffed out his chest. "This is wonderful!"

"No, it's not," she said, leading Isoke toward the stairs. "He's sick. The spell is wearing off."

"I've never heard of such a thing," he said, following. "Then again, your line does not have the best luck with men."

Yeah, well it was worse than that.

"Hurry." She urged Isoke through the door upstairs.

Dante lay on the recliner. He looked like death. His eyes were sunken behind dark circles. His skin had gone pasty and his entire left hand twitched uncontrollably.

"It was an accident," she insisted, crouching close and taking his hand. "I woke him as part of a love spell." But now? She'd never touch him again if that's what it took to save him.

Isoke landed on the arm of the recliner and leaned forward to inspect Dante. He was shaking badly. Blood trickled from under his bandage.

She'd thought she wanted love, but she didn't. Not this way.

Isoke looked at Amie as if he blamed her too. "Something is very wrong. I have seen soul mates raised. It is a beautiful thing. This is not."

"I know." Amie touched her hand to Dante's forehead. It was cold. He shivered, and she wanted to curl up in his lap and cry.

He was going to be taken from her forever. There would be no one else. She couldn't handle it. Besides, she knew there would never be another man like him.

Isoke leaned his head against her. "It is powerful magic to bring back the dead. You must need him very much."

Needing was one thing. Having was quite another. "I'll leave him alone forever if you can help me fix him."

She swore she'd never follow in her mother's footsteps and she wouldn't. It was going to be safe and boring from here on out.

Isoke drew away from her. "I'm sorry," he said, "there is no spell for reanimating a zombie. And if he dies again, he is truly and forever dead."

Her heart stuttered. "We have to do something." She couldn't lose him. Not yet.

"I will leave you alone," Isoke said, waddling across the room. "Follow your heart, *bembe*." He closed the door softly behind him. "This is something you must do on your own."

He'd said Dante was her soul mate.

"Amie," Dante murmured, his lips barely parting.

Not here. Not now. The tears welled in her eyes as she squeezed in next to him. He was cold. She wrapped herself around him, trying to keep him warm. "We have another day," she said, embarrassed at how her voice cracked.

"We don't," he said.

"Dante. Please." There were so many things to say and she had no idea how to go about them all. He'd showed her so many things about herself in such a short time. She needed more of him. She needed to know if she was truly meant to be with him. It couldn't end this way. "I don't want you to die."

"That's not enough," he said, on what might have been his last breath.

Her heart constricted. "But I don't want you to leave."

Dante's eyes cracked open, dazed. "That's not enough."

Her tears flowed freely as he closed his eyes once more.

He wasn't moving anymore. He was barely breathing.

He was leaving.

"I love you," she whispered. Heaven help her, she loved him. And it was awful. She already felt the loss, the dread. Amie took his face in her hands and kissed his cold lips, his cheek, his chin. She felt her magic build inside her as she opened herself to him, in honor of him.

Amie closed her eyes and savored the moment, her last time with him. She focused on the beauty and the happiness she'd found as the love magic thrummed through her. She touched her lips to his and released it in one glorious wave.

It poured into him, brilliant and whole. The air around them shimmered as pure love glowed between them. She held nothing back. For the first time in her life, she gave everything. She had to think that he felt it, that he knew.

This magic would never come back and she didn't care. She gave it to him, brilliant and true, because she loved him. It was the most natural gift she could give. It was her love spun out like silk. She needed him to have it before he died.

Amie laid her head on his cold hard chest, drained, yet more at peace than she'd ever been.

Her heart fluttered as traces of her love magic sizzled between them. Her breath caught. She didn't know exactly what she was feeling, only that her magic was slowly growing instead of diminishing.

The traces weren't flowing to him, but from him and through her and back to him. She could see it like golden cords between them. She raised her head and discovered him watching her. "Dante?"

He cocked a weak grin. Amie wet her lips. His face had regained some color. He still looked tired, but . . . "What's happening?"

"You love me." She went weak as he reached for her, his arms holding her tight.

She buried herself against the warmth of his chest. "Yes," she sobbed against him.

"And I love you." He leaned forward and kissed her lightly, tasting the salt of her tears. "More than I can ever say." He pulled her to him, kissing her long and hard. She felt the power this time, a soul-deep tug as it spiraled through her. It warmed her, fulfilled her and . . . "Oh my." She drew back. If he hadn't been weak and bleeding, it would have her doing indecent things to a chair-ridden man.

"I'm going to be fine," he whispered. She followed his gaze to the empty place on her bookshelf. His wedding ring had disappeared.

"Really?" Her heart squeezed. "You're really going to be fine?" She almost couldn't allow herself to hope.

"Fine," he said against her lips. His arms slipped around her and he demonstrated exactly how he had recovered.

It was beautiful and intense and—confusing. "Wait. How?"

He drew her back down to him. "Because you love me."

Chapter Ten

Dante had never met a woman who had mirrors over her bed. Then again, he'd never encountered anyone like Amie.

He drove his feet into the tangled sheets and hissed out a breath as she flicked her tongue over the sensitive spot at the base of his ear. Warmth flooded him.

"That's it." He flipped her over onto her back. "I can't take it anymore." He ground himself against her, naked, and more ready than he'd ever been.

"What?" she asked. "You've waited two hundred years for this and you can't take another twenty minutes of foreplay?"

"Something like that." He lifted her and in one swift motion, pinned her against the antique cherry headboard.

She wrapped her arms around his neck and skimmed her lips against his before drawing him down for an utterly lethal kiss. He felt her power burning between them, hot, wild, and sexy as hell.

Her love magic had sealed the spell that had brought him back. It had healed him, made him fully mortal once again. But more than that, it had given him the woman he loved, one who could—at last—love him back.

And while he had her here . . .

Amie never imagined feeling this way in her safe, warm bed. Dante was everything she didn't want—wild, unpredictable, and undeniably hers.

She was about to tell him that when Dante lowered his mouth and began doing spine-tingling things to her neck, her ears, her breasts. Her magic flowed into him, warm and steady, and rocketed back to her, spinning and sparking, catching on the ribbons of pleasure that wound through her until she thought she'd die from the pleasure of it.

At long last, Amie managed to lift her head and croak, "You. Here. Now."

She flung her head back. "Dante," she pleaded as he kissed and nipped his way up her body.

"Yes, dear?" He nuzzled her neck, gasping as she ran her tongue along his ear.

"I love you," she whispered.

His voice caught. "I know," he said hoarsely, and drove home.

Zombiewood Confidential

Marianne Mancusi

To Jacob—DBQ and Zombie Hugs forever!

Prologue

An arid wind swept the street, kicking up dust and debris. A man stumbled forward and stopped for a moment, scanning, taking in the dried-up fountain in the center of the deserted town square and the dilapidated shacks all around. He scratched his head. Where was he? How had he gotten here? And . . . why the hell was he so hungry?

An almost overpowering scent wafted through the otherwise stale air, a heavenly scent, the scent of roast chicken slowly revolving on a rotisserie of deliciousness. The man wiped away the drool that had somehow pooled at the corner of his mouth and took another step, hesitant, trying desperately to discern the source. Because he had to have some of whatever it was. Wherever it was, whoever *he* was, he needed to feed. Er, eat. As soon as possible. He was *sooo* hungry.

Movement across the square; he saw it! Lurching forward on unsteady feet, arms outstretched to keep his balance, he made his move. Light flashed in his eyes, blurring his vision, but still he stumbled in the direction of that irresistible smell. At the back of his mind he realized someone was shouting, but all he could focus on was that mouthwatering scent. And then, suddenly, his quarry was standing right in front of him: the biggest, most succulent chicken he'd ever beheld in his entire life. A fierce hunger overpowered him, and he lunged, nails digging into the creature's flesh as he opened his mouth wide, desperate for that first bite of juicy, finger-lickin' good—

"CUT! GODDAMN IT, YOU MORON, what part of CUT don't you understand?"

Ty Briggs looked straight up into the face of Mason Marks. The action star and Hollywood legend was glaring down at him with an extremely annoyed expression, most likely because, for some unfathomable reason, Ty's fingers were currently digging into his bare shoulders. Some British guy was shouting from just off to the left.

Face blazing with embarrassment—had he actually drawn blood?—Ty let the actor go and took a wary step backwards. "Sorry, man," he muttered.

It all came back: He was Ty Briggs, a thirty-three-year-old accountant from Reseda, California, who was currently taking time off from crunching numbers to live out his life's dream—playing Zombie 43 in the new Romeo George flick *Isle of the Living Dead*. Evidently, he was getting way too into the role.

"Okay, that's it, we're going to take five," Romeo barked into his megaphone. He'd been the shouting guy with the British accent. "Zombie Forty-three, try to get it the fuck together, okay?" The young director ran a hand through his shock of bleached blond hair and turned to an extra standing just off set. "Thirty-nine, get your makeup on. If Forty-three fucks up my shot again, you're in." He slapped the other actor on the back and walked away to confer with the cinematographer.

Ty started after him—to explain, to apologize, to beg Romeo not to replace him in his one big scene. After all, he didn't want to lose his only chance to be featured in the picture . . . but his chase was cut short as a small, angry dog leapt into his path, barking its head off. It looked like some sort of white rat terrier mix.

Ty recoiled. "Hey, someone get this mangy mutt away from me!" he cried, waving his hands in front of him to ward off the beast. The dog advanced, growling.

Ty was about to retreat—live to fight another day and all that—when he suddenly caught another whiff of the delicious smell that had plagued him earlier, the scent of roast chicken slowly spinning on a rotisserie. Was it coming from the dog? Ty took a wary step forward, sniffing the air. The canine, evidently not appreciating the fact that its threats were going unheeded, stepped things up a notch, raising its hackles and baring sharp white teeth. Ty knew that it would be wise to step back and let non-sleeping dogs do whatever the hell they wanted, but that smell . . . oh, that smell! Against his better judgment, he reached out to grab the snarling critter—

"Hey! Leave Chico alone!"

Before Ty could make contact, a muscular, manly figure swept in, scooping the dog up in his arms. The animal went from Cujo to cuddly in three seconds flat, and started licking his master's face.

Oh, shit. This was Mason Marks's dog?

Mason glared at Ty. "What did you do to him?" he demanded.

"Dude, he just attacked me!" Ty protested. "Out of nowhere!" Great. Now he'd be fired for sure. First he'd accidentally attacked the leading man, and now he'd pissed off the guy's dog.

"That doesn't sound like Chico," Mason said, nuzzling the dog's snout and then grimacing in distaste. "He likes everyone except paparazzi. Don't you, boy?"

The dog snorted happily in reply, opening his mouth and panting an affirmative. Ty's mouth watered as the smell of roast chicken wafted from Chico's breath.

"What do you feed him?" Ty couldn't help asking. "He smells so damn good."

Mason shot Ty an odd look, grimacing again. "You're joking, right?" he asked. "He's been rolling in some kind of garbage out on the island somewhere, and I'll be damned if I can figure out what it is." He sniffed Chico. "Rotten chicken or something, huh, boy?"

"Um, right. Of course." Ty reached out to give the beast a pat. Chico snapped at him, baring his teeth once again, and Ty recoiled. "Uh, I think I'm going to go down to the catering cart," he muttered.

He walked off the set, still confused about what the hell had just happened. His brain felt like mush. Maybe he shouldn't have stayed up so late at the party the previous night. All he knew for sure was that he was still pretty hungry. He hoped like hell the catering cart was serving chicken.

Chapter One

"I clearly told you I wear *only one thing*, and yet here you've used Candy Glow!" Actress Cissy Max grabbed the lipstick tube from Scarlet Patterson's hand and hurled it across the trailer, mouth twisted in an angry pout. "Where's my Cherry Blossom? Do you have any idea what my sponsors will say if I'm seen in this other shit?"

"Sorry, Cissy," Scarlet replied, running a frustrated hand through her bangs. She'd only been on the set of *Isle of the Living Dead* for three days now, and each day she felt less qualified to be there. "Just let me wipe it off and I'll fix everything."

"And my skin—it's drier than the Sahara on this godforsaken island! Where's my Armani Obsidian Mineral Regenerating Cream?"

"It's on order," Scarlet explained, using a baby wipe to scrub Cissy's lips. "It'll likely be here this afternoon on the two o'clock boat. Tomorrow by the latest."

"You know, I should call my agent on you guys," Cissy snarled, grabbing a hand mirror and holding it up to her face. "According to my contract, you're required to have Armani Obsidian Mineral Regenerating Cream on hand at all times."

"It was *back-ordered*, Cissy," Scarlet tried, not knowing why she even bothered. The temperamental star would never listen. "If we had waited for it to come in, that would have held up production even more, and we're already three weeks behind schedule."

Cissy scowled at her reflection and swore loudly. "God, I

look terrible. Seriously, where did they find you? Beauty-School-Drop-Outs-dot-com? I mean, I knew they were scraping the bottom of the barrel, but really! My freaking great-grandma can apply less clumpy mascara, and she's got an acute case of Parkinson's."

Scarlet winced at the jab. She hadn't technically dropped out of cosmetology school, but after the past month, losing her boyfriend and having to pay all her own bills, she wouldn't be able to pay for her final semester. The Hollywood Makeup Academy was the only school Grandma Jo would have respected; too bad it was so damn expensive, and she hadn't left Scarlet any money when she'd passed away last year. In fact, if Scarlet hadn't been needed for this film by her best friend, award-winning monster-makeup artist Derek Keyes, she would probably be stuck behind the MAC counter at Macy's, trying to work up her final semester's tuition.

Luckily, Derek had been desperate. It was evidently tougher than one would think to get a real makeup artist to agree to spend weeks trapped on this deserted island for the money this particular film had budgeted. So, after his first makeup artist had fled, stowing away on one of the daily, two PM supply boats, reportedly because of the heat, Derek had fudged Scarlet's resume, name-dropped her grandmother and told her to get ready for her big break.

At the moment, Scarlet had to admit, she felt pretty broken.

Cissy tossed her hand mirror back onto the counter. "My fans love my flawless skin," she huffed, as Scarlet attempted to repaint her lips—a tough assignment when the actress's mouth remained in perpetual motion. "What are they going to think when they see dry flakes on the big screen? Especially if this goes to IMAX. You can see every single pore on IMAX!" She turned to look at Scarlet. "You *are* using HD makeup, right?"

Scarlet resisted the urge to roll her eyes. IMAX, indeed. Cissy would be lucky if this low-budget zombie flick didn't go straight to DVD. Or, even more likely, VHS.

Meticulously painting Cissy's lips with Chanel's totally inappropriate Cherry Blossom color, Scarlet let her mind wander to what Dame Jo Patterson would think if she saw her granddaughter now. The former makeup artist to the stars would probably roll over in her grave. In fact, if she knew Scarlet was working on the trashy celebutante who'd gained most of her fame five years ago as slutty Nurse Susan on the hospital drama *Red's Anatomy: Full Frontal*, she might even rise from the dead to protest. The show had been cancelled after its second season, and Cissy had declared she'd take some time off to "find herself"—or, you know, to at least find someone desperate enough to hire an actress better known for her tabloid adventures in Vegas than for any theatrical talent.

It hadn't been like that back in Grandma's day; that was for sure. Scarlet remembered all the fascinating stories her grandma had told about the Golden Age of Hollywood, when stars acted like stars and not high-price hookers one rolled-up dollar bill away from a four-week stay in rehab for "exhaustion." Betty Grable, Joan Crawford, Elizabeth Taylor, Lana Turner—over the years, Grandma had worked with them all. Oh, how things had changed.

"Hey, Scarlet, you ready for me?"

Mason Marks.

Scarlet drew in a shaky breath as her childhood idol sauntered into the trailer, wearing a pair of thigh-hugging black leather pants and a damp gray T-shirt that clung to his washboard abs. She'd had a crush on Mason since she was twelve years old, back when he was still a young actor working for "The Muskrat" as they'd say, referencing his film company's cheesy mascot. He'd grown up since, abandoning his recurring television and film role as Trey Rey, the singing and dancing track star, for hot, sweaty action flicks where he would run around shirtless, blasting monsters with machine guns and shouting testosterone-laden if not particularly nuanced one-liners like "I'm gonna kick your mutherfuckin' alien ass," which ended up printed on countless T-shirts and quoted on junior-high-school playgrounds across the country.

That someone of Mason's renown was working on a piece-of-shit film like this had confused her from the beginning, when Derek had used the fact to further entice her into taking the job—not that she needed much encouragement beyond the paycheck—but she wasn't about to look a gift horse in the mouth. Unless, you know, said horse was willing to open said mouth and invite her to peek. Then, admittedly, she might risk it. After her latest dating experience, a boyfriend she'd labeled Slacker 2.0 before she'd realized he was Dickface Mark 1, she could use a little thrill in her life. Mason Marks was nothing if not thrilling.

"No, she's *not* ready for you," Cissy shot back, before Scarlet could find words. "The incompetent bitch discolored my lips with Candy-fucking-Glow. Seriously, I think our new makeup artist might be color-blind."

"And I think she must be a saint, putting up with the likes of you," Mason shot back, giving Scarlet a sympathetic look as he plopped down in the second makeup chair. Such unkind words for his girlfriend surprised Scarlet, but then she'd read many times that their affair was on again, off again. Currently it was on. More's the pity. She wondered if that was how he'd gotten suckered into doing this film.

Mason's little dog, a black-and-white mutt named Chico, hopped into his lap and started licking his face. According to the gossip rags, he'd found Chico a few years back while filming the box office bomb *Sparkly Vampires from Hell* down in Mexico. The dog had been wandering the streets of Baja, homeless and hungry and desperate for love—or at least for a fish taco or two. Mason had scooped him up and brought him back to LA, where he'd fattened the canine up and took him on "walkies" down all the most exclusive events' red carpets. Scarlet had never seen anything cuter, though several other students at cosmetology school cited it as proof that Mason was secretly gay, despite his much-publicized connection to Cissy and other women. As if.

"Hey, Chico!" she greeted, attempting to divert attention from what was fast becoming a hostile work environment with Cissy. She leaned over and gave the dog a little pat on the head. He licked her fingers in return.

"Ew!" The celebutante screwed up her face in disgust and huffed, "That dog stinks. You really need to wash your hands before you touch me again. I do *not* want dog germs on my delicate skin. If I break out in a single zit, I'm so having my lawyer sue you for everything you've got."

Which is absolutely nothing, Scarlet grumbled as she forced herself to walk calmly to the sink and wash her hands. Pumping the liquid soap, she tried to imagine Cissy's flawless face erupting into a molten pool of dog-germ-induced craters. It made her feel a little better.

"Come on, babe, you look beautiful," Mason was saying to Cissy as Scarlet returned. "Now get your skinny ass out of that chair and let the girl work on me." He glanced up and gave Scarlet a saucy wink. "After all, I need it more than you do."

Cissy scowled again. Scarlet took pleasure in the fact that the witch was going to get deep frown lines before she turned twenty-seven. "But—"

"We start filming in ten minutes, you know," Mason added, smiling sweetly.

"Ten minutes?" Cissy shrieked, leaping out of her chair. "But I'm not even dressed! What's wrong with the people on this movie?"

The actress lurched toward the exit, a heavy cloud of Chanel No. 5 wafting after her, but her exodus was blocked as the trailer door swung open. She slammed headfirst into the set's maintenance man, Jesús De La Cruz. "Ow!" she cried, losing her balance and teetering on heels that were way too high for her. Jesús dropped the broom he was carrying and grabbed her arms, effectively preventing her from crashing to the floor. It earned him no thanks.

"Get your hands off me," Cissy snapped. She smacked at his arms with her well-manicured fingers. "And look where you're going next time, asshole."

Jesús let go, giving her a sly grin. "Oh, I'm looking, *chica*," he replied, giving her a thorough once-over with lusty, amber-colored eyes. "I'm looking *muy* closely."

"Ugh! Gross. Go away!" Cissy pushed past him and out of the trailer, the door slamming shut behind her.

Jesús watched her go, a small smile playing at the corners of his mouth.

"Nice one, man," Mason said, tipping his head in respect.

"You just wait, senor." Jesús grinned back at him. "Someday I become an action star like you and I get all the hot mamas."

Mason laughed appreciatively. "I wish it were up to me, man. You'd be in for sure."

The maintenance man smiled and picked up his broom and set about sweeping the trailer floor, whistling as he worked.

"So, wait," Scarlet said, remembering what Mason had said before the interruption. She glanced at a clock. "You're filming in ten minutes? I thought it was more like a half hour."

Her onetime crush chuckled and stretched his muscular arms out behind his head in response. "Actually, her scene's not 'til three," he admitted, running a tan hand through his wavy blond hair. "I just figured you'd had enough of her for one afternoon." He grinned at Scarlet via the mirror.

Cautiously she smiled back, appreciating his effort but not sure how to react. After all, she'd read on PerezHilton.com about how turbulent the relationship between the two stars was. And as her grandmother had taught her, a movie makeup artist should always keep open ears and a closed mouth. Make the stars shine but never let them burn you.

"Are you ready to get started?" she asked, reaching into her makeup kit for a bottle of foundation and a sponge.

"Sure. I guess."

Scarlet looked down, surprised. If she hadn't known any better, she'd say he sounded disappointed. She supposed he was just used to fans fawning over him, and had probably been hoping she'd gush like a schoolgirl over his heroic gesture. But she had more self-respect than that. Not to mention, she knew her place here on set: crew, plain and simple. Crew and cast did not mix.

Still, that didn't diminish the tremor in her hands as she dabbed foundation on his forehead. He was so *hot*. She could see why he was always compared to a young Matthew McConaughey. She tried to think of global warming and the world's economic crisis and anything else that might distract her, but nothing worked. She was touching Mason Marks, her teenage crush! And her fingers were shaking because of it.

Maybe he wasn't paying attention?

He was.

She gasped as he grabbed her hands in his own—large, callused, utterly masculine hands—and a bolt of electricity shot straight to her core. "Are you okay?" he asked, looking directly up at her this time, instead of through the mirror. Those blue eyes pierced her, as if he sought to peer into her very soul. "You're shaking. Did she upset you?"

Scarlet let out a breath she hadn't realized she was holding. Thank god! He assumed this was about Cissy.

"Um, yeah, a little," she lied, reluctantly pulling her hand away. She could feel her face burning under his intense regard, and for the umpteenth time in her life she wished she weren't a pale and freckled redhead who blushed at the drop of a hat. "It's okay, though. I'll be fine."

Mason observed her for a moment. His eyes were twinkling, and his lips quirked up at the corners. "You know she's just jealous, right?"

Scarlet dropped her makeup brush. "Um, w-what?" she stammered, scrambling to pick it up. "J-jealous?"

"Of you, of course," Mason replied. "After all, no one wants a makeup artist who looks as gorgeous as you do—especially without any makeup."

Scarlet almost dropped her brush a second time. "Oh. Uh . . ." She was suddenly incapable of coherent speech. "I'm sure she . . . I mean, I'm not . . . I'm actually wearing lots of makeup," she finally managed to blurt after swallowing hard. As soon as the words left her mouth, she wanted to smack herself upside the head.

Mason just chuckled. "Well, whatever it is you're wearing, I suggest you keep it up." He settled back in his chair and closed his eyes, his hands wrapped around Chico, who snuggled down into his arms. "'Cause it's working. It's definitely working."

"And then he said, 'No one wants a makeup artist who looks as gorgeous as you do—especially without any makeup,'" Scarlet gushed an hour later, as she washed off her brushes and sponges in Derek's sink. Her friend was at the other end of his trailer, working on one of his zombie masks. This particular mask was of the post–shotgun-bullet-to-the-head variety and particularly gruesome—"gruesome" meaning "awesome" in special-effects-guy language.

Shuddering, Scarlet turned back to her brushes. "Of course, I was wearing makeup at the time. I mean, not a ton, I suppose, but I did put some on this morning. Though maybe I'd sweated most of it off by then. It's hotter than hell outside today. But then he said—"

"Not that I'm not *completely* invested in hearing a play-by-play for the fifteenth time, sweetie," Derek interrupted, holding up his mask, which was dripping with a mixture of fake blood and other bodily fluids. "But what do you think of this?"

Scarlet made a face. In the original, black-and-white *Night of the Living Dead* film, the production guys had literally used chocolate syrup as blood. Of course, that kind of thing no longer flew on today's zillion-color, high-def screens. So Derek had developed his own award-winning formula that involved corn syrup, red dye, and a super-secret ingredient he refused to reveal to anyone under penalty of death. Well, anyone but Scarlet, that was, after she'd played wingman through eleven and a half martinis at a particularly decadent West Hollywood gay bar one night after Derek had wrapped his last Clive Barker flick.

As it turned out, the secret ingredient to his super-realistic fake blood was, in fact . . . blood. It was animal blood, bought in bulk from a butcher in the Valley who traded it for tickets to horror movie screenings, and treated with a special anticoagulant. For some reason the whole revelation seemed a bit anticlimactic to Scarlet, not to mention disgusting. Good thing she wasn't the one being doused. Those poor extras.

"So?" Derek shook the mask, causing gore to spatter the floor.

"Ew?" Scarlet suggested, shielding her eyes. Sometimes it was tough to be BFFs with a monster movie makeup artist. "Gross?"

"Wait, wait, you haven't even seen the best part!" Derek cried, his eyes shining. "The eyeball's detachable and I can, like, have a fake maggot wiggle—"

Scarlet covered her ears, and at the top of her lungs she sang, "MARY HAD A LITTLE LAMB, LITTLE LAMB—I CAN'T HEAR YOU—LITTLE LAMB!" Otherwise, there was a good chance she would have been sick.

Derek dropped the mask on the table, rolling his eyes. "I can't believe someone as squeamish as you is working here," he chided.

"Well, you only have yourself to blame," she reminded him. "Seeing as you got me the gig. And anyway, I'm perfectly fine as long as I stay off the set—and out of your trailer."

"Well, I didn't exactly summon you here," Derek grumbled. "You're the one who pranced over here to gush about Mr. Marks."

Scarlet sighed. "Did I mention he said I looked gorgeous? Without makeup?"

Derek shot her a shocked look, slapping his hands over his cheeks á la Macaulay Culkin in *Home Alone*. "No! Oh my god, really? And *then* what? Tell me more, tell me more!"

Scarlet laughed, grabbed a prosthetic arm off the table, and threw it at him.

He dodged easily. "Trying to give me a hand?"

She groaned at the pun, sinking into a nearby chair. "I

know I'm being silly," she admitted. "But you gotta remember, I've had a crush on this guy forever. I even had Mason Marks bedsheets. My Aunt Peggy bought them for my twelfth birthday."

"Aha!" Derek accused. "So you've already slept with him!"

Scarlet snorted. "God, don't repeat that near any paparazzi. I don't want to end up reading about myself in *People*."

Her friend grinned. "'TANGLED IN THE SHEETS WITH MASON MARKS.' Come on, you've got to admit that'd be pretty awesome. You'd be famous! Maybe you could even become a web star. By any chance, do you have any videos of yourself singing Stevie Nicks tunes that we could exploit on YouTube?"

Scarlet shook her head, mortified. "No! The last thing I'd want is that sort of silliness. Even if Mason did make a move, there's no way I'd go for it. For one thing, Cissy Max would claw my eyes out."

Derek *pshaw*ed. "Honey, you could *so* take that skinny bitch."

"And for another," Scarlet continued, ignoring him, "I know better than to let myself be used, thank you very much. You know Mason's type. Love 'em and leave 'em. Bang 'em and bounce. I'm looking for something a little more permanent in my life, and you don't get permanent from any Mr. Hollywood. I mean, look at how many girls he hooked up with before Cissy. He was a one-man woman-wrecking crew."

"According to who, *Star Magazine*? The same rag that claims Angie is pregnant with sextuplets this week?" Derek paused, then added, "Of course, that could be true . . ."

"Anyway—"

Before she could continue, however, the trailer door creaked open. One of the zombie extras walked in, and Scarlet promptly shut her mouth. It was time for all talk of Hollywood hotties to cease. As her grandmother had always taught her, Scarlet would be discretion itself.

The extra stumbled over to a chair, looking pale and miserable, sinking down without saying a word. Derek walked to his makeup table and grabbed a can of bluish white paint. "Guess you hit that cast party last night, too, huh? I'm pretty hung over, myself." He chuckled. "At least you're easy to make up. You're already pasty white with dark circles."

The actor groaned in agreement, and Scarlet shook her head. There were times she was very glad she wasn't a drinker.

"Anyway, I'm going back to my trailer," she told Derek. "Maybe take a nap before dinner. You still want to meet up at craft services around seven?"

"Well, I'd been planning on eating at Ivy's . . . but since that's located in, like, the civilized world and we're stuck on a freaking desert island, I guess the catering tent will have to do." He shot her a grin. "Guess I'll see you there. I wonder what they're serving. Not that it matters, as they always burn everything."

Chapter Two

"Oh my god, three new Google alerts about me have come in since this morning!" Cissy squealed. She was sitting cross-legged on the bed in her trailer, laptop on her knees, a sexy, ripped-shirt costume from the afternoon shoot still draping her scrawny frame.

Mason rolled his eyes. "How nice for you," he replied. "Now, can you get changed so we can grab some food?" he asked, for what seemed the thousandth time. He didn't know why he even bothered. It wasn't as if there were any paparazzi on the island. He should be taking advantage of the rare opportunity to avoid hanging out with her.

"Damn in—the Internet's out again. Why do I pay so much for satellite Internet access if it's not even going to work when I need it?" Cissy cried in frustration, hurling the laptop across the bed. "I mean, The Superficial could be posting pictures of me in a bikini right this very second and I wouldn't even know it!"

"Cissy," he almost begged.

She glanced up, as if noticing him for the first time. "Oh baby, you're hungry," she cooed. "You should go without me. I've got all the food I need right here." She reached over for the tub of strawberry jam on her dresser.

"That's what you're eating for dinner?" Mason frowned. "You've got action scenes to do tomorrow. You need carbs and protein, not freaking strawberry jelly."

Cissy stuffed a spoonful in her mouth. "This is no ordinary jelly, I'll have you know," she declared. "These limited-edition preserves are handmade by monks in the Himalayas.

They're packed with essential vitamins and minerals. I had them imported, because they're impossible to find in LA." She waved her now-empty spoon in the air. "Healthy and delicious."

Mason rolled his eyes. "Whatever." LA's crazy food trends never failed to amaze him. "I'm going to get a real dinner—or at least some of the burned crap they serve around here."

"Wait!" Cissy cried as he turned to leave.

He stopped, his shoulders slumped. "What?"

"You're coming back tonight, right?" she asked, her voice suddenly plaintive, almost like a little girl's. "*Sleeping* here?"

He let out a frustrated breath and turned to face her. "Cissy, we're not going out. We're not boyfriend and girlfriend, no matter what you read in the latest US *Weekly*." He couldn't believe how many times he'd had to remind her of this fact. "Our relationship is just for show. To sell movie tickets. I don't even *like* you, remember?"

Cissy thrust out her lower lip in a pout. "Well, I don't even like you, either," she retorted. "You're boring and stuck-up and stupid, and I'm calling my agent first thing in the morning to ask him if I can break up with you again."

Mason sighed. "You know what he's going to say. We're stuck together until this disaster of a film gets released to DVD. So just suck it up and enjoy the fact that we're currently out in the middle of nowhere and don't have to spend any time getting photographed together."

"You know what? I hate you!" Cissy cried, grabbing a pillow and throwing it at him. "Get out of my trailer!"

"Gladly," he muttered. Dodging the pillow, he yanked open the trailer door and stepped outside.

He'd known he should have never let the studio talk him into this craptastic deal. Talk about selling your soul to the devil! But Mason had needed fast cash after his former money manager—aka his father—fled to Acapulco the previous year, Mason's lifetime earnings stuffed into his Louis Vuitton luggage. With the money he'd had left, Mason had paid to keep the story out of the papers. After all, no one wanted to hire an action star who got duped by his dear old dad. Then he'd begun searching for solutions.

The Cissy contract had been a quick ticket to new financial freedom. He'd accepted a large lump sum to simply spend time with her in the public eye—fortifying her waning sex appeal with his own—and star in this crappy zombie movie she'd already landed. He'd written in the ability to break up with her several times a year, provided he didn't date anyone else, and at least he'd gotten them to cut out the clause that involved them actually consummating their fake relationship. That had been a deal breaker for sure. But he still had—what was it inmates called it?—time left to serve.

A full moon hung low in the sky, casting an almost silver glow over the film-set ghost town. Across the way he could see a few bright lights still blazing, and could hear the fans whirring, which meant the second unit crew was likely filming a scene or two with some of the minor characters. Being three weeks behind schedule meant taking advantage of every waking hour. Those extras must be racking up some serious SAG overtime at this point. But that wasn't his problem. With any luck Romeo George would be able to wrap by the end of the week, and they could all go home and forget this disaster of a film ever happened—at least until the premiere party next year. Mason wondered if attendance was stipulated in his contract with Cissy.

"Hey, have you seen Derek?"

Startled by the voice behind him, Mason whirled. His eyes fell on the film's new makeup artist. God, she was pretty. She was gorgeous, in fact, in a girl-next-door way that was patently unlike the typical bleach-blonde, boob-jobbed, Botoxed Hollywood babes he normally encountered. Long auburn hair spilled down her back, and she had big, catlike green eyes that turned up at the corners. Full lips, high cheekbones . . . and her body! Man, she was a total throwback to the Golden Age of Hollywood, when women had flaunted soft curves rather than razor-blade pelvic bones. Just looking at her made Mason want to run his hands over her sexy silhouette, take his time to explore every luscious inch. He'd trail fingers up her narrow waist to her soft, full breasts, cup them in his hands and—

Get a grip, man!

This was starting to border on pathetic. Maybe it was due to his seemingly perpetual celibacy, thanks to his contract with Cissy, but ever since Scarlet had come on set, he hadn't been able to stop these lusty thoughts from invading his mind. There was just something about her. He'd even started accidentally-on-purpose ruining his makeup just to get back in her chair.

You're losing it, man. He was a big Hollywood star, after all. The kind of guy who could effortlessly score high-end tail. So why was he so hung up on this makeup artist?

Perhaps more importantly, he admitted to himself, why did she seem so completely uninterested in him? He was used to having a certain effect on women: Walk into a room, they all clamored for his attention. Scarlet didn't. She hadn't even blinked the time he'd spilled coffee on himself just to take his shirt off in her presence. In fact, instead of gaping at his perfect six-pack abs, the girl had merely offered him the use of a Slanket, in case he got cold. (And let's face it, no red-blooded American male ever got *that* cold. Especially not with third-degree burns from spilled coffee.)

No, no matter what he did, Scarlet remained professional, courteous, and completely oblivious to his supposedly irresistible—according to *Elle* magazine—charms. If her insides were at all turning to mush at his presence, she hid it well. Which, truth be told, made him like her all the more.

"Derek?" he repeated, realizing he hadn't answered her question.

"The monster makeup guy," she clarified.

"Oh, right. No, haven't seen him since this morning," Mason admitted. "Sorry."

"It's okay. I'm just . . . Well, he was supposed to meet me for dinner, and I haven't been able to find him." She absently bit her plump lower lip and scanned the area.

Mason felt a tightening in his throat. He imagined getting a chance to nibble on that luscious lip, and admitted he'd be happy to skip dinner altogether to indulge in such a delectable dessert. But then he shook his head. *Get a grip, cowboy*, he reminded himself. He had to stop these crazy fantasies. He was here to finish a movie, not mack on the makeup artist, however hot she might be. He had a contract with Cissy, and even if he hadn't, the last thing this poor girl needed was someone like him. She seemed like a sweetheart. One flash of a camera and her normal world would turn into a crazy, paparazzi-fueled circus where she couldn't even blow her nose without being mocked by TMZ.

But there were no paparazzi here. And also, there was no reason they couldn't be friends, right? Friends who, like . . . hung out and stuff. And maybe got dinner together?

"My date ditched me, too," he informed her. "Want to go grab a bite together, instead?"

"Um . . . I don't know," she hedged.

Mason frowned. Damn, what did he have to do to reach this girl? Some cancer charity had scored twenty grand by auctioning off a lunch with him last month, and here she didn't even want to go for free?

"Come on," he urged. "I hate eating alone."

"Me, too," she admitted. "And I really don't know anyone here but Derek. But come on, I'm sure you have plenty of people to eat with."

"Maybe," he admitted, giving her a casual shrug. "But I want to eat with you."

He caught a flash, then: something in her eyes. A glimmer, maybe, of interest? But a moment later it was gone, and she'd masked her expression with a careful smile. Had he imagined it, or was there something beneath her cool, calm, and collected exterior? Something like excitement?

"Well, thank you," she said finally. "I think I'll take you up on your offer. If you really want my company, that is," she added, looking up at him with those big eyes of hers. "And aren't just being nice."

He grinned, enjoying the thrill of a small victory. "Honey, haven't you read the rags?" he drawled. "I'm never nice."

Though for you, he thought, as they walked together to the catering tent, *I might just make an exception.*

"Wow, you've done an amazing job decorating this place!" Scarlet exclaimed. After a fun-filled dinner (or she should say "pun-filled," because Mason had had her laughing until her sides hurt), he'd suggested they grab Chico and take him for a walk. At first she'd felt a little weird, entering the trailer of such a big star—especially one whose posters she'd fake made-out with in seventh grade—but the awkwardness dissipated completely once she stepped inside.

She didn't know what she'd expected; maybe a trailer packed with ego, decorated with memorabilia from his own movies and posters of himself. After all, the guy did seem pretty cocky, always looking for excuses to take off his shirt and flex. Instead, the place was like a museum of old film stars, with framed pictures of John Wayne, Clint Eastwood, and even Cary Grant lining the walls. These legends smiled down at her, and they made the trailer warm and inviting.

"Thanks," Mason replied. "My grandma gave these to me back when I was a little kid, just starting out in Hollywood, to give me inspiration."

Chico circled his legs, barking excitedly. Mason scooped the dog up, and the beast rewarded him with a face full of kisses. He kissed the dog back, once on the snout. *Lucky mutt*, Scarlet thought.

"When I have a bad day on the set, I like to come back here for a little encouragement," he said, with an approving glance at a photo of James Cagney. "These guys never let Hollywood chew them up and spit them out, that's for sure."

Scarlet walked over to an autographed photo of Humphrey Bogart. "Well, don't let their tough-guy exteriors fool you," she remarked, running a finger down the frame. "They had their share of troubles, too. The general public just didn't hear about them. The studios tightly controlled their stars' images back then. And scandal was something to be avoided at all costs, rather than exploited to sell movie tickets like it is now."

"You don't know the half of it," Mason muttered.

Scarlet turned, not sure she'd heard right. "Sorry, what?"

Mason didn't repeat himself. "Old movie buff?" he asked instead, quirking an eyebrow.

She smiled, walking over to examine a young Charlton Heston. "Sure," she said. "But most of the stories I know are from my grandmother. She was a makeup artist, too, just like me, and worked with all the Hollywood greats. And let's just say a makeup artist is a little like a priest on a movie set. The stars would confess their deepest sins to Grandma, knowing they could trust her never to spill to the public. She could have written a bestseller. Instead, she took it all to her grave." Scarlet shook her head. "The things she knew . . ."

Mason stepped forward, grinning. "Oh yeah? Like what?"

She looked up and laughed. "I'll never spill, either."

"Aww." He groaned, punching her playfully on the arm. "You're no fun."

"Yeah, yeah." She reached over and stroked Chico's head, asking, "You ready to go, little guy?" The dog barked in affirmation.

"All right," Mason exclaimed. He grabbed the leash off a hook by the door. "One desert walk coming right up."

It was a beautiful night. Warm, dry, quiet. Light from the full moon spilled onto the pathway they took, enabling them to walk farther from camp than they might otherwise have been able. Soon the ghost-town set fell away into the distance, and they found themselves surrounded only by sky, which sparkled with stars. Scarlet, who spent most of her time in smog-filled LA, was speechless.

Chico ran ahead, bounding from rock to rock in a perpetual search for the best place to pee.

Scarlet watched in amusement as he lifted his little doggie head in the air and sniffed the wind. "I wonder what he smells," she remarked to Mason.

The actor groaned and said, "Probably that nasty chicken he found." At Scarlet's questioning look, he explained, "I followed him after filming yesterday, trying to figure out where he's been disappearing. I found his secret stash. I think that when the boat guys were delivering that last huge shipment of food, a crate fell off their cart and smashed on the ground. The area is now an all-you-can-eat, all-you-can-roll-in rotten-chicken buffet." He shook his head at Chico and called out, "Tomorrow you get a bath, oh little doggie friend."

His little canine companion wagged a tail in reply, his grasp of English too limited to know when doom was in store for him.

Scarlet laughed, twirling around, enjoying the warm breeze and moonlight. "It's so amazing out here," she raved, feeling intoxicated by the night. When Derek had first suggested she come, she hadn't realized she'd be wandering around the island with her favorite movie star, talking about dogs and their obsessive canine love of all that stank. Talk about a lifetime dream come true!

And Mason was different than she'd first assumed. Sure, he was still arrogant and cocky, as she'd suspected, but he was also funny and kind of sweet. And he was pretty darn nice, too, no matter what he claimed; offering to get that steak for the key grip, after the cook had grouched that the "good stuff" was for actors only, had been pretty damn thoughtful.

"I almost feel like breaking into song and dance," she admitted.

Mason laughed. "Far be it from me to stop you," he teased. "As long as you don't make me join in."

She turned, surprised. "What? No singing and dancing? But you were Trey Rey, for goodness sakes!"

He groaned. "My point exactly. I've already sung and danced enough for a lifetime. Maybe even more. I can imagine my corpse dancing in its grave, unable to stop."

Scarlet laughed. "Working for *The Muskrat* ruined music for you forever, huh? That's very sad."

Mason chuckled, before his expression became serious.

"Once I turned thirteen, my voice dropped and I could no longer sing worth a damn," he explained with a small shrug. "'The Muskrat' as you so sweetly put it, severed my contract and kicked me out the door without so much as a 'Nice knowin' ya,' moving on to grub millions off the next prepubescent prodigy he could find."

"Ugh."

"Ugh, indeed." Mason grimaced. "I thought my career was over before I'd even begun to grow facial hair," he admitted. "I went back to regular school—which was not easy, let me tell you. Turns out high school boys don't really enjoy the company of former child stars who once made a living singing show tunes, not unless it's to beat them up. On a daily basis."

Scarlet blinked. She couldn't imagine going from teenage heartthrob to punching bag in three seconds flat; she'd barely been noticed at school. "I'm sorry," she said, placing a hand on his arm. "That must have been rough."

Mason nodded. "I swore then and there that if I ever starred in another film, it'd be one where the death count outnumbered the dance numbers. Three years later, I got my big break with *Max Ledd 2: Pain to the Max*. I never looked back." He suddenly seemed a little embarrassed. "Sorry. I don't know why I'm telling you this."

"Because I'm the makeup artist, remember?" she replied. She gave him a wink, and he smiled.

"Oh yeah," he said. "So I can tell you my deepest, darkest secrets and you'll never breathe a word."

She made a zipping motion over her lips.

"Well, then . . . I guess I *can* admit that I do miss a good synchronized dance number every now and then." He grinned and made jazz hands. "Just between you and me."

"Well, then, let's see one!" She scrambled up a nearby boulder and placed her hands on her knees. "Come on, Trey Rey. Let's see some daaaaaaaaaaance magic."

"Oh no!" he cried, waving his hands in protest as he recognized her parody of the high school principal from his movie musical days. It was odd to see such boyish embarrassment juxtaposed with a body that was clearly adult—and so strong and masculine. "No effing way."

"What, afraid it'll end up on YouTube?" she teased. "We're in the middle of nowhere. No one's gonna see." She gave him her best cajoling look.

It worked. His eyes twinkled. "Okay, then. But on one condition."

"Which is?" Her heart began pounding.

He held out a hand. "Dance with me."

Now it was her turn to protest. "Oh no! No, no, no!" she squealed. "I am so not a dancer."

"Maybe," he allowed. "Or maybe you just need a good partner." He bowed low, the grace of his strong body reminding her of Gene Kelly. "May I have the honor, ma'am?"

She gave in. How could she not? After all, when was she going to get another chance to dance with her teen crush? She jumped off the rock and approached him, forcing her body not to shake like a leaf as he slid his hands around her waist. His touch was gentle but firm, and it sent chills through her body. Gorgeous, sensuous shudders.

He led her in a waltz, his steps as graceful as Fred Astaire's. She'd forgotten just how talented he'd been back in the day. She was no Ginger Rogers, but he didn't seem to mind, not even when she stepped on his foot for the fourth and fifth times. Chico bounced around them, barking, evidently in want of a dance partner himself.

"I always wanted a boyfriend who would dance," Scarlet found herself saying, suddenly feeling the need to confess a few of her own secrets. "The last guy I dated never wanted to leave the couch or his video games. Not exactly the type you can sign up for ballroom lessons."

"Was that why you broke up?" Mason asked, giving her a little twirl.

Scarlet shook her head. "No. Though in hindsight it would have been a good reason. We broke up because he met another girl online, and I caught them one night having cybersex in a chat room." She scowled. "He claimed it wasn't cheating because it was virtual. That he felt he should be able to have both online and offline women. Not to mention he was always poking fun at my dream of becoming a Hollywood makeup artist—telling me I totally sucked and should just get a real job. Preferably one that paid a lot of money so I could support him."

Mason made a face. "What a jerk. So you dumped him, I hope?"

"Hell, yeah. That was a month ago. And then Derek called, letting me know about this job. I jumped on it and came out here. Even though I'm way out of my league with all the monster-makeup stuff."

Mason stared at her, managing to appear sympathetic without any hint of pity. "Your ex was an idiot," he finally murmured, shaking his head. "Cheating on someone like you . . ."

Her heart leapt into her throat as she suddenly realized they were no longer dancing. His hands tightened around her waist, forcing her close until she was flush against his frame. She swallowed hard, wondering for a crazy second if she might be dreaming. Surely Mason Marks, *the* Mason Marks, wasn't really holding her in his warm, strong arms—right?

She felt his hard stare and looked up, instantly losing herself in intense sapphire eyes. They were even more brilliant in real life than on the big screen. Her breath caught as he studied her carefully. Then he leaned down and brushed his lips across hers. It was the lightest whisper of a kiss, but it instantly electrified every cell in her body. It was heaven.

Chico shattered the moment, barking. A shuffling noise followed, coming from somewhere behind them.

"What was that?" Scarlet asked. She turned around and around, but clouds had suddenly appeared, obscuring the moonlight and her vision.

Mason leapt back, pushing her away from him, eyes searching the darkness. His expression held horror. "Oh god," he cried. "Was that . . . a photographer?"

Then he ran off into the gloom, seeking whoever had been spying on them, leaving Scarlet with reality crashing over her head. An ugly reality, because, she suddenly realized, this wasn't a romantic night. This wasn't some glamorous old-Hollywood love story. This was an arrogant, womanizing action star seducing a stupid, naive makeup artist. And all it had taken was a minute waltz.

She fought the urge to throw up. Instead, she forced herself to gather her last scraps of dignity and run back to the set, back to her trailer. There, she would try to forget all about that kiss and the bastard who'd given it to her.

Chapter Three

Mason's fist connected with the photographer's face. The man went down, sprawling backwards, arms flailing as he lost his balance and went crashing to the ground. But then, as Mason searched for a camera, he realized the guy wasn't some paparazzo looking to ruin his or Scarlet's life; it was one of the zombie extras, still in full makeup. And the dude was lying on the ground, groaning miserably.

Oops!

Chico bounced around the extra, barking like mad. Mason called off the dog and held out a hand. "Er, sorry, man," he apologized, praying the extra wasn't one of those litigation-happy types who'd start filing assault charges from his iPhone on the way back to camp. "I thought you were . . . er, well, you shouldn't go sneaking up on people like that. It's not smart."

The man agreed mournfully, saying something that sounded like "No brains," and taking Mason's hand. Mason pulled him to his feet.

The guy's skin felt cold and clammy. *Great,* Mason thought. He'd probably sent the dude into shock, sucker punching him like that. Maybe he should offer to buy him a beer back at camp, make it up to him somehow.

"Yeah, well, no big deal. We all have brain-dead moments once in a while," he said, slapping the guy on the back.

"Brains?" the man echoed, squinting at him and cocking his head inquisitively. Then, before Mason could inquire as to what the hell he was talking about, the dude lunged, hands clamping around Mason's throat, applying pressure and cutting off his breath.

Mason reacted on instinct, throwing his hands into the Hapkido front choke defense maneuver he'd learned for a fight scene in *Anaconda Six: Snakes in Space*. Damn, that had been a slow year. And it turned out the defensive maneuver was a tad harder to execute against a real-life opponent who hadn't read the script and been cued to go down quickly, so that Mason could move on to his next scene and "Kick that mutherfuckin' snake's ass"—a line he'd never really supported, seeing as most snakes he'd encountered didn't have asses, per se.

Luckily, all his weight training paid off. After a brief and breathless struggle, Mason managed to get into position. "Gerrroffffame," he croaked, as the extra's thumbs dug into his windpipe. "Orl'llbreakyergoddamnwrrists!"

The actor either didn't hear, didn't understand, or—and this was most likely, Mason feared—just didn't give a shit, angry as he was about being sucker punched, and kept choking away. Mason could smell the man's fetid breath, could feel it moving nearer and nearer. So he did what he had to do. He slammed his arms down on the guy's wrists, cringing at the sickening sound of cracking bone.

The actor's hands dropped away from Mason's throat, and the dude gave a groan of agony. But then, to Mason's surprise, instead of giving up, the extra took another step forward, arms outstretched, hands dangling uselessly from broken wrists. Mason stared, unable to believe his eyes. What the hell? Was this guy on PCP? It figured: The one time he might actually have a use for the pistol his agent had demanded he get after the Internet threats last year (he'd refused to hire a bodyguard), and he'd left it in his suitcase. He'd start carrying it everywhere from now on, at least while on this stupid island. He imagined brandishing the thing would be a fairly strong deterrent to this kind of aggression.

Not having any other options, Mason punched the extra

as hard as he could, knocking him backwards a second time. Then he punched again—and again, because the guy kept coming. The extra wobbled, groaned piteously, then started convulsing, falling to the ground, eyes rolling back in his head and foam bubbling from his mouth. Mason watched in horror, wondering what he should do. Was the guy having a seizure? Should he try to keep him from swallowing his tongue? Would the man try to kill him again if he did?

Suddenly, the convulsions stopped. The extra sat up slowly, examining his limp, broken wrists. In horror, he looked at Mason. He clearly had no recollection of what had just happened.

"Oh, god," he said, confusion and panic in his eyes. "I think I hurt my wrists somehow."

Mason just stared, speechless.

Deciding the guy was no longer any threat, Mason reached down and helped the extra to his feet, careful to avoid the man's broken wrists. "Let's get you to the med tent," he said. "Get you bandaged up."

The extra nodded miserably, stumbling toward camp on unsteady feet while clutching his hands tightly to his chest. Whatever had possessed him a moment earlier was definitely gone. Which was good, Mason admitted, if a bit disconcerting. Was this the same guy from the other day who had attacked him on set, Zombie Forty-three? No, Forty-three was a skinny guy with brown hair. This guy was bald and kind of fat.

Chico growled menacingly, slowly circling the extra. The man looked down at him, sniffed once, then groaned. "Damn, that dog smells good," he muttered. Then, moaning in what Mason assumed was terrible agony, he lurched off into the night.

Ohhh-kay, then. Mason supposed the guy wasn't going to sue.

Suddenly, he shook his head. Scarlet! Now that the crisis was over, memory of what had happened rushed back. Shame and annoyance overwhelmed him. He had to find her. What had he been thinking? Kissing her like that, out in the open for God and paparazzi to see? Sure, they were on a deserted island, but he'd seen slimy photographers slip into stranger spots. Heck, that Adrian Ghalib guy had somehow charmed his way into Britney Spears's bed! Had Scarlet headed back to camp? Was she pissed?

If only she hadn't smelled so damn good, like warm cinnamon and sugar on freshly baked bread. Dancing so close to her, breathing in that scent, hearing her sad tale about that bastard ex boyfriend . . . well, he'd lost it. The idea of a girl as sweet as Scarlet being unappreciated made his blood boil.

But that needed to stop. At least, he couldn't be pursuing his attraction to her. He'd signed a contract, and he was pretty sure the studio wouldn't hesitate to sue him for everything they'd paid if their terms weren't followed to the letter—or maybe even for more than they'd paid. Pain and suffering, and all that.

Speaking of pain and suffering, he didn't want to pull poor Scarlet and her naive dreams into his ugly reality. If scandal hit, she might find herself blacklisted on movie sets forever. He didn't think she was interested in a career based on infamy, like Cissy's, so one kiss from him could ruin her whole career. It wasn't worth it. *He* wasn't worth it.

As he reached the small enclave of trailers, and his own, he whistled for Chico to follow him inside. They would get a good night's sleep.

Tomorrow, he would apologize and explain all he could. Scarlet had claimed makeup artists never squealed. Well . . . he'd have to trust her on that. Because he couldn't let her go on thinking he was a jerk.

Mason's not a jerk, Scarlet was telling herself. *He's a prick.*

As she reached her trailer she was still fuming, furious at Mason but more angry at herself for being stupid. To fall for the lines of a slick Hollywood actor? Her grandmother would have been so ashamed. She'd warned Scarlet time and time again.

But this wasn't just *anyone*. This was Mason Marks, her dream. That was the reason she'd allowed herself to lose her head out there, daring to imagine a reality where a Hollywood prince might actually notice a toad like herself. She'd created a fairytale story in which he would whisk her away from her lowly reality to live in his beautiful castle in the clouds—or at least his three-bedroom bungalow above Mulholland. He would caress her by candlelight and whisper how lucky he was, after years of searching red carpets and fancy parties with his faithful hound, to have finally found his soul mate in his very own makeup trailer.

But that was a fantasy. In reality, Mason was a self-absorbed, womanizing jerk who had figured it'd be easy to get some action off the naive, pathetic makeup chick while his beautiful girlfriend waited back in her trailer, dreaming of ginormous engagement rings, weddings in Cabo, and adorable baby pictures sold for a mil to *OK!* magazine. She'd get it all in the end, and Scarlet would find herself discarded like yesterday's dailies. Sure, she'd have a story to tell, but it'd be one that would only serve to scar her own reputation. After all, in Hollywood, boys would be boys. But makeup artists who slept with them? Sluts.

She shook her head and put her hand on the door to her trailer. This was *it*. She needed to avoid Mason for the rest of the filming. Maybe she could even have Derek do his makeup from now on.

A voice cut through the darkness. "Ah, Scarlet. There you are." A moment later, Romeo George walked into view. "I've been looking everywhere for you."

"You have?" she asked, surprised the director even knew her name.

"Have you seen Derek?"

Her insides churned uneasily. Derek still hadn't come back? "Did you check his trailer?" she asked. "If you guys are working late, he might have decided to take a nap," she suggested.

Romeo sighed. "I've had my assistant check everywhere.

He didn't show for the usual touch-ups this afternoon. I . . . I'm afraid he's gone."

"Oh my god," Scarlet murmured.

"Bugger! So he didn't warn you?" Romeo snapped, slamming his fist into the nearest trailer. "It's not just him. I think half my crew stowed away on the boat out this afternoon. Not that I blame them. It's fucking hot and horrible in this shithole." He wiped his brow. "But we're wrapping in two measly days! Couldn't he have waited?" He shook his head.

Scarlet furrowed her brow. She was pretty sure she'd spoken to Derek after two PM, when the boat would have left. And he hadn't said a word about leaving. In fact, he'd seemed downright cheerful, excited about his new masks. "That doesn't sound like Derek," she said. "He's very responsible."

Romeo shrugged. "I told you, I had my assistant check everywhere. We're on a desert island. Where the hell can he be hiding?"

The director was right. There weren't a lot of options, other than wandering down the beach of the tiny, half-mile island. And Derek would never have done that. After all, sand was very hard to get out of one's Armani loafers.

"In any case," Romeo continued, "we need to shoot tomorrow morning, with or without your buddy. It's vital to the picture. The grand finale—exploding building, dying zombies . . . it's going to be fucking brilliant." He pointed a finger in her direction. "And I need you to do everyone's makeup."

She stared at him, horrified. "Everyone's? But . . ."

"Yes, that includes the zombies. I have fifteen of them I need made up by eight AM. Full makeup, lots of blood. Remember, this is the money shot. They've got to look mad good."

Scarlet gnawed her lower lip. How the hell was she going to pull off something like this? She could barely get the normal cast's makeup to look *mad good*. There was no way she'd be able to create fifteen authentic-looking zombies.

"I'm sorry, Romeo, but I'm really not qualified—"

"Brilliant!" Romeo interrupted, clearly not listening and

slapping her on the back. "The first extra will be in the makeup trailer at six." Then he turned and walked away, not awaiting her reply.

Scarlet slumped against her trailer, letting out a frustrated breath. This was so not good. How the hell was she going to create a realistic-looking zombie? But it wasn't as if she had a choice. This was a make-it-or-break-it moment, she was sure. Hollywood didn't give second chances. Six AM tomorrow, there'd be an extra walking into her trailer, ready for his close-up, Mr. DeMille. And Mr. DeMille had better be happy about what he looked like.

There was a rustling behind the trailer, and then a groan. It sounded as if someone were banging around, trying to find his way through the dark. Maybe he'd stubbed his toe? Either way, it was none of her business. Scarlet sighed, determined to just hit the sack. She had a big day tomorrow.

There was another clang, and then silence. Then:

"Psst! Hey, you!"

Now what? She whirled around, looking for whoever had spoken. She assumed it was the guy who'd stubbed his toe. A mustachioed man she didn't recognize, dressed all in black and wearing three cameras around his neck, one with a huge telephoto lens, appeared out of the darkness and motioned for her to approach. He was sweating profusely and rubbing his foot.

She walked forward cautiously, wondering what he wanted. He wasn't one of the crew, she was pretty sure. "Er, may I help you?" she asked.

He put a finger to his lips. "Listen," he hissed. "How would you like to make some money?"

She squinted, unsure of his game. Of course she wanted to make some money! Who didn't? That was why she'd signed on with this dumb picture, with its big dumb star, Mason Marks. Rent, electricity, phone, cable. All those bills she used to split, and they were now her responsibility alone. She also needed her cosmetology license if she ever wanted to work on a better movie than this one.

"I'm from *E-Snoops*," the guy said, naming one of the newest celebrity tabloids. "I saw you hanging out with Mason Marks earlier. You two looked pretty close, what with all that canoodling at dinner. He took you into his trailer. Any little tidbit you can give me? How's his relationship with Cissy Max? He hasn't spent much time with her—not as far as I've seen. Trouble in paradise?" He reached into his pocket and pulled out a huge wad of cash. "Five hundred dollars," he told her. "You can stay completely anonymous. Just give me a tip so I can get off this damn island."

Scarlet stared at the money. It would be so simple: She could get Mason back for being such a sleazeball, and would earn a big chunk of next semester's tuition all in one shot. And, as the guy said, no one would know. Maybe he'd even been out on the beach, earlier. Maybe he already had photos but wanted verbal confirmation.

"Come on." The man reached into his pocket again. "A *thousand* dollars. Just one little comment about Mason and Cissy, and it's yours. No strings attached. I gotta get off this island. I've started seeing things."

Scarlet had to admit that it was pretty hot out. She looked at the money longingly, then finally shook her head. She just couldn't do it. Her grandmother had taught her better. Mason had done her wrong, but accepting this money and telling tales would be just as bad.

"Sorry," she said, shrugging. "I've got nothing to say."

Chapter Four

"So, have you been enjoying work on the film?" Scarlet asked.

It was early the next morning, and she was sitting across from a zombie extra, attempting to make conversation to distract herself from the gore she was applying to his face. The fake yet real blood was making her ultra queasy. The actor wasn't helping much, moaning a raspy reply and staring off into the distance. Evidently, he wasn't much of a talker.

She dabbed some black paint under his already bloodshot eyes and critically studied his face. "You know, you're really not supposed to put your bloody contacts in until I finish your makeup," she reminded him. "I don't want to get any paint on them." The actor just shrugged, slouching farther down into his seat with a groan.

Scarlet sighed and reached for a tube of premixed blood. If only Derek would come back. She'd checked his trailer that morning and found it completely undisturbed. Everything was still there, still in its proper place: prosthetic limbs, makeup trays, even his precious masks. There was even some extra-gory glop over in the corner, which he'd clearly just been perfecting; it looked like half an ear. Because of that, Scarlet knew he hadn't hightailed it on yesterday's supply boat. She knew her friend well enough to know he would never, ever leave his masks and gore props behind. They were his babies. His disgusting, deformed babies. Something was definitely wrong.

She wiped the sweat from her brow—the day was already proving to be a scorcher. She'd tried calling him, but her cell phone still had zero bars. And the security guard she'd tracked down refused to use the film's satellite phone, as it would put the production even more over budget. After all, he said, Derek was a grown man. He'd probably just taken off, like everyone one seemed to be doing. It wasn't, he'd added, as if Derek were the only guy missing. Half the crew had gone AWOL over the last week, fleeing this thousand-degree hellhole, this sinking ship of a motion picture. It was awful, because Scarlet knew in her heart that something was definitely wrong.

Letting out a worried breath, she handed the extra a blood packet and instructed him to put it into his mouth and bite down. The actor bared his teeth, and she recoiled.

"Did someone already make you up?" she asked warily. "You don't seem like you need much work . . ." Either that, or the guy had never seen a dentist in his life. Blackened teeth, malformed bloody gums. Yuck! "Maybe just a little more eye makeup," she decided, knowing this had to be perfect.

But as she dabbed a little black around his left eye, it suddenly fell out of its socket and onto the actor's lap.

Scarlet screamed. She ran to the sink just in time to puke her guts out. Only after washing her sick down the drain did she dare to glance back at the actor. He still sat in his chair, looking completely nonplussed, eye staring accusingly up at her from his lap.

Suddenly, she remembered Derek's eyeball-mask trick from the day before. She let out a frustrated breath. "Bastard," she muttered. "Got me again."

Sure enough, a slimy maggot poked out from the extra's empty eye socket. Scarlet shook her head, grimacing, grabbed the prop worm and stuffed it back into the hole, followed by the eyeball, both disturbed and impressed by how realistic both felt. "Dude, don't be wasting Derek's props when the cameras aren't rolling," she admonished. "He'll kick your ass."

"Braaaainsss . . ." the extra groaned.

"Yeah, Derek's got brains all right," she agreed, dabbing a

little black cream under the actor's repositioned eye. "At least, he's got brains if he ran off like everyone thinks he did. Of course, those brains are totally sick and twisted."

"BRAINNNS!!!" the actor repeated.

Scarlet rolled her eyes. "Oh, I get it. You're practicing your line. Sorry, please continue. Just try not to move your mouth so much when you—"

The actor lurched to his feet, knocking over her makeup tray. Supplies went crashing everywhere.

"Oh, geez, now look at what you've done!" Scarlet snapped. "God, I hate you method actors! Sit back down and—"

But she didn't finish the sentence. She couldn't. The actor had his hands firmly around her throat, cutting off her air.

"BRAINNNS!!!"

Fear filled Scarlet as she struggled to free herself. This wasn't method acting; this guy had gone completely psycho! She struggled to pry his hands from her neck, but his grip proved too strong. Finally, realizing she had no other choice, she drew back her right leg, then kneed him in the groin, hard. As hard as she could.

The guy didn't even wince.

Uh-oh.

Her vision began to get spotty. She continued to struggle, but the extra's grip on her throat was too strong. He leaned in, one good eye wide and bloodshot. The other had fallen out again, leaving a black pit of decay . . . and up close, she realized this was no mask but a true and grotesque face.

He tried to bite her. She screamed, dodging just in time, and desperately clawed at her assailant's face. To her horror, the man's good eye popped out of its socket, connected by a thread of goo, sproinging like an activated jack-in-the-box. The guy scarcely seemed to notice. He continued choking her, and looked as though he was just about ready to have her for breakfast.

As her vision started to fade, the last thing she heard was, "Scarlet, is that you?"

Mason's eyes almost fell out of his head. There in front of

him was Scarlet, and she was being attacked by an extra, just as he'd been attacked the previous night. It was as though everyone had gone insane and this cheesy damn horror movie had come to life. As if that could possibly happen.

He dove forward, yanking the extra away just as the guy tried to chomp Scarlet's arm. She crashed to the floor. The man turned, rotten zombie mouth twisted in a scowl. His mask's eyes were black, sightless pits.

"BRAAAAINNSSS!" the guy moaned. God, Mason was tired of actors getting too into their parts.

He threw a punch, fist making contact with the extra's nose. There was a sickening crunch and gore splooshed out, dousing the actor's face and shirt. But the man was unfazed. He wore a crazed expression, just as the guy had the night before. Mason wondered if the nutjob could see anything through his bloody-eyeholes mask.

The extra clearly could see—or hear—enough to keep coming. Mason punched him again and again. Unlike yesterday, this crazed actor didn't regain his sanity. Maybe the PCP buzz was lasting even longer? Mason realized there was only one thing left to try.

With a side kick, he sent his assailant flying backwards to the far end of the trailer, and he pulled out his gun. He'd found it in his luggage last night, and now he was glad he'd taken the time to do so. He silently thanked his agent. "Stop right there or I'll fucking shoot you!"

The extra kept coming.

Mason swallowed hard and aimed for the guy's leg, hands shaking. He had to force himself to squeeze the trigger. He'd shot a billion fake guns in his storied career, but this was the first time he'd fired for real. It was tougher than he'd imagined. He didn't even want to think about the lawsuit that might be headed his way. Would he ever be able to explain how this dude had jumped him and Scarlet and then not given up? Would anyone believe the story about this rash of PCP abuse among low-budget horror actors? Why had this never been reported?

The crazed extra's thigh muscle exploded as Mason's bullet hit; the wall behind him was spattered by a burst of crimson. Bone was showing. The extra stopped in his tracks . . . then took another step forward, clearly not going to stop.

"BRAAINNNNS . . ." he moaned.

No kidding, Mason thought. *You could definitely use some. That's gonna smart when the drugs wear off.*

At least he'd slowed the guy down. Mason turned and found Scarlet dragging herself to her feet, face chalk white, eyes as big as saucers. She shook her head as if to clear it, staring at their assailant in shock. Mason could see angry red marks on her neck from where the guy had choked her, and it was all he could do not to shoot the crazed actor in the head right then and there.

"We need to get out of here, Scarlet," he shouted. "We need to find security. Now!"

She didn't react.

He grabbed her hand, startling her out of her trance and dragging her from the trailer. The already broiling morning sun beat down, and apart from his own sweat Mason caught a whiff of dirt and decay in the air. Behind him, he could hear the crazy extra shuffling after them.

The security trailer was close to the ghost-town film set. He and Scarlet ran toward it, weaving through the maze of residence trailers, looking for anyone else, cast or crew, but the whole place seemed weirdly deserted.

"Where is everybody?" Scarlet asked, evidently thinking the same thing. Usually the area was bustling with production guys.

Mason furrowed his brow, looking everywhere. "Still in bed, maybe? It's only seven o'clock . . ."

"But Romeo said we were starting early." Scarlet frowned. "This all just seems . . . wrong."

It did indeed. But Mason didn't know what the hell was going on. "Come on, we need to get to security. I . . . I could have shot that guy again, but I didn't think it'd be right. When whatever he's on wears off . . ."

Scarlet shuddered and nodded. "I still can't believe he just attacked me like that. Thank goodness you had a gun."

Mason silently agreed, though he was sort of sickened at having had to use it. Funny, that he'd react like that after killing so many people and monsters in all the movies he'd made. But he hadn't had a choice. This extra had been nuts. And so had the guy last night. And the dude who'd tried to choke him on camera the other day. Jesus, had all the extras gone crazy? His PCP theory explained the guys' almost supernatural strength, but . . . He decided not to discuss it with Scarlet. She seemed freaked out enough as it was.

They reached the security trailer. The door was open. In fact, upon closer examination, Mason saw it had been ripped off its hinges entirely. Fighting back incredulity, he followed Scarlet inside.

"Oh my god!" she cried, grabbing his arm. Her fingers dug into his flesh.

The place had been ransacked. It looked as if it had been overrun by wild dogs searching for a hidden steak. The rug was shredded, all the coffee mugs cracked, and the security monitors were smashed. File cabinets lay horizontal on the floor, folders spilling everywhere. The guts of the satellite phone were strewn everywhere.

But the mess wasn't what had Mason truly scared; it was the bodies at the back of the trailer. Two security guards lay sprawled on the floor. One's skull was ripped open. His brain was missing. The other's guts were torn out.

Brains? Mason immediately recalled the guy in the makeup trailer. And the one last night. *Braiinnnnss.*

Shit.

Scarlet staggered backward, bending over and retching. His own stomach seeking the same relief, Mason grabbed her hair and held it out of her face. He had to stay strong. For her. And for himself. Whatever the hell was going on here, he needed to figure out a way to get them out. Get her to safety. That was all that mattered now.

He spun about the trailer, gun locked and loaded, searching for any sign of remaining trouble. He found nothing. Whatever had attacked the security guards seemed long gone. He sucked in a breath, pushing his fear deep down inside, then led Scarlet over to a chair and helped her sit down to regain her composure.

"Are you okay?" he asked, holstering his gun. He knelt in front of her and took her hand. She was shaking like a leaf, and tears stained her beautiful face.

"What's going on?" she shrieked. "It's as if the movie's really happening!"

He nodded, not knowing what else to do. "We've got to get help. We've got to find the others and get to safety." The words were cheesy to his ears, but he had to admit they were better than Romeo George's script.

"But what . . . ?" Scarlet paused, then quavered, "W-what if they're all dead? Like these guys?" She pointed at the corpses.

Mason swallowed hard. "Then we'll find a way to get the hell out of here alone."

"The supply boat won't be coming 'til two. That's seven hours from now. It's already like a hundred degrees out, and there's no shelter anywhere else on the island. But we can't stay here. Not with those crazy . . . guys running around."

"We'll just—"

A loud noise outside cut off Mason's reply—which was good, since he didn't really have a solution. "Wait here," he instructed, drawing his gun. He inched to the door and peered out. To his horror, he saw the eyeless extra limping toward the ghost-town set, a trail of blood in his wake.

And it was worse: he'd found some friends.

Mason stared out of the trailer, unable to believe his eyes. There had to be a dozen zombie extras out there, lurching here and there, moaning piteously. It was clearly some kind of joke. Seeing his movie falling apart, Romeo had decided to film a bizarre new scene at the last minute. It was either that or things were just as Scarlet had claimed: this awful movie had become a reality.

Scarlet screamed. Mason whirled, gun raised. He almost dropped it when he saw the threat. Namely, one very-dead security officer crawling toward her, face bloated, eyes bloodshot, teeth bared.

"BRAINSSSS!" the zombie groaned.

Yes, it was a zombie; Mason no longer could deny the truth. And the monster reached out for Scarlet with stubby fingers.

Mason slammed his foot into the guard's chest, kicking the monster as hard as he could away from Scarlet. The creature crashed against the far wall and fell. Then Mason raised his gun and aimed. At its head. That was the money shot when it came to zombies, according to the movies. At least, according to Romeo George's script.

Shit.

He didn't miss. The bullet struck the zombie in the forehead, and gore exploded out the back of the thing's skull. The guard collapsed to the floor, body twitching for a moment; then the corpse fell silent, clearly having lost all animation.

Mason let out a breath and lowered his gun. He turned to Scarlet, who was staring at him, wide-eyed. "He . . . he tried to," she babbled. "But he was . . ."

"Dead. Yes," Mason agreed. He closed the distance between them and pulled her into a hug. She burrowed her face in his shoulder and he could feel her heart beating wildly in her chest. An overwhelming feeling of protectiveness washed over him. No matter what happened to him, he would keep her safe.

She pulled free. "We have to get out of here. In case . . ." She gave a nervous glance at the second guard.

Mason didn't think the second guard would be an issue, seeing as his brains had already been eaten. But there *was* a problem they had to face. "Right. But, um, there's a bit of a complication," he admitted.

Scarlet blanched. "Complication?"

He motioned for her to follow. At the doorway, he peeked out and pointed to where the group of zombies milled. For some reason, the gunshot hadn't alerted them, as he'd feared it would. He prayed his luck and Scarlet's would hold out.

Her jaw dropped. "Oh my god," she whispered. "There must be a dozen of them. What are we going to do?"

Mason's mind raced. What would someone in a horror movie do?

"Well, um . . . first I need to go to my trailer and get Chico," he told her. "I can't leave him behind as zombie bait," he added apologetically. After all, the little guy was his best friend, and you didn't leave your best friend behind. Not ever. Not even in a zombie apocalypse. In fact, if those creatures touched even a hair on the little guy's head, Mason was going to single-handedly take down—to borrow a line from his last movie, *Mad Matt 5: Even More Pissed Off*—"every last muth-erfuckin' one of them."

"Then we'll head over to Romeo's trailer," he suggested. "Maybe he keeps a second satellite phone there, and we can call for the supply boat to come early. I thought I heard him say he kept one there." He didn't bring up the fact that the director's trailer was on the other side of the set, past all the damn zombies.

Scarlet just nodded, not protesting the long walk or the dog rescue. Her face, however, was still white as a ghost.

Mason grabbed her and turned her to face him, massaging her shoulders and trying to keep her calm. He locked her gaze with his own. "Don't worry. We're going to get out of here," he told her. "No matter what."

"No matter what," she repeated. Her scared expression slowly morphed to one of determination. Good girl.

"After all, I'm Mason Marks," he pointed out, giving her one of his cocky, trademark smiles. "I always get the happy ending."

Chapter Five

"Okay, stay close to me," Mason instructed, as they stepped out of the security trailer. They had waited until all the zombies had shuffled out of view, then decided to make a break for it. She bumped up against his back as he suddenly stopped.

Even as frightened as she was, Scarlet couldn't help being a little turned on. Maybe it was the adrenaline, or maybe it was that Mason exuded masculinity from every pore. He had his gun raised and ready, and he truly looked like an action hero. But . . . what did that make her in this little zombie film come to life? Was she the damsel in distress? Or was she the tough sidekick who could kick a little ass?

Oh, let's face it. She was no kick-ass heroine. Hell, she was probably the stupid girl who lost her shirt early in the movie and had to run around the rest of the film in only a bra. Damn it, why hadn't she worn a nicer bra? She had that pretty green one with—

She shook her head, forcing herself to concentrate. Whatever was going on here, whether it was really zombies or some other insanity, two men were already dead. She'd been attacked twice, and there was no quick way off the island. What had Romeo George been thinking when he chose this godforsaken place? Epic fail, on so many levels.

She turned back to Mason.

". . . I'm going to walk a few steps ahead," he was saying. "If you see anyone—and I mean *anyone*, even if it's someone you know—let me know, even if you have to scream. And don't let them bite you."

"Because I'll get infected and turn into a zombie?" she asked. She almost couldn't believe it. Almost.

Mason shrugged. "I don't know," he admitted. "But we're better safe than sorry, don't you think?"

She *did* think so. Remembering those guards: that brainless corpse and the other somehow come to life . . . Thank god Mason had shown up at the makeup trailer when he had; otherwise she might have found herself either eaten or wandering around with a severely diminished vocabulary.

Mason beckoned for her to follow, and he flattened his body against the trailer to inch his way forward. When he got to the edge, he peered around the corner. A small group of zombies had congregated just beyond, in a clearing. They were facing each other and groaning, not doing much else. He slowly stuck his hand out and waggled his fingers. None of the zombies seemed to notice. He made the motions a little more exaggerated. Still nothing.

Drawing a deep breath, he took Scarlet's hand in his. He lifted his pistol and flexed his other hand around it. Then, after turning to give her a meaningful glance, he tugged on Scarlet's hand and they made a dash for the next trailer. Their luck held. The zombies didn't seem to have noticed.

"Hmmm. I wonder if they're nearsighted," Mason remarked in a low voice. "Maybe they were buried without their glasses?"

Scarlet snorted. "Do you know how crazy you sound?"

He leveled a quelling look at her. "You got anything better, you let me know."

It was quieter on the other side of the second trailer, away from the teeming mass of monsters they'd just run past. Scarlet used the opportunity to take a deep breath, wondering how long they could keep up this game of hide-and-seek.

Mason studied her. "Are you all right?" he asked.

His voice was thick with concern, so she nodded wordlessly, grateful for his patience. Grateful to have him by her side. After all, when it came to monster-hunting, you couldn't ask for anyone better than Mason Marks, action hero extraordinaire. Even if he *was* a womanizing jerk in real life.

She set her chin, determined. "Let's go get Chico."

The sun beat down on them as they circled the perimeter of the residence trailers, soaking Scarlet with sweat. She looked longingly out into the ocean, praying for some sign of rescue. A boat. A Jet Ski. Something, *anything* that might mean an escape from this deathtrap. But no. There was nothing but blue-green water stretching out to infinity. She and Mason were on their own.

"Scarlet!" Mason's urgent tone snapped her back to reality. He'd stopped in his tracks. Following his gaze, her eyes fell upon a lone man limping toward them.

Her mouth dropped open when she recognized the Armani loafers. "Derek?" she cried. "Oh my god!" She ran toward him, heart in her throat. Tears of relieved happiness began streaming down her cheeks. "I thought you were—"

She was jerked backwards as Mason caught her by the shirt.

She spun, scowling. "What the heck are you doing? That's Derek. My best friend."

Mason raised an eyebrow. "Is it?" he asked. "Or is he one of them?"

A jolt of horror stabbed through her, and she turned back to take another look. *One of them?* That was ridiculous. Derek couldn't be a zombie. Mason was just paranoid.

Her trembling hands clenched into fists as she studied her friend more closely. Sure, he looked a little bit pale, but he didn't look like the others. They'd had flesh hanging from their bones, and maggots and stuff . . .

Unfortunately, just as she opened her mouth to argue that Derek was fine, her friend went and proved he was nothing of the sort; he made an almost superhuman lurch forward. Mason fired, but the shot only struck Derek's shoulder, releasing a spray of blood. Derek slapped at Mason's gun, which skittered to rest several feet away. Scarlet watched, paralyzed with shock as her two friends began a wrestling match of life and death.

"Derek, stop!" she cried when her friend started choking Mason. "You're hurting him!"

Oddly, Derek—who, despite being a horror movie fan, was usually quite the pacifist—seemed to have lost a bit of his Quaker mentality.

"Scarlet!" Mason gurgled. "My gun!"

Scarlet leapt for the weapon, grabbing and pointing it in Derek and Mason's direction. Her hands were shaking. Tears flowed freely down her face as she tried to reconcile herself with what Mason wanted. Because . . . what if Derek really wasn't a zombie? What if he was just pissed off about being shot in the shoulder? That seemed natural. Didn't it?

"Scarlet!" Mason cried.

"Derek! Please!" she begged, praying with all her might that her friend would come to his senses. "Can we talk about this? I really, *really* don't want to have to shoot you. After all, you're my best friend. Who am I going to bitch about my loser boyfriends with? Who's going to split my sweet-potato fries back in LA? You know that my thighs can't take a full serving . . ." She broke off, too choked up to continue.

Derek stopped choking Mason for a moment, looking over at her with his big brown eyes. For a split second she thought she saw something there, some glimmer of remaining humanity, but then his eyes clouded over and Derek—her best friend, Derek—vanished. He was nothing but monster. That monster bared bloody teeth and tried to bite Mason's arm.

"Scarlet, it's not your friend anymore," Mason begged, desperately squirming to stay clear of Derek's jaws. "It's a monster. You need to shoot him now."

Scarlet knew he was right. There would be time to mourn her friend later. She had to put Derek out of his misery now.

"On the count of three, I'm going to flip him over," Mason said. "You shoot as soon as you have a clear shot." He gritted his teeth, clearly straining with every ounce of his strength. "One, two . . ."

On three, he swung his body, the sudden force carrying Derek off balance. The zombie lost his grip and went one way; Mason rolled the other.

"Now!" Mason cried.

Scarlet squeezed the trigger. Derek's head exploded in a mass of gore.

Scarlet collapsed to the ground, sobbing, and Mason was immediately by her side. "It's okay," he soothed.

"It's not okay!" she cried. "I just killed my best friend!"

"Come on." Mason pulled her to her feet. "We're right by my trailer."

She allowed him to lead her up the metal stairs and through the front door, his strong arm wrapped securely around her waist. A moment later she was once again surrounded by posters of old-time Hollywood heavy hitters. She sucked in a small, shaky breath. The smiles of John Wayne and Clint Eastwood somehow made her feel a bit more at ease, just as they had the night before. So did the scent of freshly brewed coffee, which lingered in the air. Had Mason just been having breakfast less than half an hour ago? He must have been.

Exhaling loudly, Scarlet eased herself down on the couch, watching Mason search the trailer and secure all windows and doors. Air conditioning blew gently on her skin, turning sweat to ice.

A scratching at the bedroom door jerked her back to attention. *Oh god, more zombies?* She looked fearfully at Mason, but to her surprise he just laughed.

"Not a zombie," he told her. "Just one pissed-off pup." He walked over to the door and pulled it open.

Chico burst through, bouncing excitedly from Mason toward Scarlet and back to Mason again, then heading over to investigate his food bowl to see if someone had deposited a steak while he had been cooped up in the bedroom. Sadly, no one had.

The dog looked up at Mason and barked hopefully. His master scooped him up and squeezed him tightly in his arms.

"Good boy," he murmured. "What a good boy." Scarlet heard Mason's voice crack on the last word, and she had no remaining doubt—if she'd ever harbored any—that the actor loved his dog unconditionally. Too bad he wasn't as unswerving with his women.

Still, she was glad Chico was safe. Even if her own best friend wasn't.

"Derek," she whispered. "I'm so sorry."

Mason sat down beside her. His dog, which he'd released, circled three times on the couch, then curled up in a ball.

Mason ran a hand up and down Scarlet's back, soothing her with slow strokes. "Don't beat yourself up," he said. "That wasn't Derek; that was a monster. A zombie. If you hadn't shot him, he would have killed me." He swallowed hard, then continued: "You saved my life, Scarlet."

Her eyes met his beautiful blue ones. She'd stared at those eyes on the big screen for years, longing for the time that Mason Marks might look at her in just the way he did right now: with kindness and affection. And with concern.

Still stroking her back, he lifted his other hand to brush tears from her cheek. His touch was warm and soothing, and she felt herself relax. "It's going to be okay," he was murmuring. He scooted closer.

He ran a finger over her lips, and she shivered. She shouldn't feel so turned on. They were in a freaking zombie apocalypse, for goodness sake. But at the same time, it felt good to let go of her fear and sorrow, if only for a moment. To feel something as normal and natural as desire. A desire she'd felt almost her entire life.

Mason evidently felt the same. He leaned in, pressing his lips lightly against hers. Cool tingles crept through her, and she sighed into his mouth. He took the invitation to press his advantage, his tongue slowly tasting, exploring, worshiping, and a sudden need overtook her. Scarlet found herself kissing him back, feverish, desperate for his mouth to make her forget the death and horror outside, if only for a moment. It wasn't until his fingers grazed her breast that reality snapped back.

She pushed Mason away, scrambling angrily to her feet. "Stop it!" she cried. "What the hell are you doing?"

He stared up at her, his eyes glazed and confused. "What do you mean?" he asked, his voice husky with desire. "Why can't I kiss you?"

"Why? *Why?*" Fury oozed through her like molten lava. "Because you have a fucking girlfriend, that's why! Apparently one whom you've left to die."

She waited for an excuse. Guys always had excuses for cheating. Maybe he'd even be ballsy enough to play the "We're all going to die, so what does it matter?" card.

His answer surprised her. "Oh. You mean Cissy?" He shook his head. "I meant to tell you . . . I was planning to tell you . . . I mean, well . . . she's not my girlfriend."

Scarlet narrowed her eyes, scoffing. "Oh, let me guess: You broke up. She just doesn't know it yet." As if she were going to fall for *that* one.

"No! Goddamn it, Scarlet, we were never together," Mason blurted, frustratedly running a hand through his hair. "It was all a fucking scam. To sell movie tickets."

What? Scarlet stared, pretty sure her mouth was hanging open. "Wait. What? A *scam?*" she repeated.

Mason sucked in a breath. "About a year ago, the studio approached Cissy's agent and then mine. They wanted to make a deal. Apparently, test audiences liked the idea of us together in real life. Cissy's agent took care of the particulars, and . . . well, I accepted a lump sum to pretend we were dating. I agreed to attend award shows with her, get caught making out in clubs. We'd break up a few times, make up a few times—it would sell a bunch of tabloids, and it would all culminate in the release of this movie."

"But that's . . . that's . . ."

"Crazy? Stupid? Yes. But it would help her career. And for me? Well, it was a lot of money."

She stared at him. "You're Mason Marks. You need more?"

He flushed bright red, dropping his head and staring at the ground. For a moment, she thought he wasn't going to answer. "I was broke," he said at last. "My old manager emptied my bank account and took off for Acapulco. Left me with a pile of debts and no liquid assets."

"But I thought your manager was your father."

He looked up at her, silent.

"Oh." *Wow.*

"Yeah," Mason muttered. His grin had lost some of its cockiness. "Anyway, both Cissy and I were broke. She'd just gotten out of rehab after putting most of her life savings up her nose. Since neither of us was seeing anyone else . . ." He shrugged sheepishly. "I guess it just seemed like a good idea at the time."

Scarlet struggled to understand. "So . . . you were never with her?"

"You mean, did I ever have sex with her?" he asked, then swore under his breath. "Hell, no. I wouldn't touch that skanky bitch with a ten-foot pole."

"But you always left those clubs together, and you'd go back to the same place . . ."

"We'd have the limo drive around and lose the photogs, then they'd take us to our respective homes," he explained. "Hell, I've never even seen the inside of Cissy's house, let alone Cissy naked." He shuddered. "Well, except for that time my cousin rented *Poison Ivy Five* and I walked in at just the wrong moment. Took days for my eyes to recover, let me tell you." He gave Scarlet a sheepish grin.

"Oh my god." Scarlet sank down in a chair. "So you've been lying to everyone this whole time."

"You have to believe that I wanted to tell you," Mason said. "I've wanted to tell lots of people, but with the contract the way it is . . . Well, I'm sure you can imagine. The other night, out there on the beach . . . I haven't wanted anyone as much as I wanted you—not for a long time. I would have explained, but I wasn't sure I could trust you. After all, my whole life has been filled with people ripping me off: My mom, signing me up into child-star slavery; my friends selling personal, embarrassing stories to the highest-bidding tabloid. And my dad . . ." He choked. "I had to spend every last penny making sure everything stayed out of the paper. It was just too embarrassing to admit my own father had betrayed me, too. Just like every-fucking-one else."

Scarlet stared into his eyes, trying to determine if he was telling the truth. Her heart said yes. And while Mason Marks was a hell of a dancer and an action star, he wasn't the world's best actor. She had a feeling she'd know if he were lying.

She swallowed the lump in her throat. She couldn't imagine living such a difficult life. No wonder he always acted like a cocky hard-ass: Whenever he let down his guard, it ended up on Page Six.

"Thank you for putting your trust in me," she said quietly. "I promise you I'll never take advantage."

He looked up. "I believe you. That paparazzo came and talked to me last night. He was pissed you wouldn't spill, and he tried to trick me into giving something away."

"Oh." She giggled nervously, pleased that her instincts had paid off. Remembering the slimy guy with the camera offering cash to spill secrets about Mason just made her angry. "I didn't realize he'd . . ."

"No, I'm sure you didn't. Which is why I'm all the more grateful. At first I was sure you'd told him everything, despite what you'd said about makeup artists keeping secrets. I would have deserved it, too, after kissing you without explaining my situation. You probably thought I was a total jerk."

She gave a small smile. "Something like that," she admitted. "But still, your secrets aren't mine to tell."

"Not everyone feels that way, let me tell you. But now I know I can trust you," Mason replied. "And so I'm telling you now: I'm done living this lie. I *like* you. And I'm not going to hide it anymore. If—no, *when*—we survive all of this and get back to Hollywood, I'm going to invite you to the biggest, showiest premiere I can find and walk the red carpet with you, hand in hand, doing interviews with every reporter I see. I'll let each and every one of them know I've finally found someone special." He gave her a shy grin. "What's the worst that can happen—I'll lose all the money I've made off the deal? There are worse things in life than being poor."

He looked at her with adoring eyes, and she found herself unable to speak.

"What do you say, Scarlet?" Mason asked, his voice husky. "It's not easy to date me, what with all the stupid tabloids, but will you give it a try? I'll try to be everything you deserve."

"I've loved you since I was twelve," she blurted in reply, feeling ridiculous but relieved at the same time. "I watched every *Trey Rey: Singing Trackstar* sequel a thousand times. I had Mason Marks bedsheets so I could sleep next to you every night of the week. And now . . . now I see you're even better than I imagined."

He burst into laughter, grabbing her and dragging her close. His strong arms squeezed her lovingly, and she felt as though her heart was going to explode. She felt Chico licking his master's fingers and also her back and arms, apparently unwilling to be left out of the action.

"Awww, Scarlet," Mason murmured, running his fingers through her hair and causing her whole body to tingle. "I'll sleep next to you any night you ask."

Chapter Six

If this were a film, Mason grumbled to himself, the zombies would have stood around offscreen and waited patiently while he took Scarlet in his arms and made mad, passionate love to her. It was not a film, however, and the zombies seemed not particularly patient. They didn't break into his trailer, but they kept passing by outside, moaning and groaning, and it was surprising how much of a mood-killer it was to hear slouching noises along with an unholy chorus of "*Brainssss*." For that reason, after some way-too-brief kissing, Mason reluctantly unwrapped himself from Scarlet and suggested they continue on to find Romeo George's satellite phone. Scarlet, seeming just as reluctant, agreed.

They left the trailer, Chico securely strapped to his back in a custom pack Mason sometimes used when hiking with the pooch. The dog squirmed a bit, but thankfully didn't whine or bark too much. After all, the last thing Mason needed was his own pet calling attention to them.

First they checked Cissy's trailer, because he couldn't reconcile himself to leaving her for dead. He felt a moment of relief when there was no one inside, not wanting to cart the celebutante around, then a moment of shame for having indulged his meaner instincts. Praying Cissy was somehow finding her own way to safety, he and Scarlet returned to their original plan.

They had to make their way across the town square to the director's trailer. Mason glanced at Scarlet as they crept onto the set, keeping hold of her hand. No matter what happened, they were in this together. Her trembling fingers clutched his tightly, but her expression betrayed no fear. She was brave. Most of the girls he'd known would have cracked. Cissy would have been shrieking her fool head off.

As for himself . . . Well, even in the face of this nightmare, he had to admit that he felt almost exuberant. A huge weight had been lifted from his shoulders, knowing he'd never have to go back to pretending about a relationship he couldn't stand. He couldn't wait to get Scarlet to safety so he could properly demonstrate just how much he liked her. The way he imagined it, this would involve a lot of time spent naked, without any fear of interruption by zombies or paparazzi. A very good reason to stay alive, indeed.

As they inched into the square, Mason's eyes widened with shock. Cissy? She was casually hanging out by the fountain in a pair of Daisy Dukes, a tank top, and high heels. Didn't she realize the danger? Or had she already turned into one of the undead horde?

"Cissy?" he called, clutching his gun in a sweaty grip. "What are you doing out here?"

His alleged girlfriend looked up, noticing him for the first time, and scowled. She hopped off the fountain and approached. "Where the hell *is* everyone?" she demanded, hands on her hips. "We were supposed to start my scene fifteen minutes ago. I checked the schedule twice."

An overpowering cloud of floral scent washed over Mason; Cissy had clearly been a bit self-conscious about the heat and the smell of her own sweat. Which meant she wasn't a zombie. But evidently, she was completely oblivious about what was going on. "Your scene?" he repeated. "You want to film at a time like this?"

"Well, duh. You may like hanging out on this deserted island for the rest of your life, but I have reservations at Mr. Chow's next week. I want this movie over so I can get the hell off this rock." She rolled her eyes. "Of course, I can't find anyone important. The only people wandering around are extras."

"But they're not—" Scarlet started to say.

Cissy glanced over, seeming to see her for the first time. Her eyes narrowed as they took in that Scarlet and Mason were holding hands. "What the hell is this?" she demanded.

Mason swallowed, hard. Here went nothing. He lifted Scarlet's hand and said, "Cissy, I'd like you to meet my girl-friend . . . Scarlet."

"What?" Cissy cried. "She can't be your girlfriend. *I'm* your girlfriend. We have a . . ." She paused, looking suspiciously at Scarlet. "We have a thing. Remember?"

"She knows about the contract, Cissy," Mason admitted. "And when we get back to LA, I'm going to break it." God, it felt so good to say that aloud. To be free.

Cissy's face twisted with rage. "I'm going to sue your ass off, Mason Marks," she swore. "You traitor! You'll be sorry you ever even met me!"

Mason felt Scarlet squeeze his hand, but she said nothing. The quiet gesture of solidarity gave him courage to continue. "I'm sorry, Cissy," he said calmly. "But I'm done living a lie." He paused, then added, "Come on, you should come with us to Romeo's trailer. It's not safe out here. We're trying to—"

"Are you kidding me?" Cissy interrupted. "I wouldn't go anywhere with *you*, asshole. Have fun slumming it with your fat-ass girlfriend." She turned and rushed off toward her trailer.

His ex was fast in high heels, and before Mason could spin and retort, she'd reached the line of trailers. Unfortunately, three zombies jumped out of nowhere, staggering toward her, eyes wild and jaws dripping.

Mason raised his gun, but the monsters were too close to take a clean shot. "Run, Cissy!" he called out. "Get away from them!"

But Cissy stood her ground, evidently unfazed. She turned to the zombies, disdain written clearly across her face. "Ew," she snarled. "Go away. If you want an autograph, come back after you've taken showers. I swear, the people they have working this goddamn movie—"

Mason cringed. Cissy was dead for sure, and there was

nothing he could do about it. He turned his head and fought a wave of nausea, imagining his ex being torn limb from limb. While he'd considered it once or twice himself, he'd never really wished her any ill.

Scarlet's hand touched his forearm. "Mason, look!" she cried.

He forced himself to do just that. To his shock, Cissy was still there, in one piece, and the zombies were shuffling hurriedly in the other direction.

"How the hell . . . ?" he murmured. "Cissy, are you okay?" he called out.

The actress turned and looked back at him, her face filled with emotion. "Go away, Mason. I have nothing more to say to you." Then she sauntered off into the maze of trailers, quickly disappearing from sight.

"What the hell? Why didn't the zombies attack her?" Scarlet asked. She sounded as puzzled as Mason felt.

He shook her head. "I . . . I don't know. I mean, I'm glad they didn't, but—"

A noise behind them cut off Mason's reply. The three zombies who'd been focused on Cissy had somehow circled around and were now standing nearby, bloodshot eyes zeroed in on them. "BRAAAINNSS," one of them hissed.

"Ah, *that's* why they didn't attack her," Scarlet commented. Then: "Sorry, that was mean. But she did call me a fat ass."

Mason's laugh was cut short as the other two zombies joined the first. "BRAAAINSS," they chorused. All three took a step forward.

"Let's get out of here," Scarlet said.

Mason didn't ask for a second invitation.

The first thing Mason noticed as he approached Romeo George's trailer was that it was a double-wide, twice as big as the trailer of any of the cast, and he wondered why he'd never been invited here before; he *was* the star of the picture. The second thing he noticed was that the front door had been ripped from its hinges.

"Romeo?" he cried, stepping cautiously into the darkened trailer and wondering if the director had already become a zombie's breakfast. "You in here, man?" Light filtered in from the door, just enough to make out the scene. The place was completely trashed. Overturned food bins, empty beer bottles, crumpled scripts—garbage was strewn in all directions.

"Is anyone here?" Scarlet asked, stepping in behind him. "Oh my god," she added, surveying the mess. "I guess the zombies got him."

"Not necessarily," Mason replied. "This is how Romeo kept his hotel room in LA. He lives a bit hard."

Kicking through the rubble, Mason searched for signs of life, praying those signs wouldn't turn out to be the undead. A sudden moaning came from behind them, and both Mason and Scarlet whirled. Scarlet pointed to the closed bathroom door.

"In there," she whispered, her eyes wide.

It wasn't a fuzzy white dog making the noise this time; Chico was still strapped to his back. Mason nodded, pulling out his gun and padding slowly toward the door, motioning for Scarlet to stand away. Taking a deep breath, he whipped it open.

"Argh! Don't shoot!" cried Romeo, tumbling out of the bathroom. He held his hands in the air. "It's only me!"

Mason lowered his gun, exhaling in relief. "You okay?" he asked.

The director scrambled to his feet, brushing off his jeans. "Just brilliant, mate," he replied. "As top-notch as anyone could be during a zombie outbreak."

"So you know about that," Scarlet said.

"Yes."

Romeo George looked surprisingly sheepish, and Mason narrowed his eyes. Something was going on here, something the director didn't want to admit. "Romeo," Mason said in a tight voice, "why have the extras turned into zombies?"

"Well," Romeo said, "technically they didn't."

"Didn't turn into zombies?" Mason growled, grabbing the

director by the shirtfront. "There's a guard with his brains chewed out in the security trailer. Scarlet just shot her best friend. The people who started this seem pretty goddamn zombielike to me!"

"Oh, well, er, they are," Romeo admitted meekly. "They just . . . well, they didn't just *turn into* them. They were zombies from the start. Technically. If we're going to be technical, I'm saying."

Mason stared at him, glowering, hands on hips. "I think you have some explaining to do, Mr. George."

The director sighed deeply, looking miserable. He walked over to the kitchenette and poured himself a shot of whisky. A large one. He tipped it back before answering. "Well," he said, clearing his throat. "It all started when that bastard executive producer completely chopped the hell out of my budget."

"Budget?" Scarlet interrupted. "What does a budget have to do with the living dead?"

Romeo padded over to a nearby chair, the bottle of whisky still in hand. He sat down. "I wanted a big film," he explained. "One that would get me more than just an annual invite to Fangoria's Weekend of Horrors. That meant I needed *lots* of zombies. I mean, anyone who knows anything about horror knows you can't have a good zombie film without a lot of zombies. More than ten, at least." He took a swig from the bottle, no longer bothering with the shot glass. "Unfortunately, the powers-that-be don't know anything. They refused my original budget. They actually told me I should work with half the number of zombie extras and just reuse the footage." He shook his head. "As if. Where would we get the believability if it's the same four zombies again and again? We'd have to rename the film *Island of Bill, Bob, Frank and Merwyn, Four Guys Who Come Back to Life and Get Shot Over and Over While Trying to Eat Brains*. Fucking ridiculous."

"Ohhhh-kay . . ." Mason's gut was starting to churn. "So what did you do?"

Romeo stared into space for a moment. "There's a company," he answered at last. "Dirt-Cheap-Labor-dot-com. It's a startup by this voodoo priestess who wasn't making enough moolah with the whole sticking-pins-into-dolls gig. I heard about it in a *CEO Magazine* I was reading, about how companies are reacting to the downturn in the economy." He shrugged. "A few years back, she started raising people from the dead and renting them out in bulk. She always chooses the freshest corpses, though they do eventually begin to deteriorate. They work for a few weeks, then go back to the grave. They're really popular with farmers at harvest time, as technically they're not illegal aliens, and also with those telethons for PBS. They're the ones manning the phones. Anyway," he continued, "these reanimated corpses are a lot cheaper than hiring living people, since you don't have to worry about pesky things like unions or SAG rates."

Mason and Scarlet exchanged shocked looks. He hadn't thought it was possible for the day to get any weirder. "So you're saying that the actors playing zombies are actually zombies."

"Very meta, right?" Romeo said. "I figured it'd get me points down the road with horror fans, once I revealed the truth. Imagine, a zombie film with real zombies! It'd be the first of its kind!"

Mason and Scarlet just glared at him, and his face fell.

"Anyway, I was told they would be completely under my control," Romeo continued. "And at first they were. As advertised, it was impossible to even tell they were corpses. I had Derek working overtime, making them look like what they were, and they acted just like the people they had been when alive. In their minds, they *were* still alive. The dead don't often remember their deaths, turns out." He smiled again, weakly. "Then, last week, while we were filming some of the action scenes . . . well, things started happening. It was small at first. They'd get a bit dazed, not following directions. You must remember. As the week went on, some started to get violent. Like Zombie Forty-three on the set a few days ago," he reminded Mason.

"And you figured it was perfectly okay for us to keep on working," Mason clarified.

The director hung his head. "You don't understand!" he cried. "This may just be another movie for you, Mason Marks, but it's my entire life. I leveraged my house to make this film. I took from my kids' college fund. If I don't finish it . . . I'll lose everything."

"Everything? Like . . . your brain and your life? Sort of like most of your crew? Like *Derek?*" Scarlet reminded him.

Romeo scrubbed his face with his hands. "You have to believe me," he moaned. "I never thought it would come to this. I mean, I read all the warnings in the contract and followed all the directions to the letter," he added. "Don't feed them after midnight. Don't get them wet."

"Are these zombies or gremlins?" Mason interjected.

Romeo gave him a look, then continued. "Don't let them taste blood . . ."

"Wait, what?" Scarlet interrupted, eyes wide. "'Don't let them taste blood'?"

"Yeah. I guess they're raised from the grave using organic, free-range chicken blood or something, and coming in contact with any other type of blood disrupts the control spell and sends them batty. But *trust* me, they didn't taste any blood. We made sure of it. The cook was even instructed to make sure every piece of meat served was super well-done."

"So that's why the food here sucked," Mason muttered.

"What about Derek's blood?" Scarlet asked quietly.

Mason glanced over at her, confused.

"What do you mean?" Romeo replied, sounding perplexed. "But that's just corn syrup and—"

Scarlet shook her head. Then she explained how she'd learned during an eleven-and-a-half-martini night about her friend's top-secret ingredient.

Romeo stared at her, eyes wide. "Are you serious?" he asked. "Derek uses pig blood? I'm going to kill him."

Scarlet flushed. Mason put a hand on her arm to comfort her.

"Oh god. I'm ruined," Romeo moaned. "I'm never going to finish my movie. And Priestess Bertha is never going to give me my deposit back when she finds out I inadvertently broke her rules."

Mason and Scarlet glanced at one another, incredulous.

"You're worried about your damn deposit?" Mason snarled. "We need to figure out a way to destroy these zombies before they kill anyone else. Before we get on that two o'clock supply boat." He rubbed his temples, trying to stop the throbbing in his head.

"We know that bullets to the brain work," Scarlet suggested.

Romeo snorted. "Sure, but unless you know about some secret, abandoned, yet surprisingly well-stocked army base out here in the middle of the island, I think we're out of luck with that. Mason's the only one with a real gun, and I'm guessing you're almost out of bullets."

Mason nodded.

Romeo George started laughing hysterically. "Why didn't I stock real bullets as well as real zombies? We're all doomed! We're all going to die, and I'm not going to get my money back."

"Snap out of it!" Mason growled, and he slapped the director across the face. It gave him a certain degree of satisfaction. Not enough, but it was a start.

The slap worked. Romeo calmed down—at least enough to think—and ran his hands through his hair. "Let me look at the contract I signed with Bertha," he said. "See if it says anything about emergency situations like this." He went to a briefcase, grabbed a stack of papers about a foot high, and started shuffling through them.

"What about the explosives?" Mason suddenly realized. "The ones you were going to use in the final scene?"

"But I need to save those for . . ." Romeo trailed off, seeing Scarlet and Mason's expressions. "Yes, I suppose we could rig them to blow up a building or something," he agreed, still a tad reluctantly. "But there's hardly enough to blow the whole set. Let's face it: unless that dog of yours is the next Babe, schooled in herding zombies, I don't think you're going to be able to wrangle them all into one place."

Mason snorted, reaching over to scratch Chico's head. The dog snorted back. "No, he's more of a dead-chicken herder than a zombie . . ." He trailed off, an idea hitting him with the force of a ten-ton truck.

"What?" Scarlet asked. "Did you think of something?"

Mason nodded. "All this week, the extras kept telling me Chico smelled really, really good, which I kept thinking was strange, since all he smelled like was that rotting chicken he'd been sneaking off to roll in."

"That's it!" Romeo cried, looking up. He waved the contract triumphantly. "It says here to keep the zombies far away from garbage dumps, because of the high danger of them going wild. Evidently the human brain—their preferred diet—tastes exactly like decomposing chicken!"

Mason clapped his hands. "So what we do is, we go out to that rotting chicken crate Chico found, gather up as much as we can, then pile it into one of the buildings. After the zombies go in after it, we blow it to smithereens."

"I can rig the building while you get the chickens," Romeo said excitedly. "And I can film the whole thing. I'll finish my movie yet!"

"Um, great," Scarlet said. "But . . . you guys are forgetting one thing."

"What's that?" Mason said.

"It's one thing when we can outrun the zombies, ducking from trailer to trailer. But carrying that bait, we're sitting ducks. Er, limping chickens. Er, you know what I mean. How are we going to get out there and back without some zombie seeing and jumping us? And if you don't have many bullets left . . ."

Mason thought for a moment, then crossed his fingers. "I've got an idea," he said. "Chico, you stay here. Scarlet, you're going to turn us into zombies."

* * *

Scarlet allowed herself to be dragged back toward Derek's makeup trailer, she and Mason freezing whenever a zombie shuffled anywhere in the distance, but she protested the entire way. "This isn't going to work," she whispered. "As I was trying to tell Romeo yesterday, I'm a terrible monster-makeup artist. I got fired from the Halloween Adventure Superstore last October after I made some kid wanting to be Dracula into a circus clown. Not to mention that gore makes me barf. They only hired me here because they were desperate for a warm body." In hindsight, she recognized how desperate. "The only thing I can do is *people*, and not always those well. I'm practically a beauty school dropout. And—"

Mason pulled her into the trailer and sat her down on the couch. Her eyes misted a little as she looked around, seeing her friend's stuff strewn all about the room. If only Derek were still alive; he would make them into kickass zombies that even a voodoo priestess would believe. But Derek was dead, and since their lives depended on her subpar skills, they would likely be joining him very, very soon. It was as if a dam had broken; she felt a terror that she'd fought down all morning rising in her.

"Come on," Mason cajoled. "What's the worst that can happen?"

Scarlet gave a hysterical sob. "The worst that can happen? This is the toughest challenge ever! I'm not making us up for some dumb audience who *wants* to believe; I'm trying to fool the undead. This makeup has to look perfect or those zombies will see through our disguise and eat us for lunch!"

"They'll do that anyway if you don't make us up," he reminded her. "This way, at least we have a shot. Right?"

"You don't understand," she said, staring up at him with pleading eyes. "I can't do this. I'm not any good. I'll get us killed."

"I don't believe that," Mason replied.

"Well, you should. I'm a disappointment to the profession. My grandmother would be ashamed."

"Please." Mason shook his head, and he kissed her cheek.

His stubble was rough against her skin. "You don't lack talent. Just self-confidence. You don't believe in yourself." He cupped her chin in his hand and tilted her head up so that she was forced to meet his stare. "But that's okay," he told her. "Because I have enough belief for the both of us. I just found you, and I'm not letting us get killed. You won't let us get killed, either."

He leaned over and kissed her firmly on the mouth. She found herself clinging to him, soaking in his confidence as their mouths tangled. The bliss went on and on, routing the darkness and keeping it at bay.

At last, Mason pulled back, leaving Scarlet's lips pleasantly buzzing. Searching her face with hopeful eyes, he asked, "How do you feel now?" His mouth quirked into a small grin. "You know, now that I've infused you with a grand dose of Mason-Marks-style ego?"

She laughed; she couldn't help it. "Um, like I'm the best makeup artist evahhh?" she replied. "Like we're going to kick every one of those muthafuckin' zombies' behinds?"

He ruffled her hair and laughed. "That's my girl. Now let's make me into a monster."

He hopped into the main chair, and Scarlet gathered up Derek's paints. Some of his supplies had clearly been chewed by roaming zombies, but there still seemed to be enough usable to do the job.

She studied Mason's face for a moment, then added a primer of white. Her hands were still a little shaky. After all, everything—including their very lives—rode on what she was doing now. But as she worked, she looked down at Mason, into his beautiful, clear blue eyes, searching for the tiniest speck of doubt . . . but it wasn't there. He truly believed in her and her ability to keep them alive.

She let the job overtake her. A scar here, a bloody nose there. Soon she was so engrossed in her work that she forgot to be stressed out and worried. A half hour later, she stepped back and studied Mason's face. *Wow. Not bad,* she realized.

Not bad at all. Derek would be totally impressed. She herself wanted to vomit.

"Let me see!" Mason said, grabbing a handheld mirror off the dresser. He recoiled when he saw. "Damn!" he swore. "I *do* look like a freaking zombie!" He looked up at her with grateful eyes. "You did it," he said. "I knew you could."

When he rose to his feet to try to kiss her, she pushed him away, grimacing. "You're going to smudge all your makeup," she protested with a laugh.

"It'd be worth it." He grinned and handed her the mirror. "Your turn. Can you do yourself?"

"You know what? I think I can."

With renewed confidence, she sat down in the chair and started her own zombie transformation. Now that she'd practiced on Mason, she knew exactly what to do.

"Wow. You're disgusting," Mason said, when she showed him the finished product fifteen minutes later. "Good thing I know you smell and taste better than you look."

"As long as the zombies don't," she shot back playfully. Then her eyebrows rose and she exclaimed, "But there's one more thing we both need."

"If you say that eye-maggot mask over there, I'm going to smack you."

Scarlet shook her head. "Not exactly. Follow me."

Chapter Seven

"Cissy?" The starlet's trailer door was locked and unmolested, which had surprised both Mason and Scarlet. "Are you in there?"

Silence and then: "Um, go away?"

"Cissy, let us in!" Mason boomed. "Or I'm going to break down the door."

They heard a shuffling, and a moment later the door swung open, revealing Cissy dressed in a short bathrobe. She took one look at the two of them and screamed, slamming the door in their faces.

Mason pounded again. "Cissy, it's just us. Me and Scarlet."

"Sorry!" she called back. "You'll have to try somewhere else. No brains here."

"I said that earlier," muttered Scarlet under her breath.

"We're not zombies, Cissy," Mason called through the door. "We're just made up to look like them so they don't attack us."

The door opened a crack. "Are you sure you're not zombies?"

"Very sure."

"What's pi squared? A zombie wouldn't know that."

"Neither would you, Cissy. Let us in."

"Oh, fine." The actress opened the door wide and ushered Mason and Scarlet inside. She turned to stare at them, hands on hips. "Now, what do you want?"

"Your perfume," Mason replied.

"My . . . what? You mean my Irresistible?" The celebutante stared at them. "Why the hell would you want my Irresistible?"

"Because it repulses zombies," Scarlet explained. "When we saw you before, those zombies took one sniff and ran in the other direction. I figured out what happened just a few minutes ago. We need something to mask our smells—and the smell of rotting chicken—until we get to the town hall."

Cissy seemed unfazed by the chicken comment, but was clearly intrigued about the perfume. "So that's why, when I went and took a shower, suddenly every extra in the place started trying to attack me."

Mason nodded.

Cissy grabbed a bottle from her dresser, wrenched off the cap and started pouring the perfume over her head.

"Hold it!" Mason cried, grabbing the bottle. It was too late; she'd already emptied it. "We needed some for *us*."

"Of course." Cissy wrenched the bottle back. She pulled open a dresser drawer stuffed with bottles of the same perfume. "Here, take what you need," she said. "I'll have my agent send you a bill."

"Thanks," Mason said, rolling his eyes. He grabbed a couple of bottles and stuffed them in his knapsack. "Don't worry, Cis, we have a plan. We're going to take some rotten chickens and—"

"Oh, I wasn't worried," she interrupted. "I'm just fine here, alone in my trailer."

A banging noise erupted from the next room.

"What was that?" Mason demanded, reaching for his gun.

"Um, nothing?" Cissy replied innocently. "I didn't hear a thing."

"Cissy, it could be a zombie!" Mason said. "I should check it out."

"No, you should n—"

Mason yanked open the door. Jesús the maintenance man stepped out, completely naked save for a thin towel wrapped around his waist. Mason had to admit the guy was cut.

"*Hola*, senor," Jesús said, wearing a self-satisfied smirk.

Mason stared at Jesús, then Cissy. Then back at Jesús.

Cissy shrugged. "So Jesús saved me—from the zombies, that is. I was surrounded, and he showed up and kicked the shit out of each and every one of them." She glanced over at the maintenance man with lovey-dovey eyes. "My hero. And he's a monster in the sack," she added in a stage whisper.

Mason stared. "You two got to . . . ?" When he glanced at Scarlet, she flushed. Then he started laughing. He slapped Jesús on the back. "Good for you, man," he said. "Good for both of you."

"I, too, am an action star, senor," Jesús replied, brandishing a pistol of his own. "Just waiting for my big break."

"Well, maybe this is it," Mason agreed. "Since you can obviously take care of yourself, I need you to do me a favor. I need you to collect my dog."

When Cissy started to protest, he turned to her and said, "Only for about an hour. We couldn't bring him with us, and I don't want him with Romeo any longer than he has to be. It just isn't safe."

"Sorry, Chico," Mason muttered to himself, imagining his dog's face when collected by his arch nemesis. "We'll be back for you." He rose to his feet. "After we kick some mutherfuckin' zombie ass."

Scarlet steeled herself for what was to come.

"Okay, are you ready for this?" Mason asked, reaching over and squeezing her hand.

They stood at the perimeter of the ghost-town set. Beyond this point was open ground with no shelters or obstacles to hide behind. About half a dozen vacant-eyed zombies in tattered clothes wandered nearby, moaning softly. Scarlet recognized the cafeteria guy—and the makeup artist who'd supposedly run off! She really felt bad for them. They hadn't asked to be brought back from the dead, after all. And those extras who'd started this whole mess . . . to be exploited for no pay in one of the world's worst-written movies? In every way, destroying them was a mercy mission.

"I'm ready," she said. Ready as she'd ever be.

"Remember, for this to work we need them thinking we're exactly like them," Mason reminded her. "So watch them for a moment. See how they move? Slowly, unevenly. And they never run. We have to do the same. If one of them gets too close, just give them a quick squirt of Cissy's perfume. That should get them to back off. It always did me."

"No running, spray with perfume," Scarlet repeated. "Got it."

"And for god's sake be careful. Don't try to be a hero," he said, catching her eye. "Now that I've found you—now that I've got you in my life—the last thing I want is to lose you to some asshole zombie. I don't think we can have this end like *Shaun of the Dead*. Not with what I've got in mind for us."

She smiled, her heart squeezing at the thought of their future together. Reaching over, she brushed a lock of hair from his forehead. "That goes for you, too. Remember, you may be my hero, but this isn't scripted."

"Right. I'll try to channel Trey Rey instead of Max Ledd," he joked, naming two of his most famous roles. "Fast instead of furious."

She nodded. "That'll work. As long as Trey doesn't suddenly find himself overcome with the urge to break into a synchronized dance routine."

Mason grabbed her in a forceful hug, careful not to mess up their makeup. "God, I love you," he murmured in her ear. "It's crazy. We haven't known each other that long, but . . ."

"I've known you forever," she murmured, enjoying the warmth of his body. "I don't think it's crazy at all."

"Okay, let's do this," he said, releasing her from the hug. "Follow me."

He stepped out into the open, arms outstretched. Staggering a few steps forward, he moaned, "Brainnnns . . ." Scarlet would have laughed if so much hadn't been at stake. Mason

Marks was in the acting role of his career—even if the script was no better than usual. "BRAAAAAINNNNS."

He took a few steps more. And then a few more. Scarlet watched, breath stuck in her throat. Soon he was mere feet away from the wandering zombies, and to Scarlet's amazement, the creatures gave Mason a cursory glance and then went on their way.

It worked! Her makeup and Mason's acting were actually working! Now she had to follow suit.

Scarlet sucked in a breath and took her own step forward. Here went nothing.

"Brainnnnns . . ."

Chapter Eight

"I still can't believe that actually worked!" Scarlet exclaimed, helping Mason lug a final sack of rotten chickens into the town hall. "Those zombies didn't even give us the time of day."

"That's because you totally rock," Mason replied. "And because Cissy's perfume totally stinks. Your idea was positively brilliant."

She felt herself blushing with pride. "Thanks," she said. "My grandmother would be so proud. Maybe I have a career in movie makeup after all."

"Absolutely." Mason grabbed her and kissed her on the forehead. "Not to mention a career as my love slave."

"Oh, yeah?" Scarlet asked. "Does that pay well?"

He laughed. "It's more about the benefits."

She kissed him, hard. "Money isn't everything."

"Ahem. Not to destroy this touching moment, well scripted as it is . . ." Romeo George interrupted, walking into the room, film camera in hand. Mason and Scarlet reluctantly broke apart and turned to the director. "But we're all set with the explosives. So any time you want to start killing some zombies is fine with me."

"Okay," Mason replied. He glanced at Scarlet, who was holding a chicken sack. He picked up one of his own. "On the count of three, dump as much out of your bag as possible and run for the back. Take the bag with you, because we don't want the perfume we sprayed on it to dissuade any zombies from entering. Then, we'll turn on that fan to blow the smell out onto the island." They'd grabbed a couple of the industrial-sized production fans originally intended to cool down idle actors, and set them up strategically.

"Right," Scarlet agreed. She readied herself, adrenaline pumping through her body. But then she realized she wasn't as afraid as she'd been. Now she had Mason—and they were a good team.

"Okay, I'm going to head out and set up my shot," Romeo told them. "I'll find you after." He vacated the building.

Mason looked at Scarlet. She looked back at him. "One, two, THREE . . . !"

Scarlet flipped her bag. Slimy, slippery wings and legs and breasts spilled all over the ground. The stench overpowered her for a moment, but she forced herself to swallow down her sick and keep going. Once the bag was completely empty, she glanced over at Mason. He nodded and hit the button for the fan.

"Let's get the hell out of here."

They ran through the building, out the back door, then made like zombies, staggering until they were about a hundred feet away. "We should be good here," Mason announced, stopping and turning. He raised a hand to his eyes to block out the sun. "Are they coming?" he asked.

"Look, there they are!" Scarlet squealed, pointing to a parade of zombies, moaning and shuffling toward the town hall. The chorus of "Braaainnnsss" was nearly deafening. "It's working!" she cried excitedly. "It's really working!"

Mason squeezed her hand and snorted. "Hope Romeo gets his shot," he said, waving toward the director who had positioned himself on a riser about fifty feet away, detonator in hand, camera on a tripod. "'Cause this time there'll be no retakes."

Scarlet watched zombies continue to file into the building. "Maybe we should back up a little," she suggested. "I don't want any flaming zombie gunk exploding on me."

They cleared the ghost-town perimeter, climbing up a small sandy hill to get a better vantage. The town square was completely empty, deserted except for the fan in the middle blowing chicken smell into the trailers; all the zombies had entered the building. Romeo looked over and gave them a big thumbs-up.

"Here's goes nothing," Scarlet whispered, holding her breath. Mason nodded, reaching over to take her hand.

KA-BOOOM!

The explosion was like an earthquake, knocking Scarlet off balance. Mason managed to keep her from falling. She buried her face in his chest, not wanting to watch the carnage, because bits of flaming zombie were falling everywhere like rain. Other bits of wreckage crashed down around them as well.

"It's okay, Scarlet," Mason said after a moment. "It's over."

Surprising herself, she burst into tears.

Mason stroked her head soothingly. "It's okay," he whispered. "The zombies are all dead. We got our happy ending."

After Scarlet had calmed down, Mason led her back onto the set. The town hall's frame was still smoldering, though the walls had been blown apart, and the air was smoky and thick. Romeo George ran over to them, camera in hand, looking like a kid in a candy store.

"We did it!" he exclaimed, brushing soot off his clothes. "We killed the zombies, and right before two o'clock. I got an amazing final shot, too. I can totally finish my movie now. It'll be brilliant!"

"Are we sure we got all of them?" Mason asked, scanning the ghost-town street as they began walking. "We don't want—"

It was inevitable, he supposed; this always happened in the movies. There was one last zombie: the extra he'd shot in the leg earlier, which had apparently slowed the monster down in its pursuit of the chicken smell. Eyes still black pits, and slime dripping from its horrid, gap-toothed mouth, it appeared just at that moment. Lurching around a corner and screeching, it grabbed Romeo. The director screamed, dropping his camera in fright.

Mason ripped his gun from its holster and frantically pulled the trigger. Nothing happened. The gun was empty.

Romeo was struggling desperately now, holding the zombie's forearms and avoiding its teeth, but the creature's hands were inching closer to his throat. Mason started forward, knowing he had to try to do something. He couldn't just let the director die, even if Romeo was responsible for the whole mess.

"Forget me!" the director cried as Mason approached. "Save my movie!"

Suddenly, a gunshot sounded. The zombie's head exploded, showering the director in gore. The creature collapsed to the ground, convulsing for a moment and then going still. Mason let out a breath, thankful he wasn't going to have to resort to hand-to-hand combat. If he never got in another fight, it would be too soon.

Romeo George was simultaneously squealing like a girl and using his shirt to rub zombie gunk off his skin. Mason picked up the director's camera, then turned to locate the gunslinger, whom he imagined to be Jesús the maintenance man. He couldn't have been more wrong.

The paparazzo from the previous night holstered a pistol and bowed gallantly. "John Fletcher," he introduced himself to the wide-eyed Romeo George. "E-Snoops, at your service."

"You!" Mason said. "Thank god you had a gun."

"Yeah, well." John shrugged. "People in my profession aren't always the most popular. I keep one around for when bodyguards go wild." He glanced down at the gun. "I've never actually shot it before coming here, though. I don't know what the hell's been going on here, but it's crazy."

Mason was about to reply, but Scarlet's sudden horrified gasp cut him off. *Oh god, what now? Would this nightmare ever end?*

"Chico!" she cried, pointing.

He followed her shaky finger toward the dog. Chico was approaching slowly, growling menacingly. His big brown eyes were wild, and his mouth was drenched in red goo.

"Oh god—no!" Mason cried, feeling his world suddenly collapse around him. This couldn't be happening. "Chico, come here!"

The dog ignored him, taking a step toward the paparazzo, baring his red-stained teeth and snarling menacingly.

"Stop it, Chico," Mason begged. "Stay, boy. Please." Tears flooded his eyes as he wrestled with what to do. He should never have sent Cissy and Jesús for him. Never. "Chico!"

Scarlet touched his arm softly. "I'm so sorry, Mason," she murmured. "But I don't think that's Chico anymore."

He swallowed hard, knowing she was right. Just as Scarlet had been forced to kill Derek, he had to . . . But he couldn't. He turned his head in anguish. "I can't do it," he confessed. "I just can't. Someone else needs to—"

"Kill that dog!" screamed Cissy, bursting onto the scene in a storm cloud of fury. "I swear to god, I'm gonna murder him. Fucking mutt ate all my preserves! My organic, gourmet, limited-edition, can't-be-found-anywhere-in-stores strawberry preserves!"

Mason stared at Cissy, then at Chico. The dog licked its lips, slurping away the last of the leftover jam.

Mason burst out laughing, relief washing over him like a tidal wave.

"It's not funny!" Cissy shrieked, stamping her foot. "Do you know how much those things cost per jar?"

But Mason didn't care. He scooped Chico into his arms, squeezing him tightly. "You little monster," he murmured, head buried in the dog's fur. "You jelly-stealing little monster."

Chico just burped happily.

"But the growling . . ." Scarlet said.

Mason chuckled. "I forgot. My little guy hates paparazzi." He looked over at John. "No offense, dude."

The photographer held up his hands. "None taken. Now let's all get the heck out of here."

Chico was licking Mason's face, his tail wagging a mile a

minute. Scarlet cuddled up, hugging him, reaching over to pat the naughty canine. Mason smiled and kissed her. The three of them were already a little family.

"I swear to you," he said to Scarlet. "Next movie role I take will have more singing and dancing than *Mamma Mia.* I've had enough violence to last a lifetime."

"Maybe you can convince them to do a Trey Rey reunion show," she suggested with a smile, planting a kiss on his cheek.

"Wait a second," Paparazzo John interrupted. "You *are* dating her! And . . ." He turned to Cissy, who had been enveloped in an X-rated hug by the film's recently appeared maintenance man. At least it had shut the celebutante up. "You're dating *him?*"

Cissy shrugged. "I found Jesus. What can I say?"

"Wow. Oh, wow!" John cried, his eyes ablaze with excitement. "This is one big scoop. It'll make my career!" He rubbed his hands gleefully. "Listen, I don't suppose you guys would pose for a picture and tell your story in exchange for a ticket out of this hellhole? I've got a boat docked at the other side of the island, and it'll fit all of us."

Mason smiled broadly, realizing he didn't want to wait for the supply boat. The way movies always worked, it would explode at the last minute or something stupid like that. In real life, sometimes happy endings really did come from the most bizarre places.

"Absolutely," he replied to the paparazzo. "We'll give you a story you'll never believe. It's a tale of action and horror . . . and love. A real Hollywood—er, make that Zombiewood—Confidential."

Epilogue

John turned the captain's wheel, steering his boat due east toward the mainland. He still couldn't believe all that had happened. He'd arrived on the island hoping for a simple photo or two, and he'd ended up with a story that would make his career—a huge, shocking, worldwide feature for which he'd been promised the exclusive. Soon he'd be rich beyond his wildest dreams!

He shook his head. And to think he'd almost gone home the other night after he'd tried to hook up with one of the extras at the cast party. She'd choked and bitten him, the stupid bitch. Nobody appreciated investigative reporters.

He settled himself in for the long boat ride back. He couldn't wait to get home and file his story—after lunch, of course. 'Cause right now he was pretty hungry.

He just hoped the diner by the dock was serving chicken.

Every Part of You

Lisa Cach

To Doni and Nikki, the marine biologist and his goddess.

Chapter One

The man wouldn't stop staring at her.

Angelica shifted in her seat, flipped her long dark brown hair forward over her small breasts, and crossed her arms protectively. She was scared and self-conscious enough as it was, sitting in the waiting room of a plastic surgeon, awaiting a procedure that made her intestines turn every time she pictured it in full, horrifying color. It wasn't soothing her to have a mouth-breathing surfer dude sprawled in the chair across from her, gaping as if she were an unusually large wave.

Maybe he had a mental impairment. Or maybe he was stoned. That was more likely, wasn't it? He looked the type: sun-bleached shaggy blond hair, skin so deeply tanned that he had premature crow's-feet around his brilliant blue eyes, faded Hawaiian shirt worn open over a white tank, baggy shorts, flip-flops. He was huge, too—at least 6'2"—and muscled.

Okay, he was gorgeous, she could admit that, but beauty and brains had obviously not come together in this southern California package.

"You here for a nose job?" the man asked.

Angelica's hand flew to her nose, touching the peak at the center of its hooklike arch. As a kid, classmates every Halloween had teased that she should be a witch because she already had the nose for it.

She squirmed under the man's gaze. "No."

He nodded. "That's a beaut you've got there. Looks like something you'd see carved on the side of a Mayan temple."

Angelica cast a beseeching look at the receptionist—her

Japanese-American housemate Karen—but Karen was on the phone.

"Where are you from?" the giant asked.

Angelica returned her reluctant attention to him. There was a faint, untraceable hint of accent to the brute's voice. "Here. L.A."

"No, I mean originally. Where's your family from? Central America?"

Angelica pressed her lips together. "Sacramento."

"But you've got some Maya or Aztec in you, don't you?"

"Probably."

"Cool! So what are you here for, then, if not your nose? Don't tell me: a boob job. Seems like no one in L.A. can appreciate a nice little pair of half-cuppers like yours."

Her lips parted in shock. A moment later she fled to the reception desk, leaning against its high counter, her back to the guy, giving him ample chance, no doubt, to wonder if she were there for liposuction on her wide hips.

Karen ended her phone call and looked up, her oval face in its frame of glossy black hair as serenely beautiful as a Japanese geisha's in an ukiyo-e print. "You aren't still nervous, are you?" she asked, no hint of the annoyance in her voice making it to her facial expression. "I keep telling you, Dr. Velazquez is great, one of the best in Hollywood. You think all those movie stars who meet with him secretly would trust their faces to anyone who wasn't good?"

"It's not that. It's him," Angelica whispered, subtly gesturing over her shoulder with her chin. "Who is that guy?"

Karen leaned to the side to get a better look, smiled, and waggled her fingers in greeting. "I can't talk about other patients," she said quietly to Angelica. "They were very clear about that during my training." She shrugged. "Sorry. He's a good-looking guy, though, isn't he?" Small movements of Karen's eyelids hinted at brows that would have roguishly waggled before she'd had her face paralyzed with injections of neurotoxins. "Hunka hunka! I'm not surprised you're interested."

Angelica shook her head frantically. "No! He's weird."

Karen snorted. "You think every guy is weird. He's fine. *More* than fine." The phone rang and Karen picked up, shooing her away.

Angelica turned from the desk and searched for something to look at besides the alleged hunk.

The hunk-*oaf*, rather. The hoaf. She smiled to herself, imagining a cartoon version of the hoaf, a zombielike creature. He'd have a shambling gait, ragged surfer clothes, and drool spooling out of his mouth. She'd draw that rivulet of saliva coming down off the side of his too-rugged jaw with a fat glistening droplet hanging free, swaying with each zombie step, bouncing on its viscous thread of moisture. She was an effects animator for a movie studio, so she knew a thing or two about making realistic drops of monster drool. She chortled to herself and went to stand in front of one of the framed photos on the wall, pretending absorbed interest but seeing only a blur of greenery, her mind's eye filled with the hoaf.

There was a stirring of movement behind her. Her ears pricked as Surfer Boy stood and took the few steps to cross the room. She could feel his presence looming behind her, his mass blocking the light. The back of her neck and arms tingled, the hairs standing on end.

She was being stalked by a hoaf. She bit her lower lip, smothering a nervous giggle.

"I saw one of those once," he said near her ear, the rich vibrations of his voice sending a shiver down her neck despite the nasal overtones. He sounded as though he had a cold.

"One of what?" She turned slightly and looked up at him, breathing in a scent of clean minerals, like an ocean beach.

He chuckled, his smile showing white teeth. "One of those." He pointed at the photo in front of which she was standing: a small bright green snake coiled on a branch.

Angelica grimaced. "Oh. Ugh. Snakes creep me out."

"Is that why you were staring at it so hard?"

She hadn't even looked at the photo; her mind had been too busy drawing the hoaf. She murmured a noncommittal noise.

"It's a green parrot snake, and they're even more beautiful in real life. There's something about their color that almost glows, even in the rain forest."

"Yellow."

"What?"

"The snake is greenish yellow; the human eye reads yellow as light. That's why it looks like it glows, compared to the other greens. But a glowing snake is still a snake." She shuddered and moved to the next photo, this one of a butterfly.

The hoaf followed. "So are you just a little afraid of snakes, or phobia-afraid of snakes?"

Angelica shrugged a shoulder. "My brother once put a garter snake in bed with me while I was sleeping." She glanced at the hoaf. "It was an experience that stayed with me."

He grinned. "Cheeky bastard! Wish I'd thought of that, when I was a kid." He thrust his forearm toward her, and pointed at two pale scars amidst the tanned skin and bleached arm hair. "Sea krait, a type of water snake. They dive underwater and go fishing. You should see it, hundreds of them undulating through the water together, hunting," he said, contorting his arms in serpentine movements.

"I can picture it," Angelica said, feeling queasy as her head filled with the image of hundreds of long, thick snakes twisting through clear blue water like huge parasitic worms. "Too well." Sometimes a strong visual imagination could be a curse.

"The snake left its teeth in my arm, but not enough venom to do more than make me puke." He shrugged. "Doesn't stop me from liking little green parrot snakes, though. I'm Tom. Tom Haggerty," he added, sticking out his hand.

Her natural instinct toward politeness had her putting her fine-boned hand into his rough, warm paw. "Angelica Sequiera."

"*Angel*," he said softly.

"Angelica," she corrected.

"Good to meet you, Angelica." He held her hand gently in

his own, as if aware of how easily he might bruise it. His eyes looked into hers as if seeking the answer to a question, and for a moment Angelica lost herself in that brilliant blue gaze, forgetting even that his mouth was open so he could breathe.

"You're not getting your butt lipo'ed, are you?" he asked.

Angelica grunted in protest and jerked her hand out of his. At the same moment, the nurse popped out of a doorway, clipboard in hand. "Angelica?" she called.

"Here!" Angelica grabbed her bag and fled into the relative safety of the medical rooms.

"Are you ready to say good-bye to those acne scars?" Dr. Velazquez asked cheerily as he came into the procedure room. His scrubs couldn't hide the elegance of his slender frame or diminish the grace of his movements. His eyebrows arched devilishly under glossy black hair parted on the side, and his dark eyes flashed with energy and intelligence.

"Muhhh . . . Yeshhh," Angelica said, dimly appalled at the slur in her voice. In prepping her for the procedure, the nurse had given her a sedative to calm her overblown anxieties.

"Good, good! And it is such a kindness of your body to allow us to suck that unwanted pocket of fat from beneath your chin," he said, touching the hated second chin with the tips of two long fingers, "and inject it into your scars, where it can do some good."

A burning tingle of embarrassment fought through the sedative. "Yeshhh." Dr. Velazquez was so handsome, she was self-conscious in his presence even when he wasn't studying her every physical flaw and suggesting improvements.

The nurse lowered the back of Angelica's dentistlike chair until she was looking up at the ceiling and the photographic mural of Costa Rica's jungle that had been affixed there. Dr. Velazquez was from Costa Rica originally, and the nurse who'd prepped her had explained that all the plants and ani-

mals depicted in photographs on the medical office walls
were of native animals. Dr. Velazquez donated a percentage
of his profits to rain forest conservation.

He wasn't only handsome, smart, and successful; he had a
conscience, too. Dr. Velazquez was a world apart from Tom
Haggerty, surfer cretin. Not that Tom was completely horrible. There was a hunky half to the hoaf equation, after all.
Given a choice between the two men she'd choose Dr. Velazquez, of course, no question, although she had a feeling
that the doctor was the type of man who would get tight-
lipped and quiet if you spilled coffee in his car. Tom's car, she
imagined, would be full of greasy take-out bags and have a
lingering air of Taco Bell chili sauce. You'd get out of it dirtier
than when you went in. Spilled coffee wouldn't even be noticed.

She sighed softly. No one was giving her a choice of either
man. It was clear that neither thought much of Angelica's
looks. She'd expected no less from Dr. Velazquez, really, even
though there had been a small part of her that, meeting him
for the first time a week ago, had hoped he would say she was
lovely and didn't need a thing done. Acne scars filled? Well,
perhaps, if she truly wished, but in his eyes the imperfection
only served to add piquancy to the unique perfection of her
person.

Foolish, foolish fantasy. He'd quickly shattered it.

She watched with sleepy eyes as Dr. Velazquez and the
nurse arranged their equipment and checked supplies.

For the seven years she'd been living in L.A., Angelica
had fought to retain some sense of herself as an average-
looking woman who showed pretty well when she made an
effort. Bit by bit, though, her attitude had changed. The local
news spent half its broadcasts on celebrity gossip. The grocery store magazine racks were filled with Hollywood industry rags and beauty publications. The grocery store aisles
were full of women—and men—who'd been lifted, filled, im-
planted, veneered, peeled, plugged, and all-over carved and
polished into the shapes they desired. A chest measurement

larger than the hips on women looked normal to her now. Of course everyone's teeth should look ready for an Orbit commercial; noses should be narrow and straight, with the swoop of a ski jump; lips should be full; jawlines should be trim and square on both men and women; collarbones should be hollow; chest ribs and sternum should show through the skin; and never, ever should an upper arm have a chicken cutlet of fat hanging from it, or a thigh be textured with cellulite.

Angelica worked indoors, fully clothed, which allowed her to hide the greater flaws of her person. Her face, though, was always exposed, with its myriad imperfections. When Karen had gotten the job as a receptionist for Beverly Hills plastic surgeon Dr. Velazquez—and with it a sixty percent discount for friends and family!—Angelica had at last succumbed to the temptation to fix some of what was wrong with her instead of continuing to pretend she was okay with her body and face.

Filling the six shallow acne scars on her cheeks and being rid of an annoying little pocket of chin fat at the same time seemed relatively minor. No one would likely even notice the change, except herself. There was nothing wrong with doing this, was there? What harm could it possibly do?

"A pinch, Angelica, as I inject the anesthetic," Velazquez said, his dark eyes shining above his mask.

A moment later she felt the prick of the needle under her chin. His gloved hand came up and he brushed gently at the base of her forehead. "Have you thought more about these lines of worry we talked about?"

She had, staring at herself in the mirror every morning. "Mmmrr . . . Money," she managed to say, past the spreading numbness in her jaw. It was more an excuse than truth. She was afraid of having a face as expressionless as Karen's.

"I don't think money should be the reason a twenty-eight-year-old woman bears such lines between her brows. I can give you, gratis, an injection of my proprietary formula, Phi-Tox."

"I dunno . . ." Angelica equivocated.

"You worry a lot, yes?"

"Mmm."

"Maybe even too much?"

She nodded. Her friends and family always said so.

Dr. Velazquez pressed a fingertip against the spot between her brows. "The emotions follow the muscles of the face. If I stop you from making the face of worry, I will also stop you from worrying quite so much." He stroked her brow, his voice dropping to a seductive murmur. His eyes were liquid with warmth and caring. "You will be so much more at peace, and look so much more beautiful."

She was helpless under his touch and intense gaze. "Yeshh," she relented.

"Good, good."

Angelica fell into a light doze, aware of but not troubled by the pulling under her chin as the fat was sucked out with a small vacuum, the sounds of the fat being processed, and then the pinching pain of the injections into her scars and the sting of the Phi-Tox being injected into her brow.

"I want you to think about letting me do something about this nose," Velazquez said softly as he worked, his voice lulling her. "As I told you before, I am a descendent of the great Spanish painter Diego Velazquez, and I like to think that I have inherited his talent. Diego worked in oils, creating beautiful images of people. I work in flesh, creating beautiful people that he would have loved to paint." Velazquez ran his finger over the arch of her nose. "I would not give you one of those pinched nostril noses, too thin for the face. Nor would I give you the recent popular style of a perfectly straight bridge, drawn as if with a ruler. You are an artist, so you know: Nature never draws a rigid, straight line; it's unnatural. No, a Velazquez nose will be drawn with active lines, lines that ever so subtly change direction, curving. And a curve on the face or body must never be the perfect curve of a half circle; such curves are dead. Unnatural. They must be curves that constantly change, just as a woman's waist curves out into her hips. And just as your own chest should curve more fully out into breasts. I will fix that for you, too. Like Michelangelo with a block of marble, I seek to carve out of a woman the beauty I see locked within."

So he did see beauty in her, somewhere. The thought warmed her dreamy mind, even as she shuddered deep inside at the thought of having that beauty released by a scalpel.

"There! We are finished. That was not so bad, was it?"

Angelica opened her eyes, squinting against the light. She felt as if she were half asleep. "Hrrrmm."

Dr. Velazquez took off his mask and smiled at her. "You will go home and sleep, and take it easy for a few days, to let your chin heal without too much bruising. And while you rest, you will think about your nose and your breasts, and the sculpting I could do to your thighs. All right?"

What could she say to such a man, while his fingers stroked her brow and she lay helpless before him?

"All right."

Chapter Two

Five days later, Angelica's chin no longer ached and the pin-pricks on her face had healed. One of her coworkers had remarked that she looked well rested, but no one else had given her a second glance. She wasn't aware of the Phi-Tox in her brow unless she looked in the mirror and tried to scowl. Even then, it wasn't that she felt the Phi-Tox, but rather that no muscles responded to her efforts. It was like trying to wiggle her ears or the tip of her nose.

Overall, Dr. Velazquez had done as beautiful and subtle a job as he had promised. It made her wonder whether she shouldn't take him up on his offer to take care of the rest of her flaws.

What would she look like with a straighter nose and bigger breasts? Maybe a little like Salma Hayek? The thought both tempted and shamed her. It made her feel weak and shallow. Beauty was supposed to be on the inside, its inner glow transforming the outer. Or so her mother always said. "Smile, Angelica! You're pretty when you smile."

If she felt beautiful all the time, even when she wasn't smiling, might her life be different? Might she then have the courage to ask to be moved to a different department at the studio, where her artistic skills could be put to better use than removing wires from live-action flying vampires, or making dogs look as if they were talking? If she were beautiful, might she then have the confidence to find a worthy man with whom to share her life? If she were beautiful, might she be less fearful of life altogether, and more willing to throw herself on the mercy of the world and pursue her truest, deepest dreams?

She dragged herself home from yet another fourteen-hour day at work and found Karen sprawled on the couch in their living room, eating blue bunny Peeps and channel surfing. The local news popped on for a moment, the anchor describing a forty-eight-year-old woman who'd gone missing; her photo showed a fit, attractive brunette in a low-cut halter top that showed off fake boobs.

"I thought you were on a diet," Angelica said, kicking off her shoes with a sigh and setting her green cloth grocery bag on the kitchen breakfast bar.

"I was," Karen said around a mouthful of marshmallow, one bunny ear protruding from her mouth. She had blue smeared on the side of her mouth. Two empty Peeps packages lay on the floor by her feet. She flipped stations, rejecting a baseball game and a sitcom. "I must be PMSing or something. I suddenly had to have Peeps."

Angelica frowned at the detritus. "I thought you were trying to eat organic."

Karen reached for a fresh package, the cellophane crinkling under her tearing fingers. "What part of 'PMSing' don't you understand?" Karen's gaze alit on the grocery bag. "You didn't buy any ice cream, did you? I've been craving Ben & Jerry's Phish Food all evening."

"All I got is salmon and vegetables." She was trying to eat healthily, a chore that was especially hard given the long hours she worked. After fourteen hours in front of a computer screen, all she wanted was to wolf down something cheesy and carb-y and collapse into bed.

"Damn. I might have to go out and buy some."

Angelica blinked in surprise. "Jeez, Karen, you've got it bad."

"Ha! Not as bad as Kelsey Magnuson. Come look." Karen pointed at the TV screen, now displaying *Spotlight on Show Biz*, a daily entertainment industry program.

Angelica came over to see, curious. The host, Carrie Sharp, looked as though she had a bad sunburn, despite her makeup, and her upper lip was swollen. "Kelsey Magnuson is one of today's hottest young stars, her bikini-clad body appearing on the covers of men's magazines and in two movies in current release," Carrie was saying. "There are even rumors she'll be the next Bond girl; but maybe not, if she keeps *this* up!"

On screen, paparazzi photos showed Kelsey Magnuson emerging from a Costco pushing a cart that the host described as full of Red Vines, Hershey bars, and three big canisters of jelly beans. Two cardboard trays of cinnamon rolls sat atop the candy, and a chunk of unrolled bread and frosting hung from the corner of the star's mouth.

Angelica felt a tickle of schadenfreude. Like anyone else, she was delighted to see that stars were human, too. "Wow. Looks like you're not the only one PMSing."

"Those cinnamon rolls look good."

Angelica's mouth watered. "Yeah." Much better than salmon.

"Oh, hey, I almost forgot!" Karen said, suddenly grinning.

"What?"

"Guess who asked me for your phone number today?"

"Asked you for it? I don't know! Who could have?" Angelica's mind raced through the few men they knew in common. Karen couldn't mean Dr. Velazquez, could she? The thought made her heart skip a beat.

Karen's voice took on a teasing singsong. "I think someone is going to ask you on a daaaa-ate."

"You don't mean—"

"Tom! The hunk of burning surfer boy love, oh yes I do!"

Angelica's mouth fell open in astonishment. "Tom? Really? Why?"

Karen rolled her eyes. "Why do you think?"

"But he thought I was ugly," she said in confusion.

"Apparently not!"

She felt a spark of flattered pleasure, but quickly snuffed it.

She couldn't go out with him: what a horror! He'd be making rude comments about her all night. "Of course you *didn't* give my number to him."

"You mean of course I *did!*"

A flush of alarm burned through her. "But you can't! Confidentiality. You can't give another patient my contact info!"

Karen waved off the concern. "Phht! It's you. You're not going to tell on me. Besides, how could I say no to those blue eyes?"

"Karen!"

Her roomie stuffed two bunnies in her mouth, her cheeks poofing out. "Don' get awll wirginal on me," she said, chewing. "You know you want him."

"*Karen!*"

In Angelica's purse, her phone started to ring. She yelped. Karen grinned, showing bits of blue marshmallow up to her gums.

"I'm not answering it!"

"You gotta at least check who it is. It might not be him."

Her hands shaking, Angelica grabbed her purse and dug out her phone to check the display. "'Half Shell'? What the heck is 'Half Shell'?"

Karen shrugged innocently, her eyes glittering. "I dunno."

"I do have a Shell gas card. Maybe someone stole the number?" She answered the phone. "Hello?"

"Angelica! Hi!" a deep nasal voice said. "It's Tom. Remember, from Dr. Velazquez's office?"

Angelica glared at Karen, who was lying on her side, hand over her mouth to smother her laughter. "I remember."

"How are your acne scars? Karen told me you were having them filled with your own body fat. That is *weird,* man. I didn't know they could do that."

"They're fine," Angelica said flatly. "They're almost invisible."

"They were invisible before. I didn't even notice them."

"So I wasted my money?"

"In my opinion, yeah."

"Thanks?" she said faintly.

"Hey, you're welcome. But that's not why I'm calling."

"Ah?"

"I want to take you out on Saturday. Karen said you aren't busy, so how about I pick you up at nine AM? We'll make a day of it."

"I—"

"Bring a swimsuit."

"Wait, I—"

"You can swim, right?"

"Yes, but—"

"Great! See you at nine!"

He hung up before she could say another word.

Angelica pointed a finger at Karen, who had tears of laughter slipping down her cheeks. "You are so dead."

Chapter Three

Tom parked his truck in a visitor space at Angelica's apartment complex, killed the engine, and took a slow, deep breath in an effort to calm down. *Be the jellyfish*, he said to himself. *Go with the flow. Don't fight the waves.* He closed his eyes and pictured the school of giant moon jellies he'd once seen, backlit by the sun streaking through clear blue water. Their umbrella-shaped bodies pulsed with rhythmic movement, silent and graceful. *Be the jellyfish.*

He got out and slammed the creaking door, then pressed a kiss from his fingertips to its faded painting of a woman's face. "Wish me luck, Angel."

He followed signs toward Angelica's apartment number, the complex's paths taking him through lush landscaping and past a pool occupied by a sole swimmer doing a lazy breaststroke. The complex was in Marina del Rey, a community built around a marina just south of Venice Beach. The location was, he thought, a good sign.

Then again, he'd seen nothing but good signs from the moment he'd laid eyes on Angelica Sequiera. At the sight of her long dark hair and large, eloquent eyes, he'd heard something inside him, an inner voice that rarely spoke but was always listened to, say, "Yes." He got the impression, though, that Angelica had heard an equally imperative one saying, "No."

He couldn't blame her. He'd never been particularly good with words, or with expressing himself. He hadn't needed to be. Actions spoke for him just fine, and any situation requiring a delicate dance of words was not a situation where you'd find Tom Haggerty. Nor did the women in his life look for sweet nothings whispered in their ears: they knew they were getting a guy who could give them good, physical fun either on the waves or between the sheets, and that he'd give them a fond kiss good-bye when that was no longer enough. When a woman wanted a relationship containing words, especially ones like "I do," she found someone else. He'd been to the weddings of six ex-girlfriends so far, and borne the protective glares of six fresh husbands. Those six ex-girlfriends would have laughed to see him talking to Angelica in Dr. Velazquez's office—laughed, or, as his brother Mike's wife Lucy had done, slapped him upside the head.

"You said *what* to her?" Lucy cried, when he told her about his questioning of Angelica regarding her visit to the plastic surgeon. Tom had been sitting with Mike and Lucy around the iron patio table on their back terrace, sipping pale ales and listening to the kids shriek and splash in the pool. Lucy had reached over and slapped him. Twice.

"I wanted to make sure she wasn't going to do anything to deflate that marvelous round butt," Tom said, defensive. "I meant it as a compliment!"

Mike's laugh sent beer up his nose.

Lucy had handed her choking, coughing husband a napkin without taking her eyes off Tom. "You've probably destroyed any chance you might have had with this woman. You'll have to do something dramatic—something downright chivalric—if you're going to make up for such a bad first impression."

"Like what?"

Lucy waved her hands. "Slay her enemies, rescue her from monsters, sacrifice your life to save hers!"

He'd pictured Angelica being mugged on the street and him swooping in to bash together the heads of her attackers. Great idea, but difficult to implement. "I don't think she's in any danger."

Lucy blew out a breath of exasperation. "Then take her out and show her a very, very, *very* good time."

When Lucy took the kids into the house, Mike had studied Tom for several long, quiet minutes. At last he'd spoken. "There's something different about this one, isn't there?"

"Yeah," Tom said, taking a sip of his beer.

"Does that mean you're ready to settle down?"

The question hit him like a sucker punch. "Hell no!" He'd always known he couldn't live like Mike and Lucy, in a comfortable neighborhood full of backyard swimming pools and gossipy conversations about the local schools and kids' sports. He was happy to stay with Mike and his family for a few weeks while he was in town, and was grateful Mike had space to store his little truck, but living their anchored, home-owning, PTA-going life full-time would be death to a guy like him.

Mike nodded. "Didn't think so. Do the girl a favor, then. Before you sweep her off her feet, let her know it's a limited-time offer. You'll be leaving town soon."

Tom had nodded, even as the voice deep inside him had grumbled in bitter protest. He wanted to throw Angelica over his shoulder and drag her off with him, like a pirate with his booty. Any wish of hers to stay put would be inconsequential to a pirate. *Arrrr!*

Unfortunately, there were laws against kidnapping. Brute strength wasn't going to win him fair maiden, more's the pity. And winning fair maiden would be next to impossible if she knew his home was thousands of miles away, and he had no intention of staying in L.A.

He found Angelica's apartment door and took another steadying breath. His heart was pounding with a mix of nerves and excitement he couldn't remember feeling since he was a teenager. He raised his hand to knock, but then panic hit him at a sudden thought: What if she stood him up? She might not be home. She might have fled earlier in the morning.

He closed his eyes, breathing deeply. *Be the jellyfish. And don't say anything stupid.*

He knocked.

* * *

"I'm not going!" Angelica protested as Karen languidly dug a bathing suit out of a drawer and dropped it on the bed where she'd already deposited a sarong and beach towel.

"Oh hush," Karen said, shoving her Tootsie Pop into her cheek so she could talk. "Yes, you are. You *know* you are. Look at you; you already have your makeup on. Since when do you wear makeup on a Saturday morning? Since when are you even awake on a Saturday morning?"

Angelica stuck out her jaw and crossed her arms over her chest. "I didn't sleep well. I was up all night trying to figure out how to tell Tom that I'm not going out with him."

"It's too late now, isn't it? He's probably made all sorts of elaborate plans. It would be cruel to disappoint him after all that effort."

Angelica chewed her lower lip. She'd been fretting about that very issue, hating as she did to hurt anyone's feelings. What if he were really looking forward to today? What if he'd made reservations for a fancy meal somewhere, and told all his friends he had a date? He'd be embarrassed and humiliated if she cancelled on him at this late hour. She should have called him back right after he phoned her and told him no. Once she was off the phone, though, doing nothing was easier than calling and rejecting him, especially since he was obviously one of those men who couldn't catch a hint. He wouldn't perceive "no" until it was shouted in plain English, followed by a swat on the nose for reinforcement. She just couldn't bring herself to do it.

Angelica sighed in defeat and gathered her beach things into a big straw tote. How bad could one date be? At least she'd have a story to tell at the end of it, and when she said good-bye to him when he dropped her off, she'd make very clear that they wouldn't be seeing each other again. An idiot surfer dude was not her idea of long-term-relationship material, and she'd never had an interest in casual flings . . . no matter how well built the man, or how rumbling and deep his voice. A tingle ran over her skin as she remembered Tom standing close behind her in the doctor's waiting room.

A knock sounded at the door. "Hoo hoo!" Karen cried, and crunched into the center of her Tootsie Pop.

Angelica slapped her hands to her face, all her nervousness blossoming in her cheeks. She might have no serious interest in Tom Haggerty, but he was still a big, good-looking guy who was taking her out for the day. Her last date had been eight months ago, with a cheap little yahoo from the studio's IT department. He'd made her pay for her own dinner. Even though her body ached for the touch of a man, she hadn't let him put a finger on her.

"Want me to get the door?" Karen asked eagerly.

It was disconcerting to hear such enthusiasm in her roommate's voice while her face remained placid. Was Angelica imagining it, or had the Phi-Tox moved from Karen's brow down to her cheeks? Even Karen's shoulders and neck seemed a little less mobile than usual.

"Yeah, go ahead," Angelica said. It would postpone the inevitable for a moment, at least. "I have to get my sunscreen and stuff."

Karen sauntered from the room, and Angelica slipped into her bathroom to get the sunscreen, which even someone with her dark olive complexion needed if they were going to be near the water. Beside it in her vanity drawer was a strip of condoms. She stared at the blue packages. There was no way she was going to need them. Was there?

An image flashed to mind of Tom, naked, standing at the edge of a bed with her tan legs around his waist. The flush of sensation in her loins made her grab the packages and check the expiration date. They had a month left.

Out in the foyer, she heard the high chirping of Karen's voice, and the answering deep murmurs of Tom's. Without letting herself think about it, Angelica shoved the strip of condoms into her toiletries bag and stuffed the bag into her straw tote.

She gave herself one last look in the mirror: her hair was held back with an emerald green silk scarf twisted like a headband, the tails of the scarf falling over her bare shoulder along with her heavy hair. She wore a white cotton sundress with a full-tiered skirt and spaghetti straps that crisscrossed in back. Her breasts were small enough that she could get away without wearing a bra, at least as long as they weren't doing any jogging. Golden Greek goddess sandals adorned her feet, and on one wrist several thin brass bangles chimed in accompaniment of her every gesture.

The outfit would do for everything from the beach to a restaurant, and she was pleased to have an excuse to wear the dress. She'd ordered it online two years earlier and never worn it, always reaching instead for clothes that wouldn't show dirt or stains, and with which she could wear a bra. She wasn't sure why she'd finally put it on for Tom, of all people. Maybe she wanted him to goggle over her and regret being so rude at Dr. Velazquez's office.

Okay, so maybe there wasn't a big chance of that, given her "half-cuppers," big butt, or Aztec nose, but a girl did what she could. Flaws notwithstanding, she looked pretty good today. She smacked an air kiss at herself in the mirror, slung her tote over her shoulder and went to face the Visigoth.

She found him declining an offer of a treat from Karen's jumbo box of Mike and Ike candy. "Are you sure?" Karen said, shaking the box, candies rattling around inside.

"Yeah," he said, grimacing, but his face lit up when he saw Angelica. His white smile was fluorescent in his tan face. "Hi!" he said. He was wearing a ragged old T-shirt with the faded image of a turtle and some indecipherable writing on its front; loose orange swim trunks, and black flip-flops. Worse yet, the ends of two plastic tubes protruded from his swollen nose, and sickly yellow bruises, visible even under his tan, surrounded his electric blue eyes. The color combination made him look like the undead.

Angelica shrank in embarrassment. She was overdressed.

He'd obviously meant this date as a casual thing—if he even meant it as a date! "Hi," she said miserably.

"Wow. You look great."

"Thanks."

"I thought maybe you wouldn't be here. Do you usually accept invitations from idiots who call you up and don't give you a chance to say no?"

If her brows could still move, they would have raised in incredulity. "Are you implying that I'm a pushover with low standards?"

He winced and slapped his hand to his temple. "No! Sorry! Don't pay attention to anything I say. Just . . . come out with me." He gave her an imploring look, his face ridiculously vulnerable with pleading blue eyes above the swollen, tube-filled nose.

She softened, her vanity appeased. "Yeah, okay. Where are we going, anyway?"

"I'm not telling; it's a surprise."

Angelica gave Karen a sharp look.

"Don't worry," Karen said. She had enough stranger-dating experience to correctly interpret Angelica's look. "I have all his contact info and his credit card number. If you disappear like those women on the local news, the police will know who their number one 'person of interest' will be."

Tom's jaw dropped, and he gaped in horror at them both.

Angelica suppressed a smile. Tom suddenly seemed ridiculously large and harmless in the small space of their foyer. The poor man was an innocent, in the most naive sense of the word. He was, she was beginning to suspect, a bit of a simpleton. He probably lived in his parents' basement. And ate Pop Tarts for breakfast. Probably hadn't ever had a real girlfriend.

Angelica felt her confidence returning. The day was going to be a lark, a frivolous outing about which to laugh with Karen, when she came home. "C'mon," she said to Tom, hooking her arm into his. "Let's go see this surprise destination."

They said their good-byes to Karen and headed out. Angelica dropped his arm as soon as they were past the door, and let Tom lead the way toward his car. She guessed it would be an old VW Vanagon, complete with surf rack on the roof and calico curtains in the windows.

"So, what happened to your nose?" she asked.

He touched it gingerly. "I was hit by a tank."

"I beg your pardon?"

"Tank. Wham! Right in the face."

"A *tank*? As in, armored vehicle?"

He laughed, the sound a deep rumble in his chest. "No, an air tank. As in scuba diving. It broke my nose, which I didn't care about until I realized it had healed crookedly and I couldn't breathe. So I had it fixed."

Ah. That explained the mouth-breathing. "Are you happy with Dr. Velazquez's work?"

"Can't tell yet. I was told he was one of the best, but he gives me the willies." He mock shuddered.

"I thought he was charming."

Tom snorted. "I'll bet."

"What's that supposed to mean?"

"A handsome, unmarried plastic surgeon has got to be the wet dream of every woman in L.A."

Angelica sucked in an offended breath.

"Don't let him get his hands on you," Tom continued. "I've known a few plastic surgeons, and they're all obsessed with sex. Sex, sex, sex, that's all they talk about. And they tell the filthiest jokes you'll ever hear."

"That wasn't the impression I got from Dr. Velazquez," she said stiffly.

"Of course it wasn't; you're female. He charmed you, just as any womanizer would, even if he doesn't want you. It's an ego thing."

"Well, thank you very much for that information, Dr. Phil," she snapped, miffed. He was making it clear that someone like Dr. Velazquez would never be interested in someone like her.

"Who's Dr. Phil?"

"Never mind."

"Womanizers *seem* like they love women," he went on, "but they'll never truly love *a* woman."

"I got your point!"

Tom subsided into silence.

They reached the visitors parking area and Tom's car. Angelica stopped in her tracks when it became clear which vehicle was his.

"Meet Mr. Toad," Tom said proudly, his open hand pointing at an ancient, small, faded green Toyota Hilux pickup truck with a hand-fabricated rack over the bed.

"Mr. Toad, as in 'Mr. Toad's wild ride'?"

His smile once again lit his face. "*The Wind in the Willows* was my favorite book as a kid. It made me want to talk to animals."

Her heart softened a little; wanting to talk to animals was kind of sweet. "Did you? Talk to them, I mean?"

"Sure."

"Really?" she asked, surprised.

He gave her a mischievous look. "Can't say they answered, though."

She smothered a laugh. The little brat!

Tom went to the passenger door and started to open it.

"Wait," she said, seeing an image painted on the door. She pointed at it. "What's that?"

"Not 'what.' Who," he said fondly. "That's my angel on the half shell."

She remembered the name that had come up on her cell phone. "Half shell?"

"You know, like that painting by Botticelli, of the birth of Venus? Where she's naked, standing on half a scallop shell?"

"Yes, of course I know the painting." She inched closer to get a better look, intrigued. The Venus in this case was a brown-skinned, dark-haired girl wearing nothing but a scuba mask pushed up above her brow. She held a pair of flippers in one hand, strategically hiding her private parts, and with the other hand she held dark locks of hair to partially cover her breasts. She looked a lot like Angelica herself. "Is there a meaning behind her?" she asked, feeling a flutter of uneasiness in her stomach. Was he obsessed with someone from his past and looking for a replacement?

"One of my diving buddies back when I got the truck was a graphic designer. He thought Mr. Toad needed dressing up, and that a pinup girl like airmen painted on their bombers in World War Two would do the trick. He asked me to describe my idea of the perfect woman, and Angel there was the result."

"Is she based on someone you knew?"

"Nah. She's just a fantasy." He opened the passenger door for her.

His unconcern relieved her of her worries, but they were immediately replaced by others when she saw the inside of the truck. Angelica stared with dismay at the dusty vinyl bench seat and thought about her pristine white dress. Would it be rude to take out her sarong and spread it on the seat?

Yes, it would.

With an internal sigh of resignation, she slid into the barebones cab of Mr. Toad. Sand on the floor gritted beneath the soles of her sandals. The seat was no more than four feet across, and if she tilted her head back her skull touched the glass of the rear window. There was no headrest. The dash was green painted metal and black cracked vinyl, and the cab smelled of a curious mix of spilled coffee, seashells, and coconut oil.

"How old is this truck?" she asked as he climbed into the driver's seat, his big frame barely fitting.

"1970. It was all I could afford when I was an undergrad." He pulled out the choke and turned the key in the ignition mounted on the dash. The engine made sad whining noises as it tried to start. After six or seven tries it finally caught, chugging to life.

Jeez, were they even going to make it out of the parking lot? "You never thought of replacing the truck with something, er . . . more reliable?"

"Replace Mr. Toad?!" he cried. He patted the dash soothingly and addressed the steering wheel. "Don't worry, she didn't mean it." He cast her a sidelong look and spoke out the side of his mouth. "You can't let an old vehicle hear you talk like that. It upsets them, and next thing you know you're blowing out a clutch."

Oh Lord, the man was crazy. Angelica hesitated before buckling the seatbelt, realizing this was her last chance to flee.

"But don't worry, the toad gets you where you want to go. Usually." He frowned, jerking the gearshift around until he could wedge it into reverse. "If your destination's not too far away." He suddenly turned to her and grinned, his face boyish and delighted, and rapped the horn twice: *Beep beep!* "This is gonna be a great day, isn't it?"

Angelica couldn't say no to that face. "Yup!" She clicked the buckle closed and sat back, abandoning herself to his enthusiasm.

Mr. Toad bounced and chugged down the driveway to the main street, Via Marina, and they pulled out, Angelica silently praying that Tom wasn't going to take them on the freeway in this thing. Rattling down the boulevard with the windows down, wind whipping her hair around her face, the motor growling and whining as Tom took it up through its gears, it felt as though Tom was driving at a recklessly high speed, at least fifty. But when she glanced over at the speedometer it read a measly twenty-five. She laughed.

"What?" Tom asked.

"It really is a wild ride, isn't it?" she said, holding flying hair down with one hand.

He nodded, clearly loving it. She realized with surprise that she was enjoying it, too. It had the same jouncing appeal of an amusement park ride.

"So you scuba dive?" she asked over the noise of car and road.

"Yeah."

"Around here?"

He shook his head. "Not anymore. It's not that great for recreational diving, although I spent a lot of time off the coast while I was getting my PhD."

She did a double take. "Your PhD? Are you serious?"

He gave her an *of course* look. "Yeah. Marine biology. Scripps."

He meant Scripps Institution of Oceanography, down in La Jolla; it was one of, if not *the,* top ocean sciences research institutes in the world. She gaped at him, flabbergasted. "You're a scientist?"

"Nah. I liked the diving way more than the nuts and bolts of science. After I got my degree I started operating live-aboard dive trips, and I've been doing it ever since. Some of my clients are scientists, and a couple times a year I organize excursions especially for them, based on their areas of interest."

"What was your dissertation on?"

He flashed a smile, and turned onto Admiralty Way, the road that continued around the north side of the marina. "Scallops. More specifically: *The early pelagic larval life history of three eastern Pacific scallops.*"

Angelica grimaced. "Gack."

"I know. A topic only a devoted scientist could love. I blame my angel on the half shell for that choice; she made me think I was fascinated by scallops. Maybe I thought I'd find her in one." He gave her a wry, self-deprecating smile. "It took a while, but I eventually discovered that most women live on land."

She bit the inside of her cheek. "Very perceptive of you. Do you regret all that work you did for your degree?"

"Nope. It led me to where I am now, so it's all good."

She glanced at him, envious of the easy peace he'd made with his erratic path in life. It was so different from the constant second-guessing she did with her own decisions, her regrets, her should-haves. "Where do you go for the dive excursions?"

"The islands have some fantastic spots—world-famous, really."

"Which islands? The ones off the coast here, like Catalina?"

"No, I—" he started, and then seemed to catch himself. Instead of finishing his answer, he turned the truck off Admiralty Way and down a side street toward a private marina. Tom pointed through the windshield. "We're here!"

"We are?" she asked, surprised. They were no more than a mile from her apartment. "What's here?"

He pulled into a space in a parking lot. The lot was edged on the water side by a tall chain link fence, in the center of which a gate with a keypad lock sat beneath a small sheltering roof; a gangway led from the other side of the gate down to the moorage.

"My brother's boat's here."

"We aren't going diving, are we?" she asked in alarm. "I don't know how to dive!"

Tom pointed at his nose with its protruding tubes. "This wouldn't fit in a mask."

She felt foolish. "No, of course not."

They got out of the truck and headed for the gate. "Don't worry," Tom said, punching in the code to unlock it. "I'll teach you to dive after I'm healed up. You'll love it, I can tell."

Angelica didn't miss the hint that there'd be another date. She'd been out with guys who said things like that before, though; all it usually meant was that they were careless with their promises and told women what they thought the women wanted to hear. They never followed through. Was Tom one of those guys? Half an hour ago she would have said yes. But he had a PhD. That didn't speak of a careless man with no follow-through. And as she followed him past the gate and down the gangway, she wondered if she might have judged him too quickly. Maybe there was more to this shaggy, sunbleached beach boy than she'd thought.

Today would be her chance to find out.

Chapter Four

"Prepare to come about!"

"What?" Angelica cried.

"Come about! Release the starboard sheet!"

Angelica panicked, looking frantically around the deck of the sailboat, no bed linens in sight. "Sheet? What sheet?"

"The rope, remember?" Tom hollered at her. He was in the cockpit of the sailboat, manning the wheel.

Her confusion cleared. "Oh, right!" Angelica threw herself up the slope of the tilted deck to the left side of the boat, reaching for the rope wound around a cleat.

"Starboard!" Tom shouted. "Starboard!"

"Isn't this starboard?"

"That's port! Port on the left, starboard on the right!"

Embarrassed, she scrambled to the other side and unwound the rope as Tom turned the wheel and the boat changed direction. The jib luffed, the small sail flapping in the wind.

"Haul the port sheet!" Tom yelled.

Feeling like a bumbling incompetent, she staggered back to port and winched in the sheet, the sail filling with wind and stretching tight. The sailboat tilted to port now, seawater running fast and green alongside where Angelica worked, salty spray hitting her face. They were sailing north, up the California coast.

"Good! That's good! Tie 'er off!"

Angelica wound the end of the rope around the cleat in something vaguely approaching the same way Tom had shown her, then coiled the extra rope in a neat spiral on the deck. "Okay?" she called back to him, praying for a nod of approval.

"More than okay! You did it! Good job! I knew you'd be a natural sailor!"

Angelica stumbled back to the cockpit and flopped onto one of the blue-cushioned seats. She was sweating, her heart was racing, and her hands were shaking. She hoped to god they wouldn't be tacking again anytime soon; she hated feeling that she didn't know what she was doing. "You said the same thing about me and scuba diving. Your opinion obviously can't be trusted, and I'll drown the moment I put on a pair of fins."

He glanced at her, his eyes flashing down to her chest, then away. "I wouldn't let anything happen to you. Besides, I meant it. You'd be a natural."

She was flattered, despite herself. "What makes you think so?"

"I dunno."

When he neither elaborated nor looked at her, she looked away herself, disappointed. The last hour had been spent preparing the thirty-five-foot sailboat for their outing, casting off, motoring slowly out of the marina, and then finally hoisting sail. It had been all work, no conversation.

"I guess it's intuition," Tom finally said.

She turned back to him, raising her brows.

"How I know you'd be a good diver, I mean." His gaze flicked between her face and the bow of the boat, as if he were afraid they'd suddenly hit a whale, even though the water was empty for a half mile in any direction. "I've taken so many people out, taught so many, too; you get a sense of the types of personalities that would do well."

"So what's my personality?"

"You're careful, for one thing. Cautious. You probably follow instructions well, and you don't take unnecessary risks."

She pressed her lips together. He must think her a stick in the mud.

"That's a good thing," he said. "Careless divers are dead divers."

She murmured a vague agreement.

"And you're adventurous; that's good."

She snorted in surprise and disagreement. "You really don't know me at all, do you?"

"You *are* adventurous. You're here, aren't you? You've never been sailing before, but here you are, giving it your all and learning quickly. And you're enjoying it, aren't you?"

"No! It's horrible!"

He gave her a hurt look. "Really?"

Angelica chewed her upper lip, scowling, but then almost against her will became aware of the mist of sea air on her skin, the warmth of the sun, the easy pitch and roll of the boat, and above all the brilliant light that glanced off the water, the deck of the boat, and the distressingly delicious figure of Tom himself. "Maybe I'm enjoying it a little."

He nodded. "On top of all the rest, Karen told me you're an artist. Anyone who loves beauty will love diving. There are colors down there like you've never seen before."

"Yeah?"

"Vivid, pulsating colors, and all moving to the rhythm of the ocean. The only danger for someone like you would be nitrogen narcosis."

"What's that?"

"An intoxication from the gas and air mix you breathe, which can leave you so entranced by your surroundings that you forget to surface in time. Beauty becomes the death of you. But don't worry, I'd never let that happen!"

"So you're immune to beauty?"

His gaze dropped to her chest and he visibly swallowed, then looked away. "No."

Feeling a little cocky now, Angelica leaned back, resting her elbows on the gunwales behind her. As she did, she felt her dress chafing against her breasts. A quick glance down showed her what Tom had been so studiously avoiding. The salt spray had misted more than just her face. Her white dress had turned transparent, her dark nipples staring out from her chest right at Tom.

Embarrassment washed over her. She cursed and sat forward, pulling the fabric away from her skin. Her cheeks were burning. "Why didn't you tell me?" she cried accusingly.

"I didn't want to embarrass you."

"Or you just wanted a free show!"

He gave her a chiding look. "Well, yeah, but you know I wouldn't take advantage of it."

"Because they're too small to be worth staring at?"

His brows shot up. "No! They're perfect! God, it's all I can do not to grab them! And kiss them! Those nipples . . . Christ! I want to lick them!"

Angelica gaped at him, too shocked to do anything else. As the shock and embarrassment faded, something warmer took their place, her belly clenching in hungry response to his words. Her sex felt full and heavy. "No one has ever talked to me like that before," she said hoarsely, not sure if she should be angry, or at least pretend to be.

He grimaced. "I'm sorry. I told you not to listen to anything I said! I shouldn't be allowed out with civilized people."

"No, it's okay," Angelica said weakly. She fluffed the front of the dress as she held it away from her skin, encouraging it to dry.

Tom wedged his knee against the wheel, pulled off his T-shirt, and handed it to her. "Here."

Her throat went dry as she took in the muscled expanse of his torso. His body was not that of a gym rat, with six-pack abs, a twenty-inch waist, and over-developed pectorals. No, his body was that of a man who led a heavily active life, ate right, and thought free weights were for sissies. He looked as if he belonged on the ceiling of the Sistine Chapel, in one of Michelangelo's frescoes.

"Thanks," she said, taking the shirt and pulling it on. It was warm from his skin and the sun, and as she pulled it over her head she was enveloped in the musky, mineral scent of his body, and inhaled deeply. A primitive part of her reveled in it. When her head popped through the neck opening a moment later, she was slightly dazed.

"Better?" Tom asked.

"Yes," she murmured, pulling the soft cloth down around her.

"Take the helm," he said, coming around the wheel and holding it with just one hand.

"What?" she cried.

"Take it!"

She scrambled to take his place, putting her hands on the wheel. "Where are you going?" she asked in alarm, as he started down the steps into the cabin. "I don't know what I'm doing!"

"Just hold her steady, and don't let the sails luff. I'll be back in a sec."

Angelica muttered choice words under her breath and chewed her lip. He might as well have left her to fly a plane! What type of date was this, with him making her steer the boat and hoist sails? She wasn't a sailor!

She heard a hint of ruffling, flapping noise in the sails, and a wash of hot panic dumped down her spine. Luffing! That was luffing, wasn't it? She whined deep in her throat. Mewing in uncertainty and distress, she inched the wheel slightly to port. The ruffling noise turned to vicious snapping in the sails. Angelica cursed and gently turned the wheel the other way. Several long seconds later the sails went taut and silent. As the minutes went by and they stayed that way, she started to relax and enjoy herself.

Tom emerged from the cabin with a tray of cheeses and fruit, white wine and glasses. "Looks like you've got the hang of it," he said. "Do you need a break?"

She surprised herself by shaking her head. "No."

He smiled, looking pleased with either her or himself, she wasn't sure which. He poured her a glass of wine and handed it over, then settled back with his own glass. "Karen said you were an artist; what kind of work do you do? Paintings?"

"I wish. I'd starve if I tried to make a living as a painter. No, I work for an animation studio." She nibbled a piece of cheese.

"Cool! So you get to create characters like Wall-E or the Little Mermaid?"

She shook her head, resigned to explaining her job as she had explained it to so many disappointed people in the past. "I mostly do effects animation. Things like making cats and dogs look like they're talking, or removing wires from actors as they 'fly.' When I work on animated films, I'm usually doing things like creating the dust clouds from a herd of cattle, or the raindrops in a storm."

"Oh. Sounds kind of boring."

She grimaced. He was sure blunt. "It is."

"Why do you do it?"

"Money," she said, and immediately felt ashamed. "I make a good living, better than I ever could as a fine artist. Sure, the hours are long and there's no creative freedom, but at least I can provide for myself. I have health insurance and a 401K. How many artists have that?"

"I dunno."

"Not many," she said fiercely. "I'm not a sellout. I'm realistic."

"If you say so."

"I do say so."

"Whatever makes you happy. So, what movie are you working on right now?"

She took a gulp of wine, thinking about how she'd spent seventy hours a week for the past three months. "You don't want to know."

"Of course I do!"

"It's a romantic comedy."

"With talking dogs?"

She shook her head. "There aren't any special effects. I'm doing a correction."

"To what?"

She took another gulp of wine. "To an actress's breasts."

"What's wrong with them?"

"Breadloafing."

"Huh?"

"Breadloafing," Angelica repeated, and sighed, deflated. She was defensive about her job because she knew how horrible and soul-sucking it really was. "It happens when a woman gets implants that are too big for her. Instead of having a valley between her breasts, the two breasts merge into one. The valley part rises, like—"

"Rising bread," he finished for her, looking horrified.

"It happened to this actress at the start of filming, and they couldn't stop production for her to go get it fixed. So I'm fixing it, frame by frame."

"And this uses your artistic talents how?" he asked, appalled.

"You do need to know how to properly shade a sphere," she said wryly.

He shook his head.

"I admit, it's not what I dreamt of in art school."

"What did you dream of?"

She closed her lips and shook her head. Those dreams were too childish to share.

"Tell me," he insisted.

"You'll laugh."

"Maybe," he said. With his hair blowing in the wind and the tubes in his nose, he looked like an innocent goofball, man-god torso notwithstanding. "Won't know until you tell me."

She laughed. "Guess not." What did it matter if he thought her art school fantasies were stupid? She sensed he wouldn't think any less of her, even if he did laugh. "I wanted to be like Gauguin, who went to Tahiti to live and paint. I thought I could find an island somewhere with a low cost of living, and send my paintings to New York to be sold, and live off that income."

"You're kidding," he said in obvious disbelief. He looked as though she'd slapped him with a two-by-four.

"Ridiculous, I know!"

"No, it's not. Not at all! You can do it, you know."

She shook her head. "It's not that easy."

"Sure it is! What's so difficult? There are hundreds of islands in the Pacific where you could live cheaply and paint. I even know a place where you could stay for free, on a little island that's surrounded by some of the best diving in the world."

She shook her head. "Maybe someday, when I have enough money socked away."

"But you're young and healthy now. Who knows what tomorrow holds?"

"I've only got myself to count on for financial support," she countered. "I have to earn my nest egg while I can. Gauguin died penniless in Tahiti."

"Hurrah for him! At least he did what he wanted."

"Of syphilis," she added.

"Oh. Well, they hadn't invented penicillin yet. You can't blame *that* on poverty." He sat forward, earnest. "Angelica, money can be a prison. Yes, yes, I know you need a basic amount for survival, but beyond that you have to beware the golden handcuffs. The more money you make, the further you are carried away from the work you love. I know; I've been there myself."

"When you were a marine biologist?" she asked skeptically.

"Nah. I mean with the diving tours. The more trips I booked, the more paperwork I had to do, the more people I had to manage, and that meant fewer chances for me to go diving."

"So what did you do about it?"

"Hired a manager to take my place! Went back to work as an expedition leader, for a smaller salary but a better life."

"But what type of future can you build like that? What's going to happen to you if you get sick? Or when you get old? What if you have an accident?"

"Life's for living. You can't spend it locked in a protective box. You're not a china doll; you're not going to break if you fall down a few times. Take a chance; let me take you to the western Pacific! Take a year off, bring your paints. Talking dogs will still be here if you come back."

Her mind filled with the possibility, and she saw herself in an open-walled thatched house with dark wood floors, jungle on three sides and a view out over turquoise waters on the fourth side. The canvas on her easel would be filled with brilliant color: tropical flowers, local people, birds . . . Tom, naked, standing like Adam in the Garden of Eden. And she would be his Eve.

At least, for as long as he stuck around. But when he took off, returning back here to his regular job, what would happen? She would be alone, thousands of miles from anyone who knew her, and her bank account would slowly drain. Even if she could sell her paintings when she returned to L.A.—assuming she had enough talent and voice to create art that was better than a gaudy tourist souvenir—she wouldn't earn enough to make up for all the money she'd lost. She'd be lucky to cover her airfare. She'd have to find a new a job and a new place to live. She'd have to start over.

She slowly shook her head, letting the tropical vision of paradise fade. "It's too risky."

"I'd take care of you."

"No!" That was a trap too many women fell into, to their regret. "I have to take care of myself. I can't count on some guy to do it."

"But that's what men and women do for each other."

"When they're married, maybe. But there are no promises made in one date and a wildly impulsive scheme to live the life of a starving artist in the tropics."

"You'd do it if we were married?"

She laughed. "That's a huge 'if'!"

"But you'd do it?"

Given that she would only marry someone she loved, and she could only love a responsible, stable, capable man, the possibility that she would ever marry Tom seemed remote.

But in the unlikely event that after a couple years had gone by, he had proved his stability to her and they were in love, and if they married, then, "Yes, I'd do it."

"Marry me."

"No!"

"Why not?"

She gaped at him. There was a hint of embarrassed smile on his lips, but his eyes looked serious. "I barely know you! You barely know me!"

"Sometimes you just know it's right."

"I don't know it's right! Far from it! The fact that you would seriously ask me to marry you on our first date is good evidence that it's *not* right for me. Not right at all!"

He looked wounded. "What would convince you?"

"There's no 'convincing.' It's something that has to be proved over time."

"How much time?"

"A lot of time."

"A couple weeks?"

"Now you're just teasing me," she said. "Can we talk about something else?"

To her relief he let her change the subject. The next two hours passed pleasantly, finishing off the cheese and fruit, chatting about where they'd grown up, their families, their friends, and places they'd been. He told anecdotes about his experiences scuba diving, often poking fun at himself and making her laugh again and again. She shared with him how hard she'd fought to convince her parents to let her go to art school, and how proud they were now that she worked on films they could see at the theater and tell their friends about.

Lunch was a picnic from a Greek deli, served with a rustic red wine and finished off with baklava that melted in Angelica's mouth. She used her fingertip to capture every last crumb of sweet pastry on her plate.

"Want the rest of mine?" Tom asked. He was still shirtless, half lying on the bench opposite her in the open cockpit of the boat. He'd taken in some of the sail and tied a rope to the wheel to keep them on an easy course.

His offer was barely out of his mouth before she'd scooped the pastry off his plate and gobbled it up.

"Jeez, you've got a real sweet tooth."

"I don't, usually," she said around her full mouth. "And I shouldn't be eating this."

"Why not?"

She gestured toward her hips.

He snorted. "You know what a girl with some curves looks like to a guy?"

She swallowed and shook her head.

He gave her a slow smile full of suggestion. A subtle alteration changed his posture from idle lounging to open invitation. "She looks like a lot of fun."

Angelica felt her body responding to the suggestion, her eyes traveling down his belly to his shorts. Alarmed at her attraction, she snapped, "Well, I'm not a lot of fun!"

He laughed, the muscles of his torso flexing.

"That didn't come out right," she muttered, her eyes glued to his body. "And I've had too much wine."

"You've had two glasses."

He sat up and started gathering the detritus of their meal. She moved to help, but he shooed her away. "Relax."

She did as bidden as he went below with the dishes and clanked around in the galley, cleaning up. She took off his T-shirt and lay back on the bench, her knees up, one arm over her forehead to shade her eyes as she squinted up into the blue sky and watched the clouds. The movement of the boat and the quiet slosh of water against the hull were lulling, and she felt herself starting to doze.

"Have you got any lip balm I can borrow?" Tom called from below, some minutes later.

"In my bag," she called back. "Help yourself." So peaceful . . . A girl could get used to days like this. A girl— She bolted upright. "Tom, wait!" she cried, and scrambled toward the hatch. "I'll get it! Don't . . ." The words died as his upper half emerged, her toiletries bag in his hands.

"I got it," he said, digging through her things.

She grabbed at it, but between his surprise and her desperation the bag went tumbling through the air, spilling its contents on the deck at her feet. The linked packets of condoms unfolded like a bright blue snake in the midst of face powder, lip balm, sunscreen, and comb.

"Ah, jeez, I'm sorry," Tom said, and hurried out of the hatch to pick up everything.

"No, let me," Angelica said, but her reflexes were strangely slow and he beat her to it, his big hand landing on the condoms. For a long moment he seemed not to recognize what he was holding, and started to shove them back in her toiletries bag, but just when they were about to disappear inside, his hand stopped, then reversed direction.

"You brought—?" he started to say.

Burning embarrassment scorched her skin. Angelica grabbed his hand and tried to pry the packets away. "Gimme those!"

He was too strong and too curious. He held the condoms out of her reach. "You want to sleep with me!"

"No, I don't!"

"At least three times, by the looks of it!"

"No!" she protested, her whole soul cringing in embarrassment.

"You knew before I even picked you up that we would end up in bed together."

"*No!*"

"That's why you packed them."

"Tom, stop it!" she pleaded, verging on tears of humiliation. "I just threw them in. I wasn't thinking. I just . . ."

"Shh, sweetheart," he said, lowering his arms around her.

"I just . . ."

He nuzzled her ear, his breath warm on her skin. It sent a shiver down her spine and she melted against him.

"Of course you weren't thinking," he said. "You didn't have to think. You already knew."

"No," she murmured, slowly shaking her head, but sharply aware of his hand on her lower back, holding her gently against him. The hand slipped lower, caressing the curve of her buttocks and sending a shot of arousal through her loins.

She rested her cheek against his bare chest and closed her eyes. She heard him toss the condom packet on the bench, and then his other hand slid up her back to the nape of her neck, where his fingertips brushed at her hairline. She lifted her face from his chest and looked up, smiling for a moment as she caught sight once again of the ludicrous nose tubes; but then her gaze was caught by his eyes, electric in their intensity, and she forgot about everything except his body against hers, his hand pulling her hips tight against him, his hard thigh wedging against her sex. Her eyes fluttered closed as his fingers slid up into her hair, pulling out her green scarf and then cupping the back of her skull in his strong palm. His lips lowered to hers, kissing her tenderly, persuasively, asking her to give herself over to him. She wrapped her arms around his neck and returned the kiss, and the moment she did she felt him release the reins on his hunger.

His lips devoured hers, his tongue plunging inside, roughly stroking her own. He leaned back against the cabin for balance, his knees slightly bent, and pulled her thigh up against his hip, bringing the mound of her sex against his rigid arousal. The pitching of the boat against the waves created a rhythmic pressure everywhere their bodies touched, her sex rocking against his, her breasts brushing his chest again and again with each movement of the boat.

With a few tugs Tom untied the lacing of her dress, loosening it enough that he could push the straps over her shoulders. The bodice fell to her hips, leaving her naked from the waist up. He groaned, taking in the sight. He gripped her thighs in both his hands and hoisted her up to where his mouth could reach her breasts. His waist was locked between her thighs and she clung to his shoulders as he lowered his head and laved her nipples with his rough tongue. She dug her fingers into his hair, tugging on it in delight, like a happy cat.

He painted every inch of her breasts with the brush of his tongue, and gently rolled her nipple between his lips, flicking its end with the tip of his tongue. When she moaned in pleasure, he lowered her slowly to her feet, letting her sex slide against his body while his mouth trailed up to her neck, nipping and licking.

As soon as her feet touched the deck he spun her around so that her back was against his chest. His left hand cupped her breast, playing with the nipple, while his right pulled up her skirt and then slid inside her silky underpants. He kissed her neck as his hand brushed over her folds, as lightly as the confines of her underwear would allow. She raised one arm and wrapped it around his head as she arched her back, her hips moving in rhythm with his delicately stroking hand. She could feel the peak of her folds catching against his palm, the friction magnified by the moistness of her flesh. His palm grew slick as he stroked her, but his movements remained maddeningly slow and light. She moaned again, rocking her hips against his hand, begging for more.

In answer, he suddenly slid his finger deep inside her, thrusting, then curling forward to stroke that oh-so-sensitive spot. Her knees went weak, and her hand gripped his hair so tightly that he flinched.

He gave her a few more thrusts and then slowly withdrew his finger. She mewled in protest and turned around, ravenous for more. She captured his lips with hers while her hands yanked down his shorts, freeing a huge erection. Her greedy hands closed around it, the velvet shaft as thick as her wrist. It bobbed in her grip and she dropped slowly to her knees, letting the head brush against her breast as she went.

She looked up at him as she dawdled, swirling the head of his penis with its drop of moisture against her nipple.

"Angelica," he breathed, his hands hovering near her head as if to stop her. With her eyes locked to his, she dropped down a few more inches and took the head into her mouth. He jerked against her, and in answer she swirled her tongue around him. He grabbed her head and weakly tried to pull her away. She sucked him more deeply into her mouth.

"Oh, god," he groaned, and then with obvious effort forced her to stop. He kicked off his shorts as he raised her off her knees and pushed her to lie back on a bench. With a few tugs he had her underpants off, and then he was reaching for the packets, tearing into the foil with his teeth.

"Anything medical we need to stop and talk about?" she asked in a hoarse breath.

He shook his head. "You?"

"No."

"Thank god." He grasped her ankles and lifted them to his shoulders. Her dress pooled around her waist. With one knee on the bench and the other foot braced on the deck, he lifted her hips to meet him. She helped guide him into her opening, and then stretched her arms above her head, using her hands to brace herself against the gunwale.

With slow, shallow thrusts he began to enter her, stretching her to the edge of pain. But as each thrust brought him deeper inside her, the awkward angle of their joining brought the end of his shaft against that place inside her that his finger had so recently stroked.

"Oh my god," she moaned, and locked her feet behind his neck. "Oh my god . . ."

He thrust into her like he meant it, his face taut with desire, his whole body straining against her. She felt herself building toward a climax, slowly, surely, but as his speed increased she started to fear he would get there before her.

He read the need of her body, and a moment later she felt the pad of his thumb against the peak of her folds, stroking lightly against her with each thrust of his hips. For several long seconds she hovered on the brink, her body locked rigid with passion, and then she tumbled over, falling in pulsing waves of pleasure. He fell a moment later, crying out as he held motionless inside her.

And then he had his arms around her, rolling her onto his chest as he took her place on the bench. They gently separated their sexes, then fell into a doze, naked in the sunlight.

Two more blue foil packets later, they were at last on their return trip to Marina del Rey. They'd eaten what was left of their picnic between their joinings, and Angelica was pining now for something sweet. She'd ransacked the galley, but there was not a chocolate chip or jellybean to be found.

"You okay?" Tom asked from behind the wheel. They'd raised more sail, and were speeding along at a good clip.

"Yeah." She sat at one end of a bench, her back against the cabin, her knees pulled up under her skirt. Except for the sugar craving, she was floating in a blissed-out haze of good sex. She was enjoying the moment for once, and not letting herself fret about the future.

"You sure you're okay?"

"Yeah, of course. Why?"

"You look . . ." he said, gesturing at his own face, "I don't know. Blank."

She scowled, or tried to scowl, anyway. "I, er . . ." she started, and then grimaced, not wanting to confess. Or she *tried* to grimace. She touched her face, trying to feel what emotion was displayed there. She couldn't feel any change. A hot flush of alarm flamed to life inside her. "While I was having my scars filled, Dr. Velazquez gave me a free injection of his Phi-Tox formula, to keep me from frowning so much."

"Phi-Tox? What the hell is that?"

"It's like Botox, but it's not from botulism. It's his own secret formula."

"You let him put that in your face?" Tom asked incredulously.

"He was very persuasive."

"Well, don't let him persuade you anymore! It's not permanent, is it?"

"It's not supposed to be," she said, feeling her cheeks and trying to smile. She still could, barely. "I don't know what's going on; my face seemed fine this morning!"

"It's migrating," Tom said darkly. "There's no way to keep a toxin locked in one spot in your flesh."

Her panic increased. "It can't migrate to my heart or something, can it?"

"I don't know; depends on the toxin, and how it travels in the blood."

"You're scaring me!"

"You're not the first person he's given this to, are you?"

She shook her head. "No. Dozens, if not hundreds of people have gotten it. It's all very hush-hush."

"Any of them die?"

She shook her head.

"There you go. I assume it's FDA approved?"

"I don't think so," she said meekly.

He gaped at her. "You're super cautious about everything in your life, but you let a doctor inject an experimental drug into your face?"

"Like I said, he was very persuasive," she mumbled defensively, ashamed. She wrapped her arms around her knees. "They'd given me a sedative, too. I wasn't thinking clearly."

"This is unethical on so many levels, I don't know where to start."

"Please don't. I feel stupid enough as it is."

"No doctor should—"

"Please, Tom!"

"But the AMA should—"

"Tom! Please! Don't!"

He ground his jaw. "I need to have a few words with him."

"Tom! He's Karen's boss. I don't want to cause trouble for her."

"This is bigger than that. You can't let him harm people in order to keep someone's job."

"But I'm not really harmed. I'll go in and see him, and I'm

sure he can give me some sort of antidote for it . . . or at least reassure me the effect will go away in a couple weeks."

"You can't trust that guy!"

"*You* have to trust him, too. He's taking those tubes out of your nose on Monday, isn't he?"

He grunted in assent. "Although any doctor could do it, I bet. Hell, I could do it, with the right pair of scissors to cut the sutures through my septum."

"Oh, for heaven's sake. Just go to your appointment! He's not Dr. Evil."

"Looks enough like Satan, with that slick black hair," Tom muttered.

Angelica shook her head, exasperated.

"Prepare to come about," Tom said a few minutes later.

Angela got up, ready to scramble forward and deal with the jib, but she caught herself and turned. "How about you do the jib, and let me take the wheel?"

He shook his head. "There's the mainsail to deal with, back here. It might be too much for you to do at this point."

"Oh." She turned toward the bow, disappointed and wondering if he were punishing her for not letting him go off on Dr. Velazquez.

"Angelica, wait! You really want to take the wheel while we tack?"

She nodded.

"Okay, here's what we'll do. You take the wheel, but I'll stay here with you and deal with the mainsail. It won't hurt to let the jib wait until we're done."

She grinned. "Really?"

"Sure."

She took his place at the wheel, and he told her how many turns to take while he hauled on the lines to move the mainsail.

"Ready?" he asked.

"Yup!"

"Go on, then. Make it so."

She turned the wheel as he'd directed, and he hauled lines. She ducked as the boom at the bottom of the sail passed over them and swung out to the other side, lurching into place as the boat turned and the sail filled with wind.

"One turn to port," Tom said.

Angelica spun the wheel with confidence, and the boat changed direction.

Tom looked up. "Did you turn to port?"

She nodded.

"One more turn."

She repeated the motion, turning the wheel to the right.

"Port!" Tom cried. "Left! Left!"

Angelica jerked the wheel, but the boat was slow to respond. It had already turned enough in the wrong direction that the mainsail spilled its wind, and the boom lurched back toward the boat. "Tom!" she screeched in warning, pointing.

He turned his head just in time to be walloped on the nose by the boom. He fell back across the bench, blood pouring from his nose and violent curses from his mouth.

"Tom!" Angelica cried.

"Left!" he gurgled, and let out another stream of expletives.

She corrected course, checking that the mainsail was back where it belonged before tying off the wheel and going to Tom's aid, wadding up her skirt to press against his nose.

"Ow! Stop it! Never mind my nose; go tend the jib!"

Angelica hurried forward as bidden, then returned to the cockpit to find Tom leaning out over the water, his blood chumming the sea. "I'm so sorry!"

"My fault," he said tightly, obviously in great pain.

"You'd think I could get port and starboard straight!"

Tom reached out a hand and patted her thigh. "It's okay."

"But your nose! Did you re-break it?"

"Probably."

"Oh god!" She felt horrible.

"Angelica."

"Yes?" she said eagerly, desperate to help.

"Could you get me some ice from the galley?"

"Okay! Anything else? Bandages? Painkillers? What can I do?"

"Just one thing, my dear."

"What?"

"You're going to have to sail us home. I'm not sure I'll be conscious."

Chapter Five

You let your guard down for a minute, stopped being careful and started enjoying yourself and getting cocky, and this was what happened. Disaster! Injury! Terror on the high seas, and on the road in Mr. Toad, and where did it all end? In the emergency room, that's where.

Angelica shook her head and bit back tears. She was in the waiting area of the emergency room. They'd taken Tom in ten minutes earlier, despite his protestations that the bleeding was much less now, really. They both looked as if they'd been vacationing in a slaughterhouse, and the blood was especially conspicuous on Angelica's white dress. Her skirt was a red Rorschach test, her bodice a field of Flanders poppies.

Tom had stayed conscious during the sail home, but she had been the hands that did as his mind commanded. Her body was shaking from nerves and exhaustion by the time they tied up at his brother's slip. She'd thought her trials were over until Tom pointed out that she'd better be the one to drive to the ER. He got Mr. Toad started, but then it had been her tired muscles against the toad's drum brakes and manual steering. She was grateful she knew how to handle a stick shift, although even so the toad had thrown her a few curves, not least of which was his habit of jerking either left or right when she touched the brakes. She suspected the little green truck had been difficult on purpose; it had remembered her unkind words earlier in the day and taken revenge.

Tom had called his brother en route, asking him to check

on the boat, as Tom wasn't confident he'd left it sufficiently secured.

"Skittles! I need more Skittles!" a woman in the waiting area moaned.

"Shh, you ate them all," her husband said.

Angelica sneaked a peek at the couple, who were sitting about fifteen feet away. The man was balding and chubby but well-groomed. His wife was badly sunburned, and strangely swollen in her upper lip, chin, and breasts. The flesh in those areas looked inflamed and angry, and there was an open sore above one breast, visible above the low neckline of her shirt.

"Skiiiiii-ttles," the woman moaned, her face curiously immobile despite the distress in her voice. "Skiiiii-ttles." She lumbered from her chair toward a vending machine in the corner. "Skittles?"

Her husband chased after her, digging in his pockets for change. "How about Reese's Pieces, dear? Would those do?"

"Reeeee-se's . . ."

Angelica was distracted from the couple by an attractive woman in her early thirties who had stopped in front of her. "Angelica?" the woman asked.

Angelica nodded in surprise.

The woman, a dark blonde with freckles and green eyes, smiled. "I'm Lucy, Tom's sister-in-law."

"Oh! Hi! They took Tom back about fifteen minutes ago."

Lucy's gaze traveled over Angelica's dress. "Wow. You're never going to get that out."

Angelica closed her mouth, working past her surprise. Lucy was worried about her dress?

Her date's sister-in-law sat down beside Angelica and took her hand, patting it. "I've known Tom for ten years. I know it'll take more than a smashed nose to do him any lasting harm. I'm more interested in how you're doing. Are you okay, honey?"

Angelica looked into Lucy's concerned green eyes and felt herself crumbling. "No."

"Aww, honey, come here," Lucy said, and put her arms around her in that way that only mothers could do.

Angelica dissolved into tears, crying quietly into Lucy's shoulder. It was her stress finding an outlet, purging her system of the fright and struggle of the last several hours.

"I know a date with Tom is hard on any woman," said a man's voice, "but this goes too far."

Angelica dried her eyes and sat back.

"This is my husband, Mike, Tom's brother," Lucy explained. "Mike, this is Angelica."

Mike was a dark-haired, paler version of his brother, with the same bright blue eyes. "Pleased to meet you, you poor devil." He shook her soggy hand.

"I'm sorry I smashed your brother's face with the boom."

"He probably deserved it."

"No, he didn't."

"I'm sure someone somewhere thinks he did. At any rate, if anyone was going to smash his new nose, I'm sure he's delighted it was you. Did you have a good time with him out on the boat? Before the boom thing, of course."

Lucy surreptitiously kicked his foot.

What? Mike's expression seemed to say.

"I was having a wonderful time. I'd never been out in a sailboat before."

"You didn't get seasick?" Lucy asked.

"Not at all. And Tom served a wonderful lunch, a Greek picnic."

Lucy blinked in surprise and looked up at Mike.

"He served you real food?" Mike said, clearly astonished.

"Of course he did," Lucy answered.

"Dr. Velazquez!" the chubby man halfway across the room suddenly called out. "Oh thank god."

Angelica, Mike, and Lucy all turned to look as Dr. Velazquez strode into the waiting area, dressed in casual clothes that probably cost more than Angelica made in a month. His hair was perfectly in place, his movements smooth and assured. He held up one finger to the chubby man, silently asking him to wait a moment, and strode past the intake desk into the ER proper.

"Bit of a slick customer," Mike murmured.

"Stop it," Lucy chided. "He did an excellent job on Tom's nose."

Mike grunted.

The swollen woman started groaning, drawing all eyes. Angelica stared in horror as the sore on the woman's breast opened up and something white started to emerge. Angelica's heart caught in her throat, but it was the woman's chubby husband who started to scream, the sound girlish and piercing in the confines of the waiting area. The white thing swelled, pushing through the widening opening in the woman's breast as she lay moaning in the chair, her bag of Reese's Pieces falling from her hand.

"Dr. Velazquez! Dr. Velazquez!" the chubby man screamed. "Somebody help her!"

The woman's breast suddenly seemed to contract, squeezing tight, and the white thing flew out the top, arcing through the air toward the three of them. They all shrieked and covered their heads with their arms as the thing bulleted toward them, then landed with a wet noise on the tile floor. *Splat.*

Angelica lowered her arms and stared. Mike inched toward it, then cautiously poked the blood-streaked, white, jellyfish-like mass with the toe of his shoe.

"You know what that is," Lucy said in a hushed voice.

Angelica nodded, both revolted and fascinated. "It's that woman's breast implant."

Nurses and orderlies rushed over and took the woman and her implant away. Someone mopped up the spot on the floor, and swept up the Reese's Pieces. The chubby man had returned to his seat, only now his face was in his hands, his shoulders hunched.

Angelica got up and approached him. "Excuse me, sir?"

He looked up at her, and then blinked at the state of her clothes. "Yes?"

"I just wanted to ask, if you don't mind, did Dr. Velazquez perform your wife's surgeries?"

He shook his head. "No, some quack in the Valley did them. We were hoping that Dr. Velazquez could fix whatever went wrong. We had an appointment to see him next week."

"Oh. Thank you." She scuttled back to Mike and Lucy, feeling reassured.

"That's a relief," Lucy whispered, echoing Angelica's own thoughts.

A few minutes later Tom emerged from the ER, wads of gauze bandages fastened under his nose and a new brace attached to the bridge. Angelica rushed over to him. "What'd Dr. Velazquez say? Is your nose going to be okay?"

"I'll be fine," he assured her, his voice newly nasal from the bandages. "Good as new in no time; maybe even better than new." He grinned, but it didn't look reassuring under the new bruising that was developing in his face.

"Tom, I—"

He laid his finger on her lips. "Stop. I'm okay. And I had a wonderful day with you."

"You did?"

"Can't beat this for a first-date story, can you?"

She chuckled. "I suppose not."

Mike and Lucy joined them. "She's a good one, Tom," Mike said. "I can see why you're sorry you don't have more than ten days left."

"Ten days left for what?" Angelica asked, as Lucy again kicked Mike. Angelica looked up at Tom. "Ten days for what?" she repeated.

"Ten days left to win your heart."

"Why ten days?"

"Tom, you didn't tell her?" Lucy asked, censure in her voice.

"Tell me *what?*" Angelica pleaded.

Tom grimaced. "In ten days I fly back to Micronesia, in the western Pacific. That's where I live, full-time."

"Full-time? What do you mean? I thought you did dive tours somewhere around here, or Mexico."

He shook his head.

"No? But you must fly back and forth to L.A., right?"

"Only once every two or three years. It's too far, and too expensive."

She digested that, stunned. "So in ten days you're out of here. I'll never see you again."

"Not unless you come with me."

She shook her head, her heart understanding before her brain could. Fresh tears sprang to her eyes. "We did *that*, all day, and you didn't tell me you were leaving? You asked me to *marry* you, and you didn't tell me you'd be gone from my life in a week and a half?" She kept shaking her head as she backed away. "You should have told me!"

"I was afraid you wouldn't go out with me if I did."

"I wouldn't have!"

"See?"

"But it was my decision to make, not yours! How could I ever love a man who treated me like that?" Sobbing, she turned on her heel and fled.

Chapter Six

"Good evening!" a skinny fake blonde on the TV screen said. "And welcome to *Spotlight on Show Biz*. I'm Bethany Williams, in tonight for Carrie Sharp, who is out sick."

Angelica slouched on the opposite end of the sofa from Karen, each of them working through her second bowl of cookie dough ice cream. It was Friday night, and neither had gone to work for two days. Angelica had a severe sunburn on her face and chest that refused to fade, and that was making her feel tired and ill. Or maybe it was thoughts of the intimacy she'd shared with Tom, and the feelings for him that she had started to develop, that made her feel ill.

He'd called her every day since, trying to persuade her to see him again. She hadn't yet relented, but she felt herself weakening. She'd liked how he'd made her laugh with his stories, and the way he'd made her body feel. She'd liked the way he'd challenged her to learn to sail the boat despite her fears of incompetence. Even with the disastrous, bloody ending to the day, she'd felt more alive with him on Saturday than she could remember feeling for years. And she'd liked his brother and sister-in-law, too.

Against all that, though, was the feeling that he'd lied to her by omission, that he hadn't allowed her to make her own choice about getting involved with someone who would be leaving the country in a few days. As Maya Angelou said, "The first time someone shows you who they are, believe them." But was Tom a man who habitually hid the truth, or was he, as he kept claiming on the phone, a man who had fallen in love for the first time in his life, and acting like an idiotic adolescent as a result? And was one answer really any better than the other? She didn't want an insecure lover, one whose weakness made him try to control her. Nor did she want a lover who lived halfway around the world.

She could of course move to Micronesia with him, but how could she take such a massive risk without having a better idea of his character? He'd fooled her once already. She couldn't give up her life here when it was possible he could fool her again.

And yet, their day on the sailboat had been so wonderful . . .

The show credits and intro ended, and Bethany Williams was diving into the meat of the broadcast. "We begin tonight with shocking footage of Kelsey Magnuson, who has been hospitalized. We warn you, the amateur video you are about to see is disturbing. It was captured by a fan on his iPhone late Thursday night."

On screen, an image of the interior of a candy store came up, shot from outside the front plate glass window. Candy bins had been pulled from the shelves, their contents scattered on the floor. Kelsey Magnuson lay amid the carnage on the floor, strands of something yellow, green, and red hanging from her mouth. For a horrified moment Angelica thought they were snakes, but then the videographer zoomed in and she saw that the strands were actually gummy worms. Kelsey moaned as she chewed, stuffing fresh handfuls into her mouth every few seconds.

The videographer panned down Kelsey's front to her breasts, a great inflated mound beneath her T-shirt. The shirt itself had wet, bloody-looking stains, and it looked as though something was moving under the fabric. A moment later, an implant shot out from under the hem of the T-shirt. The videographer shrieked and started to curse, his hand shaking as he focused on the white blob resting amid a mosaic of gobstoppers.

Angelica dropped her spoon into her dish with a clank. "Oh my god!"

Karen, too, stopped eating. "That's what you said happened at the emergency room!"

"Shh!" Angelica said, as the TV host came back on the screen.

"Medical authorities are launching an investigation into what has been causing a rash of implant rejections across the city. Contaminated silicone is the primary suspect, although authorities have not yet pinpointed the source of the contamination, nor what substance is causing it. If you have implants, you should call your doctor if you have any of the following symptoms: swollen flesh around the implant, open sores, fatigue, poor coordination, and possibly sunburn or an unusual craving for sweets or other simple carbohydrates."

Angelica and Karen looked at each other, and at the bowls of ice cream in their hands.

"Yeah, but what's an 'unusual' amount?" Karen asked.

"I know people who go weeks eating nothing but soda and candy bars," Angelica agreed, even as her mind cast back over the past two weeks and her increasing attraction to sugary foods. And her sunburn. And the fatigue that had kept her home from work. "Thank god neither of us has implants." Her own words did little to reassure her.

On screen, Bethany Williams was saying, "To help explain these distressing developments we have the well-known plastic surgeon, Dr. Emilio Velazquez."

"Cool!" Karen said, resuming consumption of her ice cream. "I didn't know he was going to be on. Of course, he *is* a bit of a media whore."

Angelica had called Dr. Velazquez on Monday to ask about her face, and he'd assured her that the spreading paralysis was a temporary, common, and harmless side effect. If it didn't resolve itself in a couple weeks she should come back, which he would like anyway, as he wanted to talk about working on her nose and breasts.

The show cut to an interview with Dr. Velazquez in his office. The reporter reviewed the points they'd already heard, and then asked for an explanation of how this could have happened.

"The body treats an implant as a foreign object," Velazquez explained. "Even when it is an inert substance like silicone. The body forms a capsule of scar tissue around the invader; this is the body's way of containing the danger. In some cases, this capsule contracts, causing pain and deformation. These cases are difficult to repair, as any replacement of the implant is likely to cause the same thing to happen again.

"In the case of Kelsey Magnuson and others who have been affected, I suspect that a foreign protein contaminated the surface of the implants sometime between their production and their implantation. The body has overreacted to the implants, stimulated by the foreign protein or other substance. A bacterium, perhaps. The result is what we've been seeing: not just capsular contraction, but a massive rejection of the implant by the body."

"Is it possible that something besides the implants is causing the problem?" the reporter asked. "Some medication that these people are taking, perhaps?"

"My suspicions are that it may be a toxin in the environment. Pollution and global warming could be to blame. Perhaps the Environmental Protection Agency should look into it."

The reporter blinked in surprise, then recovered and smiled. "Related to that, you are well known as a champion of conservation, especially in your home country of Costa Rica."

"Yes, my foundation has saved thousands of acres of jungle from the threat of logging and development. The rain forests of our planet are the pharmacopoeia of nature, and we have only begun to discover the cures they hold for mankind. To save the jungle is to save ourselves."

"Well said, Doctor. Changing topic, you are also known as a pioneer in the field of plastic surgery. You've developed several techniques that have been adopted by your colleagues, and there are rumors that you have a new formula under development that will rival Botox."

Dr. Velazquez frowned. "If I did, I would not speak about it until I had FDA approval to begin clinical trials. There are several drug companies that would be eager to steal my ideas. If they did, the jungles of Costa Rica would suffer. Money from such a drug could save not just the jungles of Costa Rica, but potentially all of Central and South America."

The camera switched back to Bethany Williams. "Big dreams from a doctor who just might save the world. If you'd like to contribute to Dr. Velazquez's conservation efforts, go to his Web site . . ."

Angelica licked her spoon. "He looks even better on TV than he does in person." It was true, though Dr. Velazquez's handsomeness had lost some of its allure for her. Compared to Tom's messy charm, Velazquez looked unpleasantly polished and overgroomed. Her heart gave a sad *ker-thump* as she thought of Tom and what might have been.

It was right of her not to see him during his remaining days in L.A., wasn't it? All seeing him could do was increase her hurt—and his—when he left. She had to be cruel to be kind, for them both.

"Is there any more ice cream?" Karen asked.

"No."

"Want to go get some?"

Angelica's taste buds said yes, but her creeping fear that her sweet tooth had grown abnormally large, not to mention the inertia caused by her paralytic laziness, said no. It was almost eight PM, and they'd both been in their pajamas all day. "We'd have to get dressed."

"Just put on a sweatshirt. Everyone goes to the grocery store in PJs."

She couldn't argue with that. She got up, stretched, and rolled her shoulders, which were tingling. The realization sent a cold splash of alarm down her spine, but she tried to reassure herself that they were probably stiff from her having been motionless on the couch all day. All week, she'd found herself being a lump during the day and only showing signs of life well after nightfall. The news report hadn't said anything about becoming nocturnal; surely it wasn't a symptom of something being wrong? "Do you want to drive?"

Karen shook her head. "I feel crappy."

Angelica did, too, but she seemed to be in slightly better shape than Karen, who was moving as if she were underwater. Angelica grabbed a sweatshirt and her purse, slipped on a pair of thongs, and the two of them headed to the store.

"I think thassss one of Dr. Velazzzquezzz's clientsssss," Karen slurred as they waited in line at the checkout, idly perusing the magazine rack. She was pointing to a driver's license photo of a smiling, middle-aged woman on the cover of one of the more tawdry tabloids.

"Are you okay?" Angelica asked, as she shifted their heavy handbasket full of Ben & Jerry's, Junior Mints, and hot fudge sauce to her left hand; her right one felt like it was going numb.

"My moush doessshn't sheem to be working," Karen said, putting her hand to her lips. "Hungry. Gimmee Junior Mint-sss."

"Wait a moment; we're next in line. Which photo is of one of Dr. Velazquez's clients?"

"Her," Karen said, pointing again.

The photo was under a banner headline: WHAT'S HAP-PENING TO THE WOMEN OF LOS ANGELES? Two subheads marked out the stories the tabloid was tying together as a plague on L.A. women.

The first story was about the implant crisis, and promised readers dozens of photos of stars who might or might not be at risk of implant rejection, and who had recently gone on suspiciously timed "spa retreats," according to their publicists. The second story was about the spate of disappearances among upper-middle-class women; a serial killer was suspected, although no bodies had yet been recovered. It was a woman from this second story who had caught Karen's eye.

"What type of plastic surgery did she have done?" Angelica asked.

"Thighssss liposssuctioned," Karen said slowly. "Tummy tuck."

An idea that had been tickling at the back of Angelica's mind crawled to the front. "She didn't have Phi-Tox injections, did she?"

Karen met her gaze, her voice strained, obviously understanding where Angelica was going. "Don't know. Givesss to lotsss of pashhhients, free. You don't think—"

"I don't know," Angelica whispered, her heart starting to thud as she realized how possible it was that Phi-Tox could be the common denominator in what really *was* happening to the women of Los Angeles. She put the tabloid, and two others like it, in their basket.

The checker, an older woman with gray hair and the vertical mouth wrinkles of a smoker, started to ring up their purchases and chortled. "I think the backlash has finally started," the checker said gleefully, hefting the jar of fudge sauce.

"Backlash?" Angelica asked.

"Against vego-, lacto-, organo-, gluten-free sprouted whatever-ya-call-it diets. Stores have been selling so much candy and ice cream, the local distributors are running out of stock. I knew it would happen!"

"That's weird," Angelica said, swiping her debit card.

"Drinking wheatgrass juice is weird," the checker said. "What are we, cows? People don't eat grass. Nothing weird in people eating ice cream."

Angelica smiled uneasily. It wasn't a taste for ice cream that she'd meant was weird.

As she and Karen walked back to the car, she voiced her real concern. "Even if it's the Phi-Tox that's causing these problems and making people crave sweets, how could so many women have been affected that the city is running low on candy? How many injections of the stuff could Dr. Velazquez have done?"

"Mintsssh!" Karen demanded, pawing at the bag.

Angelica got the mints for her and opened the box. Karen grabbed it and poured the candies into her mouth, standing still with her eyes blissfully closed as she chewed. A happy growling sound came from her throat.

When Karen opened her eyes again, they were slightly brighter, and her speech was clearer, although still slow. "He's only been doing them for about a month, as far as I know. I don't see how more than a few hundred people could be affected."

"But there's some connection, isn't there?" Angelica insisted. They got into the car, and Angelica took the tabloids out of the grocery bag and handed one to Karen. "Do you see anyone else in there who is a client of Dr. Velazquez?"

Karen took another mouthful of Junior Mints and thumbed slowly through the pages, leaning near the window so the parking lot lights could illuminate the photos. Angelica started the car and backed out of their spot, then drove toward the end of the row. She rolled her shoulders; they were still stiff. Her whole body felt stiff, actually.

Exactly how far had the Phi-Tox migrated?

A Cadillac Escalade suddenly backed out of a parking space, its giant rear end barreling right toward the side of Angelica's little white Lexus IS. Alarm shot through her and she jerked the wheel, but her action came too slowly, her arms not responding to the demands of her panicked brain. There was a sickening crunch of metal and the muffled explosion of airbags deploying all around her, the inflated surfaces striking her from all sides. The Escalade kept going, shoving the Lexus across the aisle and into the Suburban parked opposite, sandwiching the smaller car like a marshmallow in a s'more.

It had happened too quickly for either Angelica or Karen to scream, and then for several long moments the only sounds were the deflating airbags and the Suburban's car alarm. Angelica's heart was beating in her throat, her breath coming in shocked gasps. She looked wide-eyed at her friend. "You okay?"

Karen shoved the airbag off her and started pawing around her seat, looking for something. "I dropped my candy. Where are my Junior Mints? *Where are my mintssssss?!*"

Angelica giggled, the sound desperately close to hysteria. At the same moment her cell phone started to ring. She dug her purse out from behind her seat and answered, her voice a squeal. "Yeah?"

"Angelica?" Tom said.

"Yeah!" she said, and made a sound that was either a sob or a giggle.

"You okay?"

"I've just been in a car accident, and I think Karen is turning into a candy-fiend zombie. Yeah, I'm great!" She started to laugh, her vision going blurry. Was she crying? How funny!

"Angelica! Where are you? Tell me where you are!"

She told him, but then the driver of the Escalade was in front of her car, staring through the windshield at her, and Angelica's laughter stopped on a gurgle. It was a 30-something woman with swollen cheekbones and suppurated sores under her eyes. She had a half-eaten Hostess fruit pie in one hand—cherry, by the looks of the red globules spilling over her hand.

"Oh god," Angelica said into the phone, dread coming over her. "There's another one."

"Another what?"

"Zombie! They're everywhere. What's happening?" she cried.

"You stay right where you are! I'm coming to get you!"

The Escalade woman tilted her head, looking in at them. "You have fruit piesssss?"

"Hurry," Angelica whispered into the phone, and then screamed as something white started to emerge from the sores beneath the woman's eyes. "*Hurry!*"

Chapter Seven

Tom worked Mr. Toad's shifter, forcing the little truck to strain its way up to fourth gear. The engine's growl was overlaid with an ascending whine. "Come on, Toad," he urged. "Don't let me down now!"

Fortunately, he had only six blocks to cover. For the past week he'd been staying on his brother's boat; he'd told Mike it was because he felt more at home sleeping on the water than on land, but that hadn't fooled either Mike or Lucy. Their eyes had said they knew he wanted to be close to Angelica, in case she relented and agreed to see him.

An emergency wasn't the reason he'd been hoping for, but he was grateful to be near enough to come to her aid. He couldn't bear the thought of her being in distress, hysterical by the sound of it, and possibly injured. She'd said something incoherent about zombies; she must have hit her head, and was hallucinating.

A fresh bolt of adrenaline shot through him as he approached the grocery store parking lot just off Admiralty Way; a fire engine and paramedic unit were converging on the accident, red lights flashing and sirens crying. The sirens were cut off mid-screech as the vehicles pulled up to the scene. Tom parked Mr. Toad in the corner of the lot and ran toward the commotion. He could see three cars pushed together and some milling customers, but there was no sign of Angelica. The thought that she might have fallen unconscious due to her injuries sent a sword of terror slicing through his gut.

The firemen and paramedics jumped out of their vehicles

and hurried toward the scene, but Tom beat them to it, instinct drawing him to the small white car sandwiched between the others, the SUVs preventing the car doors from being opened. He had to circle a woman sitting on the asphalt, her blank face marred by open sores, to get to the front of the car. He threw his hands down on the hood and visually searched the compartment, seeking Angelica. Only white mounds of semi-deflated airbags met his urgent gaze.

"Angelica!" he shouted. "Angelica! Angel! Can you hear me?"

There was movement, and a tan hand batted down the driver's side airbag. Angelica's face appeared in the shadows of the car interior. Her voice came through the glass, muffled. "Tom?"

"Angelica! Are you hurt?"

"I don't think so, but Karen's acting weird. And stay away from that woman with the fruit pie; I thought she was going to attack us!"

Tom looked back at the woman sitting on the asphalt, motionless and moaning, an empty fruit pie wrapper in one hand. The paramedics got to her and went to work, but she barely seemed to register their presence, and started to crawl away from them, back toward the grocery store. "Fruit piesssssh . . ." she moaned, as the paramedics tried to restrain her.

Tom looked back through the windshield at Angelica. "Did she try to hurt you?"

"No. She collapsed before she got to the car."

A pair of firemen approached the Lexus, while two others got into and moved the Suburban and Escalade, freeing the smaller car. Tom dashed to Angelica's door and yanked it open with a screech of metal, and then he was on his knees beside her, his hands tracing over her in search of any hint of injury. He heard her breath catch on a sob, and then her arms were around his neck, holding him tightly to her. A hot rush of love, relief, and protectiveness drowned his senses, and it was several seconds before he was aware of the fireman's hand on his shoulder, trying to pull him away. He reluctantly dis-engaged Angelica's arms from around his neck and let the fireman do his exam before allowing her to exit the car.

"Tom," she said weakly as soon as she was standing, her dark eyes imploring.

He started to swoop her up into his arms, determined to carry her away from all danger, but she pressed her hand against his chest, stopping him. "Something's going on," she whispered, "and I need your help to figure it out."

"Anything!"

She led him a few feet away from the car. Another fireman was helping Karen. Tom heard the girl asking the fireman if he could retrieve her Junior Mints.

Angelica was shivering. He started to put his arm around her, but she gave a tight shake of her head and pulled away, wrapping her own arms around herself in lieu of his. Hurt stabbed him at the rejection. "I think Dr. Velazquez is doing something very bad to women with his Phi-Tox," she said, distracting him from his hurt. "I think he might have caused *that*," she said, nodding stiffly over her shoulder at the woman on the asphalt, "and every other case of implant rejection in the city."

"Thank god you don't have any implants yourself!"

"I need you to help me prove that the Phi-Tox is behind what's happening."

For a moment his blood surged with the thrill that she wanted his help, but rationality quickly intruded. "You don't have to prove anything. Tell the paramedics. Tell the police."

She shook her head. "It's just a suspicion. They'll never be allowed access to Velazquez's records without a court order, and god knows if they'll ever get that. But *we* don't have to jump through legal hoops. We have Karen, and her keys to his office."

Tom looked over at the Asian girl, presently fishing the last of her Junior Mints out of a box while ignoring the fire-man's questions. "You mean to break in?"

"It's not breaking in if we have keys, is it? I want to get into his office and check his records. I want to see how many of the stars who are having implant rejections have also been clients of his Phi-Tox."

"Can't Karen check on Monday?"

Angelica laid her hand on his arm, her touch stealing so much of his attention that he barely heard her words. "Tom, I don't think Karen'll make it until Monday. Something bad is happening to her. It's happening to me, too."

That caught his attention. "What's that slick jackass done to you?" he whispered urgently, gripping her upper arms.

Angelica lowered her voice, eyes slowly checking to right and left to see that no one could hear her. "I think we're turning into a sort of zombie. *Carb*-scarfing zombies!"

"*What?*"

"We're gradually becoming paralyzed. Like, like . . . like from that puffer fish that people eat in Japanese restaurants! Look at me; I can barely move my face or my neck. I can't even move my eyes easily." She demonstrated.

Fear for her made Tom's heart skip a beat, and then that fear transformed to anger surging in his blood. *Velazquez!*

"I think sugary foods work as a temporary antidote to the Phi-Tox," Angelica went on. "But that sounds crazy, doesn't it?"

He fought back the anger so he could think for a moment, his mind picking through things he'd learned as a biologist. "Not necessarily. Sugar is quick energy for the cells; maybe a high enough dose of it gives you enough energy to fight the effects of the Phi-Tox."

Angelica looked over at her friend. "Then we're going to have to keep Karen in Junior Mints until we get into Dr. Velazquez's computer."

One of the firemen examining Karen called out to Angelica. "Ma'am? Could I talk to you for a moment?"

Angelica and Tom went over to him, as Karen went back to the Lexus and started rooting around inside.

"Ma'am, is your friend on a prescription medication?" the

fireman asked, his face studiously bland, although his shoulders were tight.

"No," Angelica said.

He sucked his teeth for a moment, looking at her. "Did she take something non-prescription?" He raised his eyebrows suggestively.

"No! Karen doesn't take—"

"Yeah," Tom interrupted. "Yeah, she did. Kind of obvious with her munchies, isn't it?"

Angelica slowly turned to look up at him, angry denial in her eyes. He widened his own at her. "She has an appointment to see her *doctor* about that problem of hers," he said meaningfully, and saw comprehension clear the anger from Angelica's eyes. If the paramedics took Karen to the hospital, he and Angelica might not be able to get into Dr. Velazquez's files.

The fireman nodded, relaxing. "All right. Her reflexes are messed up, and I wanted to be sure it wasn't from the accident. Keep an eye on her; if she doesn't seem quite right when the drugs wear off, take her in to get checked out."

"Yes, sir," Angelica said.

Karen emerged from the back of the car with the pint of Ben & Jerry's. She had the lid off, and was squeezing the carton to bring the ice cream up to mouth level, where she slurped it off in great gulps. Cream smeared like clown makeup around her mouth. "What?" she said, as the three of them stared at her. "It's going to melt!"

It was another hour before they could leave the scene, what with gathering information, talking to police—who gave Angelica the hairy eyeball because of her slow movements, but seemed to decide her behavior didn't fit with intoxicants—and arranging for removal of the car. As they waited, Tom's worry grew as he saw firsthand how Angelica's physical stiffness gradually worsened. The Ben & Jerry's was long gone, and she and Karen had already shared the jar of hot fudge sauce, eating it with their fingers. Even five minutes without sugar intake seemed to affect them adversely. At the rate they were declining, they'd hardly be able to walk by the time they got to Velazquez's office.

Tom had had plenty of experience with neurotoxins; the sea krait had been the least severe of the encounters he'd had with venomous creatures, chief amongst them being the multitude of jellyfish in the ocean. He himself had been stung several times by the notoriously deadly box jelly, and had endured excruciating, days-long pain even with the administration of an antivenom. At least two divers he'd known had not been so lucky, and had died.

Whatever toxin Velazquez had injected into Angelica might lead to the same fate: death. The toxin's effects seemed to be growing stronger with time, not weaker; God only knew what chain of reactions was going on inside her body. Angelica might die without an antivenom, assuming one even existed! His heart dropped into his stomach at the realization that there might not even be an antidote.

Be the jellyfish, he reminded himself, as he felt the adrenaline surging in his veins. Fear was acceptable, but panic was not. The jellyfish projected graceful calm even while trailing ten meters of toxic tentacles, destroying all in its path. *Be the jellyfish, and think!* If there were an antidote, the information would be in Dr. Velazquez's files. If there *weren't* an antidote, then the only hope of creating one was also to be found in the good doctor's office. They needed to know how Velazquez made Phi-Tox.

He got the women and their entertainment magazines installed in Mr. Toad, then jogged back to the grocery store and started throwing candy into his basket to keep the women mobile. A better idea suddenly hit him. He dumped the candy out of his basket and ran to the baking aisle. A minute later he'd emptied the shelves of corn syrup.

"Here," he said when he got back to the truck, popping the lids off a couple of Karo bottles and handing them to Angelica and Karen. "Drink up!"

Both women stared in dismay at the offering he'd put in

their hands. "They werrrre out of Junior Mintssss?" Karen complained.

"Yup." He nudged Angelica's hand toward her mouth, silently urging her to drink. He'd give her an IV of corn syrup for the next thirty years of her life, if that was how long it took to find the antidote. "Bottoms up!"

Angelica's first sip was reluctant, but then some force beyond her control seemed to take over her body and she tilted her head back, chugging the entire twelve ounces and then holding the bottle above her open mouth, waiting for the last slow dribble to leak out. She turned to him with eyes showing a glimmer of returning brightness.

"Good?" he asked, as he crammed himself into the tiny cab with the women and started the car. Angelica legs were parted around the gearshift, and the sides of his hand rubbed against her inner thighs as he fought for reverse, his hand brushing up against her crotch as he finally got the truck in gear.

"It's good," she said throatily, throwing him off for a moment, until he realized she meant the corn syrup, not his hand in her private parts. "But I'm going to pack on five pounds a day at this rate."

"Don't worry. That's just more ass for me to grab!"

From the other side of Angelica, Karen piped up, "Angelica, you have to keep him. Those are the words of a good man!"

Tom waited to hear Angelica's response, his jaw tight with hope as he drove out of the parking lot and onto the main street. Her answer came slowly.

"I might have kept him, if things were different. But to me, a keeper is by your side through thick, thin, and everything in between. I want someone I can count on to be there for me, every day. I don't want an absentee boyfriend. I'd rather be single than pining after someone I could only see once every year or two."

"You'll pine for me if I leave?" he asked, catching the one

small spot of brightness in her words. She was pressed up against his side, her left leg tucked beneath his right calf. She looked up at him, so close he would only have to bend his head to kiss her.

"'If'?" she asked, a spark of hope in her voice.

His tongue, unfortunately, got ahead of his brain in his answer. "I don't know why I said 'if.' I meant 'when.'"

"Oh," she replied, disappointment leaking out of the vowel sound like air deflating from a tire. She turned to look out Karen's window.

Tom winced, cursing himself. Couldn't he have left it at "if"? The jellyfish would have been cool with that.

Conversation died as he took Mr. Toad up the entrance ramp to the freeway; the noise of road and wind made talk impossible. Between handling the squirrelly truck and speculating on the formula for Phi-Tox, a small part of his brain became obsessed with "if."

Why had he said "if," anyway? Maybe part of him was considering staying here. He could leave the manager he'd hired in charge of the business in Micronesia and get a boat going here, running overnight dive trips to Catalina and the Channel Islands like Santa Barbara. But diving around Catalina was not in the same league as diving in the South Pacific, and living in Los Angeles was a slow death to anyone who thrived in a natural environment. Was love worth that big a sacrifice?

He was surprised he was considering staying. He knew himself better than to think it would be a good idea. How long would it be before he started chafing at life here? How long before he started to resent Angelica for being the reason he stayed? He couldn't change his wants to suit those of another.

He glanced at Angelica, feeling his heart contract at the beauty of her face. He'd been asking her to change *her* wants, hadn't he? He'd tried to make her want the footloose, precarious life of a traveling artist, even though she'd told him that what she valued was stability and security. No wonder she'd rejected him.

He urged Mr. Toad up to fifty-five, the little truck rattling and howling, giving voice to the frustration in his own heart. There might not be much hope for him with Angelica, but it didn't change this one sure thing: he would lay down his life to deliver his Angel from evil.

Chapter Eight

"Thissh issh all I have accessh to," Karen slurred, as the appointment book came up on the computer screen at her desk in Dr. Velazquez's front office. The monitor cast a blue-white tone over the girl's immobile face, and Angelica thought it made her look eerily like a stone sculpture. Karen had been sipping at a bottle of Karo, but every few minutes she seemed to forget it was in her hand, and murmured, "Junior Mintsssh . . ."

Angelica had been nervous about entering the building, a Beverly Hills low-rise with a security guard stationed in the lobby. The guard had recognized Karen, though, and Tom's nose tubes made it clear enough that he was a patient. Karen had assured her that there were plenty of late-night comings and goings in the business of plastic surgery; stars didn't want to be seen walking into a clinic in the broad light of day, and walking out again with bandages on their faces or groggy from anesthesia.

"You can't get into the medical records?" Tom asked.

"Nuh," Karen grunted.

"But you can go back in the sssschedule?" Angelica asked, wincing inside at the sound of her voice. Tom cast a worried look at her. She took a hit of Karo. "Look for the namesssh." She spread both tabloid covers on the desk.

Karen slowly started typing.

"Where are the medical records kept?" Tom asked.

Karen pointed at the door into the clinic proper. "They're digitizshed. Eash exam roooom hash a computer, and sho doessh Vewashquesh'sh offish. I don't have pashwordz."

"If the employees here are like most others, they've written them down somewhere convenient. I'm going to go check." He headed toward the door.

"Tom, wait!" Angelica said, alarm thumping through her. Digging through medical files in the office was different from accessing the appointment records that Karen was already allowed to see. If they were caught right now, the worst that would happen was Karen being fired. If Tom were caught in an exam room, digging through records, he'd be arrested. "If you're caught . . ."

"Karen, you said Velazquez was at a movie premiere tonight?" Tom asked.

"Yesh. Date with actresssh. Go to partiessh after."

Tom grinned at Angelica. "See? No problem. He won't surprise us."

The worrywart part of her was only slightly soothed. "The appointment book should tell us enough to bring to the policshe."

They both looked at Karen. "Firssht name, no luck," the girl said. "Now for second name." Her fingers slowly found the right keys.

Tom met Angelica's eyes. "Even if she finds the names, we need more than that. We need the Phi-Tox formula. You stay here with Karen; I'm going in." He pulled open the door.

A whimper of nerves strummed in Angelica's throat as she looked from Karen to the door closing behind Tom. *Curse it!* She couldn't let him take all the risks alone, not when coming here had been her idea. She chased after him, fear thrumming in her blood.

The hall beyond the door was dark and quiet, its carpeted floor absorbing sound. A dim light came from an open doorway straight ahead, at the end of the hall: Velazquez's office. Tom had headed straight for the source.

She found him pulling out drawers and lifting the blotter on Velazquez's big antique desk while the computer booted up on a built-in mahogany counter behind him. He'd turned on the dim, under-cabinet lights above the computer.

"Ha!" he declared, peering into the back of a drawer. "Found it!"

Angelica came over to look. Inside the drawer, stuck to its side near the back, was a sticky note that said:

Login: diego
Password: infanta

Angelica was impressed by Tom's quick success. This breaking and entering seemed almost too easy.

"Nice of him to label them for us, wasn't it?" Tom said, turning back to face the monitor that now displayed the login page. "Wonder what they mean, diego and infanta?"

"Diego, as in Diego Velazquez, the Spanish painter. The 'Infanta' was his most famous work. Dr. Velazquez is descended from him, and feels he inherited the family talent."

Tom snorted. "No man with a true appreciation for beauty would spend his life carving up women, trying to 'improve' them." He typed in the password, entered the system, and started poking around.

"You don't think some women could use a tweak here or there? Smaller thighs, bigger breasts?"

"If a skin-and-bones woman wants bigger breasts, she should gain twenty pounds," he said dryly.

"It's *not* that easy! On some women, extra weight goes straight to the thighs. No one wants to be shaped like a pear."

"Why not?" he asked with half his attention, as he opened and closed files.

"B-b-because!" she stuttered in shock. "Pear-shaped! Bad!"

He shrugged, clicking open a different icon.

"Guys don't want women who look like pears!" she insisted.

"Hey, I can't speak for all guys, but give some of us some credit," he said, scrolling down a page. "I'd rather have a pear-shaped babe willing to do the nasty in broad daylight—on the deck of an open boat—than a self-conscious Barbie doll who wants the lights off and spends all her free time and money on grooming herself."

"Really?"

He clicked the file closed and opened another. "I'd say most guys would rather have someone who enjoyed herself as she was than someone who tortured him with insecurities about the size of her butt. Act like you have a great butt, and we'll believe you! Happily!" He glanced up at her. "You know what they say: it's not the size that matters; it's how you use it."

"I don't think they're talking about women's butts in that."

"Same difference. You want me asking you if my dick's big enough?"

"No!"

"See?"

"But . . ." she protested, as he looked back at the screen, "don't you think the women who do take such pains with their appearance are more beautiful?"

Tom broke his attention away from the monitor to look at her. "Angelica. The women in L.A. look like freaking plastic monsters. They make my skin crawl. They aren't real. *You're* real. You're beautiful."

"I've got small breasts . . ." she started weakly, wanting to believe him but doubting his words.

"And you've got a big butt and a hooked nose; yeah, I know. And I love them. I love *every part of you*." He grabbed her hips, turned her around, yanked down her pajama bottoms, and planted a noisy kiss on her butt cheek.

Angelica squeaked in surprise.

"Every part of you," he said again, pulling her PJs back up. He turned back to the monitor. "Which is why we've got to find out more about Phi-Tox."

Angelica turned slowly around to watch him work, her mind a welter of thoughts and emotions. He thought she was beautiful! He loved every part of her. Did that mean he loved *her*, Angelica, the sum of her parts? He'd asked her to marry him, sure, but he'd never said he loved her. She'd taken his proposal for an impulse.

Angelica had always believed that *true* love at first sight, that rarest of loves, could only happen if the people were right for each other and subconsciously understood each other's natures when they met. She'd thought Tom wasn't right for her, and thus that his apparent attraction to her was not based on anything approaching true love. If she didn't love him, he couldn't love her; not really, truly, deeply.

She watched him scanning through files, his focus so intense that he seemed to have momentarily screened her from his awareness. She hadn't thought he was capable of such determined concentration; his goofy manner precluded such behavior, PhD notwithstanding. And his efforts now were all to save her, even though she'd given him no hope that they could have a future together. She lifted her hand, intending to rest it on the back of his neck.

"I'm not finding anything related to Phi-Tox!" Tom growled in frustration.

She dropped her hand, an idea coming to her from the depths of her unconscious. "Try hissh browsher."

"You want to see what porn he's been surfing?"

She took a swig from the Karo bottle she'd set on the desk when she came in. "No. Maybe he keepsh hish information in the cloud."

Tom's brows rose. "Huh?"

She took a few more glugs of syrup. "Information cloud. Online. Personal computers can be subpoenaed, their hard drives dug through. Maybe he feels safer hiding things online."

Tom clicked open the browser. "But if his computer says where he's been, how is the information safer?"

"*I* don't know. Maybe it's not. But maybe *he* thinks it is, or maybe he has some sort of elaborate security system."

"Let's hope not."

She watched as the browser opened. "Check History."

The menu opened, and as they both scanned the list of Web sites Tom started to chuckle. "Porn! I *told* you plastic surgeons were obsessed with sex! Want me to go to one of these sites, to make sure?"

"No! Check his bookmarks."

Tom shut the history menu and went to Bookmarks. It was full of porn sites, other plastic surgeons' Web sites, about twenty sites related to Costa Rica's rain forests, a bunch of government sites including the FDA and the National Center for Biotechnology Information, and a file called, simply, Testing. Under it was one Web site: BB. "Click there," Angelica said.

A pink and white site opened with the banner headline: BEYOND BOTOX! The subhead read: *Be young forever, with the super secret new formula developed by the world's top plastic surgeon: Phi-Tox!*

There were several Before and After photos of women's faces, transformed from scowling prunes to serene Madonnas. *The Fountain of Youth has been discovered!* the caption declared.

Another photo showed a group of attractive young women lounging around a richly decorated living room, laughing and sipping wine. *Arrange for a Phi-Tox party in your own home. Groups of twenty-five or more receive a special discount.*

"Why did he put this under Testing, I wonder?" Angelica said. "Looks more like a cash-generating machine."

"That son of a bitch," Tom growled. "Don't you see? He's using the women who sign up for Phi-Tox parties as his lab rats! He's testing the formula on them in an uncontrolled experiment."

Angelica sucked in a breath, understanding. "That'ss how he'sh managed to inject sho many women around the schity that L.A. ish running out of candy!" She struggled to make her stiff lips work. "Velashquesh could do a hundred women a day, going from party to party!"

Tom looked at her in concern as she finished off the bottle of Karo syrup. "Angelica, you're getting worse. We've *got* to find that formula. There's nothing about it on this computer. He must be doing his research elsewhere."

"Karen sayssh he hash a big private eshtate in Malibu. Maybe there?"

Tom nodded. "It would make sense. No nurses, no janitors; he'd have complete control over access. Complete privacy." He glanced at the computer's clock. "It's a quarter after ten. Karen said he was going to parties after the premiere; how late do those usually go?"

Angelica thought back to all the office gossip Karen had shared about Velazquez's love life over the past couple months. "It dependsh on hish mood. He could shtay out all night if he likesh hish date, or be home by midnight."

"We'll have to risk it." He spent a couple minutes finding Velazquez's address on Google, and then pored over the satellite shot of the estate. "Jeez, would you look at the size of this place?" He zoomed in on the sprawling mansion as far as he could.

"What's that big round dark area on the roof?"

"I'd guess it's an atrium or greenhouse." He shifted the screen view slightly. "There's also a long rectangular run of glass over here, maybe above a gallery or a pool. Velazquez sure likes his natural light." Tom pointed to an area next to the atrium, where large cubes cast shadows on the roof. "By the size of these units, this must be commercial-grade HVAC equipment. I'll bet this is where his lab is."

"How arrre we going to get in?" She didn't realize until she said it that she fully intended to go with him. Seeing the Beyond Botox! Web site had pushed her over the edge: Velazquez was experimenting on women without their consent, and that was so *not* okay. He had forfeited any right to privacy or the protection of the law, as far as she was concerned.

And, too, the thought of being separated from Tom right now was more frightening than the thought of invading Velazquez's estate. Tom's determination to save her and her growing faith in his strength and intelligence were all that were keeping her from panic.

"I'll bet he has an extra set . . ." Tom said, spinning around in the chair and going back to Velazquez's antique desk. He dug in the drawers again, and a moment later came up with an automatic garage or gate opener and a ring of keys. "Ha!"

Tom printed out a map to the estate as well as one of the satellite images, and shut down the computer. On their way back to the front office they checked out the day-surgery and exam rooms and the dispensary—opened with a key from the ring—but there was no Phi-Tox to be found.

"Karen musht be done by now," Angelica said as they pushed back through the door into the reception area. The tabloids were still spread on the desk, and the computer screen lit, but there was no sign of Karen.

"Done and gone," Tom said darkly.

Worry crept up Angelica's spine. This was *not* the time for Karen to go missing! "Maybe she'sh in the bathroom?" she asked without any real hope.

"Maybe."

Angelica checked the restroom, but it was empty and dark.

"Look at this," Tom said urgently, when Angelica returned. He held up one of the tabloids. There were messy red ballpoint notes scrawled next to the columns of print in several places. "She wrote down dates of the women's visits to Velazquez."

"Sho the implant rejectionsss *are* related to the Phi-tox!"

"It's *worse* than that," Tom said. "Most of the dates are written next to names in the *other* article."

"Not—" she started, overcome by a feeling of horror as she looked at Karen's empty chair.

He nodded. "The article about L.A. women who have mysteriously disappeared."

"Oh god. Karen! Velashquesh musht have come back—" She cut herself off, stopping her fears from running away with her. "Wait. If Velashquesh wahsh here, he would have checked his offishe."

Tom nodded. "He would have caught us, too. Which means he either *wasn't* here and Karen wandered off on her own, or . . ."

"Or?"

"He's taken Karen and retreated to the lobby to call the cops."

Alarm set Angelica's neck hairs on end. "Either way, we've got to get out of here."

"Agreed!"

They found the fire stairs and hurried down, but Angelica's stiffening body slowed them. Tom scooped her up into his arms. "It's faster," he said against her protests, and she put her arms around his neck and let herself be carried.

On the ground floor Tom set her down. The door leading outside was attached to a fire alarm. "We've got to try the lobby first," he said, and carefully pushed open the door to the lobby and peered through the crack. Everything was quiet. "Stay here," he said, and slipped out.

Angelica waited tensely while he tiptoed to the end of the elevator bank and peeked around the corner toward the guard and his desk. Tom looked back at her and shrugged his shoulders, then gestured for her to come forward. She obeyed, and then he put her hand on his arm and led her out past the desk, where the guard was reading a book.

"Hey!" the guard suddenly said.

They stopped in their tracks. Angelica's heart seemed to freeze in her chest. "Yes?" Tom said, a faint quiver in his voice betraying his tension.

"The Asian girl. She didn't look too good. Is she okay?"

"Uh, not really," Tom said.

"She shouldn't be walking around alone like that. Someone should be looking after her."

Angelica felt Tom's arm relax under her hand. "That is exactly what we intend to do," he said. "Did you see which way she went?"

"Left."

"Thanks." They started to leave.

"And, hey!"

They both stiffened and turned back. "Yes?" Tom asked.

The guard's shoulders were hunched, his face uncertain. "I've kind of had my eye on her for a while. Is she, er . . . single?"

Angelica chuckled, her nerves straining at the odd sound. "Her name'sh Karen, and shhhe lovesss men in uniformsssh. You shhhhould asshk her out."

The guard's face brightened. "I just might do that. G'night."

"'Night."

"Christ almighty," Tom said under his breath, as they fled into the night air. He dragged Angelica across the street toward Mr. Toad.

"Wait, he shaid Karen went left!"

"You need more syrup, and we can do a faster sweep for Karen from the truck."

Angelica saw the logic and allowed herself to be helped into the toad.

Tom popped the top on the second to last bottle of syrup and put it in her hand. She glugged it while he fiddled with Mr. Toad, coaxing the truck to start. *Rrr rrr rrr*, the engine said. *Rrr rrr rrr!*

"C'mon," Tom muttered. "C'mon!"

At last the engine caught, rumbling to life, and then they were easing down the road. This part of Beverly Hills was quiet at this time of evening, with all of the retail shops closed. As they turned onto Brighton Way, though, they saw a small group of women mobbing the front of a shop. One of them was familiar.

"Karen!" Tom shouted, rolling down his window.

She didn't seem to hear. As they approached, a pair of women threw something at the plate glass of the front window, shattering it. A moaning cheer went up from the group, and they pressed forward, knocking out the last of the glass and invading the shop.

"What the hell are they doing?" Tom said, pulling over.

"Karen!" Angelica hollered out her window.

Tom yanked on the emergency brake but kept the truck idling. "Stay here!" He jumped out and jogged to Karen, grabbing her by the arm just as she was about to go through the broken window with the others.

Angelica smelled the heady scent of chocolate. She looked up and saw TEUSCHER OF SWITZERLAND above the door, and didn't even mind the pretentious lower-case T. These were chocolatiers, famous for their truffles. Her mouth watered. Chocolate was so much tastier than Karo syrup.

"Truuuuuffles," she moaned, and fumbled with her seatbelt. "Truuuuffles!" She creaked open her door.

Tom was trying to drag Karen back to the truck, but, like Angelica, she was moaning her desire. "Chahhhhcolaaate! Chahhhhhcolaaate!" Angelica stumbled past, drawn irresistibly toward the scent of cocoa butter and sugar.

"Angelica! Get back in the truck!" Tom said, grabbing her arm.

"Truuuuuffles!" she whined.

"Chahhhhhcolaaate!" Karen cried.

Together, they started again toward teuscher, Tom dragged along by the superior force of their combined hunger.

"Goddammit!" he swore, and released Karen.

The next thing Angelica knew, her feet were off the ground and she was being manhandled back into the truck and strapped in. Karo was poured into her mouth, and then Tom was in the driver's seat, forcing Mr. Toad at maximum speed away from the chocolate shop. As the scent of chocolate cleared from the air, her senses returned. She sucked down syrup and then put her hand on Tom's arm.

"What about Karen?"

He turned a corner. "I can't handle both of you."

"But we can't leave her there!

"I'm sure the police will arrive at any moment," he replied, turning onto Santa Monica Boulevard. "They'll put her somewhere safe. Jesus H.!" he shouted, slamming on the brakes as a mob of women stepped into the road in front of the truck. Mr. Toad jerked and bounced to a stop.

The women ignored the little truck and stumbled onward toward K Chocolatier. One of them started dragging a trash can toward the plate glass.

"It's *Night of the Living Dead*," Tom said, his voice hushed.

"And I'm turning into one of them," Angelica whimpered, her heart in her throat.

"Not if I can help it," Tom vowed, his voice full of dark determination. He put Mr. Toad back in gear and hit the gas.

Chapter Nine

It was midnight when they rolled up to the gate in front of Velazquez's Malibu home. The estate was at the top of a bluff between the Pacific Coast Highway and the ocean, and they'd only seen one other driveway off the unlit, one-lane road leading up to the gate.

"Jeez Louise, I didn't know plashtic shurgery paid this well," Angelica said. They'd stopped at a supermarket on the way to refill their supply of Karo. "No wonder my parentsh wanted me to go to med shchool instead of shtudy art."

"I don't think plastic surgery *does* pay this well. He must have family money." Tom cranked down his window and reached for the buzzer to the gate.

"What are you doing?" Angelica cried.

"Seeing if anyone's home. Better to find out now than when we've snuck in."

She couldn't argue with that.

He hit the buzzer and they waited. Seconds ticked by without a response, and then Tom jabbed the buzzer several more times in a row.

"If he was ashleep, he'sh not now," Angelica said.

"Exactly." Tom gave the buzzer another jab for good measure. After a couple minutes went by, he pointed the automatic opener at the gate and pressed the button. The gate slowly swung open, and Mr. Toad chugged through.

The cobblestone drive wound under a canopy of trees up the hill, coming out at last in a courtyard with a four-car garage at one end, and a massive portico at the other. Tom ignored both and pointed the toad toward the left end of the house, where a path led through the shrubberies.

"What are you doing?" Angelica whispered anxiously as bushes scraped the side of the truck.

"The satellite image showed a path around the house. Better to have the truck out of sight of the front entrance if he comes home."

Angelica gurgled in response.

They came out of the bushes onto a wide green lawn, illuminated along the landscaped edges with up-lights that showed off the forms of trees and bushes. The far edge of the lawn disappeared into night air: the bluff over the Pacific. The lights of distant ships twinkled near the horizon, and overhead a half moon sent its watery light through a thin layer of hazy marine air. Tom parked Mr. Toad under the branches of a eucalyptus, the truck's faded green paint blending with the menthol-scented leaves of the tree.

"Leave your door open," Tom said. He fished a flashlight from the glove box and then got out, leaving the keys in the ignition. "I want a quick getaway if it comes to that."

Angelica looked at him, then at the truck that never started in less than a full minute. There was no such thing as a quick getaway in Mr. Toad.

"Don't say it!" Tom warned, knowing her thoughts. "The toad has ears!"

Angelica shook her head and lugged her clinking grocery bag of Karo out of the car. "According to the shatellite image, the lab shhhould be over there," she said, pointing.

Tom nodded, and they sneaked their way along the edge of the house for a hundred meters, slipping past windows and across a terrace. They came to a block of the building without windows, the beige stucco wall broken only by a single, unassuming steel door. Above them, they could hear the whirr of HVAC equipment on the roof.

"This has got to be it," Tom said, and started trying keys on the door. The fourth one worked, and he turned the knob and opened the door a crack. Silence greeted them.

"No alarm shyshtem?" Angelica whispered hopefully.

"Don't know. Could be silent." He poked his head in the door, then chuckled softly.

"What?"

He opened the door wider and showed her. There was an alarm system, but it wasn't activated. Its LED lights glowed green in welcome. "He seems kind of complacent about security," Tom said.

"There are probably houndsss about to attack ush."

Tom took a quick glance back over his shoulder at the quiet grounds of the estate, as if it were a real possibility. "No barking."

"The deadly ones bite firsht, bark later."

He gave her a dark look, all the more menacing for the tubes that still protruded from his nose. "You're giving me a hard time, aren't you?"

If she could have grinned, she would have. "Jusht trying to relieve the tenshion." She took a swig of syrup.

He grunted, and held the door open for her. Together they slipped into the dark hall, and Tom switched on his flashlight. Its ellipse of white halogen light illuminated an institutional tile floor and utilitarian doors set into the walls. He raised the beam, and the light glimmered on solid glass double doors at the end of the hallway.

"That looks like something," Angelica whispered.

"Let's see what."

They crept down the hall. Angelica, feeling the same nervous dread she'd had when going through a Halloween haunted house as a child, reached for Tom's hand. It was warm and strong, and he gave her a reassuring squeeze.

Two of the doors they passed seemed to lead to service rooms: behind them, the muffled hums and rhythmic thumps of compressors and fans were dimly audible. As they came to the end of the hall, they saw it continued for a few feet to the right, ending in a mahogany door with a worked-iron handle.

"Probably goes into the house proper," Tom said, and

turned back to the glass doors. He put the flashlight up against the glass, peering through. "It's an antechamber." He grabbed the chrome handle on one of the doors and pulled it open. Angelica felt a rush of warm humid air scented with flowers and forest mold.

"It musht go to the atrium," she guessed, following Tom into the antechamber. It was only five feet deep, ending at another glass door, set in a wall of glass. Through the door they could see a steel catwalk stretching straight ahead, tropical leaves overhanging the handrail. The moon sent just enough illumination down through the round skylight for her to make out the silhouettes of a few trees. "Good Lord," she whispered in awe. "He's sure serious about his house plants!"

About fifty feet away, across the atrium at the other end of the catwalk, was another glass door, this one leading to a lit area beyond. "Do you think someone is home?" Angelica whispered, holding tightly to Tom's hand.

"If that's the lab down there, he might always leave some lights on. Or it could be a grow operation, if he gets the PhiTox from a plant."

"Or he could be home."

"Well, yeah. If you want to be pessimistic about it." Tom tilted his head. "Listen!"

Angelica did. Through the glass she heard the muffled trills of some animal; the quiet chirps of insects; a solitary, angry squawk; and rustling. "It's not just plants in there," she said.

"No." He pushed open the second door and led her forward.

Their footsteps clanged on the catwalk, and the atrium fell into silence at their intrusion. Angelica breathed in warm air as thickly humid as a steam bath, the scent of jungle even richer and more floral than in the antechamber. She pressed close to Tom, then muffled a shriek as something fluttered close to her head with a sound of rustling taffeta and then away again into the darkness. "What was *that?*"

Tom shone the flashlight into the foliage, searching for creatures. "Bat? Bird? Giant moth?"

Angelica groaned softly. "Don't let it be a bat."

The beam of the flashlight lit on a creature, and stopped. "Uh-oh," Tom said.

"What?" Even as she said it, Angelica's eyes followed the beam and saw what. A fat yellow snake lay on a branch not three feet from them, its rings of coils dripping over the sides of the branch like melting frosting. Revulsion rose from Angelica's gut to her throat, lodging there with the sickly sweet taste of stomach acids and Karo syrup. She gurgled.

Tom flashed the light away from the snake and pulled Angelica forward along the catwalk. "Let's not look at that."

A bird squawked, and then a few insects began their hum. A moment later a creature *beep-beeped* loudly on their left, and Tom flashed his light toward the sound. A small brilliant orange frog glowed against a green leaf the size of a platter.

"Beautiful," Angelica breathed, stunned by the hue of the frog.

"Mm," Tom murmured. "It looks like a type of poison dart frog."

"Poison dart, as in, used to make poison darts?"

"Yeah. Most of them are harmless, but some varieties are deadly. One frog can make enough paralytic toxin in its skin to kill several people. Those are the types that jungle tribes use for their poison darts."

"You seem to know a lot about them."

"I have an interest in toxins, given how often I've been bitten or stung by snakes, jellyfish, insects, spiny fish—"

"And you want me to go scuba diving? I don't think so."

The frog leapt away into the darkness. Instead of following its path with the light, Tom suddenly turned around and shone the light again on the yellow snake. "Interesting."

"What's interesting?"

He leaned over the metal rail and aimed the light down to the bottom of the atrium. Angelica followed his gaze, but saw only hints of forest floor, rich in humus. "Velazquez has an entire ecosystem in here," Tom pointed out. "Trees, dirt, insects, frogs, snakes, birds."

"He's big on rain forest conservation. He says they're nature's pharmacopoeia."

Another *beep-beep* sounded in the foliage, and Angelica laughed softly.

"What?"

"They sound like Mr. Toad."

"Mr. Toad," Tom said, his voice trailing off into thought. "Did you know, zombies in Haiti are thought to be created in part by a toxin from a toad? Toads and dart frogs . . ." His voice rose in excitement. "This whole atrium is for the poison dart frogs!"

"The frogs? Are they endangered?" Angelica asked, but even as she spoke she realized that that wasn't what this was about. A tingle of goose bumps rose on her arms, despite the humid heat. "The Phi-Tox. You think he's making it from the poison dart frogs' toxin!"

"'Phi' as in am-*phi*-bian. Most animals that produce toxins don't do so in captivity," Tom explained quickly, as he put the pieces together. "Usually they get their toxins by eating insects that produce certain alkaloids, and the insects in turn get their alkaloids from processing the plants they eat. It's a multistep chemical process, not well understood, and difficult to reproduce in the laboratory."

"So Velazquez re-created the natural laboratory," Angelica said. "He's letting the jungle do the work for him."

"Right."

"Does the jungle also produce an antivenom?" she asked, fearing the answer might be no.

"The poison dart frog has one predator in the wild, an animal that is immune to its toxins. By regularly eating the frog, this animal's blood has developed antibodies to fight the venom."

"What animal is that?" Angelica asked, even as a feeling of foreboding crept over her.

"*That.*" Tom flashed the light on the yellow snake.

"No," she begged, shaking her head.

"It may be your salvation—"

Her knees went weak. "No! Not the snake!"

Tom took a step toward the snake, dragging her along with him. "We've got to catch it and—"

"Tom, no!" she whined, as he dragged her closer and closer. The snake seemed to expand as they approached; its yellow eye opened and seemed to gaze right at her with soulless hunger. Terror made Angelica's brain go blank. "No, no! Don't make it bite me! No . . ." she moaned.

"Bite you?"

"No!"

"Angelica, I don't mean for it to bite you! I mean we should get some of its blood and separate the serum from the red blood cells. There's no antivenom in the snake's *own* venom."

His words sank through her haze of terror. "Oh? Oh!" She stood up straighter, strength returning even as her cheeks flamed in embarrassment at her error. "Then we should look in the lab first!" she babbled, ecstatic to have an excuse to get away from the snake. "Maybe Velazquez has an antivenom on hand for himself! You can give me an injection!"

Tom stopped. "You're right."

He changed direction and hurried her toward the lit door, holding her up as her feet tripped over the steel grating of the catwalk. Relief rushed through Angelica as they pushed through the glass door and into another antechamber, leaving the snake safely behind.

The exit door from this antechamber was translucent white, but not transparent. What they'd thought might be the white of a laboratory was, instead, this. "Now, what has Velazquez hidden behind Door Number Two?" Tom mused.

"Better not be more snakes," Angelica muttered.

Tom chuckled, then cautiously pushed open the door a crack and peered through.

"What do you see?" Angelica whispered.

"I think it's an art gallery."

"Really? Let me see."

He let her take his place. Angelica put her eye to the crack and saw the edge of a statue on a plinth. "Sculpture." She pushed the door open slightly wider, and saw that the statue was of a naked woman. Her eyes skimmed past it to the wall behind the art. "I see a door just off to the left; maybe it goes to the lab."

Tom pushed open the door and they stepped out into the gallery. It called to Angelica's mind the sculpture galleries she'd seen in museums, where a long white space was lined with Greek or Roman statues of men and women standing on plinths. Velazquez's statues were all of nude women, created in a medium that Angelica could not immediately identify. Resin? Wax? They'd obviously all been made by the same artist, as their style was identical: proportioned like Playboy bunnies, realistic down to the hair that flowed over their shoulders, and colored to mimic life. Several had flesh-toned bandages stuck on their bodies, and one of them looked a lot like Kelsey Magnuson. The statues all seemed embarrassingly real and vulnerable in the bright lights of the gallery.

Angelica squinted up at the lights affixed to the ceiling near the night-dark skylights. "Thishhh looksh like full-shpectrum lighting," she slurred, her tongue suddenly thick in her mouth.

"What was that?"

"Fffffull shhhhpectrum. Like daylight. Expen-shive." During art school she'd learned to see the differences between the various types of artificial lighting, as each type of light affected how the eye read colors. Bulbs that truly mimicked daylight in color temperature and color rendering were rare and expensive.

"Why'd he leave them on, I wonder?" Tom asked, while taking Angelica's grocery bag of syrup from her and opening a bottle. He held it out to her, and when she was slow to respond he wrapped her hand around the bottle and eased it to her lips.

Angelica drank, and felt only a slight tingling of improvement in her body as the Karo went down her throat. Something was wrong; *more* wrong, rather, than it had been. Her eyes slid away from Tom and to the statue behind him. Her eyes went wide, and she gagged on the syrup, coughing and sputtering.

Tom slapped her back. "You okay?"

"Unnn!" Angelica grunted, and lifted one heavy hand to point behind him.

Tom turned. "What?"

"The ssshtatue!"

"What about it?"

"Isssh not a shhhtatue!"

"It's not a statue? What do you mean, it's not a statue?"

"Isssssh woman!"

"Yes, I see that." He frowned at her. "Are you upset that she's nude?"

Angelica thumped her hand against his chest in frustration. "Tom! Isssh *living* woman!"

Tom goggled and spun around. *"Christ almighty!"*

The eyes of the naked woman were slowly opening. Her lips parted. A breath eased out between them, carrying a whisper of sound. *"Helllllp . . ."*

"Oh my god," Angelica gasped. "Faaaace in newshpaper."

"Face?"

"Her," Angelica said, pointing at the living statue. "Misssshing woman!"

Comprehension hit Tom, and he looked down the length of the gallery in obvious horror. "The missing women! These are them! The goddamn asshole has paralyzed them and put them on display."

"He shhaid he wassssh an artisht." Her mouth barely managed the words; she'd been doing well in the atrium, but out here under the full-spectrum lights she felt as though she were quickly turning into one of these statues. "They are hisssh art."

"God *damn* him!"

"Tom," she said weakly.

His voice cracked in anger and what sounded like tears of outrage. "God damn him to hell!"

"Tom, da lightshhhh . . ."

"When I get my hands on him, he's going to pay!"

"Tom!"

He looked at her. She weakly pointed upward. "Lightssshhh baaaaad."

Understanding lit his eyes. "Phototoxicity! We've got to shut the lights off!"

A popping *thwup* sound suddenly cut the air, and a thin dart with a wad of white cotton at the end appeared in the side of Tom's neck. "What the . . . ?" Tom said, reaching for his neck.

Thwup! Another dart appeared, this one in his forearm.

"Tom!" Angelica screamed.

Thwup! Thwup! Thwup! Three more darts hit his body.

Tom's lips parted as if to speak, and then his eyes crossed. He swayed before his legs gave out beneath him and he crumpled to the floor, his eyes open and dead.

Angelica felt as if her heart had stopped in her chest. *Tom! No!* She remembered his words about the dart frogs: one frog could produce enough toxin to kill several people. Her heart couldn't bear the thought. *No! Not Tom!*

Footsteps approached behind her, easy and slow. She turned. Dr. Velazquez was walking toward her, a long wooden blowgun resting in the crook of his arm. He was dressed in black tie, his hair perfectly coiffed, his face filled with quiet confidence. "There is more than one way to 'turn out the lights,'" he said, and smiled at his witticism.

"Issssh he deeeead?"

"Unless he's a superhero, yes, I imagine so. But you won't be." He pulled a dart from his breast pocket and tucked it into the mouthpiece of the blowgun. "Hold still, my dear. This won't hurt a bit."

Angelica tried to dodge, but it was no use. Velazquez raised the blowgun to his lips, and with a soft *thwup* she, too, was stuck with a dart in the neck. She stood for a few seconds, feeling the toxin spreading its numbing force through her body, and then she dropped to the floor, the world spinning around her as she fell.

When she came to rest, her eyes were still open, and she could hear Velazquez approaching. "Don't worry," he said, towering above her. "You're finally going to get those implants you need. With a little work, you, too, can be a work of living art in my Hall of Beauty." He picked up her feet and started to drag her across the smooth floor to the door at the side of the gallery. "Aren't you the lucky one?"

As he pulled her through the doorway, Angelica caught a glimpse of Tom's body crumpled at the feet of a statue. Tears spilled from her eyes. She *had* been the lucky one; she had had Tom. He'd offered her love and devotion, and a chance to live the life of her dreams. If only she had been willing to take that chance . . .

But no, she'd been too wrapped up in being responsible, and too fearful to take the bounty that life had offered her in the shape of one fearless, glorious man. And what had all her caution gotten her? Tied down in the laboratory of a madman, about to be cut up and made into a living statue. If she had it all to do over again, she would grab Tom's hand, run with him to the farthest corner of the globe, and never look back or regret.

The door shut on her view, and her heart folded in on itself. All those possibilities were over forever now, dead along with the man who had given his life for her. The pain of it was too much to bear. She shut her eyes.

If only.

Chapter Ten

Tom listened to Velazquez telling Angelica the horrors he was going to inflict on her body. Tom's whole soul screamed out against such atrocities, but his body lay paralyzed, unable to so much as lift a finger to defend the love of his life.

From the corner of his vision he saw Velazquez drag her away, hauling her by her feet as if she were a deer he'd run down with his car. He heard the door shut, and the sound acted as a starting gun in his head. The race between his paralyzed body and Velazquez's scalpel was on. As long as there was breath in his body, he would not let harm come to Angelica. If he had to pull himself forward with his lips, he would fight his way there and find a way to save her.

A single blink of his eyes was his first victory against the paralytic toxins coursing through his bloodstream. His eyelids slowly shut, bringing blessed moisture to his dry eyes. It was marginally easier to open them. Close, open. Close, open, faster each time. It was as if that one small neurological pathway were cleared of toxin by repeating the movement.

Next was his neck. Through force of will he made his head turn slowly to the right, where he'd heard Angelica's bottle of Karo roll when she'd dropped it. Millimeter by millimeter, his muscles obeyed his command until his cheek was pressed against the cold, sticky floor.

Sticky. The Karo had spilled!

He reached out his tongue and dabbed its tip in the syrup. His tongue seemed to revive under the taste and take on a life of its own, lapping at the floor. His whole body tilted to-

ward the syrup, his mouth opening to suck it off the floor like
a dog in a dirty kitchen.

Sparkles of sensation filtered through his inert limbs, and
before he knew it, he was dragging himself to the fallen grocery bag and opening another bottle.

He should have been dead from all those darts. Velazquez
had thought he was, and about the only thing on which Tom
would trust the doctor at this point was his ability to kill
someone. He could only think that the dozens of times he'd
been bitten or stung by animals while diving had resulted in
a partial immunity, like that of the yellow snake in the
atrium. He knew of a species of fish that built immunity to
sea anemone toxins so that they could live within the tentacles. The same thing must have happened with him. The excruciating box jellyfish stings had been worth it, if it meant
he had a chance to save Angelica.

A few minutes later he was on his hands and knees, crawling toward the light switches on the wall near the entrance
to the atrium, having remembered what Angelica had tried
to tell him about the lights. He was moving so slowly he
would have lost a race with a snail. He felt as if he were slog-
ging through mud, his limbs like anchors trying to hold him
to one spot.

If he was going to save Angelica, he was going to need
more than Karo syrup to fuel her rescue. What was worse, he
didn't know if he'd be able to do it alone.

He looked over his shoulder at the gallery of frozen
women. The one who'd asked for help was staring at him, an
intense, unreadable expression burning in her blue eyes. He
wasn't alone! He had a whole zombie army to help him, if
only he could help them first.

Velazquez was humming under his breath. It drew Angelica
out of her grief, firing her soul with angry annoyance. She
wanted to cry, goddamn it, and think about Tom, but that
humming was getting in the way. What was worse, she recognized the tune but couldn't immediately place it.

What was it?

Oh, good Lord. "You Are So Beautiful."

The motherf----r.

"D, or full D?" Velazquez said, appearing in her line of sight with a silicone implant in each gloved hand. "Ten-inch breasts, or ten-and-a-half-inch breasts?"

She was lying strapped to a gurney in an operating room off his lab, naked except for several lines drawn on her skin with marker to help guide Velazquez as he operated. At the moment she also had a small paper surgical blanket over her loins, a small concession to modesty that would last only until it was time to liposuction her thighs.

The doctor had changed out of his tuxedo and into scrubs. His coiffed hair was hidden beneath a paper cap. She supposed she should be grateful that he was at least practicing good hygiene.

"Full D?" He held the implant slightly above her bare chest.

No! She didn't want implants! She wanted her breasts just the way they were, just the way Tom had loved them! He'd loved every part of her, exactly as she was.

"I know, you're worried about implant rejection, aren't you?" Velazquez said conversationally. "I've been working on an anti-rejection drug cocktail that is showing some promising results. It's been three days since any of my artwork in the Hall of Beauty has rejected an implant. That, my dear, is progress."

Angelica gurgled.

"What was that? You'll have to enunciate if you wish to be understood."

"Wwwwhy?" she whispered.

"Why am I doing this? I should think the answer is obvious."

"Mmmmmoney?"

"Money?! *Dios*, no. Do you take me for a greedy philistine? My family left me more money than I could ever need. No, I do this for the betterment of the world."

She stared at him. In what crazy world could anything he was doing be seen as betterment?

Velazquez set the implants on a tray and arranged surgical equipment nearby. He'd already told her that he was going to do everything under local anesthetic; it was too risky to put her under completely while he was working alone. The horror of being awake during plastic surgery was too terrible for her mind to take in. If she could keep him talking and delay that first incision, she would.

"Hhhhow behhhhhter?"

Velazquez paused. "How do my efforts better the world; is that what you're asking? It's quite simple. I make women far more beautiful than any of them are naturally, which you must agree is a great gift to the planet. More importantly, part of this beautification is through Phi-Tox, which as you may or may not have figured out by now is derived from a variety of poison dart frog native to the rain forests of Costa Rica. As soon as the FDA approves the toxin, and I am able to sell it openly, I will make billions of dollars. Billions! And it can all go to saving the rain forests. It's a beautiful circle, isn't it? The frogs make the toxin, women pay to be made beautiful with Phi-Tox, the money from the drug goes to preserve the jungle and the frogs. It's elegant in its simplicity. It's perfect."

"I know some women who beg to differ," a deep voice said from outside Angelica's field of vision. Her heart tripped. It sounded like—

Velazquez spun around and then gasped. "You!"

Angelica's soul sang with joy. It was Tom!

"You're dead!" Velazquez gasped.

"And yet, here I am."

"But how . . . ? I gave you enough to kill *five* men! Only a, a, a . . . *zombie* could be up walking again!"

Yes, how? How? Angelica wanted to know.

"There's no way," Velazquez insisted. "No human could have survived." His voice lowered in dread. "What *are* you?"

Tom spoke slowly, his voice as deep and sure as a superhero's. "I have always told myself to *be* the jellyfish. But tonight . . . tonight, I *am* the jellyfish!"

Velazquez gaped. "A jellyfish?"

"*The* Jellyfish," Tom corrected.

"You're insane." Velazquez fumbled for a syringe on the instrument tray, and as his hand wrapped around it, his confidence seemed to grow. He moved toward Tom. "The toxins must have damaged your brain."

"Loooook out!" Angelica croaked.

"You're probably barely able to stand," Velazquez continued.

Tom snorted. "The Jellyfish is immune to your pathetic amphibian toxin."

"You can't be," Velazquez said, faltering.

"Thanks to that fridge full of antivenom in the lab, there are some women who are also shaking off the effects of Phi-Tox. Ladies?"

"No!" Velazquez gurgled.

Angelica tried to turn her head to see what was happening, but she couldn't.

"Baaad doctoooorrrr," a rough female voice said. "Baaaaad . . ."

"No! Get back in the gallery! Go back on your plinths!"

"Doctoooor neeeed to payyyyyy . . ." another voice said.

"Payyyy!" others echoed.

Velazquez shrieked, the sound high and girly. He dashed through the corner of Angelica's vision, pursued a moment later by a mob of naked women, chasing him with the same fervor they had once spent on chasing carbs.

Suddenly Tom was beside her, looking down into her eyes. She felt tears of joy and disbelief sliding down her temples.

"My love," he said softly, and then held up a syringe. "This will pinch."

"I . . ." Angelica croaked.

"Yes?"

"Looooove you."

His bright blue eyes crinkled in joy, growing shiny with

emotion. Then he nodded, and a moment later she felt the pinch of the needle in the bend of her arm. She closed her eyes and let it happen.

Tom pulled out the needle and dropped the syringe to the floor. He unstrapped her from the operating table and pulled her up into his arms, squeezing her so hard she thought her ribs would crack. "Urrrg," she said, with no breath to say more.

"Sorry! Did I hurt you?"

"No. Give me 'nother!"

He hugged her hard, and she wrapped her arms around his neck and dug her hand into the shaggy hair she'd thought she'd never touch again. She realized she was moving more easily, and her mouth was working.

"Let's get out of here," Tom said, releasing her. He spotted her clothes in a heap and fetched them, then helped her pull on PJ bottoms and sweatshirt.

They heard shrieks and something being knocked over.

"What are they doing to him?" Angelica asked.

"Do you really want to know?"

She shook her head.

Tom lifted her in his arms and carried her out of the lab, through a door into the bare hallway they had first used to enter the house. They pushed out into the night air, the feel of it gloriously cool and refreshing in Angelica's lungs.

"Geeeeet hiiim!" a woman shrieked. "Doooon't let hiiim get awayyyy!"

Velazquez let loose another girly scream.

As they came around the corner of the building they saw naked women pouring from the open terrace doors, running toward where they'd left Mr. Toad. A car door creaked and slammed, and then another.

"Oh no, he's not!" Tom said, doubling his pace, Angelica bouncing in his arms. "He is *not* stealing Mr. Toad!"

Rrr rrr rrr! Rrr rrr rrr!

"Goddamn it!" Velazquez shrieked. "Start, you piece of crap! Goddamn pile of junk!"

Rrr rrr rrr! Rrr rrr rrr!

"F—ing pile of s—!"

Tom's footsteps slowed, then stopped. He set Angelica on her feet. "Oooh. Mr. Toad's not going to like that type of language."

They could see the truck now, naked women trying to get into it and swarming over its cab. Velazquez was just visible, a shadow screaming behind the glass, waving his arms as he ranted at the little truck. Tom winced at the blue language floating to them on the soft breeze. Angelica pulled in her chin at a particularly spicy, multilingual string of curses.

"No," Tom added. "The toad is not going to take kindly to that *at all*."

As if to prove him wrong, the truck suddenly roared to life and away across the lawn. Velazquez shrieked in triumph as women fell off. One tried to get out of the way, but he howled and aimed for her. She was running as fast as she could on the grass, but the doctor trailed her, keeping the nose of the vehicle right behind her pumping thighs, although each time he gunned the engine to flatten her, Mr. Toad jerked right or left, as if deliberately missing the woman. The other women ran after the truck, screaming at Velazquez to stop. His maniacal laughter echoed back to where Angelica and Tom stood.

"Do something!" Angelica pleaded. "Stop him!"

But even as she said it, the running woman was coming to the end of the lawn. She made a last frantic dart to the side.

As the toad's headlights hit the fence, Velazquez realized he was heading for the cliff and slammed on the brakes. The toad jerked and bucked in revolt, and then the engine suddenly roared and the wheels spun, steering straight for the fence in clear defiance of its driver. With a final buck, Mr. Toad leapt, crashing through the fence and flying free into the starry night. As the little green truck disappeared over the edge of the bluff, they heard the toad's final, descending call of victory and farewell: *BEEP BEeeeeeep . . . !*

The pursuing women slowed and stopped, gathering together at the hole in the fence. Tom and Angelica joined them. Below, all that was to be seen was the white foam of surf in the moonlight.

"God rest you, Mr. Toad," Tom said solemnly. "It was your last wild ride, but through it you avenged your dart frog cousins and achieved greatness. We shall remember you always."

Angelica sought his hand and squeezed it. "Amen."

Epilogue

"Karen says that teuscher is sending her to Switzerland to learn about chocolate production, as part of her training for her new job with them," Angelica told Tom, reading the e-mail on her laptop. She was sitting on the wooden veranda of their wall-less house on the island of Yap in Micronesia. "She thinks she's found her calling."

"Good on her!"

"Who'd have thought that temporarily becoming a carb-zombie would have led her to her life's work?"

"I guess we all have something to thank Velazquez for," Tom said, kissing Angelica on the top of her head. "You wouldn't have given me another chance if I hadn't rescued you from his evil clutches."

Angelica grunted in reluctant agreement. Velazquez's work had also started a backlash against breast augmentation, and small, natural breasts were becoming the "it" thing. Breast reduction surgeries and implant removals were on the rise in L.A.

Even better, researchers were investigating the use of Phi-Tox as a treatment for Parkinson's. Velazquez *had* given a lot of people something to be thankful for.

Angelica set aside her laptop and picked up her sketchpad as Tom bounded off the veranda and into the lush tropical foliage that surrounded the house.

"You want me to pose like this?" Tom asked, leaning forward and flexing his arms. He made a face like an angry monkey.

Angelica laughed. "No!" Tom was supposed to be posing for her as Adam in the Garden of Eden.

"Like this?" He turned to the side and took an Egyptian stance. His butt was bright white in contrast to his tan everywhere else, and glowed even in the shadows of the tropical foliage.

"No! Be serious!"

He turned full frontal to her. "I *am* serious, about certain things."

"Like what?" she asked, smiling.

"Do you really need to ask?" He waggled his eyebrows. Amid the white of his upper thighs, one very important part of his physiognomy began to rise and swell. "It rises from the dead!" he declared in a Vincent Price voice. "And it wants only one thing: human flesh!"

Angelica feigned a sigh. "I'm never going to get any work done with *that* thing chasing me all day."

"Is that a complaint, my beautiful wife?"

Angelica grinned and tossed aside her sketchpad. A moment later her sarong was a puddle on the wood planks, and she bounded off through the foliage, past Tom and down the sandy path to the beach. He caught her just before she could burst free into the sunlight, swinging her around and lifting her in his arms up to where she could wrap her legs around his waist.

"No complaints, husband o' mine," Angelica breathed as he lowered her down onto himself. "You know I love every part of you." She threw her head back, feeling his rod part her flesh and fill her to delicious fullness. "Every single part."

✂ ☐ **YES!**

Sign me up for the Love Spell Book Club and send my
FREE BOOKS! If I choose to stay in the club, I will pay
only $8.50* each month, a savings of $6.48!

NAME: _____

ADDRESS: _____

TELEPHONE: _____

EMAIL: _____

☐ I want to pay by credit card.

☐ **VISA**   ☐ MasterCard.   ☐ DISCOVER

ACCOUNT #: _____

EXPIRATION DATE: _____

SIGNATURE: _____

Mail this page along with $2.00 shipping and handling to:
Love Spell Book Club
PO Box 6640
Wayne, PA 19087
Or fax (must include credit card information) to:
610-995-9274

You can also sign up online at **www.dorchesterpub.com**.
*Plus $2.00 for shipping. Offer open to residents of the U.S. and Canada only.
Canadian residents please call 1-800-481-9191 for pricing information.
If under 18, a parent or guardian must sign. Terms, prices and conditions subject to
change. Subscription subject to acceptance. Dorchester Publishing reserves the right
to reject any order or cancel any subscription.